ARCADIA
PLANITIA
HIGH SCHOOL

FORTITUDO
TENACITAS
LAETITIA

JOE R. LANSDALE

This special signed edition is limited
to 1250 numbered copies.

This is copy_**442**_.

THE SENIOR GIRLS
BAYONET DRILL TEAM
AND OTHER STORIES

THE SENIOR GIRLS
BAYONET
DRILL TEAM

AND OTHER STORIES

Joe R. Lansdale

Subterranean Press 2023

First Edition

ISBN
978-1-64524-097-6

Subterranean Press
PO Box 190106
Burton, MI 48519

subterraneanpress.com

Manufactured in the United States of America

TABLE OF CONTENTS

INTRODUCTION
TO THE SENIOR GIRLS BAYONET DRILL TEAM
AND OTHER STORIES

THIS LATEST COLLECTION of stories is, as always, a mixed bag as far as types of stories go. I couldn't write if I felt I had to be a horror writer, a crime writer, a historical writer, a mystery writer, a science-fiction writer, a fantasy writer, or any label one might apply. When I was young, I did want to be a science-fiction writer, and I've written some science-fiction related material, but as time went on I knew I would never fit comfortably in a box, or be able to write to others' expectations.

It amazes me that there are readers who only read one type of story, or expect an author to only write in the genre they prefer. I find nothing more boring than reading the same sort of story time after time. Pretty soon, even if the work is good, you burn out. You go out in the world and see what else is there, coming back to your original love gives it a boost, actually.

I'm not criticizing, just stating a lack of understanding. I've always been amazed at readers who dismiss out of hand a story that isn't in the same vein as the last few they have read. I get hung up from time to time on a genre, but the stories I like best actually mix and match, or better, blend these elements into the work so that it's hard to have easy classification.

Some works solidly fit into genres, and I love that as well, when that's my mood. But my moods, like my reading tastes, vary. That's the case here. Some stories fit labels comfortably enough, but others do not. I hope that's what you want, variety, because that's what you get.

Beyond that, I will give you story notes in the book concerning the creation or inspiration for the individual stories. If that's not your cup of blood and sugar, then skip those and read the stories.

Personally, and perhaps because writing is my profession and profound love, I enjoy that sort of thing from other authors. Introductions to stories used to be a more common thing in collections and anthologies, but as of recent years there seem to be fewer of them. For me, an introduction to a collection, individual story notes, are like a nice greeting at the door as you are invited in to relax in the living room while the coffee is made. The stories are the coffee. Here they are.

Sip up.

Joe R. Lansdale

THE HUNGRY
SNOW

In memory of Robert E. Howard, Lord of the Pulps

GREAT GOUTS OF blood on the snow. The cracking of ice. The wind so cold.

That's what he would remember.

And IT.

❧

IN THE COLD, wet, blowing snow, the Reverend Jedidiah Mercer rode his horse and led his pack mule into the midst of it. It was as if God, the mean dictator for whom he worked, had taken the world in hand and filled it with slush and ice and shook it like a petulant child.

When at last the wind shifted, he could see the world again. He was high up in the Rockies. The tips of mountains were coated in snow and the trail he was on was narrow. It was easy enough to traverse when his vision was clear, but as he rounded a precarious curve, the snow dumped again, forcing him to pull his mount and lead his mule close to the side of a rock wall. Only a few feet away to his right was a deep drop-off that fell into a cluster of snow-coated trees, and between the boughs of those trees was a long, cold drop and eventually a hard bottom of solid rock.

He cinched up the lead rope on the mule and managed it around the curve of the mountain. The wind shifted again, and for a brief moment there was a part in the blowing snow. He could see where the trail rose up and near the top of it was a red haze, like a burning match seen through greasy glass. It was a large cave and there was fire inside. There were people as well, squatted together around the fire. He only glimpsed them, and then the snow blew hard and they were wiped from view.

The Reverend heard a dribbling sound, realized it was falling gravel, small rocks, slipping ice, and then he felt a tug on the mule's rope, and then the rope burned through his hands.

The beast was sliding over the side of the trail and away into oblivion. Within an instant, the rope was gone and the Reverend held nothing but a clenched fist. It felt less like the mule slid away, and more like it was snatched away.

Most of his supplies for crossing the Rockies on his way farther west had been strapped on that mule's back. Now those supplies and his mule were at the bottom of a cliff. The mule had not made a sound.

The Reverend reined his mount to a stop, slipped off his horse and led the beast. He did this by putting one hand out to his left to feel the rock wall, clutched the reins in his other. He kept as close to the rock wall as possible, aware there could still be surprises. Breaks in the trail, a narrowing of it, but to stop moving and stay where they were was sheer frozen death.

He felt he had to make it up to the cave where the fire burned, place himself among the people there. The cave might help him and his horse ride out the blizzard.

It was like a blind man threading a needle, but he managed up the trail, and soon he saw the light of the fire again, a crimson glow against the snow. The sight of it would come and go as the wind puffed and gusted, wild and white, wet and cold.

He trudged upwards, and soon the fire and cave were visible again, as were those nestled around it. A couple of the men in the group stood up as he arrived. Another, a bearded man stayed squatted close to the fire. The remaining two occupants were a woman and a boy, sitting close together, a blanket wrapped around them.

The Reverend stopped outside the entrance to the cave. The logs in the fire were popping and crackling with a sound like a man snapping peanuts free of their shell.

"Do you got food?" one of the standing men said. He was a big fellow in a thick buffalo coat that made him seem even bigger. He wore boots topped with rabbit fur, a thick leather hat. He had pushed his greatcoat open. It was lined with a checkered blanket. His hand was on the butt of his pistol, which looked to be an old converted .44. He was slightly crouched. The Reverend believed him to be a man who thought he knew what he was doing.

The other man was short and thin. He had grown so thin and pale, blue veins could be seen in his face, like colored pencil marks on a map. His coat was thinner than the other and made of leather that had turned dark and was stained from time and wear. He had on a black slouch hat with a hole in the crown. He removed his hand from the butt of his pistol and let it hang at his side.

"It'd be right nice if you did have some food," the small, thin man said. "We done boiled and ate damn near everything that's leather except what we're wearing. Horses and mules had to go too, as did a hog and a flock of chickens we was hauling out to start a farm. We ate the goddamn seeds we had for planting. There goes the turnip crop, the beans and peas and squash as well."

"Those were our seeds," said the woman.

"Well," the skinny man said. "We all ate them."

The Reverend carefully observed the others, knowing from experience that those who did not appear threatening could be the ones to worry about. The other man was older than the rest, had a thick beard. He wore a drooping wide-brimmed hat and a weasel hide coat. If he had a pistol it was either under his coat or in one of the wide coat pockets. His head was turned to look at the Reverend. His massive beard was flecked with snow and ice and time's gray marks.

The woman had on a hooded coat. Her hair poked out from under the hood and was dark as the bottom of a coal mine. Her face was like an animal looking out of its den. She was delicate, except for her dark eyes that appeared to contain some reservoir of strength.

The boy he thought to be twelve or thirteen. He had black, scraggly hair and was snuggled close to the woman. His mouth, like the others, was cracked and bloody from the cold. From the color of the boy's hair and eyes, the Reverend decided they were mother and child.

"About that food?" said the bearded man at the fire.

"To be exact, gentlemen, much of my chuck and supplies were on a mule that made a misstep and took flight off the mountainside and into the void, like Icarus with melting wings, but in this case, with frozen ass."

"What the hell are you talking about?" said the big man in the buffalo coat.

"He's talking metaphor," said the skinny man. "I heard a preacher talk about metaphor and how it's a lot of what the Bible is. Still, I don't know who that Icarus is."

"I'm talking truth," said the Reverend. "My mule fell off a cliff."

"Why didn't you just say that?" said the big man, the one the Reverend had come to think of as Buffalo Coat. The other standing man he decided to think of as Skinny. The man by the fire became Bearded Man, and the other two were Woman and Boy. It might be best not to know names. If things went sideways, it was best not to have names for what you might have to eat.

"Let me start with a friendly suggestion," said the Reverend. He looked right at Bearded Man. "Remove your hand from the butt of your pistol. Be assured I will not ask you twice. If you do not, I will consider you hostile, and will put a bullet, perhaps two, through your head."

The man eyed the Reverend for a moment, but any show of strength in his face faded. He straightened from his crouch and dropped his hand away. His coat fell around him and concealed the pistol.

"Who the hell are you?" Buffalo Coat said.

"Call me Reverend. This is my horse, Bill."

"A goddamn preacher," Skinny said. "I'd have preferred a gambler with a deck of cards, even if I got nothing to gamble."

"Well, you have me," the Reverend said.

Without asking permission, the Reverend led Bill around the fire and inside the cave. At the back of the cave the warmth of the fire could still be felt, even if the cave ceiling was tall and wide and pretty long. It was a relatively cozy spot.

The Reverend prepared to hobble Bill with the hobble ropes that were fastened to his saddle. He did this while keeping a cautious eye on his new companions.

He pushed his black duster coat back over his matching ivory-handled pistols in their black leather holsters. He wanted to discourage any sort of confrontation, because he sensed a tension in the air that was cold as the snow.

The Reverend was proud of his pistols. He had recently bought them from a peculiar gunsmith who said they were haunted and had belonged to Wild Bill Hickok, shortly before his demise. He said the spirit of the gunfighter's aim was in the guns. Said they should always be loaded with silver bullets. That was something the Reverend did anyway. Went with his line of work.

As for them being the pistols of Wild Bill Hickok, the Reverend considered this a bullshit selling point to jack up the price, but he liked the pistols and didn't regret the gunsmith's subterfuge, if indeed it was. The guns did feel strange in his hands. He had yet to kill anyone with them, but shooting targets with them was a delight. He was an excellent shot, but when he fired these pistols he felt as if he were an even better one.

As he leaned down to fasten the hobbles to his horse's ankles, he noted a large pile of firewood, which was a good thing. He also saw a cache of charred bones not far from them. Some of the bones were those of a horse, and some were of a human; broken femurs and a skull that had been smashed open at the top, like a kid shattering a piggy bank to get at the loot inside.

The Reverend made no recognition of this. He removed his lantern from the saddle. It was contained in a thick, leather bag. He placed it against the cave wall. He never lit it unless he had to. He wanted to keep the coal-oil content as full as possible, in case it really became necessary to see in the night, if the moon and stars were not in sight, if a camp fire was not enough. The lantern itself he had washed several times in Holy Water. Water that, if to do its duty, had to be blessed by someone other than himself. He was not that holy.

He removed his horse's blanket and saddle and sat them against the back wall next to the lantern. He took time to curry Bill with a brush from a bag that dangled from the saddle horn. The others watched him as if he were a bear doing human things. He pulled the saddlebags off the back of the saddle, threw them over his shoulder and headed toward the fire.

"Food?" said the woman.

This time the Reverend answered. "Some."

He rummaged in one of the bulging saddlebag pouches and pulled out a fat mound of waxed paper wrapped around strips of beef jerky. He gave a piece to everyone. They all squatted around the fire and ate. The Reverend took a piece for himself, carefully wrapped the paper around the dried meat and put it away.

They watched him as he did this. He knew he'd have to be alert, or they would not only take the jerky, but eat him as well. From the bones in the back, he was certain they had already resorted to cannibalism, but the question was had they eaten a fellow pilgrim that had died, or had they killed to eat? One he could understand, but of the other he was less tolerant, especially if he might be on the menu.

An old sailor who had been marooned on an island told him that he and three others had been trapped in what seemed like a tropical paradise, but they couldn't catch fish. They didn't seem to be as prevalent there as expected. They lived off wild greens and fruits, an occasional crab, but nothing much edible was in abundance. When members of their group died, they ate them, raw. Cut them open and pulled out the guts and the innards, cut the flesh in strips and ate it. The old man said the strips of flesh were chewy, but tasty, and he developed quite an appreciation for it.

In the end, he said it was only him and another, and that they watched each other like hawks, hoping one or the other would die. He admitted he occasionally considered helping the other to do just that. Said he was so hungry he could see cornbread walking on the ground.

Fortunately, a ship found them, and he and his island companion were rescued. He never saw his companion after their return to civilization, but for a short time they were both famous as Robinson Crusoe. He never went to sea again. Worked the docks. Never mentioned what happened to the others until he was an old man and read that his surviving companion had died. Somehow that set him free to tell his tale.

"You know," the old marooned sailor said. "I still have me a hankering for a strip of that raw people meat. In fact, I don't think I've ever had anything as tasty. Of course, maybe I was just hungry."

The Reverend had never forgotten the story. There was also the fact eventually he had to kill the old man, but that was for righteous reasons and had nothing to do with cannibalism.

"How long have you been trapped here?" the Reverend asked.

"No idea, exactly," said the woman. "But a long time."

The older man said, "We were crossing the mountains, trying to get out West. We took a wrong cut-off."

"As did I," the Reverend said.

"We were trapped in the pass for maybe a month or more," said the woman. "We had plenty of supplies at first. Plenty of feed for the horses. And then we didn't. We ate what we could find. The men hunted. We scrounged for anything edible, even the bark off trees."

"That bark was better than I would have thought," said the boy.

"Hell," said Buffalo Coat, "we picked grain out of our horse's shit to eat. Even that tasted pretty good. What I want to know is how come you look so good, and you got that sleek horse?"

"I got trapped in a valley, and it wasn't terrible there. There was plenty of game and the snow wasn't so bad, but I couldn't get out until the other day, and when I did, I soon wished I'd stayed. The storm that had gone away came back with a vengeance. I believe I'd have been alright had I stayed on the original trail, but I'd heard of this cut-off, that it took days off the trip. It might in fact do that if the weather is perfect and you hold your mouth just right. Left the valley too early, decided on the wrong trail, and here I am."

"We studied the trail you was on," Buffalo Coat said. "Decided it might be worse than here. Cave is at least a sight better than being out in the bad weather. Thing is, though, we ain't got no supplies."

"You probably made a better choice," the Reverend said. "If the snow were to blow over and out, the ice melt some, then I'd try and go back the way I came. But not otherwise. That trail takes the brunt of the North Wind. And it is narrow as the edge of a butcher's knife."

"Up here, there hasn't been a break in the snow in weeks, maybe it's been months," said Buffalo Coat. "Oh, there was that one day when we could see the sun. I remember. I had gone out of the cave to shit, was squatted doing my business, and the sun hit me like a bullet. It was so warm for a couple of minutes, I thought I'd cry. Instead, I looked through my shit for something edible. I think I found a seed. The sun got covered in clouds and the wind blew snow, and that moment was gone."

"Don't talk like that in front of a lady," said Bearded Man.

"She ain't no lady no more," Buffalo Coat said. "Ain't none of us nothing more than survivors."

No one challenged this. Night slithered out of the sky and began to choke out the sun. The Reverend noted that as it did all the pilgrims looked at the gathering darkness as if watching themselves bleed out.

"At least it's nice and warm in here," the Reverend said.

"We chopped some trees growing alongside the cave," Bearded Man said. "There's no more to chop. This wood runs out, then it's just us and the cold and that won't play out so well. And then there's the real reason we've stayed here close to the fire."

"And what would that be?" the Reverend said.

"IT," said the woman.

There was a loud cracking of ice out in the night. Everyone looked out into the darkness.

"It's out there, and it's coming closer," she said. "But it doesn't like fire. We have to seal the entrance with it. We do it every night. Why the wood goes quick."

The Reverend helped them spread the fire-licked wood about so that the front of the cave had a barrier of flame in front of it. Bearded Man and Skinny went to the back of the cave and pulled some firewood forward, stacked it on the fire.

When that was done, Bearded Man squatted back down by the fire, looked out of the cave at the night. "It don't come in daylight, but just night. It always does. It's hungry, like us."

The wind sighed. All that could be seen from the mouth of the cave was the swirling of the snow. The Reverend sniffed. There was a stench of evil the Reverend knew so well. It had a stink not common to human experience. Even with all that he had faced, vampires, werewolves, walking dead and monsters from the edges of time, he felt his skin crawl.

Bearded Man said, "We have another day or two of firewood. Like Jane said, it doesn't like fire, though it's gotten bolder of late. Comes closer."

"Jane," the Reverend said, now having a name to call her. "Can you tell me more about this IT?"

"You'll think we're crazy, but you'll know soon enough what I say is true," she said.

"I've seen strange things in my time," the Reverend said. "You might say strange things are my business."

"Very well," Jane said. "We started out in fine weather, and there was a much larger number of us, twenty or so. We had horses and mules and were well stocked. The trip was fine. Then Mr. Meeker thought we might do better to take a short-cut he'd been told about. It would cut days, even weeks off our travels, he said. But it was only a good way to go when the weather was good, and it wasn't good. We were trapped by bad weather, and after some time we begin to run out of food. We were eating bark off trees and eating all our leather. Of course, the horses and mules were killed and eaten, and then it was just us."

"You don't have to say," Bearded Man said.

"It's all right," Jane said. "I'm not happy about it, but I'm not ashamed either. We began to eat the dead, Reverend. Meeker was the first. I know how that must sound to a man of God."

"I'm not judging you."

"Then it went from worse to worst. Someone among us began to kill. They would strike in the night, drag their victim off in the woods. Next morning, we'd see bloody drag marks in the snow. Whoever killed their pick for the night ate all of them, save for a few bones. Can you imagine? One person eating a whole human body in one night, leaving only crushed skulls where the brains were taken out. Leg and arm bones cracked and the marrow sucked. Of course, when one of us died, it was understood they would be eaten by the rest of us. It was a matter of who was to be last. That was letting nature take its course, but this was someone outside of nature. And he wasn't sharing. We quickly realized the killer was Gabriel Johnson. He was a terrible man to begin with, before he became what he became. Greedy and lustful, a thief and other things worse that were rumored."

The Reverend said, "It is known there are mountain spirits, spirits of the cold and snow and the cutting wind. Starving spirits that seek a host. They prefer the malicious, the desperate and the greedy. We all have those components, but they float at a higher level in some."

"Gabriel Johnson was all those things," Jane said. "Always eating more than his fair share and talking about how he planned to open up a mining-camp store when we got out West, jack up the prices for goods, water the whisky. He asked me if I wanted a job serving miners, and he wasn't referring to me waiting tables. He was proud of that kind of thinking. As we traveled, he kept apart from us more and more. Would wander into the forest alone.

"He was stealing flour and salt and smoked meats from our stock. A little at a time at first, and then a lot. By the time we found out it was too late. He had stashed it away. We went to confront him, but he disappeared into the dark. Didn't come out during the day. At night he would call to us. Taunt us. But over time he sounded strange. Like himself, but not exactly. I know how this will sound, but he became immune to the cold. He was never around the fire. And when we did catch a glimpse of him, moving between the trees, in spite of having our supplies and having killed and eaten folks in our group, he was thin. Skeletal."

"His eyes were odd," Bearded Man said. "They glowed in the night, but could turn dead black in a moment."

"Got so we didn't see Johnson," Jane said. "Merely saw his shadow. It would fall down on the snow just before complete dark. But he wasn't to be seen. Just that shadow. Then the night would come in solid and the shadow would blend with it. It was unnerving.

"Then one night a man lit a torch, stepped outside the heat and light of the campfire. In the torchlight we could see the shadow rise on hands and knees, then scuttle off like a lizard. Then it rose up and ran, like a human, but it was growing in size as it went. And the snow was flying to it. Almost immediately the shadow was turned into a creature made of snow. It ran off into the woods. It sure didn't like that torch, the light and the heat from it.

"From then on it would come in the night. It would call in Johnson's voice, and there was a smell about it. I noticed you wrinkle your nose. That is the smell, right there. Right now. And then we'd see it coming closer. Not right up to the fire, but close enough for us to see there was no more Mr. Johnson. It was a kind of snow man. And it was hungry. It would whistle and stomp and frighten the few mules we had left. They tugged their halters loose. And then they were gone. Johnson would get to them some way or another.

"We built bigger fires. And we kept the mules close to it. It helped. But we had to eat the last of the mules ourselves. Then this thing followed us as we moved along. Oh, maybe not during the daylight, but it would catch up come night. Nightfall, it made promises in Johnson's voice. Some of our group couldn't keep from leaving the fire and going off in the woods. Starving, exhausted, not thinking straight, they lost their will. They walked out into the dark and never came back."

"And then we came to this cave," Bearded Man said. "We only have the front of it to guard. The fire takes care of that. We're down to nothing to eat, and my belly is full of empty. Perhaps giving Johnson what it wants is better than starving to death."

"No," the Reverend said. "It isn't. Your soul will continue to be pained after your death. What's out there isn't Johnson. He's its catalyst and host, but now he's something other than what he was. Johnson has become that mountain spirit I mentioned. It's called the Wendigo."

"Wendigo," the boy said.

"The Indians know of it. The Cree, Ojibwe. The tribes that live in cold places and have known starvation and darkness. The Wendigo goes by many names. It kills and cannibalizes. It entices others to do the same. It's a taboo that breaks a soul down. Untethers it so that it may more easily fly away. But it's not a flight to escape. It's a flight into darkness and eternal pain. Johnson was chosen to become its host because of who he is, or was. The Wendigo exists without a host, but its powers are limited. Cold wind. Hunger. That's all it has until it occupies a soul. Then it lives off other souls and becomes stronger. It's never satisfied. It is always hungry for meat and for human essence."

"None among us are innocent of ravenous hunger. Starvation," Bearded Man said.

"But we didn't murder for it," Buffalo Coat said. "Though I admit it has crossed my mind. Just as a thought, you see. Those that died. That was different. We were starving, and it was the only thing to do. Not let the meat go to waste when we could eat and live and not die out here with ice on our bones. But the other, you know, sometimes I think about it."

"That's the Wendigo," the Reverend said. "It gives those urges to you."

"It calls out for us to break apart the circle of fire and let it in," the boy said.

"And sometimes we want to," Skinny said. "There is something about that voice. It promised we could eat. That we would have all the food we wanted. Way that thing talked, you almost believed what it was saying. Then you would see it standing outside the fire, bigger each time. In the morning we would find the bones of bears and elk and all manner of beasts. Now and again, someone would make the mistake of listening to that thing, and would go mad, go outside the fire. Next morning, their bones and blood were on the snow. Sometimes there was a bit of meat still on the bones."

"We took some of those bones," Jane said. "God forgive us all."

"God is a soulless terror," the Reverend said. "His will is my business, and His will is one of suffering and pain. It's hard to know what His plan is, or if there is one. There's no end to His punishments. I deserve them. But He doles them out to the good and the bad, the sinners and those without sin in equal amounts. He is both God and Satan. He's unreliable in his intentions."

"Blasphemy," said Buffalo Coat.

"Perhaps, but you don't know Him as well as I do," the Reverend said.

"Still, we ate human flesh," Jane said. "And if someone died, I would do it again. I would feed it to my boy by my own hand. What does that say about me?"

"It says you are hungry," the Reverend said.

"Bones in the back, ones I saw you eyeing," Bearded Man said. "They belong to Old Man Carruthers. He was a good man. He knew his fate. He was dying, and he knew we were eyeing his flesh as if we were in a meat market. We had already killed and eaten his horse. He told us to think of him as a gift."

"You did what you had to do," the Reverend said. "Johnson did what he wanted to do. I can assure you of that. Had he not, there would be no Wendigo following you. Johnson fit the bill for what the Wendigo needed. No doubt about that. He was a Wendigo's dream. If indeed they dream. The Wendigo is the opposite of warmth. That's why the fire holds it back. But even so, in time, it can become bolder. You want to survive, then you will have to leave this cave. Take your chances traveling. Possibly find game. Building fires as you go. We can find fallen wood as we travel, and I have plenty of lucifers to strike up a fire with me. They are well wrapped in wax paper and made waterproof inside an oiled water-shedding pouch. I also have flint and steel. You can stay here and die, or you can take a chance and leave. I'll be leaving soon. Stay if you like, but if you go with me, from that moment on I will make the choices for all of us."

"What gives you the right?" Buffalo Coat said.

"I take the right and do not ask your permission," the Reverend said. "If you have a different point of view, you may express it, but it will do you no good. I can leave you and be fine. And if you come with me, I can offer you no guarantees. Just the sum of my knowledge, which to be immodest, in these matters is considerable."

There was a cracking sound like a limb burdened by too much snow, and then a more terrible stench than before. A stench like a pit full of rotting meat and vegetables, overlayed by a too-sweet smell of fermenting fruit. The fire wavered as if pushed by the wind. But there was no wind. The Reverend's horse nickered. Then came a voice, strangely close and simultaneously distant. The mere sound of it chilled the bones.

The voice said, "Pull back the fire. Let a cold man in."

"It's Johnson," Skinny said.

"It's the Wendigo," the Reverend said.

There was a laugh more like a cackle, and now the wind was back. It twirled the snow and danced the flames. The cackle seemed to tumble downhill and away, crashing along like dropped dishes shattering on the rocks below.

The Reverend stood from his squat and rested his hands on his revolvers, tried to see through the high-burning fire. And he did see something. Something that had a near human shape, but larger. It shifted, and then it was nothing more than the twirling of the driven snow and a lingering reek that made the stomach shift.

"When we run out of wood, it'll get in," said the boy.

"It's all right," the woman said, but the boy was not reassured. He looked out at the dark as if he were about to mount the gallows.

Some time passed. The odor dissolved. There were no more voices. Buffalo Coat, who had been squatting, stood up, took off his hat and held it politely in front of him as he spoke to the Reverend.

"May we eat your horse?"

"No," said the Reverend. "And if you try to harm that horse, it will be you who is eaten."

"All right, then," Buffalo Coat said, and put his hat back on.

∾

THEY BUILT UP the fire, and though there was still wood, the Reverend could see that one more night, and that would be it. A small fire would not contain it. Bother it, perhaps, but not contain it. Over time no fire would hold it. There were other methods, but even they had their limits. He would consider those later.

The Reverend curried his horse and put oats in a feed bag and fed him. He fastened a cloth over Bill's face and eyes to soothe him, then unrolled his blankets and sat with his back against the cave wall and drew his blankets over him. Back there, away from the fire, it was cooler, but not exactly cold. Comfortable enough, all things considered.

He pulled his revolvers and clutched them by his sides under the blankets. Kept a loose eye on Buffalo Coat. The big man was sitting near the fire with his back against the side of the cave. He was watching the Reverend, waiting for him to drift off, he figured. Skinny was doing the same, eyeing him like a greasy porkchop soon to be dipped in blood gravy. Their own weaknesses and the power of the Wendigo were having an effect.

The Reverend pulled his hat down so that it partially covered his eyes, but he could still see. He was exhausted and feared he would drift off. If he did, if they moved toward him, his horse, Bill, would hear them and snort and stamp. It wasn't exactly like having a watch dog, but it was some comfort.

🖙

THE REVEREND CATNAPPED. But when Bill snorted and stamped, he came wide awake. Buffalo Coat and Skinny stood close by, awkwardly looking at him. The others were asleep near the fire.

"Howdy there," Buffalo Coat said.

"I will warn you but once, gentlemen. If you make your move, you'll never make another. Go to the fire and stay there. I see your hand on your gun, or you come close again while I'm resting, I will shoot you without investigation or guilt."

Buffalo Coat pushed his coat open to reveal his pistol. "You talk a good game, Reverend, but I think you're all blow."

That was when the Reverend moved, flipping the blanket aside and bringing up his revolver in his left hand, he fired. A hole appeared in the middle of Buffalo Coat's head and there was a spray of blood and brains flying toward the fire like a clutch of insects. Buffalo Coat fell backward and hit with his ankles crossed.

Jane, the boy, and Bearded Man were suddenly awake, sitting up. They looked at the Reverend and the body with open mouths.

The Reverend waved the gun at Skinny. "You take out your pistol and you lay it at my feet, so I don't have to get up and take it from you or give you a third eye like loudmouth there. You have another gun, let me assure you, you had best divest yourself of it. I find you are carrying after this moment, then I'll kill you."

"Yes sir," Skinny said and gently pulled his pistol with his thumb and forefinger and laid it on the ground. "Is it okay if we eat him?"

"That is your prerogative."

"We'll save you a piece."

"No. I will maintain. Jane, boy, I'm sorry you had to see that."

"It's all right," said the boy. "I didn't like him, and I'm hungry. And I done seen worse."

All of them had left the fire and were creeping toward Buffalo Coat's body. "I claim the coat," said Skinny.

"No," the Reverend said. "That belongs to the lady."

"Who says it belongs to her?" Skinny said.

"Who did you hear?" the Reverend said.

Skinny nodded.

"Boy," the Reverend said. "Bring me that pistol. And bring me the one underneath the buffalo coat."

The boy brought both pistols to him, then hurriedly returned to Buffalo Coat's body.

The others had begun to pull off the dead man's coat and were removing the dead man's clothes. The coat was given to Jane as instructed.

"Take him closer to the fire," the Reverend said. "I don't want that going on near me."

"You'll grow hungry yourself," Bearded Man said.

"I am not there yet. Do as you do, but not close to me."

❧

BY MORNING MOST of Buffalo Coat's corpse had been cooked and devoured by the hungry travelers. The entire middle of the man had been cut open and his innards ripped out, blood and fecal matter from his body was all over the front of the cave, and the eaters were covered in blood. A blood-stained rib cage lay nearby.

Having slept very little, the Reverend was surprised at how refreshed he felt by the sunlight and the cessation of the blowing snow.

He fed Bill and tried not to step in horse shit. When finished, he walked over and kicked the rib cage through the fire and out into the snow. Then he edged the fire aside on one end with a stick of firewood and went outside the cave and looked at the snow. There were no tracks. That didn't surprise him. A creature like the Wendigo wouldn't leave any.

The snowy trail below had been replaced by ice. Trying to skirt down to it would be impossible. Even if they could make it, the trail was so precarious they would be trapped on it before night fall, and there might not be a place as protective from the Wendigo as the cave. He had to find another route.

He stepped back inside the cave. "I'm going to take a look around. I will leave my horse where he is. If the horse is harmed, I will kill every last one of you without consideration. Understood?"

They all agreed it was understood.

"Sir," said the boy, "may I go with you?"

"You may if your mother approves."

The boy looked at her.

"I believe you may be safer with him than us," she said.

The Reverend picked his saddlebags off the ground where he had used them as a pillow, threw them over his shoulders, thinking the jerky in his bags might be too much of a temptation for the group. There were other things in them as well. Silver bullets. A spare revolver. A few odds and ends of string and leather strips. He left the lantern.

The boy stood nearby, as if waiting for the school bell to ring. The Reverend said. "Do you have an axe?"

"We do," said the boy. "We got a hatchet too."

"Get them both."

A moment later, the Reverend and the boy stepped outside the cave. The boy was holding the axe and had the hatchet handle tucked through his belt. The air was as sharp as a razor and cold as a polar bear's nuts.

There was a little trail that went up and around the back of the cave, then led farther up into the mountains. The Reverend started in that direction.

"Why go up there?" the boy said. "That leads back to the trail that brought us here. It's just more of the same."

"You did ask to come with me. If you are going to spend your time giving me pointers, perhaps you should stay in the cave."

"Sorry."

"We need to go higher to have a vigil where we may peek out at the land. Perhaps we can find fuel, as well as another path."

Climbing, they ended up in a cluster of cedar trees, both short and tall. From that angle they could see down a five-acre wide three-acre deep slope covered by a sheet of ivory colored ice. At the bottom of it was a mountain lake, also covered by ice. The water beneath it made the ice look sky-blue.

The Reverend considered the terrain. Beyond the lake was a trail that was considerably clearer of snow than the trail the Reverend had used to arrive at the cave. It split through the mountains. Boulders and trees bordered it on both sides. If one could get past the acres of slanting ice, cross the frozen lake, the trail looked to be a better way out. But the ice slope looked deadly. And how thick was the ice over the lake? Was it thick enough to walk on?

Unanswered questions.

"You thinking about that clearer trail down there, ain't you?" the boy said.

"I am."

"It might not be any better once you get down it a piece."

"I was thinking the same, but unless we can chop an immense amount of wood daily, haul it to the cave, soon there will be no fire. Even if we can keep the fire going, there is no food, except one another. And, of course, there's the Wendigo."

"I have kind of gotten used to eating people," the boy said.

"There is your mother. Should you eat her or she you?"

"I done told her she can eat me if I die."

"Eventually, we will run out of people. There is only one choice, and I intend to make it. Leave. You and the others will do as you will. Give me the axe. We spend our time chattering, the day will run away from us."

~

THEY SET ABOUT finding suitable trees or dead wood. After a few hours, the Reverend had a considerable pile of wood chopped and shortened. There was plenty of dead wood as well. The boy had used the hatchet to clear the chopped wood of limbs.

The Reverend used some of the evergreen limbs the boy had chopped, and lashed them together with leather strips from his saddlebag. He added some green poles they had cut, and turned them into runners.

The Reverend studied the boy. He seemed strong for all he had been through. Then again, on this very morning he had eaten a hardy meal of Buffalo Coat's remains. That was bound to brace him a bit. Buffalo Coat's blood was still on his face and stained the front of his coat.

"Now, saddle and bring my horse. By the way, what's your name?"

"Evan," the boy said.

"Evan, you may ride him back. But be careful of the trail."

After a while, Evan came back riding Bill, the hobbles fastened to the saddle horn. As Evan climbed down, the Reverend removed one of the two coils of rope he carried on his saddle. He cut pieces off of it and used them to fasten together a travois made from the wood runners and limbs he had salvaged.

It was a simple device, the evergreen limbs fastened between the runners to make a bed for the wood. The Reverend then fastened the long runners to the sides of the saddle.

They loaded up the chopped logs, but there was still wood they had to leave due to lack of space and the device's inability to carry huge loads. The Reverend let the boy lead the horse down the trail and back to the cave. It was slow work.

When they were inside the cave, they removed and stored the travois in back, stacked up the wood at the sides of the cave.

"We going back for more?" Evan asked the Reverend. "We left some."

"The day is darkening. We would do all right going, but coming back we might find ourselves in the dark with IT. We have plenty for the night, so let's lay low and keep the fire high."

The Reverend went to the back of the cave and leaned his back against the rock wall. He took jerky from the saddlebags, chewed on a piece. Sitting by the fire, the others watched him, licked their cracked lips.

"You ate a whole man, just about," the Reverend said. "Had some of him for lunch while me and Evan were occupied. If you are still hungry, I spied some toes and a hand you missed over there. But I warn you. Share. Me, I have not had any nourishment but this, so you can turn your gaze away."

In short time the hand and toes were found, cooked and eaten. The Reverend enjoyed the smell of the meat cooking.

❧

IT CAME IN the night and called in Johnson's voice, but it made other noises as well, and the noises were enticing, like the flute-playing of the Pied Piper. No one succumbed.

It prowled and called and darted in front of the cave, cackled, and was gone before daylight. When the first rays of morning came, the Reverend used his coffee grounds and the small pot he had wrapped in his bedroll to make coffee. He offered some to the others. Poured it in bowls and cups they provided. Skinny drank his from Buffalo Coat's skull, from which all the flesh had been stripped. He gave them all a chunk of jerky from his saddlebags, then he and Evan went back up the hill with the horse and travois, loaded the wood that was left from the day before, and brought it back to the cave.

There was still plenty of daylight, so he and Evan returned with Bill to cut more wood, but this time the Reverend had the boy help him cut a large pine. When it fell it shook the snow and ice and caused birds to fly up and squirrels to scamper from the fallen top of the tree.

The Reverend took the axe and cut the tree in sections. The top section extended over the slope of ice. He cut the limbs off of it, and he and the boy chopped them up for kindling. Finished, they looked back at the icy slope, the blue lake sheeted by ice, the trail beyond. It seemed so close and yet so dangerously far away.

Evan stood on the front end of the fallen tree and wobbled it.

"Do that, and you will soon take a trip down the slope. Broken bones might well be in the offing."

Evan stepped off the section. He said, "Should I care?"

"You get to choose."

They hauled the firewood back to the cave. The Reverend and Evan began to build the fire up with the help of Jane and the Bearded Man. Skinny threw a few sticks onto it. Skinny had begun to take on an attitude that reminded the Reverend of Buffalo Coat.

Just before night, Jane began to cough a lot. She had been coughing before, but not consistently, but now the cough was more frequent and deeper within her chest.

"She ain't been doing good all day," Bearded Man said. "Cough has gotten considerable worse." He spoke like a man hopeful she might soon die.

The Reverend took some horse liniment from his saddlebags, had Jane came to the back of the cave, told Evan to remain up front by the fire.

The Reverend held up the liniment bottle. "You can do this yourself if you're modest, or you can let me do it. I'll need your coat wide open, your blouse open to expose your chest."

"Sounds like to me you're just having fun."

"You can do it, then."

She shook her head. "You do it."

She unbuttoned her blouse and the Reverend rubbed the liniment across her chest and breasts. There was nothing erotic about it. She was as thin as a bird and due to malnutrition, her breasts were small like fried eggs. But even with the bones in her face poking tight against her flesh, he could see she was a pretty woman. Regular meals for a month, hot water and a bath, nice clothes, and she'd be a standout.

The male mind, he thought.

"It's going to burn a bit, but it'll get into your chest, maybe help clear up that cough."

"We're not going to make it, or are we?"

"I am," the Reverend said.

❧

NIGHT TIME CAME and there was a revival of blowing snow and howling wind. This encouraged the travelers to build the fire higher, to push it from one edge of the cave mouth to the other.

The fire roared five feet high. The wood crackled and oozed sap. Beyond it, through wafts of flames, rises of snow could be seen. The mounds were growing higher. Tomorrow they might need to find a way to move some of the snow, so as not to be trapped by it.

The Reverend noticed that the corners of the fire were being gently nudged. He strained to see if it was the wind. Finally, he saw that it was a stick poking out of the dark, gently pushing a log.

The Wendigo was investigating.

No one else had noticed.

"It's getting braver," the Reverend said. "I suggest we move to the back of the cave. I have a few tricks that might hold it off."

"What you mean?" Skinny said. "Best fire we've had. I actually feel warm for a change."

"Best fire because we cut enough wood to build it," Evan said. "Not like you did anything."

"You shush, boy, or I'll be eating dinner out of your belly."

Skinny produced a knife.

"Whoa," Bearded Man said. "We can't lose our heads like this."

The Reverend, without anyone realizing it, had drawn one of his pistols. "Put the knife up, or you will end up like your partner, who you've eaten and shat out into the early morning snow."

Skinny put the knife away. His eyes glowed in the firelight.

"I just ain't got no time for insults from a child," Skinny said.

"Yes, you do," the Reverend said.

They moved to the back of the cave near the Reverend's horse. Bill had been groomed, fed, and hobbled and a mask had been put over his eyes.

While Jane coughed and spat flecks of blood into an already stained handkerchief, the Reverend began to draw a large circle on the cave floor with the tip of his knife. He drew it so that they were within it. The Reverend didn't quite complete it. He stopped at the wall at the back of the cave. He then drew an extension of the circle on the wall, five feet high. Used his knife to carve symbols into the cave rock along the sides of the extended circle on the wall. Then he drew the same symbols on the floor, just outside the loop. The markings were crude and strange. They looked like stick men and dancing creatures.

Bearded Man said, "What is that?"

"Symbols of power. Cree used similar drawings, though I've added in a bit of this and that from other beliefs."

"Are you saying it makes us safe?" Bearded Man said.

"I have used similar before. But no guarantees. It might be more like a picket fence that will hold out the less determined."

"The fire has held just fine," Skinny said. "Why do we need these silly marks in the dirt? I don't see that working, preacher man."

"I think you don't see a lot of things, fellow. We need the circle and the spell because it has grown stronger and bolder. Fire or no fire, it will come through. It has been trying the fire, a little at a time. Evil is like that. It nudges, then it pushes, then it shoves. In time, it can break down barriers."

"I don't plan to sit inside some damn circle, or stand in one neither," Skinny said.

"Suit yourself," the Reverend said.

"I want to stay inside," Evan said.

Jane and Bearded Man agreed.

"To hell with your circle. I'll take my chances up close to the fire," Skinny said.

"Fine. But do not smear my line or drawings."

Skinny stepped out of the circle, making big steps, as if stepping over a snake. He moved close to the fire, rubbed his hands together, basked in its warmth.

"What do you think now?" Skinny said.

"That you should come back," the Reverend said.

Skinny, feeling bolder, cocked his head as if to say something, then stopped. A chilly wind blew into the cave. The fire's flames ruffled like red feathers. The Reverend and those in the circle could see a shape on the opposite side of the roaring blaze. It was the first time the Reverend had seen the Wendigo clearly. It was tall and broad and made of snow and sticks and chunks of ice wadded together in a rough facsimile of human form. Its face had a long line of a mouth set tight in its round head of snow. The sticks and debris poked from its body like hair and warts. There was a faint definition of a nose and two deep dark holes for eyes. It reached a long arm over the fire and an enormous hand made of snow and sticks flexed. Water dripped from it, hissed in the flames. The cave filled with its stench.

Skinny, aware now that something was behind him, wheeled toward it, knife in hand. The Wendigo grabbed him by the head and lifted him up. Skinny's legs dangled momentarily in the fire.

Skinny screamed. It was the kind of high-pitched dying-rat scream that made buttholes pucker and skin slither over a person's bones.

Skinny was lifted out of the cave.

The beast roared. The roar was even more terrifying than Skinny's scream. The sound of it filled the cave and made the Reverend's horse try to shuffle away in his hobbles. The Reverend grabbed the rope that he had fastened around Bill's nose, and pulled him back.

The Wendigo had switched to holding Skinny by one of his feet. He slung Skinny about, popping him like a whip. The third time he was popped, Skinny's head snapped off and landed in the snow. Blood gushed. A boot fell off Skinny's foot.

The creature split open its long mouth and poked Skinny into it. The creature began to chomp with teeth that were jagged like cracked ice. Gouts of blood sprayed into the fire, coated the rises of snow beside the creature like strawberry topping on mounds of fresh-churned vanilla ice cream. The face of the Wendigo was reddened with gore, spattered with chunks of flesh.

It took one long stride and picked up Skinny's head where it had fallen, began to eat it like an apple.

"Jesus, help us," Bearded Man said.

"He won't," the Reverend said.

The monster peered over the fire at them. The dark holes that served as its eyes had something in them that moved and flickered. The crackling flames caused those things to be better seen. They were miniature shapes of humans, small and fluttering about like moths in a jar.

"It's all them that came with us," Bearded Man said. "Only they're little."

The Reverend could see Skinny in there with them. Pushing against an invisible wall, trying to get out.

The behemoth parted its blood-stained lips and a cascade of voices fell out, all of them so kneaded together they were impossible to understand one from the other; they were an avalanche of sound.

Jane put her hands over her ears and screamed. The boy yelled. Bill stamped his feet and whinnied, tugged at the rope around his nose.

The Reverend said, "Evan, hold this rope," and he passed it to him.

Evan took it without thinking.

The Reverend drew his pistols and fired.

The bullets whistled and the silver-coated loads hit the Wendigo in the face and sizzled. The holes they punched exhaled smoke. The creature let out with a fresh roar. It was different this time. It was a cry of pain. The silver bullets had hurt it. It dropped what was left of Skinny's partially eaten head and went away so quickly it was hard to believe it was gone or had even been there.

Moments later, it returned. It carried a small sapling in one hand. The sapling's roots dripped dark earth. It had pulled it from the ground.

Poking the sapling into the fire, the monster lifted away logs. The fire sparked and sizzled. The beast continued to push with the sapling until the fire was parted and a wide path was made.

"It's coming through," Evan said.

"Evan, saddle and bridle Bill. Make sure the saddlebags and the lantern are fastened in place. But stay in the circle."

The boy didn't move.

"Son. Do as I say."

Evan slowly began to do as he was told, boosting the blanket off the ground, tossing it over the horse's back, preparing to lift the saddle into place. Bearded Man and Jane stood staring at the Wendigo, mesmerized.

The monster hadn't stirred from its spot. It held the sapling and stared at them. The movement inside its eyes was gone; they had turned dark. The voices were silent. There was only the wind. The thing looked at the path it had made, as if considering its chances. It used the sapling to cautiously push the fire even wider apart. As it did, it breathed out flakes of snow and flecks of ice.

Evan pulled the bridle on, cinched the saddle into place, removed the rope from Bill's nose. A scarf was over the horse's eyes, put there when they had returned from their wood chopping. Evan left that in place. He held the reins tight as Bill chomped at the bit and stamped his feet.

"No matter what the Wendigo does," the Reverend said, "stay inside the circle until I say otherwise. Evan, here's my knife. If I say 'Cut', you cut the hobbles off Bill, cut them close to the hooves. No dangles."

"A circle in the dirt don't seem like much," Bearded Man said. He was shivering, and not from the cold.

"We'll soon find out," the Reverend said.

The Wendigo's thin, long line of a mouth twisted, and it started through the gap in the fire, its snowy skin hissing from the heat, birthing a thin mist that filled the cave.

᧕

BEARDED MAN PULLED a small pistol from his coat pocket. He had been armed all along.

"Unless those bullets are coated with silver, they will not cause it injury," the Reverend said.

"This bullet ain't for it," Bearded Man said.

Bearded Man put the gun to his head and pulled the trigger. The bullet passed through his head and whizzed near the Reverend's nose as it exited. Hot blood splattered against the side of the Reverend's face. Bearded Man fell to his knees and onto his face.

Jane picked up the gun.

"Do not dare," the Reverend said, and twisted it out of her hand, dropped it in his coat pocket.

"It wasn't for me," she said.

"No thanks," Evan said. "I trust the Reverend."

The Wendigo moved swiftly to the circle. It lifted the sapling and swung it down. When the tree hit the realm of the circle, it burst into golden flame and would not pass through. Sparks of gold flared about the cave.

The Wendigo swung the flaming sapling again, but this time it came apart in its hands, shedding gold ash, none of it passing into the circle.

The Wendigo slammed its fists down against the invisible barrier. They too flamed with golden fire. The howl from the beast was loud enough it dislodged dust that dribbled from the roof of the cave and fell into the circle.

Wheeling away, the Wendigo charged through the split in the fire and out into the dark and the snow.

"It worked," Evan said.

"The dust from the ceiling," Jane said. "How can that be? That thing couldn't swing a tree through, but dust fell inside?"

"What the beast touches is tainted with the beast," the Reverend said. "Otherwise, the natural order is unaffected."

Stepping outside the circle, the Reverend hastened toward the fire. He grabbed the unburned end of a flaming log and dragged it into the circle, then used his knife to reinstate the part of the circle that had been damaged by his efforts. He chanted a combination prayer and spell.

"Evan," the Reverend said. "Get some of that kindling and firewood from the back, but stay inside the circle."

"Yes, sir," Evan said.

The Reverend studied the fire at the mouth of the cave. It roared in two sections now. He considered pulling the sections together again by using a stick of firewood, then decided against it.

He tugged the body of Bearded Man out of the circle and close to one side of the cave. For a starving man, the sonofabitch had some weight on him.

The Reverend repaired the circle again, repeated his spell and prayer. Evan had brought up firewood and kindling. The Reverend carefully stacked it onto the burning log. Soon there was a solid blaze.

"Will the circle hold?" the woman said.

"No guarantee. That thing has moved past the fire, which it fears, so its determination is growing stronger. According to legend, the more the Wendigo eats the hungrier they get. Those it eats become part of IT, part of its power."

"Then why give it more to eat?" She nodded at Bearded Man.

"Distraction. Rest while you may. Come morning we must depart. It's no longer safe here."

Jane and Evan cuddled together close to the fire, and fell quickly asleep. Even with the fear of the Wendigo, slumber had claimed them. The Reverend could not and would not sleep. He sat down in front of the fire and held his pistols in his lap.

It was only an hour or so until daylight cracked the blackness. Would it come back before the sun came up? Or was it through for the night?

The Reverend noted in the firelight that the circle he had marked was beginning to thin, the markings to fade. That was a signal that evil was gaining strength. The protection he had created was beginning to fade. There would be no redrawing it. The magic was done. From this point on it was assholes and elbows.

The wind groaned like an old man dying. Snow drifted into the mouth of the cave and fell into the remains of the fire.

Seeing that made the Reverend more mindful of the fire inside the circle. He placed more firewood on it. When the spell was gone there would only be the fire, and the Wendigo was less fearful of it than before.

The Reverend was considering options when he felt the hairs on the back of his neck lift up. The air thickened with a stench. He saw the shadows outside the cave twist, saw flakes of snow fly to them, cling to the shadows like cotton to tar. Sticks were picked up by the wind and tossed at the shape, spearing it. It was like watching an invisible sculptor build a statue from available materials. The shape was now the color of snow.

The Wendigo was larger than before. It bent at the waist, looked inside the cave. Its eyes were greater than before, deeper and black as original sin. A light came on inside of them, as if an early riser had lit a lamp. The light was the color of shit in amber. Once again, the Reverend could see the miniature souls of those it had consumed inside its eyes. They writhed, reached out, imploring rescue. Again, a thin dark line formed for the mouth. The wind blew two dents into its face. The dents became its nostrils.

The Reverend glanced at the circle. It was withdrawing. Growing closer to the fire. The symbols outside the ring were barely identifiable. They moved like crippled insects to keep up with the receding circle.

Glancing back at the Wendigo, the Reverend saw the thin line of its mouth had split open to show those horrid cracked-ice teeth. Was that a smile?

The Reverend placed his pistols in their holsters, said, "Jane."

He said her name twice. Jane sat up. She saw what he saw.

"Wake the boy," the Reverend said.

THE WENDIGO SNIFFED loudly. It smelled, then spied the body of Bearded Man lying against the cave wall. It eased itself through the split in the dying embers and moved toward the body.

Jane and Evan were both up, watching the thing as it entered the cave. It tossed a quick look at them, and then at the body. A tongue like a wet, red rope, licked out of its mouth and slathered its cracked-ice teeth with bloody saliva the texture of gruel.

"I'm going to climb on Bill," the Reverend said. "Evan, cut the hobble ropes close to the hooves. Jane, climb up here behind me. Evan, you in front of me. Stretch out over Bill's neck."

The Reverend mounted, pulled Jane up and behind him. Evan cut the hobbles, was about to climb on board Bill.

"Give me a torch," the Reverend said.

Evan picked out a flaming stick of firewood by the unburned end. He handed it to the Reverend who held it high above his head, used his other hand to help boost Evan in front of him.

The Reverend knew that carrying three was more than Bill could do comfortably, but there was nothing for it.

The Wendigo picked up Bearded Man. Just as it tilted its head back to drop its meal into its now widely-spread mouth, the Reverend jerked the covering away from Bill's eyes and yelled to him, and out of the circle they bolted.

The mouth of the cave was close, but so was the Wendigo. The Reverend flung the torch in the monster's face. It caused the Wendigo to step back, Bearded Man's legs dangling from its mouth.

Out of the cave they rode, into the cold night air. Bill's hooves slipped and the Reverend was certain they were about to go down. But Bill gained purchase on the rocks beneath the snow, and up the trail they went, riding hard toward the wood-yard the Reverend and Evan had made.

The Reverend glanced back.

Behind them the Wendigo came, seeming to glide on the wind, its legs and feet blending with the white of the snow. It was gaining.

The Reverend pulled a pistol with his left hand, leaned out and shot back. The silver bullet struck the Wendigo and sizzled like bacon in a hot frying pan. The Wendigo howled and fell back a pace. But it was like a bear stung by a bee. It was an annoyance, nothing more.

Bill slipped on the ice. They were almost to the peak of the hill when it happened. Jane flew off and tumbled backwards.

Bill rolled, nickered, and then made a noise seldom heard from a horse—a scream. The Reverend and Evan were tossed into the snow.

The Reverend and Evan stood up. They saw Jane rolling down hill, right to the Wendigo. The Reverend drew one of his revolvers, fired rapidly, and accurately. The bullets tore the air and impacted the monster, but it was less annoyed by them than before.

The Reverend's last shot wasn't meant for the Wendigo, but it found its mark as well—Jane. It was a better death than what might have been.

Jane's body was lifted limply into the Wendigo's mouth like a cheap sweet, and devoured in a mist of blood and a crunch of bone.

Evan charged past the Reverend, having grabbed a stick. The Reverend leapt after him, grabbed his coat collar, pulled him back.

"Nothing you can do, boy."

The Reverend hurried them upwards, pushing at Evan's back, pausing only long enough to stop where Bill was panting in pain. He pulled his second revolver as he replaced the first. He shot Bill in the head, finishing him off. He pulled the leather lantern pouch off of Bill, grabbed the saddlebags. Then up the last bit of the hill they went.

The Reverend glanced down. The Wendigo had stopped. It turned its great round head and looked east. The sunrise, the Reverend thought. It needs to be tucked away somewhere dark before the sun comes up.

It looked up at the Reverend, and he knew it had decided to take its chances. It rose up the hill like a windblown sheet.

The Reverend pulled the lantern from the leather case, lit it with a match from the saddlebags, flung it just as the Wendigo was almost on them. The lantern burst. The oil in the lantern exploded into flames and the Holy Water flared with holy fire and spread over the Wendigo's head and turned it into what looked like a giant blazing match.

Tugging the boy along, the Reverend ran to the edge of the ice where the trimmed top section of the pine tree rested. He pulled the boy in front of him, lifted him with one hand onto the log.

"Straddle it," he said. "Don't let your feet touch the ground. Hang on with everything you got."

The Reverend pushed the large log slightly. It tilted over the slope of ice. He jumped on as it dipped down, glancing back once to see the flame-head Wendigo gliding after them, the blaze wafting in the breeze. The Wendigo howled.

The log shot down the slope, scratching up ice in a stinging spray. The front of the Reverend's hat brim lifted in the breeze. Evan was almost flat on the log, clutching it with all his strength. He was whimpering.

The log slid like a sled for some goodly distance, then it started to wobble, threatening to tip and roll over. It stayed upright until it finished the slope and launched out onto the icy lake, tossing them loose and onto the frozen surface.

Out of habit, the Reverend drew his pistols as he rose. He yelled to Evan as the boy wobbled to his feet. "Run like a deer."

He then took his own advice. They ran as fast as their tired bodies would carry them. The Reverend felt as if his heart would burst. He wondered if the lake might crack beneath them.

The flames on the Wendigo's head had burnt out. It paused at the enormous log of pine that had been used as a sled. It picked it up as if it were nothing more than a switch. The Wendigo glided over the ice toward them, slamming the log in anger against the frozen lake.

As it neared them, it slammed the log down again, close enough the Reverend felt the wind from the blow on the back of his neck, felt a slight pressure against the heel of his boot.

Then there was a noise akin to a bull whip cracking, but the sound didn't end right away. A line in the ice formed beside the Reverend and then the line split and he could see cold, blue water in the rip. The line expanded more.

The Reverend forced himself to look back. The Wendigo looked down with its hollow eyes as the crack broadened beneath it and it plunged into it, sending up a slosh like an ocean wave. The Wendigo was about to float above it. But then the night was striped with the color of a fresh egg yolk. The light moved like a bully into the blue-black strands of night, consuming it.

The Wendigo was climbing out of the water. It was being blown apart by the wind. It was less like a wraith now, and more like a man. Small. An animated skeleton, flesh dangling from it like rags.

Johnson.

Crawling out of the icy split, Johnson turned its bare skull to look at the Reverend. From the eyes little naked bodies, souls, were leaping out and away. They scrambled like insects on the ice, then quickly melted in the sunlight, dissolved into buttery puddles.

Johnson managed to rise on bony legs and feet, and staggered over the ice. The Reverend raised a pistol and fired. A bullet nested in Johnson's skull, causing it to burst into pieces. The skeleton collapsed and rattled apart. A shadow in the shape of Johnson lay on the ice like an oil spill, then soaked into the ice and became clear.

The sun was golden. The sky was blue. The wind was gentle. The spirit of the Wendigo was gone.

The Reverend caught up with the boy.

"Is it dead?" Evan asked.

"For now. That's what greed did for it. It wanted us so badly it neglected the rising of the light. Consider this some kind of goddamn Bible lesson."

They walked carefully across the ice to where the other trail began. It was clear enough to travel. They found an indentation in the rocks just before night and made a fire with dead wood and matches from the Reverend's saddlebags. They ate the last of the Reverend's jerky. The Wendigo was no longer a threat.

Come morning they moved on. Late afternoon of the next day, the Reverend shot an elk with his pistol, three fast shots to the heart. They made a camp in a copse of trees for two days, finding a gap in the midst of them where they could build a fire from dead wood and roast and eat elk until they were full. The Reverend cut strips of meat from the elk and placed them in the snow until they started out again come morning.

Two days later, still living off the remains of the elk, the trail broke wide and slanted down and out of the mountains. The earth below was touched with ice and snow, but much clearer. Bits of grass could be seen poking up from the frost. The Reverend and Evan descended and walked the flatter trail for two more days. Then a band of noisy pilgrims with oxen, wagons, horses and mules showed up.

They were given a ride in one of the wagons. Fed beans and cornbread. Evan told a story of harrowing survival, but he left out the Wendigo, which the Reverend considered wise. Evan turned the Wendigo into a bear. He also left out the cannibalism. Also a wise decision.

The travelers reached civilization a week and a half later. Evan found a home with a family that had lost their son while crossing the mountains, dying of some unknown disease. Evan seemed happy enough. He and the Reverend never spoke again.

When the Reverend regained his strength, he took a job at the stables. He earned enough to pay for the room and board he had taken, enough to buy a horse and saddle, riding gear, as well as a few supplies.

The horse he had bought was no Bill, but it was a strong Paint and it was enough. The Reverend rode the Paint toward California.

THE SECOND FLOOR OF THE
CHRISTMAS HOTEL

I HAVEN'T MENTIONED THIS to anyone because I know how it might sound, having to do with what some might call a ghost. I am not a religious man, but I think there may well be some things we don't understand beyond this life, though I doubt they have anything to do with the common concepts of heaven and hell.

Some of us may die and merely cease to be, and some of us may remain hung between life and death, caught in a kind of limbo, captured there by intense emotions and events, retaining the dregs of life, but not life as we would want it.

And sometimes those things reach out.

This happened ten years ago, when I was seventy. Robert was the same age. He wrote me a letter suggesting we meet for Christmas Eve dinner, which was coming up within the week. It sounded like a glorious idea. There were no wives or children in my life. I had ended up that way by choice, and early on it seemed a great idea to be a playboy with no plans for children, but if I could go back in time I would alter that. It gets lonely without kin.

I had not seen Robert in some time, and we were no longer the friends we had been, and if I am being completely honest, we were probably never great friends, just friendly, so I was surprised by his invitation.

I wrote him and agreed, and met him on the decided day at a downtown hotel. It was an old hotel, and Robert's family owned it. They had been hotel owners all his life. They had a chain of them, many of them boutique or old classic hotels. They had become quite well off in the business, and when they retired, Robert took over. He had to travel a lot, examining the hotels to make sure everything was functioning properly.

We sat in the back of the hotel restaurant and dined quietly amidst canned Christmas music, multicolored lights and decorations. The place was nearly empty, people having gone off to parties or to be with their families.

We talked about this and that, recalling things that had happened to us, as well as things that involved old school chums, as they used to say.

After dinner and dessert, we lingered over coffee, and it became obvious that we really had little in common but our school and business experiences.

Just as I felt I had come up with an exit line, Robert said, "Do you remember that old hotel my family owned where we spent Christmas Eve and Christmas so many years?"

"It was an unusual place, out in the woods, down by the river. Not very large."

"That's the one. At one point it had been the location for a river stop, back when steamboats worked the water, and later on the hotel was built there. I forget when my family bought it. Very boutique. Only catered to a handful of guests, reservations only. Not too many rooms. It was full for several years, and then finally we closed it down when people quit reserving rooms.

The highway was replaced by an Interstate farther north, so there was no longer traffic coming near it, and it kind of faded. In its time we certainly had fine Christmas parties there. My parents really knew how to throw one."

They did indeed. I had only been invited once. I partied in the downstairs lobby with Robert and guests at the hotel, and some like myself who had been invited for the party, but not the Christmas Day festivities. The place was well decked out then, lots of lights and green boughs and colorful decorations. A Christmas tree that stood at the edge of the reservation desk rose up so high anyone on the second floor could have leaned over the railing and touched the glowing, silver star at the great tree's tip.

I remembered that party primarily because I met a pretty girl there, and we shared a Christmas kiss at the edge of the stairs. It was nothing more than a party kiss under mistletoe, but even to this day I remember it. She was such a beautiful and unique-looking woman, the memory of the event was cut into my brain.

"You know," I said, "I haven't thought about that hotel in years. Do you still own it?"

"I do, but it won't be around for much longer. I'm having it torn down, and then I'll look for someone to purchase the land. Hotel has gone to seed. I could repair it, but I think the time for that place has come to an end. My family had Christmas there for years, and me and my younger sister used to call it the Christmas hotel. I have a lot of fine memories, but toward the end, some not so good."

"How say?" I said.

Robert paused, sipped his coffee, and let the question ferment for a bit. Finally he placed his cup carefully on the saucer, said, "I suppose I actually invited you here to tell you the story, and perhaps gain your support and assistance, because you were there one year, and you met what I believe to be the catalyst of this story."

In that moment I was no longer ready to leave. I was intrigued.

"It was the next Christmas, the one after the party you attended, that something peculiar was discovered about room twelve on the second floor, the top floor of the hotel. I don't know if you ever went upstairs or not."

"I didn't," I said. "I was only in the lobby, downstairs, for the party. I met a young woman there."

"Amelia," Robert said.

"Yes. You remember her too?"

"I certainly remember her, and every male there most likely remembers her, for she was indeed a beauty. Wore those big gold hoop earrings, a red blouse, a short blue jean dress. You know, I believe she was barefoot."

"Hair tumbling down like an ebony shower, her skin dark and smooth," I said. "Read that somewhere in a book, and liked it."

"Accurate description of her, no matter who said it or when. Anyway, she came back the next year as well, dressed the same way, and that's when the peculiarities began. And I believe she is the catalyst for my story."

"How so?"

"Other than her first name, no one knew who she was or how she was invited, or if she was invited, but she showed up those two years in a row, and it's presumed she drowned in the river behind the hotel."

Hearing that news, it was as if that magical kiss beneath a sprig of mistletoe had been taken from me. In my mind

Amelia was still out there, as she had been that night, young and beautiful. The idea that she might have aged wasn't something I could wrap my head around, and the idea that she drowned long years ago behind the hotel was impossible to grasp. I recalled how she moved, and how the men there that night watched her, unable not to, and I remembered one young man making a crass remark as she walked by. That had made me angry. He treated her like she was a bus he meant to catch and had missed.

Other than that, I couldn't recall much about the party. I didn't even remember seeing Amelia again that night. But that kiss stayed with me.

"I hadn't heard about her drowning," I said.

"It was in the news, for a few days," Robert said, "but it was merely a suspicion. Truth is, no one knows exactly what happened to her, and I can't even say for certain she has anything to do with the story I want to tell you, so you have to keep that in mind."

I poured myself another cup of coffee and decided to nibble on a piece of bread my diet didn't need.

"Tell me about it," I said.

Robert stared at his cold cup of coffee, as if he might fish his memories from it, finally lifted his head, and began.

❧

MY SISTER AND I always called it the Christmas Hotel, because of the parties there. These days it's in ruin. I have been out there most every year, even after its closing. I always unlock the door with a head full of fond memories, but once inside they fade.

First word of strangeness in the room, discomfort on the second floor, came some many years back, the Christmas after Amelia's disappearance. The hotel was still in business then, of course. A young married couple rented number twelve, and left in the middle of the night. I don't know what their exact complaint was, but I was told they found the room "unsavory," and couldn't sleep for things "going on up there."

The room was fine the rest of the year, no complaints, but come Christmas Eve, no one could make it through a night. This seemed ridiculous to me, and I thought it best to discover what was causing the problem, so I set about spending a night in the room come Christmas Eve.

Keep in mind this was some years ago, and I was young and strong and willful. I felt that though others had vacated the room, I would not, and that I would deduce the problem, and see that whatever was causing the disturbance was repaired. A board nailed down, a creaky wind-rattled window fastened shut, what have you. Simply put, I felt the problem with the room was a natural one, perhaps compounded by the guests having indulged in too much Christmas food and liquid cheer during the annual parties.

Before I tell you about that night, perhaps I should preface a bit, and this is where you can make up your own mind about how much Amelia has to do with this, if anything at all.

On the night she disappeared and was assumed drowned, she was seen with two young men on the stairs, laughing, engaging them the way she engaged every male there, and then there were no more memories of her.

At some point in the night she disappeared and was not seen again, though her clothes were found on the river's edge, and that led to the belief she drowned, perhaps having gone skinny dipping, encouraged to do so by excess alcohol.

The police were called out the next day, but Amelia was not found. As no one actually knew her, or even knew her last name, there was nothing that could be done. The two young men said to have been with her on the stairs were investigated, but neither admitted to going upstairs with Amelia and there was no real proof they had, other than a young woman who said she saw them together on the stairs, and knew them, but admitted the next day she was terribly drunk, and was one drink shy of being able to see pink elephants carrying umbrellas. So she was a poor witness at best.

The room was looked over, but there was nothing askance. No one reported to the police, or the hotel, about a missing loved one, so that was it. There was nowhere to go with it. The very next year, Christmas time, the strange events in room twelve began, the ones that so frightened that young married couple, and they continued every year thereafter.

On the Christmas Eve I chose to check it out, I left the party early, about eleven p.m., and with my overnight bag in tow, slipped up to room number twelve. I showered and dressed in my pajamas, then set about enjoying a room-service delivery of hot chocolate and a few Christmas cookies.

The lady who delivered the snack had worked with us for some years, and she informed me that, no matter what, she would not stay in that room past the stroke of midnight. She had been at the hotel too long, heard the stories from departing guests, and was certain there was something dreadfully wrong. She was in and out like a postman.

As I ate, the clock ticked its way toward midnight. The time was easy to see, because the room had one of those old tall clocks from another era. It wasn't a clock that banged the hour, but merely a large-faced clock that could be seen even with the light out if the moon was bright and the curtains were pulled back, and that night, it was so bright it made the windows glow like lighted frames.

When I finished eating, the clock hit midnight; I distinctly remember that. I got up and went to the window and looked out. The land behind the hotel, and the river beyond, were bathed in silver, and the water seemed especially bright, like a long, wide ribbon.

It was then that I noticed a curious thing, and to this day I have no idea who was responsible for it, or when it was done, but the window was nailed to the frame in several spots, the nails having been driven in awkwardly but firmly. I know because I tried to lift the window, and it wouldn't budge. I remember thinking the next day I would have the nails removed, and the window frame replaced.

I pulled the thick, dark curtains over the windows, blocking out the moon, slipped off my house shoes, turned off the lamp by the bed, and climbed under the covers. I had already decided for all practical purposes my ghost hunt was over.

I fell immediately to sleep, but not long after I awoke, chilled. It was not cold outside, or hadn't been when I went to bed. You know how it is in our part of the country, but in that moment of awakening, it was as if I had laid down in a snow bank.

I turned on the lamp by the bed, but it had ceased to work. I got out of bed and felt my way to the light switch by the door, but the results were the same. Nothing. The electricity seemed to have gone off, and my first thought was that an unexpected cold storm had come through and caused the loss of power.

After bumping my shins a few times against furniture, I located my overnight bag, pawed my way into it, and found the penlight I had there. I used it to make my way to the closet where the extra blanket was kept, something to bundle me against the cold.

It was one of those closets that has a sliding door, and when I slid it back, I lifted the penlight. The beam caught something on the top shelf, and it seemed to me in that instant that it was a set of eyes. I jumped back, stumbled against a chair. When I took another look, there was nothing on the shelf other than the blanket I had been looking for.

In that moment I decided no matter how hardheaded I thought myself, the story of something being wrong with the room had gotten to me a bit. I took a deep breath, pulled down the blanket, and made my way back to bed.

I turned off the penlight, placed it on the night stand, and tried to go back to sleep with the extra blanket over me. This time falling asleep was harder to do. I thought about those eyes I had seen, or believed I had seen. I couldn't get it out of mind. I kept picking the penlight off the nightstand, turning it on, and poking it in the direction of the open closet.

Could a raccoon or possum have found its way into the closet? Perhaps there was an opening to the attic, and a creature had somehow come in that way. That idea got me on my feet again, and sure enough, when I poked the light back into the closet, I could see there was indeed a trap door in the ceiling, but it was closed.

Dissatisfied, I went back to bed.

I finally did go back to sleep, but a little later on I was awakened once more by intense cold, and now there was a smell like dead fish and wet weeds. The air in the room seemed heavy. I literally felt the hair on the back of my neck and arms stand up and my nostrils quivered against the stench.

Though the curtains were pulled tight, they were abruptly pushed back by something unseen. The moonlight dropped in, filling the room, but there was nothing comfortable about the lack of darkness. Instead, the feeling of unease increased tenfold. I was paralyzed with fear. I lifted my penlight again and poked it at what seemed to me to be the source of the discomfort, the open closet.

From the top shelf of the closet something dropped and smacked against the floor, and then that something began to move toward the bed where I lay.

I couldn't tell what it was, and even with my penlight on it, there was a dimness about it. It came toward me, slowly, squirming and crawling. Its general shape was humanlike, but the face was like a white grub with mashed human features. Bony arms and legs poked out from the bundle, and long fingers scratched across the floor, pulling it forward. Where it crawled it left behind a slime trail, and made a wet, squishing sound as it came.

I could not move a muscle. It was as if anvils lay across my body, pressing me down. Excruciating moments passed as it neared the bed, and finally it arrived. A fat, wet hand lifted up and clutched at the edge of my blanket. I could see right through the thing, could see the wall and closet beyond. It tilted its head and examined me, as if trying to make out my face, and then, as if disappointed, dropped to the floor at the edge of the bed.

It stood. It was so surprising I think I screamed aloud. I feared that would attract it to me, and I stuck my hand in my mouth and bit down on it to keep from crying out again.

But it didn't so much as turn in my direction. It trudged toward the window on its sticklike legs. The window lifted without its touch, and it fell out of the open gap. Wind blew the curtains, the moonlight dimmed, then brightened, and the bubble of fear that enveloped the room evaporated. I felt the weight lifted off of me.

I forced myself out of bed. I didn't use my penlight. The room was bright enough with moon glow and I could see clearly. The floor was spotted with puddles of water, and I could feel the dampness against my feet. I leaned out of the open window, looked down.

The bony thing lay there in a heap. As I watched, it stood and lurched toward the river, its swollen head nodding first to one side, then the other.

Closer it came to the water the less visible it was. The moonlight poked through it, and by the time it reached the bank it was no longer perceptible, at least to the human eye. Yet, I could clearly see footprints being made in the sand by the shoreline, and then the water splashed, as if something heavy had been dropped into it, and finally the room went dark.

And here is an even more incredible part to my story. The curtains were drawn again, without my aid or anyone or anything's aid that I could determine. They just snapped closed. The chill left the air, and I swear on everything I love and believe in, when I peeled the curtains back to try and look out again, the window was down and the nails were still driven into the wood; there was no sign that they had fallen out. The puddles on the floor were gone as well.

I stood there in the dark for a long time. When I walked back to the bed, I felt as if I had been in a hypnotic state. All the dread I had experienced was gone. A strange calm had settled on me, a kind of drained relaxation that I remembered from my youth after a hard hike or a strong run.

I climbed back in bed, crawled under the covers and slept soundly until I could feel the warmth of the morning sun cutting through the dark curtains. It was just a room now, and the events of the night before seemed dreamlike, and I considered that was exactly what it was, or at least I tried to. But I knew better. It had been there, and now the Christmas haunting had passed.

I dressed and went down to the river to look for the footprints I had clearly seen on its bank in the moonlight, but there was nothing there.

As I said, I don't know if any of this actually has to do with Amelia, but she certainly came to mind. Had she been in that room? How did she end up in the river? The thought wouldn't leave me. I took it upon myself to have the river dragged, and brought in divers to search for the remains of a body, or anything that might have belonged to her, though whatever might be left of her would now be fragmentary, and had most likely long been washed out to sea years ago. It was a long shot, but I took it.

Nothing was found.

I hired a private investigator to find the young woman who had seen the men on the stairs with Amelia, and I set him to look for Amelia herself, to find out if she was still alive.

As for Amelia, when it was all said and done, nothing new was learned about her. However, the investigator did find the drunk woman who had been at that party so many years ago, found her easily. She lived nearby, and it turned out she had been a schoolmate of my sister. I either had not known that, or had forgotten it, but she said she really couldn't remember much about the event anymore, but at the time felt she had seen the three of them going up the stairs. And she provided the names of the young men, which had been forgotten after the initial investigation. She reminded my investigator that she had been drunk beyond reason.

Once we had the names of those men, they were easy to find. One, Jim Warren, was dead, had drowned in his bathtub. He lived far away from here, another state. His death was said to be suicide. He left a note. All it said was "Sorry."

His family said he had been depressed for a long time, had been having financial problems, and was bothered by bad dreams and a pill addiction. Oddly, he wrapped himself in a blanket, covered his face and most of his body with it, and climbed into a tub full of water and forced himself under. It must have taken great determination to drown himself. It seems to me a horrible way to go.

The other gentleman was found effortlessly as well. His name is Wilbert Kastengate, Jr. He is successful and lives in the city. His parents knew my parents, it turned out, and that's why he was present that night. Once he was found, he agreed to talk to me, we met at a restaurant at, as you might have suspected, one of my hotels.

He was a lean man in an expensive blue suit with a head full of thick gray hair. He had held up well, handsome for his age. But when we began to talk about the night of Amelia's disappearance, I saw him pale, and it seemed to me that the years he had fought off for so long came down on him like a whirlwind. He sagged in his chair like a large bean bag.

I went right at him, but he denied going upstairs with Amelia, said he had no idea who Jim Warren was. Not much was gained from the conversation, as far as satisfying my curiosity goes, but I convinced him to join me later tonight at the Christmas hotel. That was a month ago when he agreed. Meaning, he may or may not show.

Come with me to the Christmas hotel. It is only an hour from here. I want you to see what is there, know that I'm telling the truth, and again, it would be nice to have a friend along as comfort. I know that we haven't been in contact that much, but you and I are about all that is left from those parties years ago, at least as far as people I know go. So, come with me.

る

WHEN ROBERT FINISHED his story, he leaned back and glanced at his watch. That was an obvious indicator that I should decide on my course of action for the night.

I could have declined, but the truth was Robert and his story had grabbed me. I have never believed in ghosts, but I have always been amused and somewhat titillated by the idea of them. And, of course, there was my connection with that night, my small but significant memories of Amelia. I was a bit bothered by the fact that he had come to me because he didn't know who else to come to. It was clear he didn't want to go to the hotel by himself.

Still, it was intriguing, and another incentive was to not spend the rest of Christmas Eve and all of Christmas Day alone. Especially after memories of Amelia had been reignited. Her sweet face, the gold hoop earrings, the short dress, that kiss beneath the mistletoe, haunted me.

Robert drove us. It was a chill night, coat weather, the sky was clear and the moon was bright.

"You think Kastengate will actually show?"

"I got the impression he wanted to come, but it may have less to do with my ghost story and more to do with me trying to link him to Amelia's disappearance. Of course, that doesn't mean he's guilty. However, just so you know, I have a gun in my coat pocket. Protection in case Kastengate thinks it might be a good idea to rid himself of suspicion. I know that sounds dramatic, but, it could be like that, I guess."

After that revelation, I was feeling less excited about the prospect of company for the night, and it even occurred to me that I may have been set up. What if Robert thought I was the one responsible for Amelia's death, and this was all a plan to get me alone at the Christmas Hotel and finish me off? What if he was responsible, and for some reason thought I might know something, an idea that had festered over the years, and now he had decided it was best I was taken care of?

This was on my mind as we arrived at the hotel, an hour or so before midnight. There wasn't any electricity, but Robert had brought a battery lantern, as well as a flashlight for me and him.

He let us in and we trudged upstairs, Robert guiding, waving his flashlight before us. When we reached number twelve, he paused, sighed, and opened the door.

The door pushed aside spider- and cobwebs and in the beam of the flashlight dust motes spun about as if in a cyclotron. Robert moved the light about the room, flashed it on the closed closet door, then the bed, which upon closer observation appeared to have a velvet sheet over it; a coating of dust, made shiny in the flash light beam.

Nothing about the room appeared odd, other than those indicators of neglect. The clock he had mentioned was no longer in the room. Robert moved to the window and opened the curtains, and as he did, dust rose from them in a cloud.

It was not a full-moon night, but the moonlight was strong. It landed on the window glass and turned the panes bright, fell across Robert like a slat of silver.

I walked over and stood by him.

"See," he said.

He was showing me the nails in the window frame, all around it, slammed in randomly. Something done long ago. You could tell because the heads of the nails were rusty and looked like copper in the moonlight.

We stood there for a while and talked, maybe for as long as an hour or more, enough that I lost my suspicion of him, and as we stood there, car lights flashed and a car turned around a wooded curve and became visible in the moonlight. It pulled up to the side of the hotel, out of sight, and then some time passed and we heard someone on the stairs, coming up. I found that more disconcerting than the idea of a ghost.

The steps ended at the open door of number twelve, and a tall, handsome man with smooth gray hair came into the room. Although I didn't actually know him, and the years had settled on him, I realized he was the man I had seen that long ago Christmas night. He was the one who had turned his head to look at Amelia, and had made an uncouth comment as she passed. There was still about him an air of arrogance and privilege. The kind of man who had done what he pleased in life and hadn't suffered consequence of any kind.

"You came," Robert said.

"Curiosity," Kastengate said. His voice was smooth as honey, his movements athletic. I hadn't realized how old-man-like I had become until seeing him, a man the years were afraid to completely destroy, a man who could still turn a young girl's head.

"I didn't know someone else would be here," Kastengate said.

"A friend," Robert said.

Kastengate smiled. "I don't think you trust me."

"Do you remember this room?" Robert said.

"I've never been in it," Kastengate said.

"Would you mind closing the door?" Robert said.

Kastengate closed it. Robert leaned in close to the window and lifted his arm so the moonlight shown on the face of his watch.

"Five minutes," he said.

"And that's when your ghost comes, huh?" Kastengate said. "Maybe I should have stayed home."

"I suppose it may be more than five minutes," Robert said. "It's five minutes to midnight, but it may be a bit after that. As I remember, it didn't come right away."

"The ghost you told me about?" Kastengate said, and grinned. The moonlight lit up his teeth, but I got the impression that in that moment he had lost some of his cocksureness. He began to look nervously around the room. Maybe not for a ghost, but perhaps by that time he had become suspicious, thought we might have made plans for his demise. The question was, of course, was he actually guilty of anything?

As for the ghost, well, I doubted that. In five or ten minutes it occurred to me we would all look pretty silly standing in a moonlit room with our hands in our pockets. Maybe Robert thought the ghost story would cause Kastengate to admit what he had done. If so, I concluded that was unlikely. But if the story was designed to scare Kastengate, why tell me the same story?

"Five minutes have passed," Kastengate said.

Robert looked at his watch. "Not quite. Please. Stick around. You came, so why not satisfy your curiosity? Sit."

Kastengate remained standing. Robert went to the windows and pulled shut the curtains he had opened. Robert switched off his flashlight, and I did the same. When we came into the room he had placed the lantern on the nightstand, and now he came over, turned it on, and went back to stand between the window and the foot of the bed.

Kastengate seated himself in a chair by the door. He didn't look in the least perturbed. He crossed his legs. Still, he had come, and that meant something. Curiosity maybe, guilt perhaps, a combination of the two.

It is impossible to convey the feeling that came next, or to describe the stench, but the best I can do is to say the air grew colder and heavier and there was a stink in the room like dead rats in the walls, and then there was the sound of movement in the closet, like something heavy turning over.

Robert switched off the lantern, picked up his flashlight, turned it on and shined it at the closet. The closet door heaved a bit, as if something inside was pushing against it. The door beaded with liquid, and the liquid ran to the floor and into a puddle.

Robert kept the flashlight on the puddle.

Kastengate stood up, let out a loud breath.

The puddle became a solid mass of what looked like molasses, and I could see a head poking up out of the slimy mess. The head was dark and rotten like a pumpkin left in the patch beyond its prime. Hair the texture of matted waterweeds hung from its skull. The damp, dead odor intensified and filled my nose and turned my stomach.

An arm moved out from the mess, a bony thing with leathery flesh and long fingers like dry sticks. Another arm revealed itself. Now there was a whole, but ravaged body lying there in a puddle. It reached out with its hands, scratched at the floor and pulled itself toward the bed.

As I was standing in front of the bed, it was coming directly toward me. I was frozen in place, but as the thing came nearer, I stepped back and sat on the mattress, swung my legs off the floor, and inched to the far side of the bed which was flush with the wall. I felt like a sailor on a rickety life raft watching a shark approach.

Robert kept the circle of light on the thing, but he had moved back to the foot of the bed and had his back against the wall.

It kept crawling until it arrived at the bed. It was so low down and close to the edge of the bed by then, I could no longer see it. After what seemed like an eternity, a bony hand lifted, the fingers rattling together like dry sticks. It clutched at the blanket, and slowly I saw its head rise like a horrid moon, and the light from the real moon filled its dead white eyes.

It paused there, seeming to look for something and not find it. I don't know how to describe it, as the face was so odd, but I got the sensation that it was feeling disappointment.

"Jesus," Kastengate said. I'm sure he hadn't meant to say that, but as soon as his voice split the cold, dead air, the thing turned its head toward him, and tilted it in a curious manner.

Kastengate stepped backwards until the chair against the wall stopped him. He fell back into it, sitting there as it was his intended plan.

The thing leaned its head forward. Its mouth opened slightly, and I can't say for sure, but I thought there was a kind of smile there, like a gash in a pumpkin. And then, it moved. It covered the distance between it and Kastengate so fast it was as if I were seeing the event on film and frames were missing. It grabbed hold of Kastengate and that caused him to scream.

Perhaps I should have sprung forward to help him, but I did not, even when he cried out to me, and then Robert for help, I didn't move a muscle. Neither did Robert.

The thing jerked Kastengate from the chair and collapsed out of my sight. I could hear it slithering across the floor. I could see Robert's face, as he looked down, watching that thing crawl, dragging its prize with it. He didn't try for his gun. He didn't move.

Then the revenant rose up from the floor like a puppet pulled upright by invisible strings. It was clutching Kastengate by the neck, as if he was a rag doll. There was nothing handsome about him now. His eyes were impossibly wide. His mouth hung open. He was the color of snow.

The window curtains slid back, as if by some unseen hand, and the moonlight shown in again. I could see the rusty nails begin to turn and lift out of the window frame, and as they turned I could feel the hair on the back of my neck stand up like a bed of thorns. They rattled to the floor and the window flew up, and then, like a large windblown leaf, the thing and Kastengate were sucked out of the open window and plunged toward the ground.

Robert came unstuck from the wall, eased toward the window. I found the courage to slip off the bed and stand by him.

We looked out and down. The thing rose up and began to drag Kastengate away by the collar of his jacket. It was obvious the fall had cracked his bones in many places. One arm was twisted in a way an arm shouldn't go, and one of his feet was turned at an awkward angle and raw bone glinted from his broken flesh and ripped pants.

"We should help him," Robert said.

I didn't reply, and Robert didn't move.

Kastengate was dragged out of view behind a row of dark, limb-dripping willows and an ancient cypress tree, on toward the river.

We stood there for a long time, then we sat down on the end of the bed and waited until the sun came up, warm and rosy. Christmas Day.

I looked up as the room darkened. The curtains had been pulled across the window again. It had happened so subtly, neither of us had noticed.

I went to the window, moved back the curtains and looked out at the newborn day. The window frame was shut and nailed down again, as if the nails had never been removed. It was as Robert had described when he had spent that lonely night in the room some years back. I could hardly breathe.

Down by the river, we found Kastengate's jacket, but besides that there was only the rolling brown water. Kastengate was gone.

We drove to a pay phone and called the police. They came out and looked, thought we were suspects in the case. But nothing was ever proven, though if you look up old newspaper accounts, police records, you will see that Robert and I are still under suspicion.

We didn't tell them what we really saw, figuring that would only compound the situation. We said we drove out there under a spell of nostalgia and discovered Kastengate's car, his jacket, down by the river. Neither of us lied when we said we hardly knew him.

Next year we went there on Christmas Eve. Nothing happened in the room that time. I fell asleep in a chair and Robert fell asleep on the dusty bed. When we awoke the next morning, we decided it was over for good. Early the next year the hotel was torn down.

I never saw Robert again, though I heard he died some years back. Went in his sleep.

So now I'm old as dirt, waiting for the shadow, thinking about how one of those men had done himself in by drowning, and how the other was taken away by... Well, I can't say for sure, but I have my idea about it. I think justice was paid.

Sometimes, when I lay down, the last thing I think of is Amelia, young and alive, bright and magnetic, dressed as she was that night so long ago on Christmas Eve, those gold hoop earrings shimmering, almost as bright as the light in her eyes and the shine of her smile.

She was and is a dark and beautiful dream.

THE
DARK THING

RONALD SAT IN the dark hallway in a large, stuffed chair he had pulled from the living room. He sat there with the back of his chair against the wall and the door open at the end of the hall. He sat and waited with a double-barreled twelve-gauge lying across his lap.

The cool night wind was blowing in from outside and he could see leaves spinning, hear them crackling across the cement walkway and the hard boards of his front porch. There was the faint glow of silver moonlight dusting the ground, the walkway, and the porch.

He waited, because he knew it was coming. It always came, though it never came inside, but tonight he thought it might. It was growing stronger. Before now he had put out bowls of food, cheese and bread, as well as water and milk, trying to lure it in. But over the past week, from the first time he had discovered it, it had only come as far as the porch, but hadn't gone onto it.

∽

EACH NIGHT WHEN it arrived, always shortly after the old clock in the living room chimed out twelve chimes, it would drink from the water bowls and milk all along the sidewalk, and then it would stop at the bottom of the porch steps. It was shadowy and hard to define. It was no shape and it was all shapes. Large as it was, it could sit like a big, stray dog and look at him over the edge of the porch with its lemon-colored eyes. It looked at him and into him, and it both thrilled and frightened him at the same time.

But it went no farther up the porch. It seemed to be waiting for something. This night Ronald had put both a bowl of milk and a saucer containing sardines on the porch with hopes to tempt it closer.

As he considered these things, he saw it at the far end of the walkway. It was moving the way it always moved, coming along on all fours, or was it all sixes? Or was it legless? It was hard to tell. It moved like dark crepe paper being blown along the walkway by a giant industrial fan.

It seemed simultaneously light as a feather and heavy as lead. The moonlight was thinner tonight as it came toward him, and it didn't pause at the water bowls or the bits of bread and cheese on saucers positioned at the edges of the walkway. It came straight away to the front porch, and tonight it placed a paw on the bottom step, paused for a moment, then placed a paw on the next step, or whatever it was that supported it, something dark and padded looking.

For a moment, only a moment, Ronald thought the thing looked more like someone crouching, someone wrapped in shadow. He could hear the steps straining under its weight, squeaking like a dying rat being chewed to death by a cat.

With another move, swift and agile, it was on the porch. It went straight to the bowl of milk and sipped loudly, lifted its head and looked at Ronald sitting quietly in the dark at the end of the hall.

Besides seeing it, he could feel it even more than before; feel it throbbing inside of him like a twisted sexual need. It felt like everything he had failed to do and all the things he had done wrong: missed opportunities, disastrous relationships, all his evil thoughts, all his bad actions and foul tempers. It all seemed collected in that foul-smelling, dark thing.

It ate the sardines, rattling the saucer as it did. Then it was coming to him. Moving impossibly slow, approaching by inches, digesting its intent. The closer it got the heavier the air weighed. The darker the night seemed. And now the thing was darker too, and in those deep down sensations, Ronald felt as if it were feeding off not only milk and sardines, but all those bad things inside of him, all those memories of plans gone wrong and mistakes made and blind hubris and unnecessary slights he had visited upon people who didn't deserve it.

His wife, Tonia, for one. In his mind's eye he could remember his finger marks around her neck, her black eyes and purple bruises. He remembered the way she limped, how she shrank from him like a whipped dog. He had delighted in it then, but now it was as if he could feel what she felt, and he wondered why he couldn't before. Why did this shadow thing arouse those feelings of regret?

Its presence made him remember the things he had pushed under and tried to forget. Like the night when he had been drinking heavily, and she told him she was leaving, and then he remembered the blood-red rage that had surfaced inside him. She had gone missing, went away and didn't come back. But Ronald knew where she was. Not far away actually. And though the cops suspicioned, questioned and searched, they found nothing, even though Tonia was right under their noses. Had they come back a week later, gone back to the creek that ran next to his property, trickling water musically over round white rocks, water covered in shadows from the trees that grew on either side of it, they would have certainly had it under their noses, for she smelled by then. He had buried her shallow, into the side of the creek, and at first it was fine, but then he had to go down there and dig her up and rebury her under a lean elm tree farther away from the creek bank.

He put lime in her grave and dug this one deep. Dug in the cover of the trees in the dead of night with only a flashlight lying on the ground by the grave to light his work. No one saw him, and the years crawled by.

He would think of her from time to time, but it was as if it all had been a dream.

All those memories washed over him and into him, and the thing left the porch and came through the open door, crept down the hallway. The smell of it was intense now, and, of course, he recognized that smell, the smell of rot and decay; the smell of something deceased and putrid.

And when it was less than a yard away, he knew what it was. It was Tonia. Or what she had become. This dark wad of menace was made of his guilt and depression, fear and anger. It was everything he had done wrong and thought wrong, and his greatest wrong was what he had done to Tonia. Sweet pretty Tonia, gone now for twenty years and at times almost forgotten, but as of late well-remembered, at least by him.

As it came closer, he could feel every blow he had dealt Tonia, every slight, and every pain she had felt at his drunken antics, his many deceptions.

It was so near now he could reach out and touch it. The eyes, though golden, not blue, he recognized as the eyes of Tonia, for the same expression was there. It was that poor, sweet woman he had laid in the creek bed, and then finally beneath the elm. It was his belief that the ground would be open there now. With each passing night, as he grew more aware of the thing's presence, her presence had gained strength and nightly left its death womb to creep closer and gain courage. It came nearer and nearer, having lost all fear of him, having turned into something made by him and of him; she was a collection of her own pain and betrayal, as well as the deep, black dark inside of him.

Ronald pointed the shotgun at it, her, cocked back the hammers. She/it was right on top of him. It was now or never. And then he lowered the shotgun and nodded at the thing at his feet, placed the twin barrels of the shotgun under his chin, and pushing his house shoe off his foot, put his big toe inside the trigger guard, and gently pushed against the trigger itself, and there was a loud bang.

The shot echoed loudly but was not heard by anyone in the sparse and widely spaced neighborhood. It echoed down the hall, out across the yard, all the way to the creek, and finally to the broken grave beneath the elm.

Next morning the mailman walked on the porch clutching a fistful of mail, accidently stepping on and breaking the saucer that had held the sardines. He looked through the open door and down the hallway. A man without a head was sitting in a chair. A shotgun lay on the floor. What had been Ronald's head was mostly on the wall and scattered about in wet, meaty droplets.

But even more curious and disturbing was the body in front of the man in the chair, lying belly-down on the floor, its arms reaching out toward Ronald, one hand touching his shoe. The stench of the body was almost enough to knock the mailman off the porch.

Clutching the mail in one hand, holding his nose with the other, the mailman moved inside the hallway and tiptoed toward the bodies. When he was closer, he saw that the body on the floor was little more than yellowed bones, wrinkled parchment skin, hanks of cloth, and long strips of greasy black hair. There were wads of roots and vines and clumps of dirt on and around it, as if it had shed those like a cocoon.

The body's head was turned, and one eye socket was visible. Roots were growing inside the socket. Red earthworms twisted amongst the little roots. Most remarkable of all was that the skull wore an impossibly broad smile that crinkled up its parchment skin at the corners of the mouth, and clearly revealed its yellowed, dirt-filled teeth.

Cluttered as it was with roots and worms, a black moth fluttered out of one of the eye sockets, and lifted upwards in front of the mailman's face.

He saw then that it was not a moth at all, but perhaps some kind of miniature bird with a squirming black worm in its beak, and up and away it went, down the hall, out into the daylight, climbing up toward the sun.

BIRD

WHEN I WAS twelve my friend James was the finest boy that ever lived. That changed when he got older and started borrowing other people's cars without asking. But before that he was all right, and I guess in the end he was all right still, but he was all right then in prison. He borrowed one car too many.

But the thing I remember most about him was how he was when we were kids.

One summer when we were enjoying freedom from school, he found a robin with a busted wing, shot by a BB gun he figured, and he began nursing the bird. I helped a little.

After he found the bird he put it in a shoebox and fed it by hand, worms and such he mashed up in a bowl and made liquid enough to pull up into an eyedropper, and then he'd shoot that mess into the bird's mouth. Everyone said once you touched a bird they couldn't go back into the wild because there was the smell of humans on it, and other birds would peck it to death.

I told James that when he found the bird, and he said, "That's silly. Birds ain't that big on smell. Where's their nose?"

He had a point, I guess.

With the bird in a shoebox, we went to the store and bought Popsicles. At the check-out the clerk said, "What you got in the box?"

"A hurt bird," James said.

"Yeah. Let me see."

James took the lid off the box and showed him the bird.

"His wing's all bent up," said the clerk.

"Yep. That's what the Popsicle sticks are for. To make splints."

"Yeah. Well, even if you could get him all right, birds will peck him to death because you touched him."

"I keep hearing that," James said.

"Cause it's true," said the clerk.

"Have you seen it happen?" James said.

The clerk turned slightly red. "Don't forget who you're talking to. Respect your elders."

"Yes, sir," James said.

Outside, us sucking on our Popsicles, the shoebox under his arm, James said, "That asshole don't know nothing."

We went to James' house, but we didn't stay there long because his father was drunk and had just knocked out James' older brother in a fistfight over a biscuit, or some such. Anyway, we didn't stay, but James got some twine and a few other things while I waited out in the yard. He managed to avoid his father, so he didn't get knocked out too. From time to time his dad drank too much, and he always knocked someone out, or got knocked out. His wife could throw a good punch too, if she could sidle in close enough and catch him unsuspecting. It was kind of a ritual, the drinking and the knockouts. The whole family was that way except James, and later he was that way too.

We went over to my house. Out in the backyard under the apple tree, we sat with our backs against the tree trunk and James opened the box and gently took out the bird.

The bird looked up at him with what I thought was an odd look, but who's to know if a bird can give an odd look, or a friendly look, or whatever, but I thought it was an odd look, and then a friendly look, a kind of don't-hurt-me look.

James was very gentle. He used the Popsicle sticks, now minus the Popsicles, of course, and he used some twine and white tape to tie up the injured wing, making splints out of the sticks. He was very professional about it.

The bird became our main interest, and in time it got so the bird could hop around and such, but it never tried to fly, because it couldn't. It was perfectly happy living in the shoebox and being let out to chase bugs and worms in the grass. After a bit, it would hop back into the box and hunker down, tired and ready to rest. James had folded up a washrag in the bottom of the box, and that was the bird's bed. It didn't mind being trapped and seemed to have decided the big wide world was too much for it, and being contained with a place to sleep and three meals a day was good enough.

I never knew a wild bird could be like that. It was like a pet. It would sit on James's outstretched palm, or on his shoulder, and it would make a kind of singing sound, but for a bird, it didn't have much of a voice. My old Aunt Nettie could have done better with wax paper folded over a comb.

James kept feeding it with the eyedropper, and the bird grew stronger.

James hid the bird in the loft of his family's barn at night, and took it out in the day. The bird went with us pretty much everywhere we went. Girls would ask what was in the shoebox, and James would show them, and they would ooh and ah, and such. James said girls liked a boy that cared about animals, especially puppies and kittens, but birds would do in a pinch. He thought it was a good way to meet girls and show them your sensitive side.

There was a cat at our house. It wasn't our cat. My mother gave it milk and bits of scraps, and it hung around. It had one eye. I didn't like it much because it scratched me the time I tried to pet it.

My mother said, "If you'd been through what that poor cat has been through, you might scratch someone too."

Anyway, we had to watch our bird when the cat was around. Letting the bird out of the box, you could see the cat under the house eyeing it with its one bright eye, thinking the robin would be one hell of a good meal. And it would have. The bird had actually gotten fat.

One day James took the splints off the bird's wing. He worked the wing gently with his fingers, and said, "He's healed up."

"Think so?" I said.

"Know so."

Next few days James would get down on his knees and toss the bird a little, nothing serious, not too high, and the bird would flap its wings and glide for a short distance. A week or so later he said it was ready to fly.

We climbed up on the roof of my house using my dad's painting ladder, taking the bird in the shoebox with us. It was a cool evening and the sun was starting to go down, and James said letting the bird loose while there was light would give it a chance to get out there, but by night it could roost somewhere and build its strength, and by the next day it could fly longer and better.

"Does it know how to roost?" I said.

"It's a bird," he said, as if that contained all the answers.

We sat on the roof near the edge, and after a bit James took the bird out of the box. It was a big moment for both of us. A lot of time and effort had gone into healing up that bird. Earlier that day it had even flown a few feet farther than the day before, though it never got any higher than six inches off the ground.

The sky was starting to fade, but there was still plenty of light. James held the bird in both of his palms, like a treat in a bowl.

"I name you Apollo," he said. "We wish you luck."

He stood on the edge of the roof, sure-footed as a goat, and I stood beside him, a little less sure-footed.

James lifted the bird as if it were an offering to the fading sun, then lowered his hands a little and brought them up swiftly and tossed the bird into the air.

The bird's wings spread immediately, but they didn't flap. It soared out a ways, then took a beak-dive toward the earth. It went down fast and hit directly on its head, a one-point landing. I thought I heard a little crack even from all the way up on the roof, a sound like someone snapping their fingers.

James looked down on the bird, said, "Well, shit."

The one-eyed cat came out from under the house like a rocket and grabbed the bird in its teeth by its repaired wing, and darted back under the house.

James stood there for a long time looking down at the spot where the bird had fallen.

"I didn't expect that," he said. And then, after another long moment we saw the cat come out from under the house with just the bird wing in its mouth. It ran past the apple tree and disappeared into a patch of woods behind the house.

James took a deep breath. I was crying a little. James patted me on the shoulder.

"Well, a cat's got to eat same as a bird," he said.

THE MOUSE AND
THE ELEPHANT

ONE DAY A mouse was entering the jungle and came upon a large and deep pit. An elephant had fallen into it. The mouse stood on the edge of the pit and looked down. The elephant looked up.

"Don't worry, buddy, I'll get you out," said the mouse.

The mouse immediately unpacked his backpack and took out his calibrating tools and such, and began working on the idea of a harness and a pulley system.

When he had it all worked out, it began to rain. The mouse took his umbrella from the pack and opened it up and thought a moment, then leaned over and looked down at the elephant.

"I'm going to have to leave for a short time, but I will return with all that's needed."

The mouse darted away.

He took a path through the jungle, and finally the rain stopped, but then the mouse crossed the desert. Sunburned and tired, he finally reached his home.

No other mice were about.

The mouse went to his house and put on a pair of work boots and dungarees, and a loose work shirt, then borrowed a few things from neighbors, even though they were not home.

Among the things he borrowed was a large pulley system that fit his calibrations, and a wrench, as well as a harness and a bulldozer, because the keys were in it. He drove back across the desert on the bulldozer, drove through the jungle on narrow trails, and made good time.

The mouse arrived where the elephant was trapped. The mouse looked in the pit.

It had stopped raining, but the elephant had water almost to his shoulders. When the elephant looked up, there seemed to the mouse to be desperation in his eyes. The mouse felt he was the elephant's only hope.

The mouse immediately went about setting up the wrench and pulley system, but found the ground too uneven. He decided to start first by using the bulldozer to flatten the ground around the pit so that the wrench could be erected on steady ground.

As he scraped the earth, and neared the pit, the mouse made a miscalculation and the bulldozer gunned forward and went into the ditch with a splash.

The bulldozer turned over and the mouse went underwater and was crushed beneath the dozer like a peanut hull, his tail waved briefly in the water as if trying to send a distress signal, and then it flopped down and went still.

It was such an impact that his little boots and dungarees were knocked off and they floated in the water. The elephant saw that he could put his back feet on the dozer, and if he did that, he could use his forelegs to pull himself out. So he did that.

Beneath the bulldozer the mouse's body was pushed deep in the mud, but the dozer proved a firm foothold for the elephant. The elephant reared up and hooked its front legs over the edge of the pit, and with considerable effort pulled himself out of the pit and started for home.

What is the moral to this story?

Mice should never operate heavy machinery.

THE SKULL
COLLECTOR

THERE WERE THREE of them, but the guy in front of me did most of the talking.

"What I'm thinking here, sweetie, is you aren't telling us all you know."

"You're thinking that, are you?" I said. "That's where you're wrong. You do all this, hurt me enough, scare me enough, then I'll tell you something, but it won't be the truth. I don't know the truth. You're wasting your time, and mine."

That was a lie. I knew where what they wanted was, but I figured once they knew, I could kiss my ass goodbye.

"Like I care about your time, sister."

"I like to get my nails done on Wednesday, so time matters to me."

"You're a tough broad, I'll give you that. Here's what I'm thinking, though, about that lie part. We find out you told us a lie, then we got to make it harder on you. Being tied to a chair and slapped around, that isn't going to be all of it. We think maybe we might have to start carving you up. Oh yeah. This is Wednesday, and Wednesday is done."

I wasn't actually that tough. I was hoping to die of a heart attack. I feared what they might do to me, feared it to the point of a possible surprise bowel movement, but there's something in me besides shit, and it makes me a smart mouth when I'm in danger. And frequently when I'm not. It's like the skunk that when frightened sprays stink. I'm frightened, I run my mouth.

"You can look all kinds of places, but I don't have it. Turned out there wasn't anything in the grave. And by the way, where'd you get that aftershave? It's making my eyes water."

"Oh," said the tall one leaning against the wall, "she's got a sharp tongue." This guy was probably six one and he went in heavy for the hair product. He had enough oil in his dark locks to grease all the squeaky hinges in creation with enough left over to grease a transmission.

"Tongue won't be so sharp if I cut it out," said the main one, the talker.

"Then you won't get to know what I know is nothing, not unless I lie to you in sign language. And I don't know sign language."

"Oh, shut up," said the man in front of me, the talker. "You're not funny." He had on what at first looked like an expensive suit, but the way it hung on him proved different. It was more like a man tent without the mosquito net. I had just noticed that. When he had been hitting me my powers of observation had been limited.

"I think she's funny," said the third man, a fat fellow with a crew cut and checkered pants that he must have bought via a time-machine trip to the nineteen seventies. He had on a shirt so green Irish grass would have been embarrassed to grow.

"Just shoot her, cut her throat, get it over with," said the tall one leaning against the wall. "She don't know nothing. She'd have said by now."

The taller one eyed me carefully. I believed him when he threatened to carve me up. After hours of being tied to a chair in the basement of an abandoned high school, I feared that heart attack wasn't coming to put me out of my misery. I was way too healthy for that.

"I say we get right to cutting her," the fat man said. "A little at a time. Everyone talks when you do that. We can get lies out of the way quick. She don't know nothing, well, we get to carve her anyway. How do you like that idea, baby?"

"Not all that appealing," I said.

The main talker nodded. "What I think we're going to do, missy, is do just that. We're going to cut those clothes off of you, put you on the floor there, and start carving. But we'll do it slow, just in case maybe you do have something to say. You talk, well, we can get it over with quick."

"What a treat," I said.

That's when I heard the door open and Ruby stepped in. Her dark hair was done up in a bun. She was wearing jeans and a droopy brown sweatshirt, holding a sawed-off ten-gauge shotgun. She looked like she could eat floor tacks and crap an anvil. Ruby's about five-five, but in that moment, she was Wonder Woman carrying a cannon.

My interrogator, who was focused on me, looked up just as Ruby cut down with that sawed-off ten-gauge. There was a roar like a lion and my interrogator's head went away, and what looked like a flight of bloody bees smashed into the wall. The body dropped right in front of me, getting blood on my tennis shoes. I liked those shoes.

The tall one against the wall started to rock forward, reach under his coat. I heard the sharp snap of the shotgun being pumped, and the lion roared again, and suddenly the tall man had a wet, red hole in his middle. Like my interrogator, he collapsed.

The fat one made a dash for the door on the far side, but the lion roared, and the shot caught him in the lower back. He hit the floor and tried to crawl, but he couldn't do it. Ruby pumped the shotgun, walked over to him and fired. Pieces of him and the shot from the load bounced around the room like someone had dropped a box full of ball bearings and a can of red paint.

Ruby put the shotgun on the floor and took out her pocket knife. She cut the ropes around my ankles and feet, then the one around my neck that was fastened to the back of the wooden chair. Oddly, it wasn't until then that I realized my ass hurt.

When I tried to stand up, I had a hard time. I didn't know if it was from being tied so long, or if it was fear. I decided it was both.

"You nearly shot me," I said. When I spoke, I could hardly hear myself. My ears were ringing from all that shotgun fire.

"No, I didn't."

"Did too."

"Don't start crying, Crystal. We haven't time for that."

"Screw you. You took long enough."

By then we were already moving toward the door.

&

MOST OF MY Wednesdays aren't like that.

I guess I ought to not start in the middle of a true-life story, or maybe it's not the middle. Hell. I don't know. But let me tell you how I got to that chair, and then I'll move beyond.

What I do for a living is I work—worked—for a fence. What the fence does—Ruby is her name—is she buys stolen goods and resales them for a profit. She works out of a pawnshop she owns, does legitimate business too. But when it's the right stuff, she does another kind of business. She knows what's stolen and what isn't, of course, and though there are some things she won't deal in (stolen show dogs), there are a lot of things she's glad to buy and resale, and she's been known to act as a go-between and do all manner of things that have nothing to do with pawnshops or fencing.

Weirdly, she once fenced some stolen bull semen from a prize bull, and this rancher guy bought it, came back later, said it turned out to be a dud. The heifer didn't fatten with calf. He wanted his money back. He was a tough old guy, Ruby said. Big, could crack walnuts with harsh language, chase a squirrel up a tree with bad breath. She had to use an axe handle to sort the guy out a little. It wasn't too bad. He was able to leave on his own, though not without a certain amount of pain and difficulty, one hand on his bleeding head, the other pressed against his broken ribs. That's when I realized not only does Ruby deal in stolen goods, she deals in violence, if the need arises. Her and her brothers, Pooty and Boo-boo.

Actually, that's not their real names. Their names are Arnold (Arnie), he's Pooty, and Benjamin (Ben), he's Boo-boo. They're two big guys, arms like Popeye, faces like car wrecks. They were always nice to me, though. I should point that out. Of course, Ruby and the boys, as she calls them, are my cousins, so they feel a bit obligated. Cousins once removed, I think. Hell, I don't know exactly. I get lost in the weeds when you get that far into family backgrounds. Dad once said, "In our family tree about the only thing you'll find is monkeys and broken limbs."

Here's how it started.

இ

SO, I'M HANGING out at the house trying to read *War and Peace* and learning I didn't like it, when the phone rang, and it was Ruby. That's how it started, with a phone call and my boredom with *War and Peace*.

"Hey, want to make some money?" she said.

I was as broke as my ethics, so I said, "Does a bear shit in the woods?"

"What if they live in the zoo?"

"Yes, Ruby, I want to make some money."

"This is a special job. It doesn't require contacts or even a lot of smarts."

"Then I'm perfect for it," I said.

"It's really not a biggie. It's not a fence, and it's not a pawn."

"Is it big enough for me to get out of bed, leave the house?"

"I meant what you have to do is no biggie, but yeah, it's big enough to get out of bed, go out to the graveyard in the middle of the night and make a whole lot of money for a short amount of digging."

I laughed.

Ruby was silent.

"Wait a minute," I said. "You're serious? A graveyard?"

"Serious as a yeast infection."

இ

THAT NIGHT RUBY picked me up in her black van and away we went. I was, as Ruby suggested, wearing work clothes. Had on boots, jeans, and a chambray shirt, hair tied back.

I looked over my shoulder to see what was rattling in the back of the van. Two shovels. A ten-gauge shotgun, a couple of beer cans.

"This is kind of out of my line of work," I said.

"I can do it by myself, but what I thought, while I'm digging, you hold the shotgun, you're digging, I hold it."

"Shotgun? What the hell, Ruby? This seems more like a job for Pooty and Boo-boo, not your petite cousin. I was thinking digging was out of my line, but gun work, way out of my line. I think you can take me back to the house."

"First, my brothers are out of town. And I take you back, you'll be giving up five thousand dollars for one night's work. Not even a whole night."

I thought about what five thousand dollars could do. Keep the lights and water on, pay the rent, buy some real food. And I needed new underwear. I washed mine much more, I'd be wearing lint.

"As long as we don't have to shoot the caretaker, grounds keeper, whatever they call those folks, then I guess I'll stick."

"It's nothing like that, it's just that, well, there could be competition, and I'd like to be able to discourage them. Also, there's no grounds keeper. I did some research. There's a lot of old stones and some weeds, and Etta Place."

"Etta Place?"

"You know, Butch and Sundance. At the end of the Old West days. They had this pretty schoolteacher with them when they were robbing banks and trains. Or maybe she was a prostitute.

No one really knows. Maybe she was a palm reader and a part time ukulele player for all I know. Anyway, the skull collector wants her head."

"Wait a minute. Katherine Ross?"

"She played her in the movie, yeah. But Etta, she was real. She left them in South America and came back to the States, disappeared. It's one of history's mysteries. Like why people used to wear turtlenecks with medallions the size of hubcaps.

"Anyway, she came back, and no one had a lead on her. Not the Pinkertons, who looked all over, not the historians. No one. But there was a rumor she had ended up in Texas, where she may have been from originally. That her name was really something else, that she went back to that name and worked in a brothel, later became a schoolteacher. All kinds of stories. And then the diary turned up. Not hers, but her sister's. There were answers inside."

In a nutshell, this is what Ruby told me. What Ball told her, and what she surmised.

Seems Etta Place, whose real name was Ethel Dodgers, was actually a former music teacher that got bored with teaching brats to play Chopsticks, and ran off with Butch and Sundance, then returned to Texas. She told her sister, Eunice, about her adventures with the robbers. Started teaching music again, died of what might have been the Spanish flu, and was buried in a cemetery just outside of Tyler, Texas, which was not too far from where we lived.

After her death, Eunice's diary ended up in a pawnshop, was bought by one Seabury Ball, who collected such things. Ball read it, and believed it. Knew from reading it that there was something he wanted. He wasn't called the Skull Collector for nothing. He wanted Etta's skull, one of the most renowned lost-to-history individuals there ever was, and he might be the only person in the world at that moment in time who knew where she was buried, and he wanted her dug up and delivered.

This, by the way, is also called grave robbing and it's not legal. But Ball had the money to buy his collector's items from the right people, and he was good at hiding his purchases. For example, rumor is he has the skulls of the Apache warrior, Geronimo, the noggins of Billy the Kid and Jimmy Hoffa, and rumor was someone ought to check Lincoln's tomb.

Problem was, Ball, an elderly gentleman, had a sugar baby, and one night when he was working on greasing the weasel, his enthusiasm for her, and for the skull, led him to make with too much pillow talk.

He told the girlfriend about the diary, the Etta revelation, but didn't mention the exact graveyard. Being someone who was out for herself, and expecting her sugar daddy to go toes up soon, she snuck around and told Repeat Pete, another old man with money, and like Ball, he was a collector of unusual items. A man who could hire people to do most anything. Including shelling peas and killing folks. He also had a rivalry with Ball. Ball wanted it, then Repeat Pete wanted it.

Ball's girlfriend ended up in a graveyard herself, but not Etta's. Rumor was Ball had her whacked when he found out she had spilled the beans about the skull, but it could just as easily have been Repeat Pete's crew, him not wanting Sugar Baby Blabber Mouth spreading the info around anymore than she already had. Anyway, she got run over by a truck. Several times.

"So, we're good. Right? I mean, Repeat Pete's crew doesn't know where the graveyard is?"

"That's right. But…"

I didn't like *but*.

"You see, they know it's an old graveyard, and Pete has hired a crew to keep them checked out, or so Ball thinks."

"Checked out for how long? Why not wait six months, see if the observers thin out, then dig her up? And why not use his own folks instead of us?"

"He may not trust them, and me and my brothers have a good reputation with him. Or he may not want to lose his own folks in the process."

I didn't like the sound of that. "So, we get killed instead?"

"I doubt anything so dramatic. But, yeah. Maybe. As for waiting, Ball wants the skull now, not six months from now, and he's got the money to get it now. It's not us digs her up, it could be someone else gets that ten thousand dollars."

"Maybe it ought to be."

"I got a vacation planned. I want to go somewhere where I can put my toes in the ocean, and I don't mean Galveston. I thought I might find a pool boy or some kind of good looking fella at a hotel who doesn't mind making some money on the side, the hard way, if you know what I mean."

"You're pretty awful," I said.

"I am. You still in?"

"Why the hell not?"

∽

THE GRAVEYARD WAS down a long dirt road where the trees gathered thick on either side and the shadows fell over the road like a blanket of night. The headlights seemed to have trouble cutting through it, and it was starting to mist, and the mist beaded on the window like little knots of pus. Finally, Ruby turned on the wipers and waved it away.

We came to a gap in the woods and there was a trail made of gravel, just wide enough for the van. Branches rubbed the sides of the van like lustful lovers. We got to the end of the gravel where we had to park. We walked in the dark and the mist, Ruby leading the way with a tow sack thrown over her shoulder, carrying a huge rubber wrapped flashlight that could have been used to beat a tiger to death, and in her other hand, a shovel. I had the shotgun and a shovel and my penlight in my coat pocket.

No one was waiting there for us, other than the dead. So much for needing the shotgun. That caused me to breathe a sigh of relief. Way it looked to me, unless you had the information in the diary, you'd never find this place.

"How old is this graveyard?" I said.

"Old. Look for a stone with Ethel Dodgers on it."

I placed the shotgun on top of the tow sack Ruby had stretched on the ground, placed the shovel on the ground next to where Ruby had placed hers, got my penlight out of my jacket, and we split up, flashing our lights around. I found some really old gravestones, and some graves that were unmarked, but no Ethel Dodgers. Then I heard Ruby call out.

"Bring your shovel. I've found our gal."

It was a grave that had collapsed a little, and there was a broken marble stone lying on the ground where it had fallen over due to erosion or vandalism. It was damp with moisture and the color of old horse teeth in the glow of our flashlights. It was hard to see at first, but chiseled into the stone were the words ETHEL

DODGERS, a date of birth and a date of death. There was something else written there, but it was so faded I couldn't make it out.

Ruby laid her flashlight beside the grave where the light would shine on it. I turned off my penlight and put it away. We grabbed the shovels and started digging. The air was still misty, and the ground was damp. There were quite a few roots, so it was serious work. In time we came to a few fragments of dark wood. Then we came to pieces of bone, and what might have been bits of cloth, but could have been old, blackened leaves. We got down on our hands and knees and pushed the dirt around. I could feel the dark earth chunking up under my fingernails, causing me to remember I had skipped my manicure today, and then I came up on the skull. Or most of it. The bottom part of the jaw was missing. I handed it to Ruby. She flicked the wet earth off of it, and made a sound like a cat rolling in catnip.

I felt around some more and found the missing part of the jaw. Most of the teeth were in it. We went the full hog, clawed around, found more bones, ribs and such. Some of them were very fragile. We carefully packed them all into the tow sack.

It wasn't until we got back to the van and put the shotgun, shovels, and the bag with the goods in it, that I began to feel true guilt. The idea of unsettling Ethel's already crumbling grave seemed way too much. Here was a woman who had ran the outlaw trail, survived it, returned and led a normal life and had been buried in what must have been a decent graveyard at one time, well-tended with regular flowers and careful weeding, but now she had been forgotten. Her grave was rich with roots and covered in tree shadow. Her stone was cracked and turned over and in the summer weeds and poison ivy most likely grew over that grave. Until her sister's diary showed up, and some asshole wanted to give us ten thousand dollars to dig up her remains, she had at least been left alone. That made me and Ruby the real assholes.

I thought about my share of the money again, got over my feelings of assholism, at least temporarily. She had been dead a long time. What was the harm?

By the time we were out of the woods and the lights of the town were visible, it was past midnight and it had started to rain like a cow pissing on a flat rock. We came to Seabury Ball's house, where he had wanted us to meet him and bring the goods. I could already feel that money in my hand.

We sat in the car with the lights out, the engine humming, looking at his house through the rain. It was large enough to contain a shopping mall and a sizable number of stray livestock. It was four stories of blue and white architecture, placed on a dozen acres that were dead center of the rich part of town, and had once been on the outskirts of it. Progress had surrounded Ball, but he was tucked well away in his great sanctuary, rolling around in his money like Scrooge McDuck.

"I don't know," Ruby said.

"What don't you know? You better be talking about math after talking me into this shit."

"Math is a problem, but it occurred to me, maybe we ought to put the bones away, meet with Ball and make a deal to deliver. I have this bad feeling he might have thugs who would just take it away from us, save him the ten thousand dollars."

"For him, that's not a lot of money."

"He didn't get rich by being generous, or honest. He has a mean streak."

"You didn't put it that way when we first talked. And you had that line about how he trusted you."

"Sometimes, for a friend's own good, you have to lie. Here's the thing. I think he hired us because we're expendable. More than the tough guys he pays bigger money to, and he may have thought, send out the patsies, and then whack them, take the goods. That way he kept his people out of it."

"So, you and Ball, you're not that close?"

"Not really."

"That's it, huh? You just now thought of that? What they might do."

"Pretty much. It's mostly instinct. Just feeling something isn't right. I may be way wrong. But why chance it when we can set this up a bit better. Meet some place that isn't his home territory. Until then, we hide the skull and bones."

"Where do we hide it?"

"I was thinking your place."

"You were thinking that, were you? How about no? How about kiss my ass?"

"Listen, dear. Ball knows me. He doesn't know you. He doesn't know I've enlisted help. Truth is, you could walk and he wouldn't know you helped me. He probably thinks I'm using my brothers. Your place makes sense."

"Why do I feel like a goat at a barbecue?"

"Truth is, I'm probably being overly cautious. But I say we stay with that ticket. No conflict, then no danger. I'd rather not shoot anyone. Again."

"Again?"

This was, of course, before she wasted the three bozos.

"Forget I said that."

❧

ON THE WAY to my place I noticed every car that was behind us or came out of streets to end up behind us. One dark SUV in particular worried me, and I told Ruby it did.

"They could have picked us up at Ball's house," she said, "could have been waiting on us to show up with the bones, but frankly I think you're being paranoid."

"You're the one that had an instinct that things weren't right."

Before she could comment, the car behind us picked up speed, zipped around us, and turned off.

"See," Ruby said. "Nothing."

My place is across the street from a three-story clock tower that was built in the nineteen thirties. The clock is on the top story and it still works. The mechanisms and the old clock tower are kept up reasonably well, though there has been talk of tearing it down. I can look out my window and see the huge, black hands turn. The clock face is lit up from the inside and glows orange at night. You can see bats and insects making dark shapes in front of the face then. Once, it had been the tallest structure in our little city. Now it's the height, or less than the height, of nearby houses.

There's still an outside metal staircase you can use to go up to the landing. The door at the top is locked, but one time I went up there for the view, just to see what it was like. All I could see were houses and buildings, and the next time I wanted to go over there, I saw they had built a metal gate at the bottom of the stairway. It had a sign on it that said to keep out. The first time I had gone up there, I made an extraordinary discovery. There's a rubber mat in front of the thick door that leads into the tower. I accidently budged the mat with my toe, and underneath it was a key. One of those large, old-fashioned kinds that you stick in the lock and turn. I thought, really? That's your secret hiding place. Under the mat.

But considering the clock no longer had tourism, and the museum that had been there in the past was long closed, who would think to look under the mat for the key other than those who kept the clock working? Who besides the workers and me ever went up there?

I used the key. The lock clicked, the knob turned, and then I was inside, amongst shadows and the dust I had stirred. The sound of the clock's revolving gears sounded like an enormous, cosmic rat gnawing at the edges of reality.

With the door open I could see inside reasonably well. I could make out a swirling, iron staircase that climbed to the third floor where the brain of the clock lived. It was too dark to venture going up there, and I didn't have my penlight with me back then, so after a moment of taking it all in, I went out and locked the door, put the key under the mat, and went home.

❧

WHEN RUBY DROPPED me off, we sat in her van for a moment. She said, "Take the bag, put it in your closet or some such. I'll get in touch with Ball, see what we can set up where there will be other people around, but not too many. Deliver the goods in a way that doesn't seem curious to others."

"You mean we won't walk into Starbucks with a bag of bones?"

"We'll find some place open to the public, some place like that, but find another way to carry the skull around. Something less conspicuous. Meantime, get some sleep."

A dark SUV cruised by us. Was it the car that had passed us before, the one I was suspicious of? I couldn't tell. It went by too quickly.

Ruby sensed my worry. She looked a little worried herself, but a moment later her worry had faded like moisture on a window pane hit by the sun.

"It's cool, baby girl. I'll call you tomorrow."

I got out of the car with the tow sack, and went inside, thinking of going to bed, but I didn't. I took a shower, washed off the grave grit, slipped on my pajamas with the teddy bears on them, and climbed up my second-floor stairs and sat in a chair by the window and looked out at the slightly higher clock tower across the street.

I couldn't sleep. I was too wired. Back downstairs I made myself a cup of decaf coffee, ate a cookie, then got some tennis shoes on, stuck the penlight in my pajama pocket, took hold of the tow sack and strolled across the street with it slung over my shoulder. I was Santa Claus for the dead.

I easily climbed over the little barrier, and went up the stairs. I found the key was still under the mat. I used it and opened the door. I turned on the penlight and climbed the winding interior stairs. They squeaked like a starving mouse.

At the top of those stairs the sound of the gears was nerve wracking, and there was another sound like the beating of a heart, another like a dying man's moan. The clock seemed quite human.

Flashing the light around, I saw an indentation in the wall, a kind of nook. Being careful not to fall into the gears, I slipped the bag into the shadowy nook, and departed.

❧

I WAS ON a spaceship to Mars, and my cabin companion was the best-looking man I had ever seen, and he was in love with me. Or it was lust, I don't know. We did some things in zero gravity, and then some things in what I guess was artificial gravity. It was great, except he started slapping me.

I was mad as hell at him, and then I woke up, and the man leaning over me, slapping me, wasn't all that good looking, and for a moment I felt I had ended up with the worst space-traveling companion you could imagine. Then I saw there were two others equally ugly standing by my bed and I wasn't on a spaceship after all.

"Get up, bitch," said the man who was slapping me. I really didn't like him.

"Where's the skull?" said a skinny one behind him.

I like to be clever, so I said, "What skull?"

"The one you're going to give us. Put on some clothes. We like to watch."

Humiliated and embarrassed, I put on jeans, a sweatshirt, tennis shoes, and finally my jacket.

To shorten up what you know, these were my friends I mentioned when I first started telling this. Ones who tore through my house looking for the skull, then when they didn't find it, took me away from my comfy home and brought me to the abandoned school, tied me to the chair in the basement, and hit me a lot. They were good at their work. They hurt me, but they managed not to mess me up too bad. They didn't want me to die before I told them the location of the skull.

You know the rest. I was about to tell them where the skull was after talking tough for a while, when Ruby came through the door with that shotgun. And now we were back in her van, riding along to somewhere or nowhere. I was as shaky as a leaf on a tree during a thunderstorm. That shotgun business was some messed-up shit.

She said, "Did you give them the skull?"

"No."

"Tell them where it is?"

"No. And if I had, it wouldn't matter now."

"True enough. I left you, I got worried, so I got out of bed and cruised over, just to check on you, and that's when I saw those lugs loading you into their car. It was just luck, kid. I followed you to the school, saw you and them go in. I did a sneak. I didn't know exactly where they were keeping you, so I had to creep around a while. Then I found the basement and could hear you and them talking."

"I was about to break. I would have given them the skull, my old teddy bear, and my ATM number. I was almost done. And all of it over some old bones."

"Those guys were part of Ball's operation. It was like I worried about. Ball decided to get the skull discount."

"How do you feel about moving to Bolivia?"

"Things aren't that bad."

"You weren't tied to a chair. You don't hurt like I do. I'm getting stiff. I can hardly move. I think they might have banged up something inside me. I know this is a bad time, but can we find a bathroom pretty quick?"

WALMART IS OPEN late. They have nasty bathrooms for the most part, being as they are constantly open and constantly used. But it was a lifesaver. Back in the car we cruised around a bit, thinking on what to do. I was still for moving to Bolivia.

"By the way," Ruby asked. "Where is the skull and bones?" I told her.

"That was a smart play for you. Had they been in your house, had they found the bones right off, they might have killed you immediately. Listen here. I been in contact with Ball. I told him I had the goods, and then I told him that we want more than ten."

"That's pushing it."

"He knows I can sell it to another bidder. And it worked. We're now getting twenty thousand. I also called my brothers, in case we need backup. They're on their way in. I don't know when they'll arrive. They're somewhere between here and Dallas. I told them we'd be at your place."

"When do we deliver the skull?"

"I'm going to call Ball and he'll send over his people. I told him not to make it a lot of people. It might make us itchy."

"Starbucks open this time of night?"

"Got a change of plans in mind. We pick some place secluded after all, but I keep the shotgun handy. I'm in the mood to shoot someone else."

⤳

AT MY HOUSE we checked in case Ball had sent someone over to wait on us. He hadn't.

Ruby made coffee, turned on her cell phone, made a call to Ball, gave him the address. Just hearing her do that made my skin crawl. "We had a spot of trouble tonight, you sack of dog shit," she said. "You like to done in my girl. Guys you send over now, they need to be friendlier. Those others, they got wasted, and I'm up for doing it again. The skull isn't here, but you send some friendly folks and we'll give it over when we get the money, take them to it."

I didn't hear what was said on the other end, but Ruby seemed satisfied.

"All right, then," she said.

Ruby sat in the dark in the kitchen with the shotgun in her lap. Her chair faced the front door, and the back door was off to her left. I sat by the downstairs window. We sat for a long while. Finally, I saw lights. The lights belonged to a big black van, newer than Ruby's. It parked at the curb in front of my house.

"Oh, Ruby," I said. "We got company."

Ruby came from the kitchen. She had the shotgun with her. She looked out the window. Two extremely large men were climbing out of the van. She pumped the shotgun.

"Open the door," Ruby said, "then step back, just in case things get funky."

I didn't like funky.

I opened the door and stepped back. The two men came in without invitation. Both were large, but one was much larger than the other.

Ruby said, "I got a shotgun on you, just in case you got cute up your sleeve. There's some comrades of yours that found out that I don't mind using this blunderbuss, and if they could give you advice, they'd tell you to avoid irritating me any more than I'm already irritated."

The biggest of the two, who looked a bit like a concrete bridge support, said, "No cute here."

"You can say that twice," Ruby said.

The bridge support smiled. "No cute here. No cute here."

"That's some funny shit right there," Ruby said. "Funny shit."

"Mr. Ball, he told me to tell you that those three you whacked, they went rogue. He didn't authorize that kind of stuff. He thinks they were going to make a deal with Repeat Pete."

"Be that as it may, stay cool," Ruby said.

The biggest one looked at me. "You the sidekick, honey?"

"Close enough," I said.

"Where's the bones?" the smaller of the two said.

"Put away," Ruby said.

"Un-put them," said Bridge Support. "I got your money here." He moved a hand toward the inside of his coat, paused. "Point that shotgun somewhere else, will you?"

Ruby moved the barrel slightly upward.

"Make sure you don't pull anything that shoots out of that pocket and you'll do fine," Ruby said.

Bridge Support pulled out a fat white envelope. "Twenty thousand. Right here."

He tossed it to me and I caught it. I turned on a lamp and counted it.

"Yep," I said.

"All right," Ruby said. "We're going to cross the street to the clock tower and get the goods. And you two, you're going to lead the way. Keep your hands by your sides. Any sudden moves and you won't remember you moved."

☙

IT WAS NO longer misting. The air had turned cool, and the coat I was wearing felt thin. When we got to the top of the outside clock-tower stairs, I got the key from under the mat and let us in, closed the door behind us.

I had Ruby's big flashlight, as well as my penlight in my coat pocket. I turned on the big flash. The dust was thick and it spun in the beam of the flashlight. I felt like I was trying to breathe a blanket and see through fog. The gears chewed and the clock ticked, banging out seconds like an ape beating a bass drum.

"You better have something we want, cause you sweet little girls don't want to get clever," Bridge Support said.

"All we want is to be done," I said.

"And we're not that sweet," Ruby said. "And it's me that's got the drop on you two."

That's when the door flew open and three men stepped inside with shotguns, twelve-gauge I believe, with flashlights fastened on top of them.

Goddamn it. I hate it when nearly everyone has shotguns.

ꙮ

THE ORIGINAL TWO thugs pulled automatics from inside their coats, and they and Ruby all wheeled and pointed their guns at the men in the doorway. I stood there with the flashlight, thinking it wouldn't be long before the undertaker was wiping my ass.

From behind the three in the doorway, appeared a smaller figure. Even in the dim glow of my flashlight I could see he wore a plaid suit. Who wears a plaid suit besides a circus clown?

The men in front of him parted slightly, and he stepped into better view. He looked as if his dark hair was well oiled twice a day and his teeth looked to be made of polished concrete. He wore brown and white spats, like an old-time gangster. I could tell then that he was older than I first thought. He had not so much aged, as he had been well preserved, perhaps pickled. He had what looked like a book in his hand. It seemed like a bad time for a bit of reading.

"What we got here is some business problems," he said. "Business problems."

"Repeat Pete," Ruby said. "I thought you turned into a bat when it got dark."

"Ruby, Ruby. My dear, my dear. I haven't seen you since last time I seen you."

"That is accurate," Ruby said. "Listen, Repeat. This is a business deal, not a gun deal, and we're in the process of finishing up business. You snooze you lose, and you snoozed and Ball didn't."

"Oh, Ball. Ball," Repeat said. "He's snoozing now in a ditch out near some farmland. Farmland. And his skull collection. Collection. It's now mine. Good stuff. Good stuff. I got more big guns than you. I even got the diary now."

He lifted the book. Now I knew what it was. Ethel's sister's diary.

"So," he said, "there's a new business deal can be made. Made. And you boys, you can get into a nasty gunfight, gunfight, or you can go home, because you got no boss now. Now. And I'm not hiring. Not hiring."

"No shooting then," Bridge Support said.

"Got nothing against you boys. Boys."

"We'll be clearing out then," Bridge Support said. "Good luck, girls."

BRIDGE SUPPORT AND his Kemosabe left out of there so fast they didn't even leave body odor.

There were still three shotguns pointed at us.

"This could get unnecessarily messy. Messy."

"I can shoot you, though, can't I?" Ruby said.

"Could. Could. But, give me the skull, the skull, as Ball don't need it anymore, then I'll take it and go, and you already got paid, right? Right? Ball, somewhere between losing his big toe and his nose, he said he was sending money to you. We can all come out happy except Ball, cause he's dead. Dead."

I was liking that idea of giving him the skull and him leaving us alone with our twenty thousand dollars. Problem was, I didn't trust Repeat.

"What say my friend here gets and gives you the bones," Ruby said, "and we all play it cool down here, pointing our shotguns at each other. She brings the bones back, and we go with your plan, and never see each other again."

"Ah, Ruby baby, baby. You done business with me before. Before. We don't have to end our business altogether, altogether. I'll have something another time, and now, with Ball gone, it's more exclusive, exclusive."

"For the moment, let's just end tonight's business," Ruby said.

"Fair enough. Fair enough. Get the goods, goods, pretty girlie."

"You mean me, right?" I said.

"I do."

"Hokeydoke then."

I trusted Pete and his gang about as far as I could throw them, but there didn't seem to be a lot of choice.

I started toward the spiral staircase that led up to the clock.

"Wait a minute, a minute," Pete said. "I'll climb up there with you. With you."

"You think I'm going to go up there and fly away?" I said.

"I just like being safe about transactions. Transactions."

"Very well," I said. "Very well."

I was starting to talk like Pete.

ॐ

REPEAT SLIPPED THE diary he was carrying into his side jacket pocket, which was big enough to house a kangaroo baby, and we started up the staircase, me in the lead with Ruby's flashlight.

As we climbed, I said, "You ought to take up stamps, coins, maybe rare pop bottles, unusual lingerie. You'd look cute in a pink bustier, something leather, and it'd be a cheaper hobby. Less murderous, by the way."

"But in the end, not as fun. Not as fun."

"You say."

I got to the top of the stairs. I looked down and saw Repeat Pete looking up at me. He had produced a little automatic from somewhere. He was pointing it in the direction of my blue-jeaned butt. He was also wheezing.

"Need to cut back on jacking off, Pete," I said. "It takes your wind."

"Just get the skull, the skull," he said.

I started stepping again. My mind was running a hundred miles an hour, trying to decide if there was an alternative to handing him the bag. I did that, I felt that might be his moment to jettison his agreeable plan and pop me, and that would be a cue for the guys downstairs to paint the wall with Ruby.

No brilliant strategy came to mind. I had to trust him.

When he was on the walkway with me, I slipped over to the nook where the tow sack was, took hold of it. Repeat Pete pulled the diary from his coat, said, "Slip this into the bag with the bones, the bones. So I can check the location later, see that you didn't just find a skull, any skull. I find her grave, and it's empty, then I know what I got. What I got."

I took the book, and had just taken hold of the sack and slipped the diary inside, when the door downstairs flew open and there was a bit of light and noise. Now there were two more men, and you guessed it, they had shotguns with flashlights fastened to them. It was an interesting trend.

It was Pooty and Boo-boo. They had arrived at my place and figured out what was going on across the street, probably saw flashlights moving around through the windows.

There were no introductions. As Pete's men turned toward Pooty and Boo-boo, Ruby's brothers let loose, their weapons sounding like cannons going off.

Ruby went low to the ground so as not to get a face full of buckshot, and took out one of Pete's men by shooting him in the side of the head as he was turning. He dropped his gun and the flashlight came loose of its attachment and rolled across the floor. As for the other two on the Repeat Pete squad, they were now retired. Pooty and Boo-boo do not play.

Repeat Pete glared at me. He had a look on his face that made my butthole suck air. I think he had decided if he was going out, he was going to take a blonde lady with him.

He raised the automatic and I swung the tow sack. The skull inside of it was heavy enough to give him a good smack, but not heavy enough to do him any real damage. Still, he staggered a little, and when he did, he said, "Shit. Shit." I stuck my foot out before he could regain his balance. He tripped over it and went into the guts of the clock like a lawn dart. He hit the churning gears and screamed as they ripped at his plaid suit and gnawed him up and made him red, and then the gears ground to a stop so violent the clock tower shook.

❧

LATER, I THOUGHT: I should have said to Pete, as the gears crunched him up, "You're out of time. You're out of time."

What I did instead was give out a little mouse squeak, turned away, went downstairs with the bones and the diary in the bag.

My legs were shaking when I got down there. Ruby grabbed at me, said, "Hang tough, baby girl. They started it."

I thanked Pooty and Boo-boo, who were dressed in coveralls and wore baseball caps. They had fat, round faces and narrow slit eyes, and it was hard to imagine that Ruby was their sister. Right then, I was damn sure glad she was. We all went out of there, closed the door and locked it up, slipped the key back under the mat like friendly neighbors who had only dropped by to water the plants.

Across the street we sat in my living room. I still had the bag. I hadn't let go of it. After a while, Pooty got up and made some drinks and put them in front of us, but I have trouble with alcohol, so I didn't drink any. I just keep it around for those who can drink.

Finally, Ruby got me up and helped me into the bedroom, pushed me on the bed, and pulled off my shoes. She said, "You might want to let go of that bag."

But I didn't. I had it clenched tight to me.

Ruby smiled, turned off the light and started out the door. I could see her shape framed there.

"Don't leave me," I said.

"Repeat and his goons are dead," she said. "Ball is dead, so no trouble there. We got twenty thousand as well. I'll put your part in the kitchen knife drawer."

"Don't leave me."

"Okay, kid. I'm sticking. Shut your mouth and close your eyes, and sleep. I'll be nearby."

WHEN I WOKE up the next morning, I left the sack of bones on the bed, found Ruby was sleeping on the couch in the living room. I looked out the window at the clock tower. The clock wasn't turning, of course. It was jammed up with Repeat Pete.

I made coffee after checking to see my money was in the knife drawer. I left it there. I made some toast and put it on plates, got out the butter and the jelly, and woke up Ruby.

We ate breakfast and sipped coffee together.

"What happens now?" I said.

"We're done for now. Next time a job pops up you can do, I'll call you. Hell, baby girl. I can see you're messed over by all this, but those bastards got what they deserved. When they find them, it'll look like a gang war. Believe me, the law won't cry over Repeat Pete being chewed up by a clock."

Right then I couldn't see myself doing another job with Ruby. I was considering a career as a hair stylist in a beauty salon. But you had to go to school for that, so maybe cocktail waitress.

"I'll hang onto Ethel, if that's okay with you," I said. "I got plans for her."

"We might could sell her again."

"I don't think so."

She smiled and nodded, knocked back the remainder of her coffee. She hugged me and left.

I sat around all day in a daze, hearing gunfire in my head and thinking about Repeat and his plaid suit being munched by the clock.

When it got night, I got the bones and a shovel, drove out to where Ethel had been buried. We had left the grave open when we dug her up. The gaping hole yawned up at me and made me sad. I took the diary out, but left the bones in the tow sack, as a kind of shroud, dropped her in the opening and covered her up. If I had been religious, I would have said a prayer. Instead, I said, "Sorry, old girl."

I placed the diary on the seat beside me, gave it a pat. It had to be better reading than *War and Peace*. I drove home then and felt better about myself, about the whole mess. As far as anyone else but me, Ruby and her brothers knew, the beautiful Etta Place was still lost to history.

CAMEL

MY SISTER, CONSTANCE, married a camel named Abdul, and I can't stand it.

Can you imagine? A camel? And a foreigner?

Oh, the camel was born here in the U. S., but still, the genetics make him a foreigner forever, even if he had been born in my back yard. Besides, his parents are from some place in Arabia, and they came here directly from there, so the way I see it, once a camel, always a camel.

Abdul is odd.

There's that terrible accent. Gets on my nerves. The hump on his back. Disgusting. He wears it with pride. I think he should get it removed. I put up with him only as much as I have to because of my sister. I keep thinking the whole thing will fall apart and she can move on with her life and remarry... Well, I don't mean to sound prejudiced, because I'm not, but maybe she'll marry the right kind of guy, if you know what I mean.

What I'm dreading is Thanksgiving.

His family. Our family. Disgusting camels.

∾

SO, THANKSGIVING COMES around, and I'm given the task of bringing a few side dishes, figs and dates, for example, and

I had to bring a lot of them, as Abdul and his family are crazy for them. They eat thorns, and they eat grass, too. I don't know. I try to avoid any of the dishes they eat at meals, and try to not be around them at all, if I can avoid it.

I stick to turkey and dressing and cranberry sauce and pies. And that's another thing. They don't eat Turkey, not even at Thanksgiving, and my sister has turned the same way. We only have a little of that on hand, the turkey, I mean, for me and my wife, but everything else is geared to their tastes, not ours.

Come to think of it, I don't think they eat meat at all, of any kind.

Me and my wife smile a lot, but we don't mean it. I think we're really gritting our teeth. Thanksgiving for the last three years has been one long day.

I mean, hell, when we finish eating, they won't watch football. They don't like it. They talk at the table, them and my sister, and they want us to talk with them, but I never really know what they're talking about. Books, mostly, I don't get that. There's plenty to see on TV, and all the time we're talking about this or that, things I couldn't care less about, we're missing the game.

It's best my father and mother are dead. If they weren't, my sister marrying a camel would be the end for them. It's damn near the end for me. Sometimes I imagine Abdul pawing her at night in bed, or should I say hoofing it, and I get a little nauseated.

Anyway, at Thanksgiving dinner they surprised me with a request. It seems my sister has to go to a wedding, and she's flying in early, because she's a bridesmaid, and the lady getting married is an old friend from college, or some such, which just makes her another one of those educated eggheads I can't stand being around.

Thing is, they can't fly together, as Abdul has to work at the bookstore he owns downtown, so come Saturday I'm supposed to drive him out because they can't really afford another flight, and it's a short trip across the desert to where he needs to go to join her. He doesn't have a license. He doesn't even know how to drive. He walks to work, which isn't far from their house, and Constance does all the driving.

Anyway, I can't stand the guy, but Constance wants me to drive him out to meet her later in the week, and I don't want to do it, but I don't tell her that. I'm sure she knows I'm not crazy about Abdul or his parents, but because she's my little sister, I agree to drive him out. It's only a few hours across the desert, so I figured I could listen to him talk about whatever, and I could talk as little as possible, and after I got him where he was going, I could have a nice dinner somewhere, then drive back home.

ABDUL AND CONSTANCE live behind the Walgreens drugstore, and the day I'm supposed to drive him, I get there and see other camels walking around the place, near the drug store and Abdul's house. Some of them have on costumes, as I call them, those bright, long dresses they wear, men and women, and the female camels have got on hair coverings and in some cases veils, and the whole area is full of them. They came over here to work in the chicken plant and such, and I just know there's some of them that's got to be terrorists, because I think that's their nature. They don't see the world like we do. They don't value life like we do. And, as I was saying, they dress funny. Potential terrorists, I tell you.

I even wonder about Abdul sometimes. Him with a bookstore, and selling the Koran, and other camels drifting around the store from time to time. Who knows what they're planning? Or what he's planning? That's how terrorists start. Congregating.

The whole idea of driving all day with him to cross the desert started to really weigh on me, and when I parked in the driveway, I sat there and considered turning around and going home and calling to say I was sick or something, lost a leg in a fight with a wolverine, any damn thing to keep from having to make that trip with him.

But no sooner am I about to back out of the drive, then the door opens and Abdul comes out wearing one of those damn dresses himself. It's colorful, I'll give it that, and he has on some kind of little hat, like a small box turned upside down to fit over the top of his head. He's pulling a roller bag, and I know then I'm trapped.

This trip is happening.

❦

I DROVE AND listened to Abdul, who talked nonstop about all manner of things, most of which I cared nothing about, and even those things I cared about, I wished to have heard about them from someone else.

He mentioned the books he had been reading, like I'd have read any of them, and then he talked about the plays he and my sister had seen in New York when they were on vacation three years ago. You would have thought he had seen them yesterday.

He was especially fond of musicals. He found it interesting to watch how graceful the dancers moved, said that was what first attracted him to my sister, how she moved.

I didn't want to hear that, and I was beginning to fear he might break out in show tunes, so I found a place where I could stop and get gas, though the tank was nearly full. While I pumped the gas, Abdul went inside. I finished up and parked the car in front of the station in one of the slots, and went inside to pee. It was one of those places that has gas and bathrooms and snacks, and there's even a couple of food chains stuffed in there, not to mention some gambling machines of some sort or another. I don't really know anything about those, but there was Abdul, sitting on a stool in front of one of them, his hairy forehead wet with sweat, feeding it coins (they are surprisingly dexterous with those hooves) like he was giving treats to a dog. He'd stick a coin in, pull the handle, and there would be a clinking sound and some fruit pictures would pop up, but they never lined up, and I knew enough to know they were supposed to.

I went over to him, "What in the hell are you doing?"

"Passing the time," he said, but there was an intensity about him that went beyond passing the time. He seemed on a mission.

"Look, grab a snack, and go," I said.

"Sure. Right there."

I went to the bathroom, washed up and came out and bought a cold drink and a chocolate bar and went out to the car to sit and eat it. After I had eaten it, I was still sitting there, and yet, no Abdul. I went inside again, went over to the machine where he had been playing, but things had changed. Abdul was there, but so were two burly apes. One was holding Abdul from behind, pulling his arms back, while the other punched him in the stomach. His little hat had been knocked off and the one doing the punching was standing on it.

I had often dreamed of punching him myself. But, hell, he was my sister's husband.

"Hey," I said. "Leave him alone."

The puncher turned around and looked at me.

"You know this foreign sonofabitch?"

"Yes. Yes. He's... He's my brother-in-law."

"What the hell, fella? A camel."

"I know," I said, "but I didn't marry him, my sister did."

"Goddamn," said the one holding him. "What kind of woman is that?"

"You're talking about my wife," Abdul said, though he could hardly say it. He didn't have a lot of wind left.

The puncher punched him again. This caused Abdul's legs to go out from under him and he collapsed to the floor and they let him.

I moved toward them, feeling like a man about to enter into a pond of alligators. "What is this about?"

"He started hitting the machine," said the puncher. "I own this place, me and my brother. We can't have nobody hitting on the machines, especially some Arab sonofabitch."

I looked at Abdul. He was sitting on the floor.

"I got frustrated," Abdul said. "The machines are rigged."

"No, you're just stupid enough to spend money, and like most everyone else, you lose," said the puncher. "Them's the odds, and that's why we rent the machines, to make a profit. We can't have some sore losing Arab whacking on them. Them machines is expensive."

I helped Abdul up.

"We're going," I said.

"Yeah, get him out of here, and if it was up to us, his kind couldn't even come in here. This ain't like America anymore, it's like some foreign country."

I found myself in agreement, and thought for a moment I might just leave Abdul with them, but I got him up and walked him out to the car, with the two burly apes following. One of them had his crushed hat and threw it toward us, but I left it lying in the parking lot. It wasn't worth much by then anyway.

"Don't come back, and I mean you too, Mr. Camel's brother-in-law," said the puncher. "And if your sister comes through, tell that camel-lover not to come in here either. We don't want her kind or the kind that don't mind their kind. This is a full-on American kind of establishment."

❧

OUT IN THE car, after I got Abdul seated on the passenger side, he said, "Thanks."

"Been up to me, I'd have let them have you," I said, "but it was my sister I was thinking about."

Abdul gave me such a sad look, I almost felt bad. I got the car going and went on down the road a piece, when all of a sudden, Abdul yelled.

"Let me out. Let me out. Leave me here. You horrible sonofabitch."

I didn't stop, but I said, calmly as I could, hoping to quiet him down, "Now what? I just saved your ass."

"Not because you wanted to, but for your sister, my wife. Pull over."

I pulled over. He didn't get out. We had reached the edge of the desert and it was hot out there.

"Let's get it out," Abdul said. "You don't like me, and I don't like you. I am as American as you are."

"You're a camel."

"And you're an asshole, but we're both Americans. I was born here."

"You eat funny stuff," I said.

"And you eat unhealthy stuff, so there."

"Well, okay. And you got a funny religion."

"Mine is true, yours is funny. Jesus was a prophet, not a messiah."

"How dare you say that. Give me a pen and I'll draw a picture of Muhammad the way I see him."

"We don't draw images of the prophet."

I had a pen and paper in my pocket. I took them out and drew a stick figure.

"There he is."

Abdul wouldn't look. "I hate you," he said.

"Good. Now, you know what. I'm going to grant you your wish. Get out of the car. You don't turn up, I'll tell God you died. The real God."

Abdul looked at me. His face appeared angry and sad at the same time.

He got out of the car and I drove off, looked in the rear view and watched heat waves rise up from the pavement and ripple his image.

❧

I GOT ABOUT five miles down the road when I saw something smashed on the highway. It had been a living mammal at one point, now it was a scattered mammal, so scattered I couldn't tell what it was. I first thought someone had dropped a watermelon, but no, it was bone and blood and viscera, and it was all over the road.

Abdul may have been a camel, and I didn't like him, but my sister did, and it was best I didn't like him while he was alive, instead of when he was dead. My sister would be a lot more aggravated about the dead situation than me not liking him.

I found a slight road that turned toward a cattle guard and gate, turned around and went back.

HE WAS STANDING beside the road. Hitchhiking. Had to do it without a thumb, but he was working on it anyway. I was coming from the other direction, of course, and when he saw me he put his arm down and I pulled up next to him.

He got in the car without a word, and I turned it around and started back down the road. We didn't speak. I turned on the radio, but all that was on it was static. I turned it off.

"I really don't like you," Abdul said.

It seemed to come out of nowhere and was a little loud, so it caused me to jump slightly.

"I don't like you either."

"I don't like you more."

"Don't be so certain," I said.

And it was right then that the front right tire blew.

We went waving all over the road and there was burning rubber from the tires as I tried to brake, and it turned out that braking as hard as I was, and not remembering the driving advice about turning in the direction of the skid, I lost control of the car.

The terrain on the sides of the road had been flat for miles, but now that there was a blowout, a ditch appeared out of nowhere just in time for the car to dive over the side of the road and into it. It was a fairly deep ditch, and the car hit it hard and flipped, and kept flipping.

🌀

I AWOKE FEELING like someone had shit in my mouth, and my first thought was Abdul had done it, but it turned out that I had been thrown from the car and had my mouth full of blood. I turned my head and spat it out.

I lay there not moving for a long moment, trying to decide if I should move. I felt banged up but I didn't feel truly damaged. I sat up slowly and looked at the car. It was resting on its roof. I had sort of hoped it had caught fire and Abdul had burned up in it, because that seemed like a win-win. I could tell my sister a blowout had got him, not me leaving him beside the road or strangling him in some filling station parking lot.

But then I saw him. He was walking toward me, limping slightly, like he had one leg in a bucket.

He came over to me and looked down. "You all right?"

"Think so."

He didn't offer me any assistance, and I was glad of it. I managed to my feet and took a deep breath and looked out at the terrain. There was a lot of it, and except for the handy ditch we had flipped in, which played out about twenty feet from where I stood, there was nothing but desert and a mountain in the distance and a hawk soaring over a telephone line. Oh, yeah. There were telephone posts out there too.

"What now, big guy?" Abdul said.

"I guess we have to walk. Maybe catch a ride."

"This is your fault."

"A blowout is my fault? I don't think so."

"You probably picked a nail up in your tire because you were driving too close to the side of the road."

"I was not.

"Was too."

"Was not."

"I hate you."

"I hate you too."

❧

WE GOT SOME water we had in the car, which was in a couple of bottles, and we had already drunk some out of them before the wreck. We started walking. The sun grew hotter. The air conditioner in the car had spoiled me.

Abdul seemed to be doing just fine, except for the limp.

Well, the day wore on, and so did we, and it seemed as if the sun would never go down. In fact, I felt that we had been walking for hours, but since the sun appeared frozen in place, it was probably only a few minutes.

I didn't have a hat, and I could feel the sun on my head and sweat was coating my body. I had already drunk all my water before realizing this walk was going to be epic, if we made it.

My guess was we were going to die beside the road and be eaten by vultures. I was sort of hoping a car would come along, and that it wouldn't stop for us, but it would hit us and put us out of our misery. Actually, I was thinking more of me. Abdul could be miserable.

But he wasn't. He was doing fine, and had hardly touched his water. His limp had improved as well. He was rather spry. I began to fall behind. Finally, I found that I was on the ground and there were ants on me, but I couldn't remember falling. The ant went up my nostril and I lifted my head and snorted, blowing it out.

I tried to get to my feet, but the best I could do was roll over and sit up.

Abdul was standing over me.

"You fell down."

"No joke. Has it cooled off? I feel cold."

"You have chills from too much sun."

"The sun can make you cold?"

"No, but heat stroke can make you feel cold."

I tried to get up, but no soap. I couldn't. I thought if I had a blanket I might lie down and sleep.

Abdul sighed. It was almost as loud as the blowout we had experienced.

"All right," he said.

"All right what?"

"Here, take my hand."

"You call that a hand?"

"You can stay here if you want. I'm going on."

I took his hand, but my grip was limp. It took a couple of tries, but he got me up and I actually started walking, or thought I was. It took me a moment to realize I was lifting my feet up and down and swinging my arms, but I was still in the same place. I lacked propulsion.

"Damn it," Abdul said. "Here, climb on my back."

"What?"

"Climb on my back."

I wanted to argue, but I didn't feel like it. I didn't feel like climbing on his back either. I didn't feel like I could stand more than another minute or two.

Abdul eventually grew tired of waiting, grabbed me, and as gentle as lifting a child, he swung me onto his back. I grabbed the front of his shirt with both hands, and wrapped my feet around his waist, and he started walking.

We walked and it was bright and Abdul's fur smelled good, like some kind of oil. I kept trying to identify it, but couldn't. What the hell was it? Why did it matter? My head was hot and throbbing and I wished I had Abdul's hat, even with it smashed. I was certain I could straighten it out and wear it. I nodded off now and then, dreamed I was wearing the hat.

On through the day we went, and sometimes I slept and clung to him, and sometimes I merely clung. I was hungry and thirsty and full of the oil smell I couldn't identify.

Abdul kept going.

It began to grow darker, and finally it was dark, but on Abdul went, walking along the edge of the road.

Not one car had passed us. Not one.

I could see lights in the mountains off to the right, and I wondered if the people who had turned on those lights were sitting down to a good dinner, and if they had to eat food like Abdul ate. I wanted a hamburger.

Finally, Abdul stopped and lowered me to the ground, gave me a swig of water from the water bottle after I sat down on the ground beside the road. When I took it, it looked like not a drop had been drunk from when he first pulled it from the car, though it wasn't a full bottle then.

I eagerly took a swing, gave it to him.

He sat down beside me and held the bottle. He didn't drink from it.

"Aren't you thirsty?" I said.

"I'm a camel. We can go miles without water."

"No shit?"

"No shit."

"I wish a big owl would come along and pick me up and eat me," I said.

"So do I," Abdul said, "but I would settle for two big owls that would pick us up and carry us into town."

"What town?"

"I saw a sign."

"How far?"

"It said twenty-five miles."

"Jesus. But I can see lights."

"They're farther away than you think."

"Did you carry me just because you're married to my sister?"

"Did you come back and pick me up because I'm married to your sister?"

"Yeah. I did."

"Then we're even."

I sat there and thought for a while, then I said, "No, we're not even."

"You're never happy."

"We're not even because I owe you."

Abdul studied me for a long moment. "Oh."

"Yeah. I wouldn't have carried you. I want you to know that."

"You can't carry me. Monkeys are strong, but not strong enough to carry a camel."

"If we were in the jungle it might be different."

"Oh. You'd carry me through the trees?"

"Okay, I couldn't carry you through the trees, but I could get us fruit. We wouldn't be hungry and thirsty."

"I'm not thirsty."

"Yeah. I forgot."

"What I am is a man who neglects his prayers to Allah, and therefore that might be why we ended up in a ditch."

"Or it could have been the blowout."

"That is a consideration," he said.

⮌

IT GREW COLDER as the night wore on, and I thought that was certainly ironic. I was burning all day, and now I was freezing all night. Abdul seemed fine. I was feeling a little better. I may not have had heat stroke after all, just a bit of heat exhaustion. Still, I didn't feel so spry I wanted to jump up and down.

"You know, I got a bit of a gambling problem," Abdul said.

"I noticed."

"They got a course or something for getting over that, don't they?"

"It's not a course," I said. "It's Gamblers Anonymous. Only person I ever knew that was in it bet on how long it would take him to quit gambling. He bet to win. He didn't win. He went back to gambling. But it has a lot to do with wanting to quit, I figure."

"I want to."

"I believe you, Abdul. I do. We don't die here, we'll get you hooked up with GA."

"That would be a good idea. I'm kind of in debt, you know, one thing or another. Cards. Roulette."

"Does my sister know?"

"She does. She told me I had to get over it, or I'm out."

"I'm sorry to hear that."

Abdul stared at me. "Say what?"

"No. I mean it. Now."

After a while we decided it might be warmer to carry on, as I thought I could walk now. Abdul's ankle had grown swollen after he sat down. Due to the injury of course, and then carrying me all day on his back. He had been getting better there at first, but I was certain my weight had compounded the situation.

He insisted on evening prayers, even though he complained he didn't have his prayer rug. I had seen it in the car, I thought it was a gift for the wedding, maybe a floor mat, then I remembered I had seen both him and my sister kneeling on rugs, praying. While he prayed I thought about French fries.

Now I could walk, though, and that was good, and when he finished praying, he started walking, and for me it was warmer to walk. I could see the lights and they always seemed to stay the same distance away.

Abdul's limp worsened, and I let him put his arm over my shoulder to help support him on his weak side. He was much taller, but it helped him. We went on like that until Abdul sat down suddenly.

"My ankle has quit. I won't be walking anymore. Go on without me. Tell my wife I love her."

"Bullshit, you're going to be fine. You stay here, and I'll keep walking. I'll find help. And I will be back, Abdul."

There was a long pause before he said, "I know...brother. I know."

I started walking, but then I saw headlights coming down the road. They were bouncing a little, and it was because they were on an old truck with sideboards that needed new shocks. The truck stopped for me. I figured it might. I was standing in the middle of the road waving my arms.

The truck stopped and the driver got out. He had a hand gun. Who didn't? He was a camel. He was wearing a get-up similar to the one Abdul wore. He had on one of those funny hats too.

He said, "What the hell, monkey?"

"We need a ride."

"We?"

"Me and Abdul," I said.

"Abdul?" he said, lowering his gun. "He is a camel like me?"

"Hearing his name and deciding that he's a camel is profiling," I said. "But yeah. He's a camel."

❧

SO, THERE I was, in a camel's truck, sitting against the passenger door with Abdul in the middle. He finally took a drink from the bottle, and then gave it to me.

"Finish it if you like," he said. "I'm fine."

I realized then he hadn't been drinking water not only because he didn't need it the way I did, he had been saving it for me.

I drank some of it and gave it back to him and leaned against the door and slept.

I don't know how long I slept, but I came awake slowly, and I could hear Abdul and the driver talking.

"Running around with an infidel," the driver said, "that seems odd."

"Ah, that asshole's no infidel. He's my brother."

❧

ME AND ABDUL had a good adventure story to tell, and he got into Gamblers Anonymous and did well with it. He does buy lottery tickets, though, but so do I.

We go fishing together now and then, though I'm the only one that eats the fish we catch, and I have to clean them too. I like fish.

Some people will tell you monkeys don't eat fish or meat, but then those are monkeys that have never been hungry. Steak. Hamburgers. Tuna fish sandwich, a grilled trout. You name it, I'll eat it. I like lots of fruit though, and I'm very stereotypical about bananas.

But about those fishing trips, those are merely so me and Abdul can hang out. We like to talk. Nothing special. But we like to talk.

I hear from my sister that I'm going to be an uncle come springtime.

SNAPSHOT

With Kasey Lansdale

Deep East Texas, Nineteen Eighty-Eight

THE HOUSE

THEY CAME ALONG through the night, the small camper running near silent over the red, damp, clay road, the shadow-bathed trees close on either side.

At the wheel, Trevor said, "Maybe we can find a good place to park that isn't muddy."

"Good luck with that," Gracie said. "Comes another rain like that, I'm going to start watching for Noah."

The headlights showed them a bend in the road, and at the bend there was a gravel turn around.

"Perfect," Trevor said.

"I prefer a hotel."

"Too far out tonight. Maybe the next night, couple towns down the road."

"We just left a town," Gracie said.

"Yep, and some houses in that town are missing some jewels, some money, and a kid's science project."

"That was mean, Trevor."

"A little. I always wanted one of those volcano things with the lava that comes out, and now I got one."

"Jesus."

Trevor parked the camper, and they were about to slip to the rear of it, crawl into bed, when he said, "Look there."

Gracie looked. They were on a bit of a rise, and through the trees, she could see the moon shining on water. A large pond, and across from the pond there was a light on a tall pole. The light showed them a house, not exactly a citadel, but the best construction an upper middle-class income could buy. Oaks grew strategically about the yard, and there was a large satellite dish on the roof.

"Thinking what I'm thinking?" Trevor said.

"Not unless you're thinking about going to sleep."

"You know what I'm thinking."

"Yeah," Gracie said. "I know."

❧

THREE DAYS EARLIER

"HURRY IT UP, would you?"

"You want to be sure it gets there, don't you?" Trevor asked.

"Not really."

"Well I do, and I didn't hear you complaining when you found that ruby bracelet."

Gracie instinctively touched her wrist, said nothing. Trevor used his finger to smooth down the stamp in the corner a final time, pulled open the blue metal door and dropped the envelope inside. It made a squeaking sound in protest, followed by a loud clang. He turned to her, pushed back a tendril of dark hair from her face.

"The only way we are going to make a name for ourselves is if we let them know who we are."

"I think we've made a name already. Well, no one knows our name actually."

"Sure they do. Our moniker, anyway."

Gracie glanced next to the mailbox where local newspapers were contained in a bright red newspaper rack. Through the plastic front, she could see the title headline. THE SNAPSHOT BURGLARS STRIKE AGAIN.

"Let me see that," Trevor said, pointing at the stack. Gracie slipped a coin in the slot, a paper dropped, and Gracie pulled it free from the chute.

Trevor held it up and began to read aloud.

"The Snapshot Burglars have struck again, making themselves known to their unsuspecting victims by sending Polaroid pictures of stolen items to said persons following the incident." Trevor let the fold of the paper fall away and continued reading from the bottom half of the page. "The Snapshot Burglars seem to target houses in middle-class neighborhoods, and are adept at entering and leaving quickly undetected. In some cases, victims of theft were only made aware that someone had been in their homes and taken possessions when an envelope containing the snapshots arrived in their mailboxes.

"It's judged there are at least two burglars. Sometimes, other than the snapshots, they rearrange household items. Frequently, the burglars take time to prepare themselves a snack, and sometimes steal food items. No fingerprints have been found. The fact that food items are removed, suggests that the thieves live

on the road, moving from one town to the next. Law enforce-
ment is looking for any information that might be provided by
the public that will lead to the apprehension of the burglars."

Trevor folded the newspaper, looked at Gracie. "We're
unknown and famous."

Back in the camper, Gracie reread the article while Trevor
drove. When she was finished reading, she positioned her seat
back so she could rest. They drove all through the day, stopping
only to buy gas and snack food, cruising in a big circle through
East Texas. Pretty soon they'd have to expand their territory.
Oklahoma, Louisiana, maybe move on out to Santa Fe where
the sun was bright and so was the rich folks' jewelry.

Gracie had always wanted to be famous, and this was the next
best thing. The Snapshot Burglars. They were like Bonnie and
Clyde without the murder, and without being known by name.

Gracie remembered her mother's remarks about how she
would never need to amount to much. "You got looks, girl. You
don't need smarts or skill. Look what it's done for me."

Gracie didn't like what it had done for her mom, a trailer
home full of ceramic chicken knickknacks, the trailer positioned
on a sunbaked concrete slab just outside a little town where the
greatest excitement was watching the red light change to green.
Then again, there had been that bit of insurance money from
her mother's last husband, ole Stan, who worked in maintenance
but seldom found much to maintain, outside of putting batteries
in a TV remote, keeping his weight up by guzzling beers, and
reaching for peanuts in a plastic bowl on a coffee table made of
an electric wire spool. One day he reached and his heart said no,
and that was it for Stan. He ended up on the floor between the
couch and the spool, his hand still clutching a wad of nuts.

Yeah. Her mother was living the life, all right, though that insurance money did provide for a larger trailer, a double-wide, soon filled with more chicken knickknacks and a new boyfriend named Clyde who worked at the chicken plant, which was perfect for her mother's collection. If she couldn't have a life-sized chicken, she could at least have a life-sized man that worked at a place where real chickens were handled, dressed, and sent to market. Her mom was living the dream.

And for a while it looked as if Gracie would be living the same one.

Then she met Trevor and the world got brighter and more exciting, and she developed skills that he taught her. Trevor's skills didn't come from community college, but he had gone to the school of burglary, and appeared to have graduated with honors.

In short time, he told her, "My daddy was a professional burglar, and he was at it for years, anything from lawnmowers to cars to roadwork machines. He stole and sold and made a good living, and then he messed up, tried to steal a Corvette from a carport and was shot by the owner. Never served a day in jail, but is now serving an eternity in the ground."

Trevor had helped him steal a number of items, but was fortunately not with him that day. He remembered advice his father gave him only the day before his death.

"Got to tell you, Trev, stealing this big stuff, it's got a good pay off, but you got to hide it, deal with a specific buyer, change VIN numbers, all that shit, and it's tiring and easier to get caught. You continue in the family business, I suggest you steal small but rich. I think jewelry and the like would be the ticket, and except for this car I got my eye on, come next week, I'm changing my method of operation. If I can't carry it out in a bag from now on, I'm not bothering."

With his father's death, and him being so young and surviving on shoplifting, he was picked up by the cops. He ended up in an orphanage, but it felt more like a prison. When he was old enough to leave, he found that, like his father, he had a knack for theft. And he followed his father's advice. Steal small.

One day his knack failed him. Got picked up for shoplifting, placed in a program to put juveniles on the right track. It was silly. There was no way a thing like that, some stupid program, could make a person change that didn't want to change. But there was one plus. Another shoplifter was there. Gracie. Given room and board and daily lectures for stealing ceramic chickens from a knickknack store.

THE HOUSE—THE PRESENT

THEY SLIPPED ON backpacks and left the car among the trees and walked through the dark using moonlight, arrived at the house a little after nine. There were no lights shining from inside. There was only the pale lemon-yellow light on the pole outside. All three stories were enveloped by the wind-weaved shadows of tall oaks and the sawing sounds of cicadas. There were no cars in the drive. Trevor moved to a window and peered inside. It was hard to see much more than his own reflection.

Gracie took gloves from her pack, handed Trevor a pair, slipped on the other pair. "Alarm goes off," Gracie said, "run like hell."

"As always," Trevor said.

She jiggled the knob gently. No alarm. She took out her tool kit and went to work on the latch. She was done quickly, and the door snicked open.

"Did you remember the Polaroid?" Trevor said.

"Of course," she said, swinging the pack off her back, reaching into it to remove the camera. She handed it to him, then repositioned the pack on her back.

Trevor took the camera, slipped the strap over his neck, let the camera rest against his chest. Gracie, silent as a silhouette, moved inside. Trevor followed, both moving stealthily through a kitchen rich with the smell of garlic, and from somewhere came a heavy pine fragrance—air freshener perhaps. Trevor remained there as Gracie slipped down a hallway that opened into a large living room with nice furniture and the intensified sick-sweet smell of that pine air freshener. Gracie stood in the gap, one shoulder against the wall, and studied the room.

The wallpaper looked new, its pink and blue flowers bright and freshly painted. There were a few unique sculptures in a cabinet, behind glass. They were cool looking, but they were too distinct to try and sell. Someone would trace them back pronto. You had to stick to jewels, folding money, a special item or two, but all stuff that was easy to move quickly and didn't require special expertise for the fence.

Gracie's eyes traced a slightly worn path in the wooden floor from the living room couch, and followed it. It was another entrance into the kitchen. A noise startled her as she entered the room.

In the light of the open refrigerator, Trevor stood, looking like a kid who had been caught with a hand in the cookie jar.

In this case, a jar of pickles. It lay shattered on the floor in front of the refrigerator, pickles scattered about, the briny liquid that had soaked them now flowed over the kitchen tiles.

Trevor was about his notorious sandwich making. It had become, like the Polaroids, a thing.

"Sorry. Jar slipped."

"I can see that," Gracie said. "No pickles on mine, please."

Trevor grinned at her, began to remove items from the fridge, place them on the kitchen counter. Various cold cuts and condiments.

"Anything?" he asked.

"Nothing jumping out at me from the living room. No fireplace, no quick-sale paintings, no safe. Some small sculptures, but too unique and difficult to carry. We need to check the other floors, search for their special hiding places."

"Let's save a bedroom for last," he said with a wink.

Gracie smiled, nodded, and watched Trevor continue his sandwich making. He opened the walk-in pantry door near the fridge, said, "Where's the bread?"

"Like I would know."

Trevor flicked on the light in the pantry.

"Don't you think we ought to rob first, snack second?" Gracie said.

"That's best all right, but I'm seriously hungry. Peanut butter and strawberry jelly, there's jars of it."

"Might be better than cold cuts. I'm sick of cold cuts. Is that a light?" Gracie said, pointing inside the pantry.

"It's something," Trevor said. He pushed aside some cans with his foot and gave the crack of light a closer examination. An economy sized bag of dog food was propped against the back wall, unopened.

"See a sign of a dog anywhere?"

"No."

Trevor pulled the bag aside, rested his gloved hands on the bare wall and pushed gently. A door in the pantry wall swung open.

❦

IT WAS AN entrance to a cellar, larger than most, and smelled even more of pine scent than the house, and there was a scent of ammonia from what Gracie thought must be some kind of cleanser or bleach.

There were wooden steps. The walls were solid, made of concrete slabs. The light inside was weak. Gracie and Trevor cautiously started down the steps, which creaked and bent beneath their weight.

"I was the owner of this house, this is where I'd hide the good stuff," Trevor said. "Maybe the bad stuff. I'd redo the stairs, though."

"It smells like pine trees live down here," Gracie said.

"Look at this," Trevor said. Near the bottom of the stairs was a pool table. It looked new. The green fabric, lush and vibrant.

"Come on, Trevor, we have to stay focused."

"Fine. But you owe me a round." Trevor walked deeper into the room, touched a thick canvas apron draped over a rectangular shape. Gracie could see the bottom of it. A meat freezer.

She was proved correct when Trevor pulled the canvas aside, let it drop on the floor.

"Had time, and wanted it, bet we could cook up some venison, pork chops and such. I bet this thing is stuffed with them."

"We don't have the time to thaw and cook meat, goofball," Gracie said. "Let's grab some goods and hike. You're starting to get too bold, Trevor."

"Surely we can look," Trevor said, and touched the lid. "I want photos. I think it's perfect to send to them, show them we were in their holy of holies."

"Sure. What the hell?"

With both hands, Gracie pushed the heavy lid upwards, let out an involuntary gasp when the light inside the freezer coated the contents.

"Holy shit, Trevor."

Peering inside, Trevor said, "Whoa. What in the actual fuck?"

There was a plastic bag full of filmy eyeballs.

"Who would eat animal eyes?" he said.

Gracie gently lifted the package from the freezer, frost fading from it as she removed it, stared at the contents through the plastic. "Do animals have green eyes?"

"Cats, I guess."

"I don't think these eyeballs belong to cats."

Trevor was leaning into the freezer. He lifted a frosty package, round and firm. He turned it in his hand. He could see a man's face inside, the nose tight against the plastic.

"Oh, shit, Gracie."

"Yeah," Gracie said. "Oh, shit. Trevor, the other wraps. They're more heads, body parts."

Now that the freezer door was open, and the frost had dissolved somewhat, they could see more body parts in bags, a number of heads, slack-jawed faces staring up at them, frost bitten eyeballs glinting in the freezer light. Two or three heads on the top row looked fresher than the others. Frost clung to their brows and hairline. The stumps of their necks were evenly cut and dark where the blood had frozen to a deep purple.

"Jesus, there's a sack of balls," Trevor said. "Take a picture. We need proof." Trevor dropped the head back inside as Gracie leaned over the grisly collection and snapped a photo, the flash making the room seem exceptionally eerie for a moment. The mechanical click and hum of the Polaroid echoed in the room.

"Take another," Trevor said.

Gracie flashed away with the Polaroid.

"God, Gracie, think what someone would pay not to have these photos released to the law? We could make a fortune."

"You have got to be out of your fucking mind, Trev," she said as she tucked the camera back in her pack, and hoisted the pack on her back. "These are people. Someone murdered them, someone who'll keep doing it. And do whatever it is he's doing with these body parts. Eating them, maybe. Shit, I need to get out of here. I'm gonna be sick. And Jesus, if they come back, we could be in that freezer before daybreak."

"Yeah. Yeah. Sure."

Trevor closed the lid gently as they backed away as if from a poisonous snake.

As they reached the stairs, Gracie said, "That smell, under the pine fragrance, the bleach, it's rotting meat. That means it isn't just the freezer."

"It's probably everywhere. In the floorboards, under the freezer, behind things. Cutting up people like that is messy. Now, like you said, let's go."

Gracie froze in her tracks. There was an opening, previously unseen below the stairwell. It was a little door with a silver handle. "I think the stink is coming from there."

"And now you want to look?"

"Can't help myself."

"Yes, you can."

But already Gracie was moving toward the door.

She grabbed the door handle. Trevor moved beside her, touched her arm, whispered, "No."

Gracie shook her head, gently pushed on the lever.

It was a larger room than expected. The air was frigid and a plume of froth puffed out of Gracie's mouth. Trever stood back, as if nailed to the floor. In the room the light bulb was pale and orange and hung centrally located over a long steel table. A woman lay on the table, her head turned toward them. Her mouth was plugged with a small stuffed animal, a pink puppy, maybe a teddy bear, and a black leather strap held it in place.

The eyes of the woman widened as they stood at the entrance to the room, and later Gracie would know that reaction was a swift flare of hope, like a firing-squad victim holding tight to the possibility that the bullets in the rifles were blanks.

The woman on the table appeared to be naked, but Gracie couldn't be certain. Her body was blocked by someone standing on a step stool in front of the table, someone wearing a hood bunched up in the back, and a leather wraparound apron that fell to the tops of bare feet, but revealed a bare upper back and shoulders. The Butcher, for that's how Gracie thought of the individual, loomed over the victim with a hacksaw in a leather-gloved hand.

A tattoo of a pink and blue butterfly was located on the nape of the Butcher. The shoulders were smooth, brown, and wide. On the floor, next to the step stool, was a crusty-bladed hatchet.

In that same moment, Gracie took in not only the Butcher and the woman on the table, but shapes in the shadows covered in tarps.

The Butcher leaned over the woman and placed the hacksaw to her throat. The light glistened on a tear on the victim's cheek as the Butcher began to slowly saw at her neck, one hand on the woman's jaw to hold her still. There was a thin line of red at the victim's neck, and then it was wider, and blood spurted and splashed on the Butcher and the floor, which was concrete with a drain positioned under the table. Gracie could see it through the legs of the step stool. Could see the blood flow into it.

The victim jerked, but she was strapped down securely, nowhere to go. The saw bit, and within seconds, the head came loose and rolled off the table and struck the floor with a thud.

Then the hooded Butcher turned and saw Gracie, dropped the saw and stepped off the stool. The Butcher picked up the hatchet on the floor and started to rush toward Gracie.

Gracie, having been frozen in place, came unstuck. She started to yell for Trevor to run. But he had already made his exit. Gracie could hear his feet pounding on the stairs as he climbed them with all the speed of a spider monkey.

Gracie slammed the door shut, pushed the weight of her body against it as the Butcher banged on the other side, nearly knocking Gracie down. Gracie felt the pressure on the door increasing, and knew she couldn't hold it for long.

She gave it one last push, then wheeled toward the stairs.

Gracie emerged from the cellar, stumbling as she went over the sack of dog food. Trevor was nowhere to be seen. She could hear the Butcher, tight on her heels, the stairs squeaking like mice.

She scanned the area for a weapon, reached for a plastic ketchup bottle, then decided against it. The pounding of footsteps was now only a few feet away. She scooped up the dog food bag using both arms, hoisted it onto her hip. The bag ripped slightly. Dog food dribbled out. It smelled of molasses and corn. She glanced down the stairs as her masked pursuer reached the top, and heaved the bag down the stairs with all her might.

The Butcher let out a yelp as the bag hit at knee level, burst open, scattered dog food in all directions and caused the Butcher to stumble backwards and fall with a sound like someone dribbling a basketball, then hitting the floor with a hollow thud. Gracie ran out of the pantry towards the back door, and then was outside, running with all her might, making good time even though she had a pack on her back.

As she ran, she glanced back and saw the Butcher exit the house, trying to run in the long leather apron. It was not an outfit designed for running. Gracie outdistanced the Butcher, and the Butcher stopped running, stood holding the hatchet, watching her. Gracie beat feet around the pond, up toward the wood line where their camper was parked. She turned her attention to that location, saw Trevor climbing the hill into the trees. At that moment she dearly wanted to coldcock him with a two-by-four.

She also feared, panicked as he was, he might drive off and leave her. Something she had never considered before.

She hurried on up the hill and through the woods, was relieved to see the camper still parked beside the road. She took a moment to look back over the moonlit pond. The Butcher was no longer in sight. She found Trevor in the driver's seat, both hands gripping the steering wheel. He looked as if he had been hit between the eyes with a mallet.

"You left me, Trevor!"

"I was going for help."

"You were going to save your ass."

"It was reflexes, all right?"

"No. Not all right. She had a hatchet. I had a bag of dog food."

"I never claimed to be any kind of white knight. I'm a thief, not a fighter."

Trevor started the camper, drove it onto the road.

"It's okay," he said. "We'll just move on. I'm sorry, babe. Really."

They cruised along in cold silence for a while, and then Gracie said, "We have to tell the police, someone. The Butcher back there murdered a woman, sawed through her neck like she was a Christmas ham."

"We talk to the law, they'll want to know why we were in the house. We can just send them the Polaroids, give them the address."

"What is the address?"

"I hadn't gathered that information yet. I planned to."

"They'll just think the Polaroids are faked."

"We can't go to the police."

"All those body parts in the freezer. Jesus Christ."

"I don't know."

Gracie stuck her foot across the seat and put it on the brake. The camper slid, nearly turned completely around.

"Are you crazy?"

"No, Trevor. What just happened is crazy, and had I been just a few seconds slower, I'd have ended up on that table. We are going to the law, and I don't care what it costs us. You're through calling the shots. I saw what you're made of back there, and it's a pile of shit. Maybe they'll give us a pass, we tell them where a crazy murderer lives with body parts in their freezer. Do that, we might get a slide, or a short sentence. Now turn this thing around, and go back to the last town we drove through."

The sheriff's office was in a trailer on the outskirts of town. It was a double-wide on about three acres with a few outbuildings, and out front a sign that said BRYANT CITY SHERIFF'S OFFICE.

Inside the office they were seated in a row of chairs, and off to the side a partition of glass had been built. On the other side of it were a few cramped desks and three people in deputy sheriff uniforms, one younger woman in plain clothes. They were in front of their computers, typing. Gracie wondered what they were typing. A town as small as Bryant was unlikely to have much crime, and then she thought about the reason they were there. Those body parts had come from somewhere. They added up to a lot of human beings. For all she knew Bryant City might be dead center of a world-class crime wave.

The sheriff was a long lean man who looked as if he had recently been polished with a rag and given a coat of wax. He had a handsome but not particularly flexible face, teeth that looked to have been built into his mouth by someone in a hurry. His straw cowboy hat was on his desk. Straw or not, it was expensive-looking. He was probably forty, maybe even fifty years old. The little placard on his desk stated his name was Sheriff Tom Wilkie.

Behind Wilkie, on the wall, was a variety of brightly colored abstract paintings that seemed out of place for a sheriff's office.

"Let me get this straight. You was robbing the place, and you're the Snapshot Bandits."

"Burglars, but yeah."

"So, you were in the house, and you found a freezer full of body parts, and you seen a person, man or woman you're uncertain, sawing a woman's head off. You kids ain't been smoking nothing, have you?"

"We saw it."

"We thought this was the right thing to do. Murder kind of trumps us stealing a few items, taking photos," Gracie said as she dropped them on Sheriff Wilkie's desk.

"I suppose it does," Sheriff Wilkie said, and pushed the photos on the desk around like he was mixing cards. "These look like what you say you saw, but who's to say they're real?"

"They're real all right," Gracie said.

A knock came at the door and Sheriff Wilkie pushed the array of photos into a pile at the corner of his desk.

"Come on in."

A young Hispanic woman with a curtain of thick black hair cascaded down the shoulders of her beige uniform. A stiff black necktie and gold badge glimmered underneath the fluorescents. The corners of her wide mouth peeled back as she spoke.

"What have we here?"

"Deputy," Wilkie said, "these here kids are the Snapshot Burglars."

The deputy scanned them both. Her face didn't show much.

"These kids claim they might can help us out with those disappearances we been having, least I think if what they're saying is true, could explain them. I'm sure they would be up for a little trade. What say you? We let a few things slide, you show us where this so-called Butcher lives."

"Butcher, huh?" the deputy said.

"They got photos of body parts in a freezer."

"Say they do?"

"Look real, too."

"We show you where we took those photos, how much of a favor will you do us?" Trevor asked.

"Well, you won't get off scot-free, but you might end up with shorter jail time and a smaller fine. I can say some good things about you, doing the right thing and all, and that might help."

"Might?" Trevor said.

"Best I can offer you." The sheriff turned his attention to the deputy, tapped his finger on the stack of snapshots. "Look, here, Ace."

The deputy reached for the photographs.

"What do you think?" Sheriff Wilkie asked.

"Look like the real deal, you ask me."

Gracie nodded, "They're real alright. Come with us, and we'll take you there."

"Alright," Sheriff Wilkie said. "We'll follow you."

In the daylight, there was a part of Gracie that felt it had all been a nightmare, but the thing was, she and Trevor could not have had the same nightmare.

They parked on the hill overlooking the pond and the house. The sheriff and deputy pulled up beside them. The sheriff got out and went around to the driver's window of the camper. Trevor rolled the window down, seat belt strapped tight across his chest, said, "The house across the pond. That's it."

"Look here," Sheriff Wilkie said. "You two are coming with us. You're felons, and I don't like the idea of you running off and leading us on a wild goose chase."

"There wouldn't be any point to us doing this, letting you know who we are, if we hadn't seen something. You have our names."

"I got your license plate number, too."

"There you are," Trevor said.

The deputy was out of the car now, her long black hair hanging down from under her hat, the sun flaring against it like a wet crow wing. She strolled over to join them.

"Be that as it may," Sheriff Wilkie said, "you're coming with us, so get your ass out of the camper and let's go."

So down the hill they went, Sheriff in the lead, Gracie and Trevor in the center, the deputy bringing up the rear.

"So you picked the lock, then what?" Sheriff Wilkie asked.

"We went in and made a sandwich," Trevor said.

"A sandwich?" the sheriff said.

"Yeah," Trevor said. "It's kind of our trademark, besides the snapshots."

The sheriff stopped walking and looked a question back at the deputy, Ace.

"Yeah," Ace said. "That's what the reports say. The Snapshot Burglars always make a sandwich, sometimes shit in the toilet and don't flush."

"That was him," Gracie said.

"One time, and that's because there was low water pressure," Trevor said. "It wasn't a statement."

They started walking again. The sheriff said, "Okay. You made a sandwich, and then you went to the cellar and found a freezer full of body parts."

"Exactly," Gracie said. "Shouldn't you be writing this down?"

The sheriff tapped his head. "All up here. Besides, it's not like you won't be answering the same questions again."

"And again and again," Deputy Ace said. "Might even ask you two to answer in interpretive dance. And you'll do it."

"In some kind of costume if we ask," Sheriff Wilkie said.

"Do you know this place?" Gracie asked the sheriff.

"I don't think so. You, Ace?"

"Nope," Ace said.

"Now show me exactly what you did to get inside."

"Don't we need a warrant or something?" Gracie said.

"Not in these parts. Not with what you found."

Gracie worked the lock with her lock picking tools. It only took her a moment, and then they were inside. The air freshener was still thick in the air.

"So sandwich, then pantry?" Sheriff Wilkie asked again.

Trevor nodded.

Wilkie walked to the pantry, opened the door. Ace stepped inside, shone her light around and pushed at the panel in the back, sliding it aside, revealing the stairs. The sick orange light from below was visible, the color of spoiled honey. The pine smell was really strong down there, so thick it turned Gracie's stomach. She thought of it as a portal to hell.

"Shouldn't you check the rest of the house?" Trevor said.

"You be burglars, we'll be police," Sheriff Wilkie said. "I want you to show me the exact place you took those photos."

"I'm not going down there," Gracie said.

Ace patted the butt of the service weapon in her holster, glanced back over her shoulder at them. "You'll be fine. We'll be with you, and we're armed."

"You lead the way, Ace," Sheriff Wilkie said, stepping aside. "I'll bring up the rear. I want to keep a check on our burglars."

Before she started down, Ace lifted her hair, slipped a band over it to knot it into a ponytail. Gracie squeezed Trevor's arm. Why hadn't they searched the rest of the house as Trevor suggested? And how had Wilkie and Ace known exactly where to go, and which door was the pantry without asking them the way in?

And then if Gracie harbored any doubts, she lost them when she saw the tattoo on Ace's bare neck.

Gracie was telling her body to run, but her legs wouldn't move, and by the time the signal from the brain was strong enough to make them function, Ace was already down the stairs, and Sheriff Wilkie, seeming to take his time about it, grabbed a can of corn from a shelf in the pantry and used it to hit Trevor in the forehead.

Trevor let out a long sigh, like the sound of a dying engine on its last road trip, stumbled to his knees, a hand to his bleeding face, said, "What the hell?"

Before Gracie could fight or flee, the sheriff grabbed her by her hair and pulled her past him, causing her to fall over Trevor, and onto the stairs where she bounced down each step, cracking one as she went, finally landing on the hard floor below, stunned.

Then Trevor came thumping down the stairs behind her, propelled by Sheriff Wilkie's foot. He stopped rolling, stopped moving, and lay in a heap on the bottom step of the stairs, not far from where Gracie lay.

Looking up, she saw Sheriff Wilkie walking casually down the stairs, grinning like a Cheshire Cat with a canary in its teeth. When he reached the stair step she had cracked, nestled his foot on top of it, the stair cracked again with a sound like gunfire, and his leg went through the break in the stairs. Gracie felt a slight bit of satisfaction when she saw the smile rip off his face to be replaced by a wide-open mouth making a scream so high and wild it made the hair on the back of her neck stand up like porcupine quills. He was hung there, and a jagged piece of the step had gone through his groin and blood was gushing everywhere.

Ace, who had been in some other part of the basement, came rushing out then, and Gracie barely made it to her feet in time to be on the receiving end of a mallet Ace was swinging.

The world turned white, not dark, and then there were stars for an instant, and then there was pain and blackness.

When Gracie awoke she was lying on her back, strapped to a table, and in an instant she realized it was the same place she had seen the woman strapped down before Ace took the hacksaw to her. A rancid smell filled her nostrils. There was a cacophony of light and noise. Banging drums and ringing cymbals. Flashing colored lights and a strobe that blinked off and on and made the ceiling crawl with light and shadow. Flies fluttered around her face, looking for a place to land.

"You little bitch," Ace said.

Gracie turned her head in the direction of the voice. Ace stood nearby, nude except for the leather apron, a hacksaw in her hand. She hadn't bothered with the hood. Next to Ace near the table, there was a tray on a rolling platform, and on the tray were shiny sharp objects.

"I'm going to make it last for you, bitch. I'm going to saw slow. I'm going to slit a hole in your stomach and ease your guts out slowly with pliers. I'm going to clip off your toes with hedge clippers. I'm going to pull out your teeth one by one. I'm going to pop your eyeballs onto your cheeks, let them dangle on their tendons. I'm going to heat you up with a leather burning set, put my initials on your lily-white ass. I'm going to—"

"That's quite a list," Gracie said, and soon as the words came out of her mouth, she thought, don't agitate the crazy person, but it was done. On the other hand, Gracie thought, if I'm going to die, I might as well get a few quips in. But now she went silent. The gravity of her situation hung over her like... Well, like the strange thing on cables above her, swinging slowly around and around, coated in colored and strobing lights.

It covered the entire ceiling. There were lots of cables used. There were withered, dried body parts, heads and arms and legs and feet, and they had all been stitched together with wire, making a unique artistic display. Intestines had been dried into dark ropes, and they twisted through the body parts like snakes. It all moved slowly on some sort of wood and metal rig coiled with wires. The colored lights and the pounding and clanging intensified the horror of it.

Then she saw Sheriff Wilkie's head. It was boiled pink and missing the eyes, which had been filled with red Christmas tree bulbs. His head was wearing his cowboy hat, and his sheriff's badge was pinned to his forehead. His penis, or someone's penis, had been fastened under his chin by red wire, sewn right into the lower jaw as if it were a wormy beard.

"It's to honor him," Ace said. "He had sensibilities you would never understand. We were meant to be together, but you killed him."

"Me? The stairs broke. He fell."

"Your fault, though. I have made him part of the tapestry of life we were working on. One of many of our artistic creations. He would have appreciated that. You need to see the rest," Ace said. "Our art project was private, but since you'll soon be part of it."

Ace came closer to the table, worked a crank. It raised the table, lifting Gracie's head and shoulders up. She tried to move her feet and arms, but the straps held her fast.

"Look and see what my beloved and I have created."

Ace did something else to make the table swivel, spin actually. As it spun Gracie saw propped up by old boards and wire the remainder of a nude, decaying man. His once-bloated body was ruptured and his guts, a putrid pile of goo and bones, were piled in a wash tub that was held up by a rope around the dead man's neck. There was a woman too. She hung limp on a spinning display of bone and wire. Her body was tightly wrapped in green Christmas wire and multicolored Christmas bulbs. Decaying flesh dripped from her headless frame as she moved around Gracie like a parade float.

There was the body of a young man, and he had been rigged with metal extensions that caused his arms to move. There were drumsticks in his hands, and they beat at a big drum fastened about his neck in the same manner as the man with the tub of decaying guts. Another body, the woman she had seen on the table the day before, was sawed apart and fastened back together with rods and wire. Like the drummer, she moved, pounded cymbals. Flies weaved in and out of the mess like a squadron of bombers.

All the bodies were linked by barb wire and electric wire of different colors. There were creaking hinges, rattling chains, grinding gears and pulsing lights. The corpse display moved around her as she spun on the swiveling table like a macabre merry-go-round of flesh and bone, guts and gristle. When she stopped spinning, Gracie felt sick and dizzy. The circle of decay continued its noisy, brightly lit parade as it dollied around her on its metal track. So not only had she been moving, so had the corpses.

Ace bent over Gracie, said, "I added my beloved to this, and soon, I'll add yours. Trevor. That was his name, right? Little fucker broke his neck when he fell down the stairs, so I missed having fun with him. But when I get to him, I plan to fill his mouth with shit and sew it up. I'm actually going to shit in his mouth myself."

"All of this is about an art project?" Gracie said. She didn't want to talk, but she feared not talking. Anything to stall for time.

"A masterful project, using the bodies of illegal aliens, strays and malcontents and assholes and criminals who had it coming, one way or another. The government could have given them their punishments for theft and murder, peeping toms and troublemakers, runaway kids who didn't under-stand the meaning of respect and family. They could have, but they didn't. We wanted those losers to be our personal, artistic display of truth and justice and the American way. We love art, our first love, but neither of us were able to express it. Didn't understand our role in art until we met. Our meeting was an artistic blossom made up of human flesh, and a fulfillment of dreams. You spoiled our work together, you little bitch. So, what I'm going to do, is I'm going to remove your clothes with very sharp scissors, and I believe I may manage to poke you with them a bit. Then I'll slowly saw one of your legs off at the knee and after I'm coated in your hot squirting blood, I'll apply a tourniquet, and that will keep you from bleeding out. Give me time for more sawing and cutting. Then I'll sew your Trevor's balls between your legs, and you'll still be alive while I do it. I've learned tricks. I'll have so much fun with you the heavens will cry. Art and revenge, little bitch."

Ace had turned ecstatic, a little girl displaying her schoolwork.

Coming up behind Ace, moving slow, staggering, was Trevor. His head dangled to one side and rested on his shoulder. One of his knees was bending out to the side as he walked. He held a chunk of the broken stair step in his hand, a solid, jagged piece of wood.

Ace, hearing the drag of Trevor's shoe, turned too late.

The board fragment in Trevor's hand flashed out. The strobe light made the board look as if its descending arc was a series of stills cut from a film. There was a cracking sound as the board made contact with her head. Ace dropped the saw, stumbled to one knee. Trevor hit her again, and this time she rolled over on her side and grunted, her ass sticking out from under the raised apron like a baby head peeking around a curtain.

Trevor, even weaker than moments before, made his way to the table, unfastened the wrist strap on Gracie's right hand.

"Oh, Trevor," Gracie said. "I'm so sorry."

As Trevor reached across her for the other wrist restraint, there was a cracking sound, and his already loose head swung forward on his chest, and he collapsed across her. He made a coughing noise, then there was a gurgling sound, like someone drowning. Slowly his body weight carried him off her and he dropped on the floor.

Gracie sat up, used her free hand to unclamp her wrist, and then her feet. She swung her legs off the table, and that's when Ace hopped up from her position, like a frog leaping for a fly, grasped Gracie's throat with both hands, and pushed her back against the table.

Gracie struggled to break free, but without results. Ace was strong.

Gracie reached out and grabbed at something on the rolling instrument table. It was scissors. She jabbed at Ace's side. Once. Twice.

Ace bellowed and leaped back. There was a hatchet under the table, and she reached for that.

Gracie grabbed the rolling instrument table, pushed it hard into Ace, knocking her back, causing her to trip over Trevor's body and drop the hatchet. Gracie picked up the hatchet Ace had dropped, and turning the blade away, hit Ace with the back part of the hatchet in the middle of her forehead like she was driving a railroad spike.

When Ace awoke, Gracie was standing nearby. The noise and lights had been turned off. The bodies were no longer spinning about the table.

"Hey there, sleepy-head. Well, it's almost like you got two heads, way you're swelled up. But I got to give it to you. You took some serious blows, and you're still spry. Or would be, if you weren't held down with those straps."

Ace, as if on cue, struggled against her restraints.

Gracie held up her Polaroid camera.

"I went back to the camper to get my camera. I figured you could use a little nap. So I took my time. Had myself a peanut butter sandwich too. Blood sugar was a little low."

"You bitch," Ace said.

"Nailed it," Gracie said.

She lifted the camera then, flashed a photo.

She waited a moment as it ejected from the camera, took it, shook it, and watched as it developed.

"Oh, that's a good one. But, woman to woman, you might want to have some work done, jaw's starting to sag a little. You know, you could get the skin pulled back to make your face tighter. Oh, wait. I can do that for you. By the way. This photo, I like to call it the *before* shot."

Gracie placed the camera on the floor with the photo, stood up straight holding the hatchet. She lifted the hatchet over her head, said, "And in a moment, I'm going to take the *after* photo."

Gracie was amazed how loud Ace could scream.

SWEET
POTATO

A soul may find its way back from the corners of
darkness by becoming part of a common thing.

—From *Everyday Items of Darkness*

THERE'S ONLY SO much a lonely man can do, so much
TV that can be watched, books that can be read, so many
moments of masturbation, before buying a rototiller and gardening seems a realistic consideration.

Though he had a good retirement plan, Tyler hadn't expected
his job to end so abruptly, the boss having gone to prison for
ass-fondling and money-grubbing from the public trust. But
there it was. She went and the business went, and now here he
was, out in the wilds of unemployment, living off his considerable savings (thank goodness), and submerged way down deep
in the cold-ass nothing.

Dreaming for a while was so fine. No alarm clock, living
in pajamas. What he liked best, at first, was that things that
seemed silly in real life seemed fine in the dream world. He
could be an old-fashioned hero in his dreams, much younger,
washboard abs, a baseball-bat dick, and balls like grapefruits.
Carrying a sword, brave and relentless, six foot five and forever

young. And then, one night, down in a dream, there was a soundless shift.

He was cruising along beneath the quicksilver light of triple moons, in an open self-operating flying craft with a drink in his hand, an olive in his martini. He had fought for and rescued the fair maiden, but somewhere in his dream, Morpheus had dropped her off, as if after a date, and he was alone. He stood in his open craft as the wind lifted his hair and he sipped his chilled drink and chewed his olive, felt as happy as a twelve-year-old with the summer off from school and plans for a trip to the carnival.

A long-shadowed moon licked at the split in the alley of trees that was his path. Leaves the size of his palms blew about, brown and gold and crackling in the air. Then at the far end of the wooded and shadowed corridor, a door in the world cleft open, and a shadow oozed out. And brave and resourceful a hero as he was, he felt a rubbery shift in his spine, a melting of resolve.

The sensation was so upsetting, Tyler couldn't hold the old dream, and awoke in his bed. He felt certain whatever came out of the doorway came back with him, blending with the shadows in the room. He could feel it, cold and damp like a water-swollen sponge, lurking. The central air hummed. The moonlight through the curtain was cloudy like infected urine. Though outside was dry, there was a sensation of a recent rain storm having passed in the night, leaving behind electric sizzles and reverberations from thunderous roars.

Tyler sat up, turned on the lamp beside his bed.

Nothing.

It had all been a dream, perhaps a dream within a dream. Or had the shadow found a mousehole?

He decided right then, he had to find something to do that would give life to his life, not just life to his dreams, for even his dreams were growing stale, and perhaps even precarious. Or at least he had begun to feel that way. Decided it was a mental health consideration.

After that night, he no longer remembered his dreams. He slept with the light on. But he still had the sensation of a crawling thing lurking in the dark recesses of the walls, the flooring, the ceiling, licking at his bones, trying to get deep inside of him.

A week later, while walking through a farm and ranch store, he bought some jeans, a chambray shirt, and decided on a roto-tiller and a gardening book. He decided he would break the ground in the spring after loading it with compost over the summer, fall, and winter. When the time came, he would plant sweet potatoes.

He was uncertain why he had chosen sweet potatoes, other than as a child he and his mother had liked them baked and split and coated in butter and cinnamon. But sweet potatoes were his choice.

He broke the ground behind his house with the rototiller, churned the grass under and heaved up the dark, dank earth and exposed it to the sun and wind and any rain that might come its way.

It felt good to be doing something physical. The tiller rocking his body like a gyrating lover. Muscles aching pleasantly, sweat glistening on his forehead like sugary doughnut glaze.

His next-door neighbor, an old woman, Carrie Baker, who looked to have one foot in the grave and the other on an oil slick, shrouded in a white cotton housedress, hair white as well, observed him from her backyard with squinted eyes while filling her bird feeder with seeds that rattled against it like gravel under truck tires.

Over the years he had never seen her other than alone, dressed in that housecoat. She would fill the bird feeder, then retire to a chair on her back porch, hidden behind flower trellises which were without flowers or vines. She would sit there with a BB gun, in a kind of duck blind, waiting for hungry birds to arrive at what they assumed was a free buffet, only to be shot for her entertainment.

The air rifle would huff, a bird would fall, and old Ms. Baker would hoot with satisfaction. She was a good shot. Killing birds was like her morning coffee.

She bagged three or four a day, except on Sunday, a time of rest and abandonment of her white cotton housedress. She garbed herself then in ancient clothes, dark skirt, blouse and shoes, a block hat made of cloth and straw that was bedecked with a yellow band with an enormous bow. She would walk off late morning with a massive Bible tucked under her arm, on down to the church at the end of the street. A few hours later she marched back again. She never lifted a hand or spoke in greeting. She merely eyed him like she was taking aim at one of the birds on her feeder, perhaps hearing in her head the puff of her air rifle.

As for the dead birds, she would gather them up, and with a trowel, dig little holes. Their bright-winged corpses ended up beneath mounds of dirt in her side yard, like clay goose bumps on the ground.

No one came to visit her. The post lady dropped the mail in the box and ran away for fear of an encounter. Tyler found this understandable. Birds, however, were slow learners. The survivors failed to spread the word.

AT NIGHT, TYLER felt as if the escaped shadow from his dream was stirring about the house, as if searching for something. When he burst awake and turned on the light, there was nothing there.

He would then turn off the light and once again he would feel an uncomfortable feeling. He flicked it back on.

That was better. He would leave it on.

Next day he bought powerful light bulbs and used them to replace the old. At night, the inside of his home was lit up like an airport runway.

ALL THROUGH THE winter he laid out a pile of hay and sawdust and horse manure he procured from a stable, table scraps, and even added a dead cat and a dead possum to his mound. It was his view, from what he read, that even the little corpses would break down sufficiently, heated in his compost bundle to such a degree there would be nothing left but nutrients for the soil.

In the spring, Tyler heaped his winter compost over his quarter-acre garden (he thought of it as his mini-farm). The soil was black from the compost. No animal bones, cat or possum fur. No discernable food scraps, no offensive horse-manure smell.

He bought sweet potatoes and cut them in half and placed them in large containers of water until green slips sprouted from them. He removed, rooted, planted the slips, and pulled compost around them. He built a standing frame around his quarter-acre enterprise, covered the sides with cheesecloth, roofed it with the same. He made a door with simple hinges and more cheesecloth, so that he could enter into his bird-protected mini-farm and tend his sweet potato flock, as he liked to think of it.

Ten long rows were sunned through the cheesecloth, watered by the rain and a water hose when days were dry. He saw the slips grow firm and green. He knew that beneath the ground the sweet potatoes were swelling and filling with nutritional goodness. They would become so big and ripe they would beg to be split open and stuffed with butter and cinnamon.

He bought a book on sweet potato recipes. He bought a metal gardening shed and filled it with his tiller and gardening tools he most likely didn't need.

One summer morning, already hot, white clouds flowing across the sky like soapsuds, Tyler went outside with a lawn chair. He entered his miniature farm, placed the chair at the end of a row, and sat and gloated over his greenery. He would have plenty to eat and plenty to sell to the farmer's market. He had visions of buying land, expanding his farm and becoming a professional sweet potato farmer. He might add corn and tomatoes. But he was worried about one section of his plot that seemed to have rejected the compost. The potato slips there sagged like an old man's dick. They were beginning to turn yellow. He had applied the same amount of compost to the ground, but that section refused to respond. The books suggested a lack of nitrogen.

He was thinking on all of this, when he noticed what looked like a deflated human-sized doll lying in Carrie Baker's yard.

He viewed it for some time before leaving his chair, walking over to the line of grass between his yard and hers.

As he grew closer, Tyler saw that the deflated doll was, in fact, a decimated human lying facedown in the yard. He recognized the housedress and the shock of white hair. It was Carrie Baker, and she wasn't imitating a snake. She was dead. A bag of birdseed lay spilled beside her. She had a spade in her hand. A hole was dug and a dead bird lay beside it.

Tyler peered down at her for a long time. Her housedress was damp and she had begun to flatten and smell. Insects crawled in her hair. She must have been lying there for quite a few days. The bird was wormy and bug-chewed too.

Why hadn't he noticed?

The self-asked question was answered immediately by his subconscious, yelling over miles of synapses. Because he didn't like her and didn't care. Didn't want to see her kill birds and snarl across her yard at him. He hadn't seen what he didn't want to see. Or perhaps he wasn't that observant, caught up in his own concerns and newfound hobby.

It was likely she had been seized by a heart attack, perhaps even as he tended his potatoes. He could imagine her clutching at the air, reaching in his direction for help, trying to speak, but finding her mouth stuffed with vomit and phlegm, her head with goodbye memories, likely all of them mean and stale and wearing a housedress.

As he was about to return home and call the police, he was struck with a thought. Who was she, really?

It wasn't as if she was in need of immediate attention, and if he hadn't found her, she would merely have faded into the grass, her cotton dress rotting around her like melting snow.

He went to his garden shed, grabbed his thick, new gardening gloves, and used them to open her unlocked back door. He was already thinking like a criminal. Leave no prints. All he really wanted to do was see inside her house, see what she was about when she was away from her bird-hunting blind, though sometimes he did see her on her riding mower, rolling over her yard like Patton rolling through Italy. Perhaps she dreamed of the mower chopping gopher heads.

Tyler slipped inside.

It was humid inside and dark. The air felt empty of life. Where there was light streaming through the windows dust motes swirled like alien parasites.

Unlike most grandma houses, there were no knickknacks, bric-a-brac or grandkid photos on shelves, or silly slogans framed and placed on the wall. The house wasn't piled up or nasty, but it felt that way. There was very little furniture, and when he opened up the kitchen cabinets, he found a plate, a bowl, a glass, a cup, and one saucer. In the utensil drawer there was only a knife, a fork, a spoon, and a spatula. There was a frying pan and a little pot on the stove.

The refrigerator was empty except for a jug of water with greasy lip stains on its mouth. Another cabinet was full of instant oatmeal, a bag of sugar, a box of salt, a shaker of pepper, many economy sized cans of pinto beans, enough to produce abundant intestinal gas that could fart her north of the moon.

In the bedroom there was only a bed, a dresser, and in the closet, on a hanger, were her church clothes. On a shelf, her hat with the bow. He wasn't sure why he did it, but he picked the hat up and held it while he punched a hole in the crown. He replaced it on the shelf.

He opened the dresser drawers. They were stuffed with photo albums.

Inside there were no family shots. Just newspaper clippings of hospital deaths, all sudden, all men. In that same album was her nursing license, one photo of her in a white nurse's dress, wearing one of those hats they used to wear. What wowed him was that he could tell it was her, but she was young and pretty. No. Beautiful. The kind of woman you dreamed of, twisted up in the sheets with her legs locked around your ass. Yet those eyes, then and before her death, were still the same. Not so nice, near insane. Cat eyes in the moonlight.

There were marriage certificates arranged next to death certificates. Her name was on the marriage certificates. Four husbands were on the death certificates. All had died of heart attacks, and in their prime. Insurance documents were also there. The poor widow had received quite a windfall. A lot of people seemed to have signed their savings over to her.

"Shit," Tyler said aloud.

Good lord. He could envision her sitting on her bed with her scrapbooks and photo albums all around, her hand on her crotch, rubbing while reading of medical deaths and insurance payouts that she had somehow manipulated.

A black widow, an angel of doom, had lived next door to him, finishing out her golden years eating beans and shooting birds.

❧

TYLER DUG THE hole. Made it deep and fairly wide, poured in some lime, not just for her, but to even out the soil. He had tested it there, and it was far too benign. It needed some acid and a corpse for the worms to grind.

Down in the hole he stacked compost on the lime, then he laid in Ms. Baker. Another coat of compost, a bit more lime, then he stood back and looked down at his work. It seemed fine. Come next spring he would put in a few more sweet potatoes. Let them grow up from her bone dust, withering skin, and his rich compost.

That night, when he laid down, all the lights on as was his custom, he thought of the old woman down in the ground. She had been awful, of that he was certain, so it was only fair that she should contribute to the rebirth of soil and vegetables. A good deed in place of all the people and birds she had killed. Surely, that wasn't so bad.

Tyler waited to feel guilty. He waited to feel sad, or disappointed in himself. But he hadn't killed her. He had merely composted her.

But once she had been beautiful. Had she always been conniving and mean? He had sexual dreams about her youthful self, and then at some point he popped awake, having felt as if he had been having sex with a barbwire doll with a shadow-black heart.

❦

VISITING A FRIEND from work, who was also out of a job with time for the coffee shop, Tyler said, after their conversation began to falter, "Have you ever had a dream that seemed real?"

The friend, gray and heavy with lips like two red earthworms, rocked back in the booth and sipped his coffee before answering.

"Of course. Though mostly they don't make sense when I wake up. But now and again, they feel real, could be real. Some of the most outlandish dreams seem real at the time."

"Just for curiosity's sake. Have you ever felt something in a dream came back with you, when you woke up?"

"No. Though I've heard of it. Some people believe your soul lets go sometimes and comes right out of you when you breathe awake. One moment you're breathing asleep, the next, you're breathing awake."

"Your soul?"

"If you believe in that sort of thing. Maybe a piece of your soul. Or something worse. A demon. A succubus, which is a kind of sex demon that rides in and out on your essence while you dream, fucks the shit out of you and takes your energy, borrows your soul, and finally keeps it. They can be created by your subconscious, or they can be night riders."

"What's that?"

"Loose souls looking for a place to light. A place to suck the energy out of. Men can be incubuses, you know."

"I don't know."

"Male sex demons. The succubus in reverse. I think succubuses and incubuses can switch hit when it comes to sexual matters. You might even have to put Scotch tape over your dog's asshole if one of them is around."

"I don't have a dog."

"That's one less worry, then."

"How do you know all of this?"

"I read a lot. I found golf too tiring."

"Well, I could use a sex demon actually," Tyler said.

"I wouldn't mind one either. But it might be like that old saying about how you have to be careful what you wish for."

ꙮ

WHILE TYLER SLEPT, the lights stayed on through summer, fall, and winter. Come spring, he felt strong, and one night he turned all the lights out. The darkness seemed immediately stuffed with something he couldn't define.

It was as if the universe were expanding inside his room. He felt stifled. But he didn't turn the light on. He was stronger than that, he decided. Stronger than being foolish about shadows and lights. Still, the sensation of the room pressing against him was so overwhelming, that without really thinking about it, he opened a window as if to let it out.

In that moment he glimpsed a wave of darkness roll out of the sweet potato patch, out of the area where the old lady lay rotting beneath dirt and plants, beneath the cheesecloth. He had an impression of something rushing past him, like a great shadowy bird taking flight. Something colliding with the fullness in the room.

Next moment he was in the bed without remembering lying down. The shadow shaped itself and mounted him, and he could feel it moving against him, and it felt good, and soon it felt better. It was draining him not only of night emissions, but something that wiggled desperately in the back of his mind, then slithered away.

"What the hell?" he said, sitting up in bed in the early morning, his pajamas around his knees, a wet spot on the sheets.

❧

AS FAR AS Tyler knew, not one soul had asked about Ms. Baker. No one from the church. No one from anywhere. He assumed seeking her out might be like seeking out a virulent strain of flu. The mail lady ceased to bring mail to the old lady's mailbox. Birds ate from the bag of spilled seed all winter, then ceased to come when spring bloomed. They were singing in trees somewhere safer, or so Tyler liked to presume.

In the garden the slips grew fast and spread their vines, twisted over the earth and climbed the cheesecloth and the board frame and made everything within emerald green. Tyler had never seen such vines, thick and pumping as if with arterial blood, puffing up little spurts of dust between the vines, as if down below the potatoes were desperately breathing, like a reformed cigarette smoker coughing out nicotine tar.

He couldn't bring himself to dig there, in the place where he had seen the dark shadow. He took smaller potatoes from underneath other vines. He baked them and split them and buttered them and dusted them with cinnamon. They were delicious.

At the beginning of each day, getting out of bed became difficult and strong cups of coffee might as well have been water. He hesitated to go to bed at night, but welcomed it as well. He would open the window and let the air and the night and the winged shadow in.

The dreams had become good, and he could imagine the younger Ms. Baker mounting him like a show pony, running him through his tricks, urging his best performance. In those moments, he felt simultaneously close to death and ecstasy.

When it came time to harvest the sweet potato section where he had buried Ms. Baker, he discovered that the earth had swollen high and rounded like an enormous burn blister filled with dark pus. Raking back the soil, he saw the orange skin of a single, massive sweet potato. One vine that grew out of it was thick and green, like an arm tipped with pea green fingers.

Leave it alone, he told himself, or dig it up and chop it up, burn the remains. Sow the ground with salt so that nothing will grow there.

But there was something so appealing about it. As he scraped dirt away, he saw the potato was in the shape of a human. His thoughts went in a different direction. What if he dug her up and brought her in the house, placed her next to the bed?

Tyler had no idea where such feelings came from, and he walked away, ducked in the house and killed time watching television. He didn't remember a thing he watched. When night fell, he took the shovel from the shed, went to the sweet potato bed, and began to dig the human-shaped sweet potato completely free.

When he broke it out of the ground, there in the moonlight, he could see green and gold vines had clustered where the top of the head would be, and there was the same where the legs parted, growing there like matted pubic hair.

Tyler hacked loose the umbilical cord vines with the tip of the shovel, then dragged the surprisingly heavy sweet potato out of its lumber and cheesecloth home. Pulled it through his back door, trailing a swathe of dirt across the floor.

He dropped it on his bedroom floor. He sat in a chair and looked at it. He was sick of eating sweet potatoes. He was sick of gardening, but this amazing product of the soil and of flesh intrigued him. Even hacked up, it would take a few days for him to eat it. He wanted to consume it in the way disciples of Jesus wanted to taste his blood and flesh via wine and wafer.

Rising from the chair, he walked to it and touched it, and ran his fingers over it. The skin of it was soft and thin, even warm to the touch. It looked less orange in the light, more golden. The appearance of legs and arms, head and body, were more pronounced. He tugged it into the bathroom, filled the tub with warm water, hustled the potato up and into the bath. He stripped off his clothes, climbed into the tub and rubbed the potato gently with a rag. The skin trembled under his touch. Dirt darkened the water.

When he felt he had cleaned it as best as possible, he pulled it out, dried it and himself off with a fluffy towel. Still naked, he lugged it into his bed and nuzzled up beside it, feeling its warmth and soft skin. He put his arm around it.

For the first time he felt he wanted the lights out, wanted to be in the dark with his companion. He rose, turned off the light and crawled back into bed and pulled the covers over them. The moonlight through the window was like a highway to heaven and the softness of the potato was like a woman, and now the vines that sprayed from the head of the potato were softer than before, and sweet-smelling, and all the darkness around them was soft like silk.

Fingers touched him. Lips kissed him. Skin warmed him. And finally, he was making love to a woman, not a sweet potato, but a woman. The younger version of his next-door neighbor.

He could hear her breathing and grunting, and himself doing the same, and they tumbled and rolled and loved together.

When they were done, he lay with his arm around her. He felt her move and throw back the sheets, and then she crawled out of bed with her hands touching the floor first, pulling the rest of her away from him. He could hear her crawling, slinking along the floor. It was then quiet for a time and then she rose up at the foot of his bed. The moonlight had shifted, but he could see her clearly. She was indeed the woman next door, in youth. Her features were cut with shadow. Her eyes were flat and black and looked like tiny holes in the ground. Her skin was the color of a golden sweet potato.

She began to sway, then she began to dance as if the room were full of music. Swirling and writhing at the foot of the bed like a snake finding position to strike. Her legs lifted. Her arms fanned. Her head cranked left, then right, then back and forward. It was sexy at first, and then he had an empty feeling. The sudden realization that the source of him was moving away.

Everything was dark. Tyler collapsed into deep but jagged sleep. As he tumbled, down, down, a silhouette of a giant sweet potato passed him, touched him lightly, damp and cold, and then the bottom of his dream fell out and he shot shapelessly into a cosmic abyss containing stars and moons and planets. Then there was nothing but the dark and the smell of butter and cinnamon.

And then there was nothing at all.

🌿

IN THE MORNING the young woman moved naked in the light. Her skin was smooth and pale. Her hair was thick and hung to her shoulders and was the color of a lion's mane. There was the lip-smacking aroma of baked sweet potato in the air.

On the counter, next to a cleaver, lay hacked sweet potato parts. They were shaped like amputated arms and legs and there was a head with green knobs where eyes should be; sprigs of vines flowed from the head like tangled hair. Two knobby hunks of potato were beside it.

The kitchen was toasty. The woman turned off the oven. She put on an oven mitt. She pulled out the baking pan containing the large wedge of potato-orange thorax and placed it on the counter. She used a knife to split it and butter it. She shook sugar and cinnamon into the split. Now the air really smelled sweet.

She put the baked sweet potato portion on a plate and then on the table next to a knife and fork. She licked her lips and sat down to eat.

After a while, satiated, she walked naked with a swollen stomach out the back way and crossed to the house next door. She removed a simple housedress from the closet, white with blue flowers on it. She slipped it on. Barefoot, she found the BB gun. She loaded BBs into it. She carried it out on the back porch and placed it on the glider.

Back inside, she removed a bag of birdseed from under the kitchen sink and hauled it out to the feeder in the backyard.

She filled the feeder, and dropped the bag on the ground. On the porch, sitting in the glider, the BB gun lying across her lap, she waited for the birds.

HATS

MASON FOUND A store with lots of hats. He had never seen the store before, and he walked that street at least five times a week, but there it was.

As he passed it walking home from work, he decided to go inside. What surprised him was how old the store seemed. It had corners full of cobwebs and it was shadowy and gave the impression of having been there for years.

Mason tried to remember what had been in its spot before, but nothing came to mind. It seemed as if this store had found a place in the block where before there was no place.

That made no sense. Of course it was here, and he had for some reason failed to notice it before today.

He walked around amongst the hats, and there was all manner of headgear. There was a little man in the back behind a desk wearing a bowler hat. He had a thin mustache and was smoking a cigar. The entire store smelled of cigar smoke.

At the counter, Mason said, "How long has this store been here?"

"What?" said the little man, pulling the cigar from between yellowed teeth. "Oh. Long time. Before me, for many years. Who knows exactly? Looking for a hat? You need a hat."

"More curious than anything else."

"Why not a bowler hat? A bowler would be good."

"I don't know."

"Well, be curious and look around. Try a hat on if you like. Pick what you fancy, try it on. There are big mirrors at the ends of the store."

Mason nodded. "Thank you."

He had no interest in a hat, but he didn't want to be rude, so he pretended to be interested in the merchandise.

Strolling about, he found a large white Stetson cowboy hat and for fun lifted it off the peg it was hung on, and put it on and looked in the mirror at the end of the store. It was a tall mirror, and when he looked in it, he saw himself wearing the hat, but he was also seated on a big white stallion and was wearing a gun belt with two pistols and there was a mountain range behind him. Cows wandered about.

What kind of trick was this? How fun. The mirrors made a story of the hat you were wearing. He stood before the mirror and looked at himself on the horse, and he could feel the hot sun on the back of his neck in spite of the hat, and the wind was dry and the air stank of cows.

He had the sensation of moving now, and in the mirror the horse and he were moving along with the cows on a cattle drive. There were other cowboys with him. They were just human shapes on horses wearing hats and cowboy gear. It was amazing and exhilarating.

But then the dry sky turned black and there was a long, crack of lightning, but there was no sound. The cattle began to run. A cowboy and a horse went down into the herd of frightened, racing cows. His own horse was now engulfed by the thundering herd. His horse stumbled. He felt as if he and the horse might go down.

Mason whipped off the hat. The sensations he had felt and the image of himself on a horse in the mirror went away. All of it, the heat and sky and stink of cattle and the other cowboys were gone. There was just him in the store holding the hat.

Placing the Stetson back on the peg, he decided to try on another. This time it was a pirate hat.

In the mirror he could see himself standing on the deck of a ship with a great black beard and a cutlass strapped to his side. He could smell the ocean, as well as a lot of unhygienic pirates moving about on the ship. He thought, wow, I am a pirate captain.

And then there was a soundless flash of light, and the ship moved and he felt the deck beneath his feet vibrate. Now he could see another pirate ship alongside the one he was on, and he realized they had been hit by cannon fire. Pirates were leaping off of the other ship and onto the one he was on. Swinging on ropes they had grappled into the sails of his ship. Swords clashed as the two pirate bands collided. A big pirate with a patch over one eye was racing toward him with cutlass raised.

Mason quickly swept the hat off his head.

He was no longer on the ship. He was no longer a pirate. He took a deep breath.

"This is amazing," he told the man in the bowler hat. "That was so real it frightened me. The stampede frightened me, but that pirate, he was so real and so close. How the hell do you do it?"

The man in the bowler hat smiled. It wasn't a happy smile, more one of resignation. "Mirrors."

Mason laughed. "Of course." What he was really thinking is there must be some kind of projection behind the glass, but how did it put him on a horse, how did it cause him to experience it all, feel the heat and smell the cows?

After replacing the pirate hat, Mason moved toward the door.

"Perhaps one more," the man in the bowler said.

"I don't know. It's a pretty powerful experience. I liked it at first, but I don't know I like it now."

"Perhaps you need something dapper to brighten your spirits. Something stylish but less exciting."

"Can you suggest something?"

"Except for a bowler, I can't. It's against company policy to suggest anything else."

"That doesn't seem like a good business model," Mason said.

"Perhaps not."

"What the hell? You keep bringing up the bowler, and I've started to like the idea. I'd like to try one on."

"Very well, if that's your choice. It is your choice, correct?"

"Correct."

"I only have this one bowler. Would you come and take it off my head, please?"

Mason thought it an odd request, but he came closer to the counter and the little man in the bowler.

"Just reach out and take it?" Mason asked.

"That's right."

"I don't like it, then I'll give it back to you."

"That's a thought, of course," said the little man.

Mason thought the man in the bowler must be liquored up, way he talked. Mason leaned over the counter, and with a smile, removed the bowler from the man's head and put it on his own. It felt tight.

He turned and looked into the mirror. He was now standing behind the store's counter wearing the bowler with a cigar in his mouth. All the other hats were gone. All that was left was the mirrors, and the little man, who he could now see was as bald as an egg. The little man was standing in the empty store smiling at him. There were tears in his eyes.

"Hey, what kind of deal is this?" Mason said.

"It's a deal alright. A done deal, and there's no peg to put the hat on. It needs a head."

"What?" Mason said.

"Wear it in good health. It gets heavy after a while, and so few customers come in and want to try it on."

The little man was walking briskly toward the door. He opened it.

Before he went through the doorway, he looked back at Mason, standing behind the counter, unable to move out from behind it. Mason was trying to take off the bowler hat, but it wouldn't budge.

"Sorry," said the little man, and he went on out and let the door close behind him. The store filled with hats again. All manner of hats, but the only bowler hat in the room belonged to Mason now.

The little man crossed the street and looked back at where the hat store had been and breathed a sigh of relief. There was only a brick wall now. The little man rubbed his hand over his bald head and liked the feel of it.

MONKEY'S
UNCLE

ONE SATURDAY MORNING while sitting at his desk, checking his email, Jim had a surprise notice arrive on his screen.

He almost didn't open the message. He didn't recognize the header. PRIMATES RULE.

The title intrigued him, so his curiosity got the better of him, and he tapped on it.

❧

HEY, MARVIN MONKEY here. This is going to be a surprise to you, and I hope a welcome one, but I'm an actual monkey, and through extensive research I've discovered that you and I are cousins.

No joke, Mr. Jim C. Jerrod.

I may be a monkey and you may be a man, but in the far past we could mate. Well, not you and I, but our kind. The results were not an obvious mixture, but some of us who are monkeys, and some of those—like you—who are humans, have the same DNA. Well, mostly.

You are my great, great, great, great, great, great... Not sure I have enough room to list all the greats, but you get the idea. You are a monkey's uncle. A great, great, great, and so on monkey's uncle. That's a joke, by the way. Bottom line. We're kin.

I was part of an experiment that grew out of how to find your Neanderthal genetics and relations that have carried over into modern times, and the next thing you know they were investigating monkeys and found many of us and certain modern humans are kin.

No joke.

I am even a more special monkey in that I have a job, can type and speak English, and currently I'm working on German. I think I'm getting there. But that is neither important nor interesting.

Here's what is interesting. I have our DNA connection, and I will send it to you, and you can verify it with the company, and then I think, being kin and all, even if it is distant, we should meet.

I work for the circus. Saw that coming, didn't you?

Truth is the circus is a dying business, and ours is very small, and mostly for younger children. We monkeys ride around in little cars and beep horns and climb things and wear funny clothes and do tricks. I should mention that it's an all-monkey circus with an alcoholic human handler named Tim.

Rumor is he's going to sell us all for further research of some sort, and as I am, to put it modestly, unique, I might garner quite a price. I can reveal a lot of interesting things about the simian mind if given the chance, so I could be a star in the program.

Then again, they might decide to test makeup on me and put my eye out, so actually, I'm thinking it's time I went into office work. I'm good with numbers, so maybe I could assist in an accounting office until I can get my degree.

Anyway, I am moving on.

Of course, none of this has anything to do with my writing you. All of the rest is a bit of an overshare, I'm sure.

So, let's set up a meeting. As I have discovered, I have abilities that are normally only attributed to humans, and these abilities only show up in a minuscule number of the monkey population. It is my belief, and that of the researchers, that direct relations also share abilities. Meaning that as a human, you are very likely to be able to do certain things only monkeys can do.

Want to know more?

I hope so, cousin. If so, let me know and we can set up a meeting and discuss things and see what abilities I possess that you also possess. They are most likely abilities that must be awakened, and I'm here to help you do that.

Are you in?

If not, very well. I can understand the concern with unknown relatives showing up, as it were, but it would be criminal for us not to meet and have our discussion.

Up to you, of course.

Contact me.

Please, cuz.

***

JIM STUDIED THE email for a long time. He read and reread.

A monkey that he was kin to?

That was doubtful.

Another email popped up.

It was Marvin again. And this time he sent a photograph attachment. Once again Jim hesitated, but finally he opened it.

It was a photo of a monkey in a small blue car, his head and upper torso sticking out of the window, one hand waving. There was a red circle drawn around the monkey and a line that led up from the circle to the top of the page where it was written THIS IS ME. In the background, near the car, standing on a bucket, another monkey was taking a dump into his hand and staring at Marvin.

Jim tried to see some of himself in Marvin, but he could not. However, his aunt Harriet often had a mustache the same color as Marvin's fur. Maybe there was something in that. And his uncle Truman was known for climbing trees.

Oh, wow, that was reaching.

Still, intriguing.

Impulsively, Jim typed back to Marvin.

Give me some time to think about it.

A return message popped up immediately.

Of course, wrote the monkey.

꩜

JIM MULLED IT over for a few days, researched the site that was making great strides in the comparison and connection of monkey and human DNA, and the truth was, the research was real.

There were a fairly large number of monkeys that had of recent shown themselves to have a lot of unique human traits. Had learned to speak, write, and think on a deeper plane than where's the next meal?

Jim was fascinated and felt a little special. He was, in fact, a monkey's uncle. A multiple great uncle, but a monkey's uncle none the less. Or, a cousin. He was uncertain, since Marvin had referred to him both ways. Didn't matter. It seemed they were indeed kin.

After a few more days had passed, Jim wrote Marvin.

Yes. I am interested in visiting with you.

The response was immediate.

Wonderful. Do you know Pecan Park?

Jim wrote back that he did indeed. It was a large patch of preserved woods with hiking trails and picnic tables. And, of course, pecan trees.

The meeting was set.

WHEN JIM ARRIVED at the park on the prescribed morning, the air was sharp and clean. As he climbed out of his car, he could taste the soft breeze, and it tasted of pine sap and oak leaves. The sky was a stark blue and the sun was burning bright. It was a school day, so no children were around, and in fact, no one was around. All there was beside himself and his car, was a little blue car with a wind-up dial at the back of it. When Jim got out of his car, the door opened on the little car and the monkey got out.

Jim was at first startled. The monkey was wearing an orange hat, blue tee-shirt, orange shorts, and was shoeless. Perhaps due to nervousness, the monkey's toes were flexing and digging into the dirt.

"Jim?" said the monkey, and his voice was strong and clear, with only the faintest hint of some kind of accent.

"Yes," Jim said, as he walked toward Marvin, his hand outstretched.

The monkey looked up at him, took Jim's hand and shook it vigorously, as if pumping water out of a deep cistern.

"My God," Marvin said. "I think you look a lot like my mother. Around the eyes."

Jim wasn't sure how to take that, so he smiled, knowing full well it was the sort of smile babies made when they released gas. All of a sudden, he felt uncertain about coming.

"I brought some picnic supplies, nothing major," Marvin said. "Thought we might pick a table, eat and visit a little."

"Certainly," Jim said, but he felt far from certain.

Marvin scampered back to the car, his tail lifted in the air like a flag, and pulled out a picnic basket and they proceeded down the park trail and found a table. They sat across from one another. Marvin was studying Jim's face like it was a road map he needed to memorize.

"Man, I see it," Marvin said. "My mother's people. The look is stronger in you than in me."

Jim was still uncertain how to take this comment, because all he could see in Marvin's face was monkey. He did remember his aunt Harriet's mustache again, but the memory didn't exactly appease him, so once again he gave Marvin his gaseous baby smile.

"Thanks for coming," Marvin said. "I know how odd this must feel. Actually, it feels odd to me. I was always different from the other monkeys, but once I fell into the circus and then into the experiments, well, I knew then that something was considerably different about me, and then I came across our connection on MonkeyBlood.com, and I knew I had to at least try and contact you."

"I was certainly surprised. I had no idea this sort of thing existed or that there were monkeys that had human characteristics...DNA."

"Let me show you something so non-monkey it will blow your mind."

Marvin stood up on the park bench and pulled his pants down and revealed a large, dangling penis. He took hold of it and lifted it with one hand.

"Monkeys don't have this. Not normally. I'm hung, Jim. Like a human. Oh, sorry. I should have warned you this was coming out into the world."

Marvin pulled his pants up and resumed his seat. "Here," he said, "let's eat."

Jim made sure to reach for his own meal out of the basket, as he had seen Marvin with his penis in his hands, and the idea of those hands on his food was bothersome. Then he saw that the basket was full of bananas. He took one.

"I know, it's classic. But monkeys do like bananas. But I eat meat. Well, veggie burgers actually, but you know, step by step. Now and again a bit of dead animal passes my lips."

Jim nodded, peeled the banana and ate it slowly.

"And you're saying I have monkey characteristics?" Jim said.

"When you were young, did you like to climb trees?"

"I did, but so did a lot of kids. I had an uncle who was known for his climbing abilities, though."

"You look spry, Jim. Long-limbed. I think if you were to try, you might find that you have a tremendous amount of, shall we say, 'lower primate abilities.' Want to find out?"

"I suppose, but—"

"No buts, Jim. Listen here. I was surprised when the lab folks took me from the circus for a while, and then tested me for this and that, concluded I had a lot of human DNA, and encouraged me to make alphabet sounds. I did. And in time, I could speak. I actually have quite a facility for language. I can drive a car well, though I often stay on the edge of the road due to the size of my automobile, but I'm thinking of buying a larger car and having an apparatus rigged up so I can adjust the gas pedal and brakes as I go."

"I see."

"Jim, I not only brought you here because this time of the day the park is often private, but because of the trees. Would you like to check out that monkey DNA that you have?"

"How do you mean?"

"Listen here, Jim. I'll say it again. I have the test results, the DNA connection. We are cousins. I have human traits, and therefore, you will have monkey traits."

"Does it actually work that way?"

"Shall we find out?"

THEY FOUND A wide trail and there were oaks and elms and pines and sweetgums and all manner of trees crowding the path. Marvin grabbed an oak limb and swung himself into the tree.

Marvin looked down. "You should start easy. Just see how you climb. Don't think about it."

Jim was hesitant, but he grabbed the limb, remembered how good he had been with the monkey bars at the playground, how much he had loved gymnastics, and swung himself.

It was easy.

He swung from the lower limb, reached out and grabbed a slightly higher limb, and then he swung his feet high and landed them on another limb, found he could slip his body to a seated position without any real effort. Was that his old gymnastic training or was it his monkey genes? Or were they the same?

Damn. It felt great.

Marvin was climbing now, moving up the oak swiftly.

With a smile, Jim followed. When they reached the top of the oak, Jim was elated, if slightly winded.

"Now," Marvin said. "We take the next step. See across the way there, that tree?"

"Yes."

"I'm going to leap from here to there and you're going to follow. It's a short distance, and I've been watching you, Jim. You have the blood, buddy. You can do it. We'll make the jump, climb down and call it a day. You don't want to do too much, but with your monkey connection it's a short jump."

Marvin jumped, grabbed the limb and swung into a fork in the tree, then moved to an outstretched limb and sat down.

"Don't think," Marvin said across trees. "Just do."

Jim jumped. He caught the limb. He swung into the fork and sat there.

"That felt wonderful."

"I know. You know what? You're ready for the twist. It's a kind of thing we do. We monkey folk leap under the limb we want, twist slightly and grab up and take hold of the limb, swing in a big half circle, let go of the limb as momentum propels us upwards, and then the trick is to come down from above and grab it again. It looks harder than it is."

"Hell, I can do it."

"I'll lead the way, then let's go to your place and have a drink."

"Lead on, cousin," Jim said.

Marvin leaped so that his head was lower than the limb he wanted, snapped out a hand, grabbed the limb above, swung way up, let go, twisted face-down in the air, grabbed the limb with both hands, swung under and over and landed on the limb on his feet.

"Nothing to it," Jim said, and leaped.

It was a beautiful leap. Marvin thought the expression on Jim's face was priceless. Proud. Certain. Comforted in his formerly unknown monkey connection.

Jim sailed under the limb, shot out a hand, grabbed the limb and started to swing. There was a sharp cracking sound, like an elephant sitting on a walnut, and then Jim's expression changed and his arm lengthened as it came out of the socket. He tried to twist and grab a lower limb with his good hand, but he missed and caught his chin on the limb and there was a sound now as if the elephant had sat on a large duck egg, and then Jim swung on his chin and his head pointed down in the position of a one-point landing and he hit the ground like a bullet. This time the elephant seemed to have sat on a box of duck eggs, the sound was so nasty and loud.

Marvin climbed down.

Jim's neck was shortened. His head was pretty much on his chest and there was a look of either surprise or disappointment in his dead eyes.

Marvin picked up a stick and poked Jim with it a few times, but he didn't come around.

Marvin looked about.

He dropped the stick and put his hands in his pants pockets and began to mosey toward his car. He hated to leave Jim, but hell, someone might think he killed him.

He made it to his car, casually got it going, turning on the radio as he drove away.

AT HOME MARVIN had a beer and got on the computer. He didn't understand it. Jim should have had the ability to make those jumps. He seemed fine at first, but now Marvin realized he had merely been in good shape. But where was the monkey blood?

Marvin went to MonkeyBlood.com, using his code to tap into it.

Yep. There it was. Jim… Wait.

Not Jim C. He had misremembered. It was Jim Z. Jerrod that was his cousin.

Well, hell. Got that wrong.

That's some stuff, right there, Marvin thought. I thought I remembered it right.

He had found the name, misremembered the Z as a C, and then gone to an investigative location site to find Jim C. Jerrod's address instead of Jim Z. Jerrod.

How silly of me, he thought.

He shot over to the address location site, found Jim Z. Jerrod easily.

He found the email address contained there, went to his email and typed in:

Hey, Marvin Monkey here. This is going to be a surprise to you, and I hope a welcome one, but I'm an actual monkey, and through extensive research I've discovered that you and I are cousins.

No joke, Mr. Jim Z. Jerrod.

I think we should meet.

JULIET
UNCHAINED

IT WAS A hot morning and Juliet opened the door to her camper trailer and looked out at the wilderness and thought it was good. The day seemed like a nice choice for the end of her days.

She picked up Derek's old walking stick, and stepped out of the trailer and started along the hiking trail.

Before long, she bound her long, brown hair into a pony tail for comfort, and continued. She went past large trees and crumbling boulders and draws that ran down the side of the mountain.

She paid little attention to direction, just walked. As she did, she thought of Shakespeare's Juliet and how she had ended things.

Juliet had killed herself because of Romeo. She understood her pain, and now this Juliet, she told herself, will do the same. She would let the pain out of her life the way you would let the pus out of a wound.

The trail split. One branch continued straight, the other climbed up into the rocks, and that was the branch she chose.

Up she climbed, having to use her walking stick to help her. The trail narrowed and the trees came in tight on either side.

Juliet looked up the trail and could see a spot of light between the shadows of the trees. It was way up and would require some time to reach.

What she hadn't thought of when deciding this would be her last day on earth, was how hungry she would be by skipping breakfast. She had assumed she would find a high point for jumping much sooner.

She paused and thought of her Romeo, Derek, and how he had jabbed a knife into his breast and had left a note saying he had died for her. That he loved her and cherished her, but that he couldn't get his head right, and with her name on his lips, he would leap into the wild dark nothing.

When Derek plunged the knife into his heart he might as well have plunged it into hers. Derek had always been covered in shadow and regret that couldn't be defined. They had an argument only hours before his final moments, something silly, something so silly she couldn't remember the gist of it.

His note read that he loved her so much he had taken his life, and now she was sure she could not live without him, that the torment she felt would crawl down deep into her blood and bones and would live there like a parasite.

Juliet did not intend to feed that parasite. She would shorten its days of feeding.

Her stomach growled with hunger, and she climbed.

The trail became so narrow and steep, she began to crawl on her hands and knees, still clutching the cane. The boulders on the trail tore her pants and scraped her knees. Sweat poured off of her, even though she was out of the direct heat and was in the shadow of the trees.

Finally, she came to the top of the trail. She managed to stand, taking deep breaths. She felt so exhausted she put her hands on her knees and bent over to recharge herself. Blood pounded in her head and made her temples throb as if something inside of her was trying to dig its way out.

When she could breathe again and the blood was no longer pounding, she saw that she was near the edge of a high cliff, and beyond the cliff the sun burned like a flaming coal. The sky was an impossible blue, and as she walked to the edge of the cliff, she looked out and saw the trees below, and on the sides of the mountain. They were green as Ireland.

She leaned over and looked straight down.

It was a long drop. The rocks stuck out from the sides of the mountain, waiting on her.

The air cooled suddenly, and a fresh wind blew across her. With the wind on her face, something changed. She knew then, in that moment, that she didn't owe Derek her life. Didn't owe anyone. The cool air, the blue sky and the burning sun, all the shadowed green before her, revived her. If the air could change and the sun could rise and sink and rise again, so could she.

It was as if a portal of truth had opened unto her.

I am not an extension of Derek and his death. I am not a follower into the gloom.

Sadness swept over her, but found a compartment inside of her. She knew she must live, because life was beautiful, full of raw spots, but beautiful.

Juliet took a deep breath, turned, and started back to the camper. She was hungry. She was unchained.

THE BRIGHT CITY
HIGH ON THE HILL

MY FERRARI'S MOTOR purred like a happy cat as I drove swiftly and surely up the twisting road beneath the hot Italian sun, on into the town of Monte Sant'Angelo, its stark, white buildings stacked in rising rows like children's blocks.

My parents had visited Monte Sant'Angelo as well, when they were young and honeymooning; a couple that married young and stayed together over sixty-five years. My marriage, on the other hand, had made five years before sputtering out like a cheap lawn-mower motor.

Somehow, the idea of walking the same streets, going to the same places my parents might have gone, appealed to me, as if I might absorb some of their mojo, lingering and waiting for me, floating invisible on the Italian air.

For the moment, however, I was short on romantic satisfaction. What I had was the fine red Ferrari, the top down, an empty seat beside me, and the end of a beautiful day.

I found a spot to park near my hotel, put up the roof, got out and walked about, viewing the city. It was a place of an older and slower time, and it calmed me momentarily, but the emotional pain came back a short time later, for I still carried the wound of my lost marriage like a weeping cyst.

I wandered around the city for a long time, went to where I could look out at the sea. It was wine-dark and so was the sky. As the day died, it was hard to tell where sea and sky separated. For a moment, it was like being in the center of a watery globe. And then there were the lights of the city growing bright as the world grew dark; the voices of people, lovers wandering past me, young and hopeful, fingers entwined, and then the spell was broken.

I strolled without purpose and came to the famous grotto where Saint Michael was said to have appeared. It was now a church. I went inside. There were two rows of pews parted by an aisle, and up front was an altar. The only lights in the grotto were candle lights. An old woman in a black shawl was up front lighting a fresh candle with a long match. She placed it by other candles, knelt with discomfort, and prayed silently, head bent.

I sat there and felt sorry for myself for a while, and then I saw the young woman with the jet-black hair and the simple white dress; a goddess can wear simple things and look better than others in expensive attire. She sat across the way in one of the pews, slightly turned, so that one of her crossed legs extended into the aisle, showing a sensible black shoe.

I was not religious, so I sat there not for a blessing, but for the exquisiteness of the place, the warm candlelight, and the woman's beauty. The way the candle light flickered on her face, warm and golden, it made her eyes look wet and luminous even from a distance. I felt as if hypnotized by her. When she rose and went out, I went out too, into the glow of lights from the houses along the streets, rising into the hills, and in some places dipping precariously toward the sea.

I tried not to seem like a stalker, but I kept her in view, and when she went into a white building with a blue roof, a restaurant, I went in too.

It smelled of good food. She was at a table to my left, sitting alone, already with a menu in hand. I glanced at her. She lifted her head and looked at me. It sounds absurd, but in that moment, I felt a thrilling sensation from head to toe-tips.

While I waited for the waiter to come and show me to a table, she said, "Would you like to sit with me? I'm an American, out on my own."

"So am I," I said, and gratefully, I accepted her invitation.

When I was seated, she said, "This is too beautiful a place to be alone."

"Agreed," I said.

"I hope I don't seem too strange, asking someone I don't know to sit with me at dinner?"

"Not at all."

"My parents honeymooned here," she said.

I laughed. "As did mine."

"What a delightful coincidence."

"Mine were married all their lives," I said. "I managed five years."

"I managed two," she said.

I had never felt more comfortable with someone. I liked to believe my mother and father had sat at this very table so many years ago, perhaps hers as well; it was a beautiful fantasy.

We talked and ate, and talked some more, finally remembered to exchange names, and then we went out and along the rough streets, and after much talking, I walked her to her hotel, which was in fact mine as well. We laughed about that. We laughed in my room all through the night, and we held each other until the morning light.

We had breakfast downstairs, and she said, "I have to go back to the States day after tomorrow, flying out of Rome."

"The same," I said.

"We are full of coincidences."

"I've never believed in fate," I said. "But perhaps I need to rethink my position."

"I came by bus. A long ride, and not very comfortable."

"I came by car. I'm having it shipped home."

"Isn't that expensive?"

"For a California style Ferrari, it's worth it. Might I give you a ride to Rome?"

Soon her luggage and mine were in the Ferrari, and with the top down, I was cruising us away from the fine white city, high on the hill, going down and around a deep curve, the painterly light shiny on the Adriatic Sea beyond, the car's engine humming, the seat beside me no longer empty, her hand on my elbow, resting comfortably.

ROOM FOR
ONE MORE

CARS HAD WHIZZED by him all day, but none had stopped, all had ignored the hitchhike gesture of his thumb.

On the edge of the town, Jackson paused at the city-limit sign, leaned against it. He was feeling the long walk. He shifted his pack a little. Catching a ride these days was harder and harder. No one wanted to stop for a stranger. Especially now that it was night and the moon was thin.

Not stopping for strangers was good thinking on their part. If they stopped, he was going to rob them. He didn't have any real wish to kill them. He wasn't a serial killer. He had the numbers to identify as one, but all of his murders were for a financial reason, not to satisfy some kind of need beyond commerce, some kind of sexual deviancy, though he was not averse to taking advantage of certain situations.

His job was simple. Stealing enough to live through the day, until he got the big score. He was uncertain what the big score was, but felt he would know it when he saw it, and to get to the big score, sometimes, on the subject of murder, you had to be flexible.

Jackson had the kind of face that was hard to remember. Still, spend too much time with someone, the women especially, and they'd probably remember too much. The little, dark mole above his right eye, the cut on the left side of his lip that had left a white scar. His mother had a good throwing arm.

You had to judge murder on a case by case basis, though lately, his judgement had mostly led to homicide. In the end, it was more certain. Take no chances. Leave no witnesses. Keep going until he figured out the big score, and then once he had it, he'd stop robbing and killing. It wasn't that he felt any moral conundrum about it, but after a while, you had to figure the odds. You could only throw good dice for so long, and eventually it would have to be Snake Eyes. So quitting was on the agenda. He thought he might even get married, settle down. Provided he had that big score. Something to live on for the rest of his life. Diamonds maybe. Gold bullion. Jackson had a lot of dreams.

He looked out at the lights of the town. The town that said on its sign that its population was twelve hundred and six. At least one of that number, maybe more, were going to wake up tomorrow minus some goods, provided he could do it without confrontation, steal something and get out. If he was confronted, well, then they might not wake up in the morning, and someone would need to subtract some numbers from that sign.

Jackson shifted the pack again, and started walking toward the lights.

◈

BY THE TIME Jackson reached town, many of the lights that belonged to houses were out. Most of the town's occupants had tucked in for the night. There were some town lights, spotted here and there. The place wasn't exactly the Great White Way.

He watched for cop cars, didn't see any. When he reached the heart of town, he stuck to the shadows, alleys behind buildings. Some cop saw him, he might be spending the night in jail for vagrancy, or some such. Thing to do was hole up a while, wait until it was late, then pick a house that looked rich enough to have money, jewels, something he could steal and carry out effortlessly. Later, when he made it to a city, he could locate a fence for what he had stolen.

Jackson found a place behind a dumpster, next to a curb. He removed his pack, sat on the curb in the shadow of the dumpster, took a granola bar out of his pack, and slowly munched on it.

There were lights beyond the alley, and they were soft and golden, belonged to Main Street, or whatever it was called: the street that ran through the center of town. After he finished his granola bar, he eased out from behind the dumpster, sat where there was a better view of the street. He could only see a portion of it, the part that ran by a theater. It was letting out, and he watched people ease outside, laughing, talking.

He couldn't remember the last time he had been to the movies. The happiness he saw amongst the crowd irritated him. Ten minutes later he was still sitting in the shadows. The theater had completely emptied out. The marquee lights were on, but the lights that had glowed through the glass doors, revealing the concession stand and a carboard cutout for a forthcoming movie, were dimmed.

After a few minutes, a young woman came walking down the street. Jackson liked the way she looked, way she walked, way her dress swung around her legs, way her heels clicked on concrete.

A long black car with a man driving, a woman in the passenger seat, slowed next to her and stopped. The passenger window went down, and Jackson heard the woman in the car offer the young woman a ride, but she declined.

The woman walked faster, and then she was out of sight behind a building. After a few seconds, the car turned and went along the street next to the dumpster.

Jackson stepped back behind the dumpster and watched it pass, rolling slowly up the street and out of sight.

He needed to wait a while longer. To be certain the town had settled.

Nesting behind the dumpster again, he leaned against a tree that grew up next to the curb and bordered a business building of some sort, closed his eyes, and fell asleep. The long day and the long walk had depleted him.

When he awoke, he felt refreshed and eager. He checked his watch in the glow of his penlight.

Two a.m.

He put the penlight away. It was time to locate a house and make his move.

❧

JACKSON FOLLOWED THE route of the long black car that had passed him, and then took a turn on a residential street with magnificent houses on either side. The rich section. There were lights in a few of the houses still, and there were street lights, but overall it was shadowy, and now that there were fewer lights, he could see the partial moon again, a cold scimitar in the sky.

A dog barked. Jackson paused, determined it was a street over, and started walking again. He stopped when he saw the black car he had seen earlier. It was parked in a driveway leading to a closed garage. Must be nice to have so many cars you could leave one in the driveway, another, perhaps two, in the garage. Jackson's guess was the ones in the garage, they would be really nice. The one in the driveway was nice enough, but it was probably the couple's around-town car. He thought he got through with his theft, he might hot-wire the car, ride off in that until he got to the next town, better yet a full-blown city to find a fence. He'd be there before the owners woke up. If they did. It depended on how things went. He felt for the knife in his pocket. It was there. It was the sort that he could pull quick, pop open. It was as sharp a comedian's wit.

The car, the house and garage were fancy-looking. There were trees in the yard, and a big oak grew up beside the house, and next to that a fence bordered the neighbors. On the other side of the house there wasn't a tree, but there was more fencing, and from where he stood, he could see along the edge of the house and spot more fence at the back.

The house was three stories, and the top story had a balcony. The ground floor had a long porch and an indented entrance, and then a doorway with colored glass in panels about head height. There was a porch light on, but it was a light so thin, you got the feeling it didn't really mean it.

Jackson tried to catch sight of any kind of camera, or security light that might pop on when he stepped into the yard. That popped on, he would feel like a nightclub act about to start up. Most likely, no one would notice him. Not this time of night, but the idea of it didn't appeal to him.

Jackson didn't see any cameras, but he walked along the sidewalk and went into the yard through the trees that grew there, paused, decided the oak might be the best way to go. Might be an alarm at the door, but if he climbed the oak, went through the window, he could be inside quiet as a mute mouse in tennis shoes. If it turned out to be a bedroom, he might change his plans. Or, he might change their dreams, wreck their plans for tomorrow.

Still, there might be an easier way. A way he could go inside and then sneak about without ever waking them. With just a knife, someone inside might give him some trouble. They might have a gun.

Best plan was in and out with goods in his pack. He'd decide on the car after that.

Easing across the yard, no burglar lights came on. When he came to the oak, he considered, then went around it, slipped behind the house, and worked his way to the other side where the garage was. There was a window there, and he leaned forward and looked in. The garage was the size of some houses he had lived in. He could see the shape of two cars, and though he couldn't tell what make and model, their sizes were impressive.

Jackson slipped off his pack, pulled a crowbar out of it, and gently slipped it under the window, cranked up. There was a popping sound, and then the window slid up effortlessly. Replacing the crowbar, he dropped his pack inside and climbed after it. He crouched for a moment, then took out his penlight, snapped it on, flashed it around.

The cars were indeed nice. A Beamer and a sleek new red Cadillac about the size of a yacht.

Jackson felt he had hit the jackpot, and his excitement raced through him. He took a deep breath, slipped on his pack, and guided by the penlight, crossed to the door across the way. He touched the knob, tried it.

The door was not locked. Jackson turned out the penlight, and entered the house.

🙢

CREEPING ALONG A hallway, he clicked on the penlight again. He entered a large room. There was a TV about the size of theater screen, lots of chairs, and there was even a platform in front of it where someone might make a speech or sing a song. The room could easily hold twenty, maybe thirty guests.

As Jackson turned, the penlight beam fell on a shape. A young woman, beautiful, well dressed, with shiny hair and a face white as a ghost in the penlight beam.

"Oh, hi," she said.

Jackson dropped the light, grabbed her, threw her down on the floor.

"Like it rough, huh?" she said, and giggled.

"What are you? Crazy?"

"Depends on who you ask."

"Don't scream, bitch, or I'll kill you. This may be your house, but I'm the master now."

"Oh, baby. This isn't our house."

Jackson sensed too late that someone was behind him. Then he felt a sharp pain in the back of his head, and the dark of the room became darker.

🙢

WHEN JACKSON AWOKE, he was tied, hands and feet, his pack had been removed, and he was sitting in a chair in the front row of the home theater. The lights were on, but the light was soft, the color of fresh butter, and with the dark curtains drawn, the room had a cozy feel about it.

For a moment.

The girl and a man had pulled up chairs and were sitting in front of him, watching him. The man was as handsome as the woman was pretty. She was dressed as if for a night on the town. Little black dress, a string of pearls, high heels. The man wore a nice suit with a bright, blue tie with red checks in it. His shoes were shiny enough you could use them to signal a ship offshore.

"Hey, there, sleepyhead," said the young woman.

"Thought I might have hit you too hard," said the man. "Karate chop. Nah, not really. I don't know karate, but I did hit you with the side of my hand, hard as I could. I've had some practice with that, if not professional training. Know what I mean?"

Jackson didn't.

"I'm Doll," said the woman, "and this is Guy. That's not really our names, but we like it, don't we, Guy?"

"We do."

"Look," Jackson said. "I shouldn't have come in. I was looking for a place to sleep. Thought no one was home."

"Oh, I don't believe that," Guy said. "Do you, Doll?

Doll shook her head, clicked her tongue. "That's a windy, dear. You are telling us a windy."

"Just let me go, and I'm out of here. Out of your house, out of your lives."

"Didn't I say?" she said. "This isn't our house."

"Yeah," Guy said, "but it's nice, right? I mean, if this isn't nice, what is? Way we like to work, is we come into a town, small one, look for some place with privacy, and if it's nice, like this, well, all the better. And we want someone to be home."

"You tried to get that girl in your car," Jackson said. "I saw that."

"You did? I'll be damned. Hear that, Doll? He saw us."

"She was so delectable," Doll said. "But she was smart, didn't get in. And it doesn't matter you saw us or not."

"Here's the thing, and I think you have the right to know," Guy said. "And this should be clear by now, as Doll has told you twice. But I'm one for clarification."

"Oh, God, is he. He doesn't care you know, darling. He just likes to hear himself talk."

Guy reached out and patted Doll's knee. "Now, now. Don't be mean."

"Sorry. Just thought she'd have better clothes. It put me on edge. That closet, for all their money, looks like something from the children's department, and her with cash to spare. And that jewelry. Costume mostly. There was money in the safe, though. Oh, go on, darling, tell him what you want to tell him. I'm just being nasty."

"No. You're right, Doll. I'm just hearing myself talk. I've said all I need to say, really."

"You can steal it all," Jackson said. "I'm not competition."

"Don't interrupt," Doll said. "Daddy is talking."

She smiled, reached out and touched a finger to Jackson's lips. "Sshhhhh."

Guy leaned in close. "We're not here just for items to steal. Items to bleed are very important to us."

Jackson let Guy's words bang around inside his head for a moment.

"We like to find a nice house and some nice people, and turn it and them to not so nice."

"We're in the papers," Doll said. "You've heard of us, I bet. The Midnight Ramblers. Sometimes the Break-in Killers. I like the Midnight Ramblers. The other sounds so basic and crude."

"All we had to do was park right out front. It's late. No one will notice. We picked the lock, found the owners upstairs. Nice-looking young couple. Soon we'll be gone from here. But you won't. And what a mystery that will create when you join them."

Guy stood up and moved his chair.

Jackson had a straight view of the stage in front of the TV, the one that had been empty when he broke in, the one that had been filled while he was unconscious. The one with two nude and well dissected bodies on it. It was wet and red up there.

"You'll be staying here with them," said Guy. "I mean, there's room up there for one more."

"No. I'm one of you," Jackson said.

"Isn't that sweet?" Doll said.

"Just a big sack of sugar, baby," Guy said, and Jackson noted that there was a tiny bit of drool running from the corner of his mouth, like a man about to eat a slice of hot apple pie.

"I am going to keep your penlight," Doll said. "Is that okay? Of course it is."

Jackson said nothing. He could hardly breathe.

"Ain't life just full of surprises?" Guy said, bent down and unzipped a leather bag at Jackson's feet. It was filled with shiny sharp objects.

Guy removed a meat cleaver from the pile, held it up. The light winked off of it. Doll pulled a long knitting needle from the bag.

"I like to start with the toes and slowly work my way up to the head," Guy said. "Sometimes, our objects of desire don't last that long. But we're learning better and better how to make them last so as to make it last. You know, do it right."

"I like to poke," Doll said, making a jabbing motion with the knitting needle.

"By the way," Guy said, leaning in close to Jackson's sweat-popped face. "Just so you don't have false hopes. This is really going to hurt."

SHRINKAGE

ONE MORNING, WHILE shaving and listening to the news on TV, Jim put his razor down and walked into the living room, wiping the shaving cream off of his face.

He wanted to be able to look at the screen, not just hear the news, because he was certain he had misunderstood something.

He watched as aerial photographs showed the earth as seen from space, listened to the announcer who said, "The earth is actually shrinking. Scientists are alarmed."

There was much more, but that was enough for Jim to decide to change channels. Surely it was a joke.

No. The other news channels were talking about the same thing.

The earth was indeed, shrinking. And it was happening rapidly.

Jim sat on the couch. He didn't even bother to phone into work. There were riots going on all over the world, a smaller world. Asia had shrunk. Africa had shrunk, and the ocean was now a much narrower mass of water than before.

The continents and islands were pushing closer and closer together. The satellite cameras were revealing that in real time.

"Dang it," Jim said. He had finally had a date with that hot lady that worked at the coffee shop, and now he was certain that was off. No one could think about anything but how small the earth was becoming.

He sat and watched, and the ball of the earth as viewed from space grew smaller and smaller. Chinese and Africans and Europeans were now all on the same piece of land, and fights were breaking out. Wars.

All of it was short lived, because the continents kept shrinking, and pretty soon the ocean was a salty river dividing the North American continent from Europe and Africa. In fact, down at the bottom of the world, Africa and South America were touching. Pacific islands were in view off the California coast. LA and San Francisco were five miles apart, and closing.

By that afternoon, New York City and Austin, Texas were within ten miles of each other, and Chicago had wrinkled up and been overwhelmed by a part of the land mass that had wadded up. No explanation. Honolulu was just outside of Lufkin, Texas, though it was now very small. There was no beach.

The scientists who remained alive had no explanation.

Preachers claimed it was God's vengeance, because He was always mad about something, but no matter what the cause, the world was growing small.

It defied common sense. It defied science. It defied religion.

Antarctica was just down the block with a few surviving penguins wandering about.

And then Jim saw people moving toward his house. There was no longer a TV station to watch, and there was no one to report by radio, but he could see people of all nationalities moving in on his property. There were yells and gunfire.

He thought he might get his gun, but that seemed pointless.

Pretty soon he realized his house and his yard might be all that was left of the earth. People and animals were floating around the edges of the earth and others were leaping up to join them. Space was close.

Then they were pushing at his door, banging on the sides of the house. A bunch of folks who appeared red-faced and red-headed, had their hands cupped and were pressing them against one of his windows where the curtains were pushed back.

He got up and closed the curtains. But now the front and back doors were cracking. They were being broken down.

Jim ran to his bedroom, which was in the middle of the house. He looked around. There was nothing he could think of to do. There was in fact, nothing to do.

He finally decided to crawl under the bed.

Soon he heard people at his bedroom door, pressing, and then the door was knocked flat off its hinges and people rushed in.

Lots of people. Far too many to fit in the room. They began to lodge together like a puzzle being shaped. He could see their legs and feet from under the bed. Tennis shoes and dress shoes and bare feet, men and women, pants legs and bare legs that were black and white and brown and colors in-between. Twisted up together like pretzels.

And then the room began to crack. He could hear it. From where he lay, seen through gaps between all those feet, he could see the edge of the room creep closer. He thought he saw polar bear paws.

He rolled over and looked the other way. More feet and legs, and between those feet and legs he could see the wall on the other side had moved closer. Then the legs were so many he couldn't see anything beyond them, and the legs began to mass together and snap. People screamed.

Now there were people on the bed, fighting, and the bed collapsed in on him as the sides of the room and all those bodies and the darkness of space slipped together to meet him with a final crunching sound and a cosmic sigh.

ON THE MUDDY BANKS OF
THE OLD SABINE

CRACK OF DAWN

IN THESE ASHES beneath a fine blue sky, you'll find bones and memories, burned by wasted love. Fine flesh has been transformed by hot licks of flame into ash and scraps of charred flesh. The ashes are buried in a heap near the river's edge. The summer has been dry and the river has been small. There are blackened bones projecting from the pile, for the wind has picked at the grave and the rain has eroded it, but for the most part, the grave has remained. Inside the grave, the ash has become sticky with mud that has partially dried after being first hot with fire then damp with dew, then baked by the summer sun, dew-licked again each morning, dried again by a new day.

These bones and ashes and spots of flesh are almost the end of the matter, such as an end can be determined.

Here is the beginning.

Carry you down at the crack of dawn to where the Sabine River flows, out where the fish can be caught with a cane pole and cheap fishing line, a floater made of a cork from a bottle of vinegar. Add a golden-colored hook, a squiggling worm, a soft lead sinker or two—squeezed onto the fishing line by pliers—draw back that cane and cast the weighted line into the river and watch the water spread in little circles around the line and slowly grow still.

The heat lies on the back of your neck and arms, which you have coated in cheap sunscreen that is more like turkey basting than a preventative. You are both warm and invigorated from having walked from town carrying your gear. Sixty years old and in fine health, retired early with a good retirement plan, and now you can do what you have always wanted to do come early mornings besides go to work. Fish.

Cast and wait.

And then they came.

In your ears the roar of an engine as the car comes down from the long Sabine River bridge, down the concrete boat track that leads to the water.

A man and a woman getting out with the man carrying a folded blanket and the woman carrying a shoulder-slung purse the size of a picnic basket, wandering down a side trail, braving brambles and water moccasins and the occasional swarm of mosquitoes. Stopping at a clearing that has been made by the flames of lightning one summer past, but is a perfect spot to spread the blanket and sit down.

A large rise of bushes grows in a green cluster between you and them. If they looked, they could see you. But they don't look. The man sets to work as if he has just punched a time clock and has a quota. He is fondling the woman's breasts through her clothes in a manner to suggest the breasts might run away. She has a black eye. A beautiful, one-eyed raccoon fondled by an ape.

From concealment you sneak closer to the swathe of bushes, peering through gaps in the limbs and leaves.

The woman lifts the strap of the purse off her shoulder, placing it beside her on the blanket.

His hands continue to move without tenderness, but with clutching precision. And then the woman, pushing him back gently, smiling, teeth shiny as porcelain, says, "Tim, I know you've been with other women. I know their names. I know when they call you and when you call them. Their perfume on your shirts is like poison to me."

"Don't be silly."

"I know you have and I don't like it."

The woman has somehow scooted back from him, and the smile is gone from her face.

The man's face is a thundercloud. "There's going to be things in life you don't like, woman. You're mine. But you don't own me."

"That hardly seems a fair proposition."

"It's how the world is made. It's God's law that the man can do as he will. By marriage, you are my property. You know what happens when you don't mind? And don't talk like that."

"Like what?"

He studies her face, her defiance new to his eyes.

"Like you have education."

"But I do. I have college. I have a degree. You have you, but you don't have me. Not anymore."

"I'll tell you again, and no other time, quit sassing me. You know what happens when you do?"

"I'm wearing it on my face."

"That's right, and such a pretty face. Don't make me do it again. Don't make me not want to look at you. That black eye is hard enough to stare at."

And in her mind the woman thinks of all the times she "made him do it," him wanting sex when she didn't, him wanting dinner *now*, and the times when he wanted things so vague, she could neither understand nor deliver. The times she trembled in her bed, her phone taken from her, not able to visit friends, her food portions monitored to keep her weight the way he likes it. Remembers so clearly being called stupid and ugly and worthless and insane.

Maybe she was in fact the last. Driven there by a truck of circumstance, fueled on insecurity and his inexplicable meanness. She could live with her own insanity, if there was such. It was him she could no longer live with, hoping for respect to take root, hoping for love and change. She realized now, those things would never come.

She pulls a hatchet from her large purse, the hatchet she has polished like a precision surgeon's tool, the one with the carefully wrapped duct-tape handle. When she pulls it back to strike, the sunlight sparks off the blade and she has a delighted front-row view of his shocked, wide eyes, his lips drawn tight, his head leaning back, as if that would help.

And then she strikes his handsome face.

The axe cuts through bone and flesh, smooth as a hot knife through a mound of warm butter.

🌀

LATER

DEEP MORNING. A Boy Scout troop will be out for a march. Their Scoutmaster is tall and lean, a cool-skinned fellow without pops of sweat, even though the temperature rests heavy and hot on the marching troop of twelve. The Scoutmaster has little moons of sweat beneath his armpits, but they are faint, and his knees are jerking out and back under the cut of his khaki shorts. Their movements have a machine-oiled precision about them, as if he had been built to order in a Boy Scout Factory, a manikin motorized and bolted, screwed together with laser beams and socket wrenches.

The Scouts who follow him in a long trail like ducks in khaki and red scarves, are made of the lesser stuff of flesh and bone, greased by sweat, swooned by heat, pumped with blood, not machine oil.

They walk along the edge of the highway toward the lake. Time of arrival planned for noon, but a pause by the Scoutmaster, as they enter the depths of the trail into the woods, to point out Poison Ivy and Poison Oak and a bluebird on a limb with a worm in its mouth, will put them behind.

The Scoutmaster likes to lecture. He knows a lot of stuff. He knows what kinds of blisters the poisonous plants make, the mating habits of bluebirds, the life of wriggling worms that do best beneath the soil. He points out a worm wriggling in dark loam.

In that moment, the worm lifts its wiggling head only slightly, as if in acknowledgement. Lifts it right where a beam of sunlight shoots like an arrow between the trees.

The beautiful bluebird, in mid-sweet song, spies it, turns into a miniature, bright pterodactyl that chokes its song and swoops down from its limb to claim its wormy prize. Soft and gooey, an avian treat.

Whoa, the Scouts say, obviously thrilled by this dark example of nature at work. Later the bird will fly toward town and rest in an apple tree in a backyard, belly full of worms. And it will sing until a redheaded kid with a BB gun and an accurate eye shoots it out of the tree and the bluebird falls to the ground. It will lie there overnight to be found by a stray cat and taken away into a wooded grove to provide a nice supper.

Next morning, the stray cat will cross a road after a scampering mouse and be hit by a car.

But back to our Scouts.

For all the Scoutmaster's observation, he fails to note a thin black wisp of smoke rising above the trees, some distance away but noticeable to all the boys, who see it through limbs and leaves but don't really give a shit. They are happy to pause beneath the shade of the woods to pretend to listen. They have lost their military-style line and have become a wavering group around the Scoutmaster. A long rat snake on the hunt crawls between the legs of one of the Scouts so swiftly and quietly, it goes unnoticed. Later, a wild hog will notice it, but that is another story, sad for the snake, happy for the hog.

❧

MEANWHILE BACK AT THE RIVERBANK

AXE MURDER IN progress.

The fisherman hears and sees it all through the gap in the bushes, the woman swinging the axe in savage arcs, the blade cutting with loud but smooth precision through flesh and bones, the blood spray seeming to burst out in slow motion; hot, copper-colored streams and drops that glisten in the sunlight, fall and spatter to the blanket, turning it wet and dark.

Her face blood-blemished, as if she is wearing a camouflage mask of blood and skin, her teeth drawn back and flecked with splashing gore.

"Oh shit!" says the fisherman.

As the words come out of his mouth, he knows he should have kept them tight inside. He drops the fishing pole as the blood-spotted woman's teeth clench and her lips crawl and wriggle. She comes to her feet in one smooth move, like an acrobat.

The fisherman runs back to the river, darts down the trail along its bank. His boots smattering mud as he runs. Sixty years old but in prime health, he tells himself. I got this.

But swift behind him comes the Blood-Spotted Lady of Death. He hears the thundering of her feet in motion, and those thundering feet are gaining, and then he sees her shadow as it falls over him and his own shadow, its dark elbows and knees bending, flowing swiftly as if pushed by the wind. Her shadow raises its arm high and swings the shadowy axe in a swift dark curve.

There is a sudden burst of crows lifting in a dark, startled flock, up and away from the trees, their little shadows clutched together, dragging the ground.

CHOPAPALOOZA

SHE DISCOVERED THAT it was easier than she thought to drag the men to the riverbank and into a muddy pit carved by water, pull off their clothes, and take her axe to their flesh and bone, chopping and chopping, so happy that once or twice, she burst into song.

Retrieving the full gas can and shovel she had placed in the trunk before luring her prey with a promise of romance renewed, obedience accepted, hand jobs and blow jobs, oral and anal, and traditional too, she brings them to where the butchered bodies lie.

She pours the gas onto the chopped flesh and bones of the men, on their clothes, then gathers dry wood, scoops the gassy, bloody remains onto the pile with the shovel, and with her husband's lighter, sets it all afire.

Flames jump so high and hot they crinkle the tips of her hair. An eyelash is toasted. The skin on the hand that holds the lighter is lightly kissed by fire.

Tossing the shovel and the gas can, even the lighter, out into the river where the current moves, she enjoys the splash, as if it is the burst of energy that created the universe. The cotton blanket she folds carefully and places on the blaze.

Flame wraps around the cotton, blood-soaked blanket, and caresses it rapidly to ash. Wood in the fire crackles. Bones in the fire burst. Flesh sizzles. Blood boils. She does a dance with her hatchet in her hand. Dances three circles around the fire. She sings again. Her voice is deep. When she stops to breathe, from where she stands, she can see the Sabine River bridge.

All the while that she has chopped the men, built the fire, danced and sang, cars have been whizzing by. No one has noticed. Or perhaps she has been seen, but no one understands what they see. Most likely, eyes were on concrete or the horizon.

My lady, she says to herself, your escape route and conveyance await. Away, my lady.

Finally, reluctantly deciding to let it go, she tosses the hatchet into the slow-rolling, brown water.

She leaves with a spring in her step and the odd feeling of having had an orgasm, made by chops instead of thrusts.

Moments later, the Scoutmaster and his troop arrive like a khaki cyclone, crashing through brush and dodging between trees, on out to the edge of the river.

The Scouts run along the riverbank and point at the smoke and yell, and one, with a droopy face, his sweat-damp hair cut close under his field cap, looks at the remains of the fire, says, "Look, bones! People bones!"

The Scoutmaster strolls to the smoking pit full of burnt wood and bones and curling black smoke, and looks. Pursing his lips, hands on hips, face puffed with satisfaction, he says, "Son. Don't make foolish pronouncements. Don't you know a cook fire when you see it? Meat has been cooked here. Animal meat. Not human meat. Hog, I believe, from the state and size of those bones. But human bones? Not at all. As a Scout, you need to know what to look for."

The boys begin to pogo around the fire like hungry cannibals.

"Eat them bones," one says, and then another. It's a ring-around-the-rosy of voices and leaping.

"Stop!" the Scoutmaster says. Then: "What is our Scout rule that has been broken here?"

The Scouts freeze, study the face of their oracle.

Droopy Face steps forward, says, "Never leave a fire burning. Smokey Bear says the same."

"He does. And what is the rest of that rule?"

"Leave the place like it was before you used it."

"Correct. It shouldn't look as if a fire were ever here. Scouts! Camp shovels."

Camp shovels are removed from backpacks and unfolded. The boys set to work digging a pit next to the existing one. They rake the remains of the wood and the bones into the pit and cover it. One of the boys leans into Droopy. "Looks like a piece of human skull to me."

But Droopy is defeated. "Scoutmaster knows what's up, not you or me."

The boy who still thinks Droopy was right, and that there is in fact a piece of human skull in the smoking pile, tucks in his thoughts, digs with the others, and covers the remains. By nightfall, he will have forgotten all about it.

Eventually, they smooth the burnt spot into a mud slab on the banks of the old Sabine.

THE HATCHET LADY

SHE REPORTS HER missing husband and the cops ask questions. She looks teary, and the tears are tears of freedom, but the cops falsely believe the loss of true romance glistens on her cheeks. A search is made all over, but turns up nothing. One of the cops is quite handsome. He wishes he could meet a woman like her. One that would cherish and hold love delicately. He is secretly smitten.

In the meantime, a fisherman's car is located near the river, well back from the big bridge. Parked on one of the red dirt trails, not too far from where the river flows. The fisherman is missing too. He has no wife. He has no friends. He's retired.

All that is known about him is he likes to fish.

His rod and tackle box and some sun-toasted worms in a bucket are found. Thoughts are that he slipped and drowned and has been borne away. The river is assumed guilty of murder.

As for the Hatchet Lady.

At the Methodist church the Hatchet Lady attends, rumor is her husband has abandoned his job as well as his wife. Ran off with another woman. Someone quick to drop their knickers and take up with wedded men. Has her own car, most likely, and they have rode away in it. It's been said by some to some others who know some others, that he and a hot blonde with a dress so short she has to powder two sets of cheeks, have been seen somewhere up in Waxahachie.

The Hatchet Lady gradually acquires the personality of a bird freed from a cage.

She sings in the choir. In time she will marry the handsome cop that came to ask questions. The search for her husband gets lost in the shuffle of time.

THE RIVER

RAIN STORMS COME and go. They wash the river and make it flow. The river expands and covers the bank where the bones lie buried. Over time, the water erodes the shore. The burnt wood, bones, and memories of murder that the shoreline knows, are washed away in a torrential downpour, dissolving wood, tumbling those hatchet-snapped bones on out into a fast-flowing current.

In the night, the full moon lies on the water like a flat polished stone. In the day the moon goes away and the sun comes up, makes the water yellow and shiny. Moonlight and sunlight rise and sink.

And the river churns along, sometimes fast, sometimes slow, carrying the remains of the men out to the Gulf of Mexico.

THE
DEGREE

THANKS FOR THE mail vibe, Len, and I'll do my best to address your question in full. I realize it may have been merely a polite way to begin a communication, and may not have been something you were truly hoping to be answered, outside of some brief homily, and believe me, you'll get that, but perhaps with a bit of window dressing. You have stepped in it now.

I'm not too far ahead of you in the game of life, cousin, but since you asked, here's part of my answer, and we'll call this the standard part of the lecture, so to speak, the homily, and then I can only offer my observations and personal experiences. Grab the seat cushions and wait for it.

If you want some kind of career, and you suggest you want the same kind I'm striving for, you have to plan for it.

Yeah. I know. There it is, the dead fish under the sofa, but in the main, that's all I got.

Now for a bit of that window dressing I mentioned.

In a way, I suppose you could say I have been planning on my career since I was quite young. Or rather my parents were planning on it for me. Dad always said, "Unless you want to live on the bottom of the food chain, be one of life's targets, you best put your nose to the grindstone."

I'm sure you've heard that from your parents, or some version of it, and maybe that's why you're asking me what to do, because of our similar backgrounds. I am what you soon will be. A college boy, but I have dreams.

My family didn't really have the money for the university. We aren't on the lower rung of the ladder, as you know, but neither are we at the top of it either. We hope to rise, and fear falling below, which is a solid kind of fear, of course.

I took out loans for my education. If you can avoid that, and I doubt you can, as I know your family's financial situation is similar to our own, then you should. Loans can eat at you. You think, well, I'll pay them off with the better money I'll make from having a degree, but that doesn't necessarily follow. There are pitfalls.

I've been studying for a while now, and I'm still not finished, and I owe tons already. The final bill will be staggering. I may be forced to do what I trained for well past my prime, and that might even mean a part-time job, and even then, I don't know I can pay it all off, so I have to decide to enjoy my work, and be happy with that. I do think about rising in the business, becoming worth a lot more than average, but I can only work for that, not count on it. I may be stuck with fieldwork all my life, or at best, rise to middle management, and at worst, I may be sweeping the place out, wherever that place might be, as where I will be stationed in the end is currently unknown, of course. No guarantees.

I'm not squawking, I hasten to add, but those are the facts, and you, cousin, will be facing the same situation. The American Dream is an opportunity, not a promise.

For years free college was talked about, or letting debts go, but frankly, the government has too much tied up in so many other things that government loans are not something they want to drop. Private loaners, and I have used both government and private, aren't in a forgiving mood either with the way things are these days.

I like the work I'm training for, as I've had a taste of it in the labs, but again, who's to say? It can also be stressful. I have days when I feel overcome, but I soldier on. Not everyone can. Keeping up grades, studying, doing lots of physical training. It's a tough gig.

A fellow I met on campus and became good friends with, Jason Rone, he got so overwhelmed with his studies, the lab projects, that one day he went up to the Top Tower, as they call the highest building on campus, and jumped.

There were people who saw him do it, and they said on his way down he was flapping his arms like wings, as if he was suffering regret and hoping to take off like a bird. He didn't manage to do that. They said he yelled one word that he stretched out to last until he was all the way down, splattering on the cement.

The word was *Shiiiiiiiiiitttt.*

That's kind of funny in a way. Jason was always a kidder. He said to me not long ago, "Wouldn't it be a severe fucking to my government loans if something happened to me and they just had to eat it?"

Looking at it that way, his jump was a kind of joke, and he cheated them out of their money. I'll miss him. He could make everyone in lab laugh.

Still, I'm sticking with my educational plan, and jumping hasn't occurred to me as a solution. I don't know if I'd have the balls to make that choice anyway. Better to owe all my life than to end it, right?

Environmental studies are a much harder degree than I imagined. When I was young, I figured it would be easy enough. Everything seemed easy then, as I was only thinking about it, not doing it.

My first class is my favorite. It's the lab class and we get a chance to get our hands dirty, so to speak. With all the environmental problems, and the fact that most are caused by overpopulation, learning how to lower the population, minimizing our footprint as they call it, seems an absolute necessity.

And you got all these people, immigrants coming in, and you got assholes having babies one after another, so something has to be done. I've nothing against babies, but some people just shouldn't have any.

Lab class is easier than the real thing. They bring specimens and experiments to you. You don't have to go out and find them. All you have to do is what you're taught. The labs are training for fieldwork, but it's not real fieldwork. Still, it gives you a taste.

When they bring in the lesser citizens or non-citizens, to lab class, the ones they nab from the other side, I find that I can overpower my experiment rather quickly. I got some size on me, but it's the training that counts. Sure, the lab's streets and building walls are merely facsimiles of the actual areas where the lesser lives dwell, but to learn how to do the job right, you have to start somewhere. Way I see it, I do what I'm supposed to do, it's just one less doorway or cardboard box with feet sticking out of it. If we ever reach zero population status, then I suppose I might be out of a job after years of study, but with the way things are going now, all the people, many of them working shit jobs, the Spartan method, as it's called in class, is one way to fix things.

The Spartan philosophy, or at least parts of it, are the main basis for what we do. You should study that before you come to the university. You may know about it, but know it well. And if you are unfamiliar with it, here it is in a nutshell.

Spartans in ancient Greece, if they could sneak up on and kill one of the peasants, it was fine. But they had to show their stealth skills, not get caught, and if they managed that, well then, killing was acceptable, sanctioned by the government. Spartans considered it training for the army, living off the land, using stealth skills to kill. That's why they call us Environmental Spartans.

We are an army of sorts, but I always feel that I'm part of something bigger than myself when I'm in lab and I catch my experiment, subdue them, and then strangle them with my preferred jujitsu choke, sometimes a garrote.

The children are easy, but you have to chase them more, and they can be quick and elusive. There's not as much room for them to run in the lab set-up, but it gives you a feel for what you'll be doing once you get the old sheepskin. In the outside world, they won't be brought to you on a platter, so to speak, and they'll have more room to run.

Another thing, and the lab instructor pounds this into you. You got to watch thinking of them as being like you and me, as they are not. Remember, many are non-white, others are dirty, and practically savage, so hey, you do what you got to do. It's the job.

And keep this in mind, as it's important. They are a resource. Sometimes I look at them and see them as the same as me, but I know that's my empathy, which is high and something of a nuisance. I try to make their deaths brief, and I try to keep in mind I've taken a potential breeder and moocher off the street, and have provided some nice cuts of meat.

Believe me, I've thought about training to be a butcher, but if we manage to do as we are trained, reach the logical end to all that training, that meat could be limited. Though, of course, some of them would be kept for breeding purposes to keep some kind of supply, so you can't say all babies made by those shitters are bad. But controlled breeding is different than willy-nilly breeding, and then them being out there trying to get over the wall into the main population. Some think they're as good as us.

There's the first bell. I have ten minutes before the second bell and class.

Got to run. I like to warm up before I go in. I don't want to get caught on the back foot, so to speak. One of the experiments got the better of a lab partner last week, put him in the hospital. The experiment was a tough one, girl about seventeen with a stutter, but I got her. I got her good. Used my hands. Oh, I train with the sniper rifle, all the other weapons. The flamethrower is fun, I admit, and man is it efficient, but it's messy, and you can catch the lab walls on fire and frequently the meat is so damaged there's no gain. That's a weapon for elimination, not utilization.

Silly accidents can happen with the flamethrower as well. Yesterday, guy in class was putting the cook on one of the experiments and burned his own eyebrows off, which was kind of funny. If that wasn't enough, a week ago another fellow using the flamethrower set the professor's desk on fire, which did not go over well, but afterwards a lot of us had a laugh about it, and the meat was recoverable, and each of us were allowed to have a piece of it. It was charred in spots, raw in others, but digestible. Our professor called it a ritual, not a meal, but it just made me hungry.

Here's a note of warning, as you may not have heard. You remember Gabe, my age, big guy? Bigger than me. He and I used to hang together. Good guy. He could cuss the vermin about as well as I have ever heard it done. The other day he twisted his ankle bad in class, during a lab exercise with one of the outsiders. Well, more than twisted it, he's really messed it up. I see him with that limp, it's hard to imagine him staying at our level. And you got to do that. You got to take care of yourself so that you have a better chance of quickly recovering from an injury.

I hate the situation Gabe is in, and if he doesn't heal up quick and solid, they may release him onto the street, behind the wall. On the other side he'll have the shit population to avoid. If he can avoid that, well, he is open game for us then.

I hope he heals up. That's all I can say. The Environmental Corps have rules, and those rules were made to make society work, to keep it on a certain economic and racial level, keep out the invalids and malcontents.

I believe that, Len. I do. We can't have inferior folks out there breathing air and shitting turds. That's not good. I don't even think it's biblical, though I haven't read the book to know. I will, of course. Eventually.

Now, keep in mind, Gabe hasn't fallen to that level, the level of inferiority, but he is pretty bad off, and I have a feeling how it will turn out. Already, I'm trying to accept that he won't be one of us much longer. It's like when you have a relative who has some kind of disease, and you know they're dying, and they know it too, and you don't plan for it, but gradually, you start to wean yourself off their declining energy. They are, at least for you emotionally, already dead. It's nature's way of accepting inevitabilities.

I think about the fact that I could end up that way as well. We're all an injury shy of being infirm, and that's almost as bad as having the wrong skin color. People with diseases, malformation and so on, they just don't fit in to a progressive society, do they, Len?

So, I think about that, sure, but I have learned through certain mantras we are taught, to slip it to the back part of my brain, as if it is behind a fence. And again, I've got those empathy problems. I have to think of it like feeding rats to snakes. They are the rats, and we are the snakes, and snakes are survivors. So are rats, but that's why we have the Environmental Corp. To make those rats part of our reptilian survival.

Damn, forgive me for comparing us to snakes. We are far better than some cold reptile. But, empathy or not, the rats are the rats, and you have to know rats can bite back and breed constantly.

We have the government behind us. They don't.

We have our degrees and our training. They don't.

We are doing something beneficial to the world. They are not.

They are the problem.

We are the solution.

We come from a better class of people than they do. They kill, it's murder; we kill, it's legal assassination. Remember, nits make lice.

This brings me to one last note. You asked about Aunty Cecily, why you haven't seen her around, and I have saved this information for the last, as I thought it would be a good conclusion to my suggestions to study hard and train hard and to stay super fit.

Aunt Cecily, she got a little short on memory. Too much had to be done to maintain her, so, they put her on the other side of the wall. She didn't last long.

Weep not for Aunt Cecily, for she had ceased to be the person we knew by the time my mother helped put her over the wall. She wandered right into them. Mother said it was quick, and when Mother knew it was certain, she looked away. We have written Aunt Cecily off. This will be the last time I mention her name.

There's the second bell. Got to go for sure now. Must end this, and therefore, let me close with this. I didn't really give you much in the way of advice, but I hope it helps you to understand it can be done, and that it's worthwhile work, and I'm glad you're interested in following in my footsteps, as you say. Well, those footsteps have taken a short trip as of now, but I wouldn't mind doing well enough as a student, and later in my job, so that you might see me as a role model of sorts. Last bit of advice. Stay healthy, for heaven's sake.

The American Dream may in fact be, as I said, an opportunity, not a promise, but it is alive and well.

Hang in, cuz,
Charles

RED
BILLIE

(This one is for Lewis Shiner. Thanks for the tips.)

THIS HAPPENED BACK when I was a kid, during a scorching summer so hot it was rumored birds fell dead and smoking from the sky, and the clouds looked like unpleasant faces.

I don't doubt it.

Those were the good old days, actually.

I'll come to that.

❧

THE GIRL WE came to know as Red Billie moved into our town one night with who we assumed were her gray-faced parents, both of them stooped and homely as moldy sacks of old sin.

They arrived during a terrible hot spell in a coughing, clattering pickup that was made of rust and a bad promise. It was so worn out, neither model nor year of its production could be identified. It had one headlight, and that one looked tired, like a sick, one-eyed monster looking forward to retirement or a quick death from an auto crusher.

Billie and the withered adults showed up along with three slinking hound dogs in the bed of the truck. The dogs were dust-colored and bony. The dogs stayed close together, as if they had just recently been unglued from one another and were unaccustomed to independence.

Folks and hounds ended up stuffed into a sagging gray house with a leaky tarpaper roof with only candlelight at night and an outside shitter that leaked out of the side of the hill like radioactive honey, steamed in the heat, and carried its aroma, which was strong enough to part your hair and call you Bobby, down from the hill and into the edge of the Dirt Yard.

The Dirt Yard was the remains of an old quarry where the ground had given up stone and earth, and then had been shit on from above.

There was a light on a pole at the top of the hill, almost in the yard where Billie lived. From down in the pit, it looked like a second moon.

All us boys gathered in the Dirt Yard beneath where the light dropped its gold spot. It was cooler at night and more bearable against what was then record heat.

We played marbles, drank stolen beers, and talked about the girls we claimed to have screwed. Class was not our middle name, not even the name of a distant ancestor. We were fifteen, just a few years above booger eating and knock-knock jokes.

From the Dirt Yard, when the moon was bright, you could see greasy smoke rising from the nearby factories. Farther along the hill were other houses, most of them built on the fly and constructed as if sacrifices to the wind.

Most of the boys in our group lived in those houses, which were only a couple of steps in quality above the one where Billie lived. That one was abandoned and no one wanted it. Billie and her folks, and those hounds, were squatters. No one rushed to throw them out, as my guess was the person who owned that house and property was either dead or had moved off, or had no more interest in that place than one might have in trying to give a rattlesnake a tonsillectomy with a pair of tweezers.

East side of town was known as Hell's Five Acres. No one was thinking a lot of brain surgeons were coming out of that section. I lucked out in a lot of ways. My parents weren't as poor as the others, and they had other interests besides beating a kid's ass and drinking a twelve pack nightly. At least my hopes and dreams didn't wear chains and concrete boots.

One night, with the bugs swarming around the pole light thicker than the Milky Way, we saw Billie out on the sagging porch up there, sitting with her hounds, looking down on us like a hawk picking which mouse she was going to swoop down on.

We kind of knew who she was, as we'd all observed her and her strange family for a couple weeks or so, but at that moment in time, of course, we didn't know her name, and none of us had spoken to her. She watched us play marbles for a while, then came down, using a path to the Dirt Yard that would be precarious even for a mountain goat. She was carrying a bulging brown cloth bag.

Billie was peculiar looking, about our age at first glance. Because of her peculiarities, one of the meaner kids, Charlie, immediately thought of her as an object of fun, way she looked and acted.

Her short, fire-red hair made tufts on the sides of her head that stuck up high like horns, and she was ruddy-faced, and her skin appeared to have been pulled back tight to her ears by invisible wires and a serious winch. She had on jeans and a dirty brown sweat shirt that her breasts poked against like a couple of door knobs. She had little feet in little black shoes.

She shook the cloth bag. It rattled like lug bolts and broken glass.

She said, "My name is Billie. Some call me Red Billie. Some call me Little Red Billie, some call me Bill, and some don't call me at all. I'd like to play marbles."

Charlie, who lived with his grandmother because his parents were in prison and his older brother had been shot dead in a washateria robbery, said, "Looks to me, girl, like you collected an ugly bill, and got paid in full."

Billie hit him in the mouth with a sharp left jab that made Charlie sit down so quick you'd have thought he wanted to.

Billie said, "Don't write a check your ass can't cash."

Charlie realized he didn't even have a check book, and stayed seated.

Billie broke open her bag of marbles then, and just to show she had style, unfastened the string that closed the bag, and dumped all the marbles into the circle we had drawn in the dirt.

Those marbles were wonders of color, and some of those colors I had never seen before. There was one marble that looked clear. I noticed it when it fell out of the bag and rolled onto the packed earth. As it rolled it turned blue and green, then it sparked with orange and red lights, like tiny fires set by mischievous fairies.

We all studied those wonderous orbs for a bit, then Red Billie dropped her empty marble sack into the circle, said to Charlie, "You. Pick those up and bag them, then let's get down to business."

Charlie moved into the circle, still on his knees. He picked the marbles up, examining them as he put them in the bag with all the caution of a collector handling miniature Fabergé eggs.

There was only one shooter marble in her collection, bigger than the rest and black as a dead man's night. Just looking at that marble made my heart beat faster.

"Now," Red Billie said, "which game do you pussies play? Straight marbles, or for keeps?"

We did a bit of both from time to time, but it was difficult to afford a bag of marbles on a regular basis, so normally we didn't play for keeps.

Charlie, now fully indoctrinated with left-jab diplomacy, said, "How do you like to play?"

"I play for keeps or I don't play. I was only pretending to ask. And we're going to play, aren't we, boys?"

We all agreed to play. It seemed better than a jab in the snout, possibly some lost teeth.

"Now," she said, "we'll play with your marbles, not mine. Not until I say so. Except the shooter. I'll use my shooter."

"That sounds good," Charlie said. In that moment he would have spit-polished Billie's little shoes with his tongue and wiped her ass with a silk handkerchief. He might have even reversed that order.

The wind was kicking up the usual stink of sewage and foundry, but I could smell Billie too. She smelled like charred wood smoke and burnt pork ribs coated in a mist of Sulphur fumes and the residue from a sticky bean fart. She added strong tobacco stench to her scent by pulling a black cheroot out of her pocket, poking it between her thin lips, and lighting it with a match she popped to fire with her long black thumb nail. Her thumb knuckle was as big as a willow tree knot and dark with grime.

Charlie poured his bag of marbles into the center. Letting them roll every which way.

Red Billie was so short she could have walked under a kitchen table with a hat on, but she threw a bigger shadow than her height deserved. That shadow lay over the circle of marbles like a rain cloud.

We all squatted around the circle to watch Billie attempt to hit her first marble. She crouched low, and the smoke from her cheroot veiled her head in a Vesuvius cloud. She eyed her target. Then with a slow release of tobacco breath, she flexed her thumb against that big black shooter marble and let it fly.

Her shooter was a tumbling shadow. It hit a green and blue cat's eye so hard it shattered it. Fragments flew about like shrapnel.

You could hear all of us let out our breath. You might run over a marble with a truck tire and crush it like that, but a thumb shot? It could happen, but not the way that happened.

Billie's shooter didn't go out of the ring. It spun about for a moment in the center of it like a happy drunk in a four-wheeler.

Since she had destroyed the cats-eye, she was up for another shot.

"I'll go light," she said.

And so, it went. Each shot banging a marble, knocking it out of the ring, but not shattering it like the first. She had been showing off, but I didn't doubt she could explode other marbles as easily as the first. Her shooter never once went out of the ring, so she kept on shooting. She shot fast, and by the end of it, all of Charlie's marbles, by standard rule, belonged to her.

When Billie completed her run, her face was popped with sweat and one got the strong impression that the only thing that might satisfy her as well as shooting marbles was stomping kittens.

Billie wanted us to shoot, so more marbles were dumped, and without her participating, normal games were played with marbles being bumped out of the ring. It seemed lethargic after her performance.

No doubt, I played the best. I could shoot hard and had a good eye, though my results were far less dramatic.

Even as the time for me to be home ticked by on my genuine used Timex watch, I didn't inch my way away from there. I was hoping to see Billie shoot again.

But that was it for the night. Her family dogs had begun to howl, and this seemed to be like a siren call for her. She smiled and told Charlie he could keep his marbles she had won. She took her bag of marbles, said goodnight mother-fuckers, and made her way back up the hill, never faltering as she went.

We couldn't have been more in awe than if Santa Claus had turned out to be real and was living as our next-door neighbor and spent his spare time fucking a stray dog in public.

When I got home, I eased into the house, past the living room where Mom and Dad were watching some sort of variety show. They nodded at me, and my dad tapped his watch to signify I was late. I nodded back. I wasn't that late, and they weren't so strict as to lose a lung over it, but they hadn't lost sight of the time. A reminder they cared about me.

On TV, cloggers, men and women dressed in cowboy shirts, jeans and boots, were dancing what is sometimes referred to as the Ignorant White Folk Dance, or Irish dancing without the good parts. Someone was playing a fiddle. I like a good fiddle. This wasn't one.

I eased into my room, which I shared with my eight-year-old brother, Lenny. He was in the process of dismantling his transistor radio with a hammer.

"Can't get the batteries out," he said.

"That's okay. You aren't going to need them."

I lay on my back on the bottom bunk, and listened to Lenny hammering away. He was destroying everything but the hammer. I could hear the TV going, and the variety show was over by then, and the news was on, and the main topic was the weather. Unseasonably hot. Tar and roofing shingles melting like chocolate, dripping off and onto the ground. That was one reason my parents weren't too hard on me about being late. During the day it was almost too hot to breathe. The air conditioner panted in the house like a dying dog, sucked that Freon as if with a straw.

I thought about what I had seen out at the Dirt Yard. I could still smell Red Billie's aroma on my clothes. It had soaked into them like dye. I finally undressed and showered and put on my pajamas and went to bed.

I dreamed that night of Billie and her odd hair tufts, her enormous thumb and jet-black nail, the big black shooter, and that exploding marble. Its fragments blowing out in slow motion, tinkling to the sun-dried earth like hailstones.

෪

I CONSIDERED NOT going back the next night, as the whole thing had both amazed and spooked me, but, then again, I had never seen such a thing, met such a person, and I had once seen a drunk guy who could dance barefoot on broken glass.

Next summer night, the moon and stars were bagged up in wet-cloud darkness, and what should have been a cool, late-night breeze had turned humid. At the Dirt Yard, something swift and flickering moved inside the light on the pole at the top of the hill. Beat at it like a moth captured in a jar.

Now and again, Billie would pause, look up at the light, sigh, bend down again, and thump her shooter and knock another marble out of the ring. She even busted one or two to show she could.

ONE LATE AFTERNOON, the sun bleeding between houses, I was walking on the little oozing blacktop road set slightly above Red Billie's house.

I was going to buy some milk and cereal, maybe a comic book. I was thinking that night I would definitely skip the marble show. I had begun to feel odd about it, as if I were waiting for something not so pleasant to happen, and I needed to abandon ship.

As I was passing Billie's house, I saw she had gone out to sit on a bench near the edge of the hill so she could look down on the Dirt Yard. She was surrounded by her dogs. Little dust-colored shadows that slinked close to her feet.

She turned her head in time to catch me walking by, called out to me.

"Hey, come sit with me a while."

There was a plaintive tone in her voice, like a child that had thrown a birthday party only to have no one show up. I thought about an excuse, decided against it, and went over.

The dogs gathered around me as I walked into the yard. They were a bedraggled bunch. With hotspot patches where fur had been. Maybe a touch of mange. One had a phlegmy eye, and that was the good one. The larger dog had two peckers.

"They won't bite you," Billie said. "Unless I tell them to. Come. Sit."

I sat on the bench beside her. One of the hounds licked my ear, like a chef testing the specialty of the house right before it was served; a chef with hot breath that smelled like a rotting carcass, and with a tongue like sandpaper.

"Are you happy?" she asked me.

Not a question I would have expected.

"I think so. Nothing hurts and I'm okay."

"I've never been happy. Not where I come from."

"Where's that?"

"South."

"What was it like to make you so unhappy there?"

"Where I'm from, time crawls like a slug. Sometimes, though, it wobbles and comes loose. There are cracks through which you can escape. My life is like a dream in a trash can."

I was as confused as a Martian tourist, but I said nothing. The air crackled and snapped slightly. In the distance I could see dry lightning dancing and the air began to taste of ozone and turn even warmer than it had been. Sweat dripped off of me.

"I slipped through the cracks. But they'll be looking."

"Who will be looking?"

"Her. It won't be long. She comes cold and snowy."

Looking at Billie and her surroundings, those horrid dogs, I couldn't figure what she was talking about. Someone looking for her? Cold and snowy? What the hell?

I said, "You have your parents to look after you?"

"The dogs do a better job. And those two are not my parents. Guardians."

I certainly had questions, but I was afraid to ask them.

As we sat there and the summer night ticked onward with the stars swarming above like the bugs at the pole light, I was possessed with a sudden thought.

Looking at Red Billie, I found I was looking past her peculiar hairdo, her strange clothes, her little feet, and I saw a girl there, scared and almost pretty if you squinted just right. Admittedly, at the age I was then, the old gear shift had a tendency to switch out of Park and into Drive at the vaguest hint of sexual attractiveness.

I said, "Would you like to go get an ice cream cone?"

It wasn't a pick-up line on the equal to how about a trip to Paris, but it's all I had. My cousin used to ask girls to wrestle. That worked pretty well, he said.

Red Billie turned her head and looked at me. In her eyes there was movement. I could almost see thoughts drive by like cars on the interstate. Then her eyes went soft, and her face turned soft as well.

"You don't have ideas, do you?"

"About what?" I said, and I felt my gear shift back into Park. "It's not marble time yet. We got a couple hours or so before we play?"

She smiled at me.

"Just thought you might want an ice cream cone," I said. "I'm getting one."

I stood up.

"Okay," she said.

~

WE WALKED DOWN the street to the ice cream shop. When we went in, the older teenagers turned to look at us. Of course, it was Billie's curious looks that drew their attention.

At the counter we ordered. Billie went for a hot fudge Sundae and I ordered a banana split. I paid for it all, just like I had money to spare. I wouldn't be buying cereal and milk this night.

We sat in the back at a lone table separated from the others. As Billie ate her ice cream, it steamed little pale clouds out of her mouth and nose.

"Are you embarrassed?" she asked.

"About what?"

"Being with me."

"No. I'm not embarrassed."

"My mom always says I was the peach that fell off the tree and lay too long on the ground."

"Your mom said that?"

"Not good for the confidence, you know," Billie said. "I run off whenever I can. But she always comes for me, and I always have to go back. I really hate it there. I keep trying to stay away."

"Your father?"

"No one mentions his name. It's not to be said. He pretty much ignores me. I don't know if that's better or worse."

We ate our ice cream, and by the time we had stepped back out into the street, the air had been touched with a chill, which made no sense.

Red Billie trembled, looked up at the sky. I couldn't see much up there because of the street and store lights. Billie seemed to see well enough, though.

She said, "The universe has shifted."

"Yeah?"

"Yeah. All manner of this and that from then and now are coming loose of their regions."

"No shit?"

"No shit."

We walked slowly back to her house. She took my hand. It felt like a hot water bottle freshly filled. Other than that, we were just two teenagers on a cool, soft night with the universe having shifted and something coming loose of their regions.

When we arrived at her house, the dogs came out to see us. Billie slowly let go of my hand, turned to look at me, said, "Go home. Don't come back. Go home."

"Oh," I said.

"It's best. You being there or not won't change a thing. Thanks for being kind."

MY PARENTS WERE on the couch in front of the TV. I went over to acknowledge I was home.

I left them there, had a sandwich, and went to the bedroom. My little brother had worn himself out early beating an old record player to pieces with his hammer. At least I wouldn't have to hear the goddamn singing chipmunks anymore.

He lay on the floor, hunched over his damage, asleep from physical exhaustion. The hammer was next to his hand. I was going to recommend to Mom and Dad that for Christmas they buy him an anvil, or some angle iron to beat on. His toys were just about extinct.

I picked up the hammer, went outside and flung it into the shrubbery. The air was warmer again, and the stars had lost their sense of wonder. Pollution from the foundry floated in front of the moon.

"Don't come back," Billie had said, but I started walking back to the Dirt Yard.

A NUMBER OF the kids had shown up, as Billie was still the number one attraction in our section of town. They stood, hands in pockets, heads bent, waiting for Billie and a display of her phenomenal marbling shooting. Charlie seemed more anxious than any of us.

Down from the hill she came. Tonight, she wore a dark leather jacket. Her hair had been brushed and the red tufts on the sides of her head had been combed back. A bit of hair dangled on her forehead in a spit curl. She looked quite fetching, if overdressed for a summer night. That coat would have smothered me.

Following her came the hound dogs, as well as her Guardians, walking like sticks in shoes. Billie came to stand by the circle. She looked at me.

"I told you not to come back."

"I know."

She gave me a thin smile that hit me in my back pocket.

Some of the kids were looking away from Billie, in the other direction.

I turned. Coming down the back trail was a tall wisp of a woman in white shirt and pants, white tennis shoes, no socks.

She had night-black hair, skin like porcelain, eyes like fire. She had a white purse; the long strap that supported it was slung over her shoulder.

Four white cats, their fur touched with frost, strolled after her. The air was not only bite-ass cold all of a sudden, there were flecks of snow blowing about. What the hell?

Up close, the woman smelled of jasmine, damp earth, and gentle decay.

"It's time to come home," she said to Red Billie, facing her across the circle.

"I don't have to," Billie said.

"I believe you do. Things are out of whack. I see you took our dog."

Dogs, I thought, there were three of them. But when I looked, the hounds were pushed up tight to one another and I couldn't see where they separated. The Guardians had bent their long bodies so that their hands touched the earth. They had the appearance of insects. Enormous white crickets ready to hop. Out of their backs grew transparent wings.

I hadn't seen that coming.

When I turned to look at the Wisp, the cats were no longer there. In their place were long, cool women, silver-haired, bare and pale with expressionless faces. There was nothing sexy about them. No gears shifted from Park to Drive. They might as well have been marble statues in a cemetery.

One of the women licked out with her tongue and touched her nose, giving it a wipe.

"You're over your time," said the Wisp. "It's time to catch the boat, honey. I have your fare."

The insects around the light buzzed like harpies, cast shadow dots on the poorly lit ground.

"I'd rather not," Billie said. "I'll take my chances with the game."

"You know how that turns out before you start."

"Not always. Remember that time in Death Valley?"

"I've always suspected you cheated."

"And Krakatoa."

"Don't talk to me about Krakatoa. Definitely a cheat, Billie."

"And Chernobyl."

"I give you that one. I wasn't feeling myself that day."

"I think I have to be home," Charlie said, his attachment to Red Billie having faded during the transformation of the dogs and Guardians. I was about to suggest I go with him.

"Everyone will stay," said the Wisp. "The night is sealed."

"Sealed?" Charlie said.

"That means you can't go," the Wisp said, "and if you try to, they'll find you inside a block of ice. Go that way, you'll be ash. So, I suggest you stay."

"Okay," Charlie said, and looked at me.

I shrugged. I was kind of hoping he'd make a run for it. I was curious which direction he might go, and how he'd turn out. Ash or ice.

"Shall we play?" the Wisp said.

"We always do," Billie said.

"I have brought the coins for your eyes," said the Wisp. She flipped two large silver coins onto the ground. They rattled and wobbled before becoming still. "Flip it."

Billie eyed the two coins. It was obvious there was a ritual here we didn't understand, and it had been happening for quite some time.

"What's going on?" Charlie said. "What is this?"

"Shush," said the Wisp. "I don't like my concentration bothered. Understand, you little worthless shit?"

"Yes, ma'am," Charlie said.

Billie picked up one of the coins, and flipped it, said, "Heads."

In those moments the Dirt Yard was all there was of the world. Hot wind blew, and cold wind followed. Snow flecked, and insects caught fire. The air swirled with Billie's smell, the sewer, the pollution, and the sick sweetness from the Wisp. The three-headed dog growled. The women mewed and swayed. Between heat and ice, I shivered and swooned.

The flipped coin sailed up high, catching the light, the edge of it sparkling like a diamond, spinning, seeming to hang for a moment, then it dropped fast.

Billie stuck out her palm and caught it. She stepped into the circle, extended her hand, showed it so all could see. Tails.

The Wisp smiled, removed her purse and dumped her marbles on the ground outside the circle. The marbles steamed like dry ice. Her shooter was a ball of blue ice. She picked it up and rolled it across her fingers, turned her hand and let it fall into her palm. She curled her fingers, straightened them, and now she held the marble between thumb and index finger.

Billie emptied her sack of marbles into the circle. The Wisp, having won the right to first shot, bent forward with her ice-blue shooter, and with her thumb, delicate and long, her nail like a chip of ice, she thumped her shot at a bright red marble.

The shooter-marble tumbled in the air, dipped within the circle, made a little mushroom cloud of dirt as it struck the ground. It smacked the red marble. There was a scratchy streak of tiny lightning and Billie's marble blew apart. Fragments rattled about like scarlet hail.

"One," the Wisp said.

I looked at Billie. Her face was a wad of wrinkled flesh. In that moment she looked ancient and less confident or attractive than before; had the look of an unwrapped mummy.

Wisp moved around the circle, and her women followed. She found a spot where she could lean down and shoot again, the player having to shoot where the marble landed.

She thumped her shooter. Like a heat missile, it found a marble the color of a harvest moon. Another explosion and a rip of lightning, and the golden marble blew apart.

"Two," Wisp said.

Charlie said, "Aww."

When I looked at him, he was touching his face. A piece of the marble had cut his cheek. Blood ran out from under his fingers.

"Damn," he said.

"Shut up, little boy," said the Wisp.

The walls of the pit were no longer visible. Looking up, there was only the light on the pole. No stars. No moon. For a brief instant I saw something move up there, a crack of light, as if night's curtain was being parted by a nervous thespian taking a peek at the audience.

On the third shot, the Wisp broke another marble. It had been all the colors in a crayon box.

"Three," she said.

The Wisp's success finally turned sour. Her shooter rested in a really bad spot, and she had to reach pretty far to thump it. Her arm stretched slightly, or seemed to in that overhead pole light, but as she reached, the circle grew wider, and the marbles were farther away from her. She missed her shot.

Red Billie stepped forward, having kicked off her shoes to show hooves, like those of a goat. By this time, I would have expected no less.

"Dump yours," Billie said.

One of the women had collected all of the Wisp's marbles and put them back into her purse.

The Wisp nodded. The woman dumped the purse again. The marbles rolled into the ring and wobbled about. These two played their own way. Perhaps somewhere they had a kind of rule book tucked away.

Billie pushed her fingers together, cracked her knuckles. Her face looked like a drama mask, the one where the lips drooped. She eyed an icy-white marble, and thumped.

I can't describe the impact, because the sound of it brought me to my knees. I felt dazed and confused. My thoughts felt as if they returned to me by rickshaw. When they did, I saw that Billie had been shooting for a while. She had destroyed half a dozen of Wisp's marbles.

Billie was examining her possibilities for a shot. Billie took a deep breath. The corners of her lips turned up. She saw a shot, and it was easy to see that she felt she would make it.

And then I knew. I can't say how. But I knew. My mind was so wide open you could have driven a train to it. The world had shifted again.

It was as if the answers, or at least some of them, were in the air. Truthfully, I merely felt something. It's only now, much later, that I understand it more. A truth is first felt before realized.

If Billie won, the earth would grow warmer, and even the air would burn. But if Wisp won, Billie would return to where she had escaped from, and the weather would balance, or at least hold on. I still can't explain how I knew these things, but in that moment, I felt a cosmic truth move through me like a dose of laxative.

And the way it looked now, Billie was going to run the circle, destroy all the marbles.

Billie looked at me.

"You'll be all right. I can take you with me," she said.

Take me? Where?

I don't know what made me do it, but just as Billie was about to shoot, I looked down at the blue and green marble she was aiming for, and stepped into the circle.

I knew then I wasn't in East Texas anymore. I was floating in the black of space and there were marbles and fragments of marbles whirling in the void, some were like stars, others appeared to be worlds. They were bigger than marbles, but I was bigger than they were. I was a cosmic parade float hung in space and time.

And then I saw one of the marbles swirling closer. Or was I coming closer to it?

It was blue and green, and when it was about to pass me by, I saw it for what it really was.

Earth.

I grabbed it. I clung to it. Hugged it like a life preserver. I felt the heat slipping from my body like water running down a drain. The only thing that mattered to me then was clinging to that marble—clinging to Earth.

A moment later. A century later. I couldn't tell you for sure, my body felt as if it were being grated with sandpaper. Still, I clung. A piece of light cracked open the darkness.

It was the pole light. I was on my back. I had the marble—the Earth—clutched in my fist. My shoulders burned. My clothes were flecked with fragments of ice. There were hands on my shoulders.

Wisp's hands.

Wisp leaned down and looked at me. That sweet smell of hers wrapped me up like mummy bandages. She smiled. It was a shiny smile of straight white teeth, reminiscent of the sheen on a glass marble.

I knew then why my shoulders burned.

Frostbite. Wisp had yanked me out of the circle.

In the next moment, her minions were lifting me to my feet, holding me steady until I could stand on my own. The Wisp took the marble out of my hand, dropped it into her purse, which a minion was holding for her, wide open.

And there was Billie. A crooked smile on her face. She was crouched, the ebony shooter marble resting against her thumb and forefinger. The three headed dog growled at me and the stick Guardians stood up and were old folks again.

Billie had refused to take her shot.

She had refused to shoot with me in that circle. She had refused to destroy me and our planet. Was it respect for what I did, though I had no real idea what I was doing at the time? Or was she suddenly thinking about our ice-cream date, that moment when we had connected?

Slowly Billie stood up straight. The marble rolled from her hand and plopped onto the dirt outside the circle.

One of the Guardians snapped it up, bagged it in Billie's sack. When I looked into the circle, there were no longer marbles there, just perfectly round gray rocks.

The walls of the pit became apparent. The stars and the moon were bright in the heavens. The air had cooled. I could smell shit from the sewage radiating out of the wall of the pit.

The Wisp stared across the circle. Her minion women were gone. White cats had once again replaced them. They leaned against her legs and purred.

"You have defaulted, Billie," Wisp said. "You didn't shoot. You refused your shot."

Billie nodded.

She looked at me. The expression on her face was hard to identify. Disappointment? Desire? A bit of anger. A bit of admiration. It all seemed to be there in that look.

"It would have been less lonely for me," Billie said, looking at me.

"It really is time," the Wisp said.

Billie found the coins the Wisp had tossed at her, placed them over her eyes, and then, as if those coins were bifocals, she turned and trudged up the hill, followed now by three hounds and the Guardians. When she was at the peak of the hill, she threw up her hand and extended her middle finger.

Not long after, we heard that old truck starting up. One cyclopean light blazed momentarily over the hill, then swung around. There was a rumble and an engine cough, and then the truck, Billie, and her companions, were gone.

I turned to look at the Wisp. Her cats were gone. Her purse was gone. There was only her. She smiled at me. Her hair lifted on the cool wind and came apart like ripped-away shadows. Her clothes jumped away. She stood naked and beautiful and translucent in the glow of the pole light before she faded into thin air.

"Now that was the shit," Charlie said.

I went over and picked up Billie's shoes. They fell apart in my hands.

WE LEFT THE pit then. As you might guess, we were all done with marbles. I threw all of mine away the next day.

My brother grew up and went into the business of demolition. Knocking down old buildings, blowing holes in the earth for mining. He never lost that gleam in his eyes when something came apart and fell down.

Me. Environmentalist. I might as well have gone into trying to catch cicada farts in a jar, for all the good I've done.

You only get to dance so much, and then the music stops and the lights go out. My music had stopped and my lights were flickering.

But maybe, I had done something. Something big. I had to ask myself that now and again.

Had I saved the world? Part of the universe with an ice-cream date?

Well, not completely. Billie hadn't totally lost. She'd knocked some things out of whack. Outside my window on the land where great pines had been, there is only a stretch of sandy earth. No birds fly. No bees buzz. Outside the air is heavy and thick, like breathing wool socks. Inside, the central air only manages to skim the edge off the heat, but not remove it.

Somewhere, between the cracks, Billie waits. Thinking how she missed her shot, building her strength, wanting all the marbles, looking for a way to escape.

If she does, this time there'll be no stopping her. It occurs to me, the way we humans treat our Mother Ship, we may be responsible for the widening of those cracks. Giving her enough room to slip through.

Yet, I wonder if now and again, in moments of nostalgic reflection, Billie thinks pleasantly of me, and our one beautiful ice-cream date.

GORILLAS IN
THE YARD

BILL WENT OUT to pick up the newspaper and saw there was a gorilla in the yard, out under the oak by the side of the street. He was a big one, a silverback, and he was staring at Bill.

Grabbing the paper, Bill hustled himself back inside, and pulled back the curtain and looked out the window. The gorilla was no longer there.

After breakfast and coffee, Bill went to check again, and now the gorilla was back under the tree, but now his yard was full of gorillas. They were everywhere, thick as Johnson grass.

Bill called the police, told them his problem. Well, he didn't mention gorillas. Merely that he was having trespassers who looked dangerous. When the police arrived his true problem would be self-explanatory.

After what seemed forever he heard a car pull in the drive and then there was a knock at the door. He opened it cautiously. Two gorillas wearing police uniforms were at the door.

"You called?" said the largest of the two.

Bill was stunned for a moment, had nothing to say.

After a moment of waiting both police gorillas sighed.

"It's against the law to make a false call," the smaller gorilla cop said.

Bill looked past them. The yard was even more full of gorillas, big and small, young and old. They had spilled out into the street.

"I was reporting that my yard is full of...here are a lot of...people in my yard."

The cops turned and looked.

"So?" said the big cop.

"Well, I guess maybe I panicked."

"I guess you did," said the big cop.

"My mistake."

"Watch it," said the smaller gorilla. "You don't want a night in the hoosegow, watch it."

"Yes, sir," Bill said.

The two cops hitched up their gun belts and walked out to their car and backed out and drove away. The gorillas in the yard stood staring at Bill in the doorway.

Slowly, Bill closed the door.

He went into the kitchen and poured himself a stout shot of gin from the cabinet and drank it in one swallow.

Then he went to the bathroom.

"What's happening," he said aloud, then lifted his head and looked up and saw his face in the mirror.

He was a gorilla.

"Oh, okay," he said to the mirror. "Now it all makes sense."

BULLETS AND
FIRE

I HAD HIT THE little girl pretty hard, knocking her out, and maybe breaking something, messing her nose up for sure, but for me, it was worth it.

I sat at the table in the bar and smelled the sour beer and watched some drunks dance in the thin blue light from behind the bar. I was sitting with Juan and Billy, and Juan said to me, "You see our reasoning, you gonna get in with us, you got to show what you got, and fighting a guy, that shows you're some kind of tough, but hitting a girl like that, her what, twelve or thirteen, way you smoked her, now that shows you don't give a damn. That you ain't gonna back up if we say what needs to be done, you'll just do it. That's the way you get in with us, bro."

"Yeah," Billy said, "it makes you tough to fight a guy, brave maybe, but to hit someone like that you don't know, just some- one we pick on the street, and to savage her up like that, my man, that's where the real stones is cause it goes against... What is it I'm looking for here, Juan?"

"What mommy and daddy taught?" Juan said.

"Shit," Billy said, "my daddy hit me so much, I thought that was how you started and ended the day."

"Hell," Juan said. "I don't know. You guys want some more beers?"

I sat there and thought about what I had done. Just got out of the car when they told me, and there was this young girl on the sidewalk, a backpack on. I could still see how she looked at me, and I was just going to hit her once, you know, to knock her out, a good blow behind the ear, but nothing too savage, and then I got to thinking, these guys are going to take me in, they want to see something good. I did what had to be done. I beat her up pretty good and then I took her wallet. I started to take the backpack, but I couldn't figure on there being anything in it I'd want. But she had a little wallet that was on a wrist strap, and she ought not to have been wearing it like that, where it could be seen. Someone should have told her better.

Juan came back with some beers and a bowl of peanuts and we sat and drank some beer and ate the peanuts. I like peanuts.

I touched my shirt and felt something wet, and started to wipe it, but then I realized it was sticky. The girl's blood. I wiped it on my pants. It was dark in there, and wasn't anyone able to see much that mattered.

I watched some more couples get up and start dancing to the music on the jukebox, moving around in that blue light to a Smokey Robinson tune. My dad had always liked that song, about seconding and emotion. Billy said, "You know, even being a black man myself, I don't like it when they play that old nigger music. How about you, Tray, you like that old nigger shit?"

I did, and I didn't lie about it. "Yeah. I like soul fine. I like it a lot."

Billy shook his head. "I don't know, it's all kind of mellow and shit. I like a nigger can talk some shit, you know, rap it out."

"All sounds like a hammer beating on tin to me," I said. "This stuff, it's got some meat to it, cooked up good, plenty of steak, not just a bunch of fucking sizzle."

"He told you," Juan said. "One nigger to another. He told you good."

"Yeah, well, I guess nothing says we got to like the same stuff, but that's all Uncle Tom jive shit to me. A little too educated, not street enough."

I remembered what my brother Tim said to me once, "Don't let these neighborhood losers talk you down. Education hasn't got a color. Money, it's all green, and education, it gets you the money. It gets you something better than a long list of stickups and stolen money. You got to have pride, brother. Real pride. Like daddy had."

Daddy had worked some shit-ass jobs to help us make it. Mama died when we were young, fell down some stairs, drunk, broke her neck. Daddy, he didn't want us to end up drinking and fighting and getting our selves in trouble the same way. He tried to raise us right, told us to get an education. That's what Tim had done, got an education. He'd gone straight, done good. I loved Tim. He was a proud man. Well, boy, really. He wasn't much older than me. Twenty-two when it was all over for him. When I thought of him, what I thought of was a proud man, and I hated he was gone.

Me, tonight, I wasn't so proud. I'd beat that girl good and taken her little pink wallet from the pocket of her dress. A pink wallet that, when you opened it and folded it out, had some pictures, some odds and ends and five dollars.

"So, you guys, to get in with the gang, you do something like you had me do tonight," I said.

I knew the answer to that, but I was just making conversation.

"Yeah, well, we did one together," Juan said. He was Mexican and almost as dark-skinned as me, and that's pretty damn dark. All I could see of him really was his teeth in the blue light from behind the bar. He said, "We did a guy, me and Billy. Did him good."

"So you do a guy, and then you have me do a girl, and you tell me that's the way to do it? What about the rest of the gang? Any of them do like I did?"

"Sometimes, something like it," Billy said. "We had one boy who loved dogs, we had him shoot his own dog. Pet it on the head and open its mouth and stick a gun in there and shoot him. Shot came out that dog's ass, ain't kidding you. Went through that dog's ass and through a wall in the guy's house and knocked a lamp over."

"I think the bullet went in there and hit the end table," Juan said. "I think the table jarred and the lamp fell off."

"Whatever." Billy said. "You know what, that guy, he don't stay in the gang long. He shoots himself. Found him dead, laying over his dog's grave. That's no shit. Can you imagine that, getting that way with a dog? You got your gang, and your family, and everything else, that's just everything else, and that includes dogs or the fucking kitty."

"So I beat up a girl and this guy shot a dog, and you guys did a guy, so now we're all equal. That the way it works?"

Juan shook his head. "Well, you got to do something to get in, but we did something big, and that made us kind of lieutenants. You, you're just like a private. But you're in, man. You're in."

"Mostly," Billy said.

"The gang, they still got to have a look at you, and our main man, he's got to give you the okay."

"So what did you do?" I said. "I've heard around, but I was wondering I could get it from you."

Juan sipped his beer. "Sure," he said.

Billy said, "Way we did the guy was the thing."

"We may be small town, baby," Juan said, "one hundred thousand on the pop sign, but we got our turf and we got our ways, and we did that boy good."

"He was young, maybe about your age," Billy said. "Worked at a little corner grocery, was a grocery boy."

"What grocery?" I said.

"One around the corner, just a half block from here," Billy said. "Or was around the corner. Ain't no more. There's a big burn spot where it used to be."

Billy and Juan laughed and put their fists together.

"You mean the Clement Grocery?" I said.

"That's it," Billy said. "Guess it was, let me see, how long we been in the gang, Juan?"

"Three years come October," Juan said.

"I know the place," I said. "Course, I'm pretty new here now, but I used to live here, when I was younger, so I know the place. I didn't live far from here."

"Yeah," Billy said. "Where?"

"I don't remember exactly, but not far from the grocery. I used to go there. I don't remember where I lived though, not exactly. Not far from here, though."

"You ain't that old, you remember the grocery, you got to remember where you lived," Billy said.

"I could probably find the place, just don't remember the street number. You took me around, I could find it. But, man, I don't give a shit. This thing you did with the grocery boy. Tell me about that."

"We should have left that grocery and the kid alone," Juan said. "It was a good place to get stuff quick, and now we got to go way around just to buy some Cokes. But, man, what we did, it was tough. We was gonna be in the gang, you see, and the Headmaster, which is what he calls himself, ain't that something, Headmaster? Anyway, he says we got to do something on the witchy side, so we went and got a hammer and nails, and when we got there, the kid was working in the store, and the place was empty, just goddamn perfect."

"Perfect," Billy said.

"So we got hold of the kid and while Billy held him under the arms, I got my knee on his foot, and got a big ole nail I had brought, and with the hammer, I drove it right through his foot and nailed him to the floor."

"He screamed so loud I thought we was caught for sure," Billy said. "But nobody come running. They must have not heard him, or knew it was best to pretend they didn't."

"Fucker kicked me with his other leg, two, three times. And I just hammered the shit out of his leg and Billy couldn't hold him anymore, and he fell over, and then I kicked him a bit and he quit struggling, but he was plenty alive."

"That's what makes what happened next choice," Billy said. "We put some boxes of popcorn on him and then we set fire to the place."

"You forget, I nailed his other foot to the floor."

"That's right," Billy said. "You did."

"He was so weak from the kicking we had given him, and all the blood that had filled up his shoe and was running out over the top of it, he didn't know I was doing what I was doing until the nail went in."

"He really screamed that time," Billy said.

Juan nodded. "That's when we got the popcorn, bunch of other stuff and started the fire. We ran out of there and across the street and in the alley. We could hear that kid screaming across the street, but nobody came. A light went on in a couple windows of buildings where people lived upstairs, but nobody came."

"Fire took quick," Billy said. "We were so close, and if I'm lying, I'm dying, we could hear that popcorn popping and him still screaming. And then we saw the flames licking out of the open doorway, and then we saw the kid. He had got his feet free, probably tore the nails right through them, and he was crawling out the door, but he was all on fire. Looked like that *Fantastic Four* guy. What's his name, The Flame."

"The Human Torch," Juan said. "Don't you know nothing?"

"Yeah, him," Billy said. "Anyway, he didn't crawl far before that fire got him and then we finally did hear some sirens, and we got out of there."

"Last look I got of that kid, he wasn't nothing but a fucking charcoal stick," Juan said.

"That's what got us in the gang," Billy said. "And the Headmaster, he said it was a righteous piece of witchiness, and we was in, big time. You sweating, man?"

I nodded. "A little. I got a cold coming on."

"Well, don't give it to me," Juan said. "I can't stand no cold right now. I hate those things. So stay back some."

"This Headmaster, he got a name?" I asked.

"Everyone calls him Slick when they don't call him Headmaster," Billy said. "Shit, I don't even know what his real name is, or even if he's got one. He's maybe nearly twenty-six, twenty-seven years old. It don't matter none to you, though. You done done your thing to get in, and we're witnesses."

"Once you're in," Juan said, "no one much fucks with you. It's like a license to do what you want. Even the cops are afraid of us. They know we find out who they are and where they live, we might give them or their little straight families a visit."

"Gang is the only way to live around here," Billy said. "Get what you want, feel protected, you got to have the gang, cause without it, man. You're just on your own."

"Yeah," I said. "I know what that's like, being on my own. So, I'm in. I've done my deed and I'm proud of it, and I want in."

❧

WE WENT OUT of there and around the corner and walked a few blocks to where the gang had their headquarters. I thought about the streets and how dark they were and figured that fast as the streetlights got repaired, someone shot them out. Maybe the city was never going to repair them again. Maybe they had had enough.

Dad told me once, that if people don't care about where they live, the way they act, people they associate with, they get lost in the dark, can't find their way back cause there's no light left.

I had taken a pretty good step into the shadows tonight.

There was an old burnt-out building at the end of the block and we went past that and turned right and there was this old bowling alley. The sign for METRO BOWLING was still there, but there was nothing metro about the place. The outside smelled like urine and there was some glass framed in the doorway and it was cracked. When we got to the doorway, Juan beat on the frame with his fist, and after a moment the door opened slightly, and a young white woman with long black hair showed her face. Juan said something I wasn't listening for, and then we were inside. The girl turned and walked away and I saw she had an automatic in her hand, just hanging there like it was some kind of jewelry. Juan gave her a slap on the ass. She didn't even seem to notice.

The place stank. You could hear music in the back. Rap, and there was also some good hip-hop going, all of it kind of running together, and there were quite a few people in there. The floors where the bowling alley had been were still being used for bowling. Gang members, most of them dressed so you knew they were in a gang, flying their freak flags, were rolling balls down the wooden pathways, knocking down pins. The little pin machine was working just fine and it picked up the pins and carried them away and reset them. The alleys were no longer shiny and there were little nicks in the wood here and there and splinters stuck up in places as if the floor was offering toothpicks.

In front of the bowling alleys were racks for shoes, but there weren't any shoes in them. Some of the gang members were wearing bowling shoes, and some weren't. The clack and clatter of the balls as the machine puked them up and slammed them together made my ears hurt. Over near the far wall a big black guy had this Asian girl shoved up against the wall, so that both her palms were on it. She had her ass to him and her pants were down and so were his. What they were doing wouldn't pass for bowling, though balls were involved.

"That there is B. G. He's slamming him some nook," Billy said.

"I kind of figured that's what was going on," I said.

We went past them and around a corner and into a back room. There was a desk there, and a guy that looked older than the others was sitting behind the table and he had a big bottle of Jack Daniels in front of him. He was a white guy with some other blood in him, maybe black, maybe all kinds of things, and he was sitting there looking at me with the coldest black eyes I've ever seen. They looked like the twin barrels of shotguns. He grinned at Billy and Juan and showed me some grillwork on his teeth, and the grillwork was silver and shiny and had what looked like diamond in them. For all I knew they were paste or glass.

On his right side was a young white girl who wasn't bad looking except for a long scar on her cheek, and on her right hand side was a guy who looked as if he might like to eat me and spit me out. On Grillwork's left was a husky looking Hispanic guy with eyes so narrow they looked like slits.

"So, you got a wayward soldier," Grillwork said.

"That's right, and we known him now a couple weeks, and he's been wanting in, talking to us, walking around with us some, and he did some righteous business tonight," Juan said.

"No shit," Grillwork said. "What'd he do?"

Billy told him and Grillwork nodded like he had just been told I had invented time travel.

"That's good," Grillwork said. "That's real good. So you wanting in, huh?"

I nodded. "Yeah. I want in. I thought I was in. I did what was asked."

"Well, that's a beginning," Grillwork said. "You showed some stones doing something like that."

I didn't think it had taken that much in the way of stones. She was a kid, something a high wind could knock over.

"Sit the fuck down, man," Grillwork said. "What's your name?"

I sat in the chair in front of the table and told him my name.

"What you want in for?" Grillwork asked.

"I don't have a family. It's tough to make it in this town. Jobs bore me."

"All right, all right," Grillwork nodded. "You got to understand some things. You come in, you got to stay in. You want to get out, well, you get out all right, but all the way and pretty goddamn final. No, final. Not pretty final. Final. Savvy?"

I nodded.

"You get in, we got work of our own, but it's different. You do stuff that makes money by taking other people's money. We sell some chemicals, man. Got our own lab."

"Meth?" I said.

"Oh, yeah. Now and again, we deal in some weed and some pussy, but mostly we got the meth. You pick dough up on the side, that's yours, but not by selling chemicals, man. The mind-mixer business, that's all ours, and I find you dipping your dick into that, you'll wind up in a ditch with flies on your face. Got me?"

I nodded again.

"You can't run your own string of whores, lessen' you hook up with some gal will pull the train for the club, then go out there and lube some johns. You got that understood?"

"I do."

"All right, the things on the side, you can do what you want to the citizens, you know. I don't care you rob them or rape them or whatever, but you get caught and dragged downtown, not a thing we can do. But there is this. Cops, on our turf, which is about twelve blocks, almost square, cause it's got an old park in it that fucks up the square thing, makes it like a square with an addition—"

"Who gives a shit," the girl next to him said. "Just tell him what you're gonna tell him."

Grillwork looked at her, and she looked back. Her eyes were pretty damn cold too.

He looked back at me, said, "Those twelve blocks, the park, that's ours… But these cops, they pretty much leave us alone, cause when they don't, we got a way of not liking it, a way of tracking them down. It's been done, man."

I nodded.

Juan was chewing gum now, and I could hear him popping it, and I felt something cold against the back of my neck. I turned. Juan had a nine poking against my neck and he was grinning and chewing his gum.

"That there," Grillwork said, "that was in case you didn't have all the right answers. Like maybe you wanted to argue a point."

"No argument," I said, turning back to face Grillwork. "I take it you're the one called Headmaster, since you're the one laying out the ground rules."

Juan took the nine out of my neck.

"No. You don't talk to Headmaster about this shit. I'm one of his lieutenants. You can call me Hummy."

"All right," I said. It was a curious name, some nickname, and I wondered about it, but I didn't really care enough to ask.

"You frisked him?" Hummy said to Juan and Billy.

"Earlier tonight," Juan said. "He ain't packing nothing but a dick and balls."

"All right," Hummy said. "Let me ask."

I didn't know what that meant, and I didn't ask who he wanted to ask, and what he wanted to ask them about. I found the best thing was just to be quiet and everyone filled things in for themselves. You said too much, then you gave them room for varied interpretation. You didn't say anything, they usually filled it up with what they wanted.

Hummy got up and went away. He was gone for a good while. When he came back, he jerked a thumb toward the door he had gone through, and we went through it, along a narrow hall by a bathroom with an open door where a guy that was maybe three hundred pounds, sat on a sagging toilet and made noises like he was trying to pass a water buffalo, antlers and all. The hallway was full of stink.

"Close the fucking door," Juan said, as we went by. "Goddamn Rhino, who wants to smell that shit, or see you delivering it. Close the fucking door."

Rhino didn't reach out and close the door, and we just kept going along the hallway. At the end of the hall was another door and this one was a thick door that looked as if it had been added recently. Billy knocked, and a voice said, "Come in," and we went inside.

It was a big stinking room and it was full of weapons. All kinds of things. I saw an AK-47 and some automatic pistols, small and large, and there were machetes and gas cans all over the place. There were some net bags hanging from the ceiling, and in the bags were human heads, and they were the source of the smell. They were jacking with me, trying to see what I was made of, how scared I was.

Way I felt, scared was not on the agenda. I was way past scared and had leveled out into a steady feeling of numbness. My body was numb, my mind was numb, my soul was numb. The world to me was nothing more than one big numb ball of grief.

I could cope with it because of the sensei I had had when I moved away from here, some years back. I had enjoyed the training so much I almost didn't move back. It almost made me mellow.

Almost.

But I had the demon inside, and I had left sensei and what he had taught me. I wasn't trying to use martial arts to learn to live my life without violence, with confidence and harmony, way he taught me. I wanted to use it to hurt someone, the thing I wasn't supposed to do. I had learned nothing that really mattered from my sensei and I knew it and it made me feel a little ill.

There was a guy in the back, and I took him for the Headmaster, way he carried himself, and there were some guys with him. Juan and Billy left me looking at the heads in the bags, and went over to the guy and talked with him. I could hear them whispering, looking back at me from time to time, so I knew I was the subject.

This went on for awhile, and I looked around and saw all the guns and the ammunition; all the representatives of power. Straight people, they tell you they like guns because they like to shoot targets, but it's the power, man, that's what it is and all it is. It's the big dick spurting lead cum all over the place. You can call it our rights or you can call it target practice or you can call it personal protection, but it's about power, and I wanted power, and I wanted a gun just like everyone else. Martial arts, Shen Chuan, it gave me power, but a gun, that was the ultimate power.

I put that all out of my mind as the crowd back there broke off and I got a really good look at the guy they were surrounding. He was a little blonde guy with a burr hair cut and he came strutting around one of the racks of weapons. He was covered in weapons himself. He had holsters filled with automatics all over him, and his eyes darted from side to side. He was as paranoid as a staked goat at a Fourth of July picnic. And like the goat, just because he was paranoid didn't mean they weren't out to get him.

"You're the Headmaster," I said.

"They call me that," he said, and he didn't offer me his hand when I offered mine. I put my hand away, feeling as if I had offered him a fish. He looked me up and down. He was short, but he was broad and he had legs like tree trunks. They were supported on little feet in little black boots with silver tips; with those things he could kick a cockroach to death in a corner of the room.

"I got some word you done some things," he said.

"You mean the girl?" I said.

"I mean the girl. You hit her good?"

"Yeah. I broke her little nose."

"That shows you got some grit. I'm not saying it takes anything to beat up a little girl, but I'm telling you it takes balls to do it."

I had already heard this from his guys, but I didn't say anything.

"We need guys like you, can follow orders, do what needs to be done."

I said, "Okay."

"Those heads you're looking at," Headmaster said. "They strayed. They started trying to hustle their own business, our drug business and their piece wasn't enough. They wanted more. They wanted to sell a little pussy on the side. The pussy is in the river, these guys, well, you see what's left of them."

"Run a pretty tight ship," I said.

Headmaster laughed. "That I do. What we got to do, man, is we still got some things to try with you."

"Try with me?"

"Yeah," Headmaster said, "come back here."

There was another room beyond this one and I let the Headmaster lead me back there, and when he did, his guys followed me in. Juan hit me a hard one behind the head and made my sight go black, and then my vision jumped back with white dots in it, and I staggered a little. Then someone I didn't see, kicked me up under the butt from behind and got me in the balls.

I swung out and hit someone, and then the Headmaster, he was on me, slamming one in my stomach, and I guess instinct took over, because I kicked him in the groin and stepped forward, popped my palm against the side of his head and he went down.

I whirled then, and tried to hit another guy with a jab, but he slipped it, and I caught one under the belly. I jammed an elbow into the back of his neck as he stooped, and he grunted, and I slapped my hands over his ears, and he screamed and turned away. I kicked out at Billy's knee, and he screamed. I hit Juan in the throat and he dropped, and I smelled shit on the air.

I hit another one of the guys with a knee to the inside of his leg, and that dropped him. I poked my fingers in another guy's eyes, not enough to blind him, but enough to make him less interested in kicking my butt.

And then the Headmaster yelled, "That's it, that's enough."

He got up holding his nuts with one hand, grinning at me, holding his other hand up in a stop motion.

"All right," he said. "All right, you got what it takes."

I wiped blood off my mouth.

"We got to see you can take it same as dish it out, and man, you can dish it out. Can you teach that chop socky to the rest of us?"

"So this was a test?" I said.

"Big time," Headmaster said, and then he frowned and looked at Juan. "Man, you shit your pants?"

Juan nodded.

"Go get some fresh drawers," Headmaster said. "Damn, Juan, he didn't hit you in the belly."

"When you get hit hard, throat, any kind of place," I said, "you're carrying a load, you'll drop it."

"Ain't that something," Headmaster said. "I've seen and smelled them do it when they're shot, but I didn't know about the hitting. That's some shit you got there."

"No," I said. "It's Juan that's got the shit."

Everyone, except Juan, who was waddling out of the room, laughed.

I GOT RESPECT when everyone in the bowling alley heard about how I had fought, though truth was, had they fought back a little more persistent, martial arts training or not, I would have been toast. They weren't willing enough. Me, I thought I was in for it, like maybe I was just a test for them, way the girl was supposed to be for me, so I was fighting back big time. Them, they were just testing. I was glad they quit when they did, cause I felt like my balls were trying to crawl out of my asshole from that kick I got.

Anyway, I was in.

So, I guess a week goes by, and I'm doing some little things, like I had to break a guy's leg to get some money that was owed for something or another the gang had going. I don't know what. I didn't ask. I didn't care. I just stomped the side of his knee with my foot and it cracked like a fruit jar tossed on the sidewalk and he gave up the money. He was ready to give anything up. I asked him to suck my dick and lick my nuts, he'd have done it. Anything to keep me from breaking his other knee.

Another week and they gave me permission to go in the gun room, cause you had to have one of the main guys open it with a key, and you had to have permission to go in. They took me in there, Headmaster, Billy, and Juan. They gave me a gun, or rather they told me to pick anything I wanted. I picked an automatic pistol out of the pile, and I pulled an AK-47 off the rack. I got some ammunition. Clips for the AK-47 and the automatic pistol. I should have got more clips, but I was nervous. I ended up with an extra load for the AK-47, one for the automatic.

"You're gonna need that shit," Headmaster said. "Things we got going. We got a little gang on the other side, bunch of spicks—"

"Hey," Juan said.

"Not our spicks," Headmaster said, and then he looked right at Juan, "and thing is, I don't care to please you anyway, beaner. I'm the man here, and that makes you the boy, you got me, you fucking pepper gut?"

Juan made a face that looked as if he had just been handed a dead rat to eat. He had been using that kind of talk all along, but it had caught him funny going right at him and mad like that.

Headmaster leaned forward till his nose was almost on Juan's. "I said, you got me?"

Juan nodded. "Sure, man. I got you. No hard feelings."

"If there is, you'll live with them," Headmaster said. He turned to me then, said, "We're gonna have to cut down on them spicks from out and away. I thought you ought to get your shot to get some blood in, you know. Something serious, not poking some little girl in the nose or breaking a leg. Something serious."

"All right," I said. "What's the plan?"

"We're gonna get you and Juan and Billy to saddle up, go over there and take a little cruise-by, spread some lead. These guys, they got them a little meth thing going, and that's our finance, baby, and I don't want them sucking any of our chocolate."

"A drive-by?" I said.

"That's what I said, only more than that, really. We're gonna drive by, and then when they think it's over, we're gonna come back on them."

"They'll be ready," Billy said.

"What about civilians?" I said.

"Hell," Headmaster said. "There ain't no civilians. They're the same as that girl you popped, the shit these guys nailed and burned to get in the gang. There's us and there's them. You pop a few wives, girlfriends or kids, that's the price of doing business, price of fucking on turf ain't yours."

"I got you," I said.

Headmaster nodded, said, "You boys get what you need?"

Billy said, "We got guns, and we got these."

He grabbed his loose pants where his balls were, and acted like he was shaking them.

🌀

I SAID I was going to the can, and I reluctantly laid the rifle back in the rack, said, "Give me a minute to deliver my last meal," and I went out of the gun room and into the little bathroom off to the side. It was cleaner than the big bathroom right next to the lanes. And the big fuck wasn't in there stinking it up. I mean, you wouldn't want to eat off the floor or nothing, but compared to the other one, it was like it had just been sanitized. The other, it never got cleaned, smelled bad, and the toilets all had dark shit rings inside of them. There were boogers on the wall and things written in pen and pencil, blood and snot, and maybe even shit. You went in there, you might step on a needle, a rubber, or find some guy bending a girl over the sink, doing their business, needling horse—enough to call it a Clydesdale.

I went in and put the lid down on the toilet and sat there and tried to catch my breath. I was in. I belonged to the gang. It's what I wanted.

I took out the automatic, a nine, and looked at it, felt cold sweat trickle down from my hairline and run along my face and drip off my chin. I laid the automatic on my knee. I thought about my brother. I thought about my father. My father, he never got over it. Killed himself. Shot himself.

My brother, in that store, his feet nailed to the floor, and those two jackasses having set a fire just so they could be in a club, a gang. And now here I was having punched a little girl in the face and taken out a guy's knee, about to do some real damage. Of course, my reasons for being here were different. I didn't want to be a member because I respected them, but because I didn't. I hated them. Especially Juan and Billy, and then the head guy. I wanted what my sensei said was useless to have, vengeance.

After my brother was dead, and we had moved away, my dad had tried to get it together, but couldn't. He put a gun in his mouth and blew his worries asunder. I was mad at him, hated him for awhile, but then I got over it, because I realized how hard it was to carry on. I was doing the same thing, but in a slightly different manner. Throwing it away. But unlike Dad, it wouldn't just be me and some blood on the living room floor. There were some guys I was gonna flush with me.

If I got out all right, that was good, but I knew this: I was going to make my mark for Dad and for my brother. They were gonna get some blowback on that business they done.

I picked up the automatic and laid it on the sink and lifted the lid and took a piss. I zipped up and washed my face and got the automatic and stuck it in my waist band and went out of there. When I came back into the gun room, the door still open, Juan looked at me kind of funny, said, "Man, we thought you fell in."

"I was seriously packing," I said.

I picked up the AK-47. I had shot one before. I had learned a lot about guns from my sensei, the one who told me that guns are about romance and power more than they are about self-defense or constitutional amendments. He also said, "Boys like their toys, the more dangerous and explosive the better."

He said he liked them too and went to bed at night bothered by it.

I went to bed at night bothered by everything. I didn't see my brother die, but I could imagine how horrible it was. Him crawling and that fire eating at him and that goddamn popcorn popping, and across the way, those two fucks laughing, getting a kick out of it all.

I looked at Headmaster and Juan and Billy, and I thought, these three, they're the main guys I want. I could just do it now. I could open up and they wouldn't know shit from wild honey, and then it would be over.

But I didn't want to do that. I wanted more than that, and though I was willing to give what it took to get even, I preferred the opportunity to stay alive. Didn't happen, didn't happen.

I was ready to play either way.

"What now?" I said.

"I'm thinking," Headmaster said, "we should probably arm a couple of the other guys, take them with you. It's best not to take a whole wad. You do that, you're more likely to end up butt fucking one another. Too many, that's a fucking crowd. A small hit force, that's the way to go."

"You going?" I asked.

The Headmaster looked at me as if I had asked if I could stick my finger up his ass and fish for shit.

"No. You're going. You and Juan and Billy, maybe a couple of others. I go when I want and if I want. You aren't questioning my chops, are you?"

"No," I said. "I was just wondering."

"I'll do the wondering for both of us, blood."

"All right," I said.

"Damn right, it's all right. Juan, you go out there and pick you some wham-bang-dangers, two of them, and then let's get them fixed with some tools and some lead, and then you guys, I'll lay it out to you. The whole shebang of a plan."

One way, I thought, one easy way, is I isolate Juan and Billy, take them out. That would be the good way, the smart way. But it wasn't satisfying to me, not even by a little bit. I imagined Tim squirming with his feet nailed to the floor screaming, the unbearable heat, the flames licking, him ripping his feet apart to get loose.

While I was doing this, Juan went out of the room. I thought, shit, I got to get it together and keep it together. Here I am in my head and outside my head the world is moving on.

"I'll go with him," I said.

And I was out of the door and going down the hall, could see Juan's back as he turned the corner into the room where I had met the guy I thought was the Headmaster. I was almost to the door when I heard Headmaster yell at me.

"Hey, I tell you to go anywhere?"

I didn't look back, said, "What's it matter?"

"It matters cause I say so," Headmaster said, in that way of his that lets you know even when it isn't important, he wants you to know he's the swinging dick of the operation.

I looked in the room, and there behind the desk was Hummy, guy I thought originally was the Headmaster, and was probably his replacement. One day, the Headmaster would look south and a bullet would come from the north, probably out of Hummy's gun.

Or that's the way it might have gone over had I not decided to change everyone's plans. I was the fucking fly in the ointment, the crab in the ass. I was gonna mess things up worse than a politician.

Headmaster yelled at me again, told me to stop. I shifted the AK-47 to my left hand and pulled out the automatic and turned and looked at him and Billy, and then I fired. I was a good shot, and I was proud of that, because my first shot caught Headmaster between the eyes, and he went down so fast it was impossible to believe it. Billy, blood and brains from Headmaster splattered across his cheek, tried to pull up the rifle he had in his hand, but I shot him through the heart before he got it lifted, and then I was in the room with Hummy by the time Billy hit the floor.

Juan had already gone through and was at the far door, and he had turned, drawn the automatic he had, and now there were guns coming out from under coats and out of pockets, and from behind the desk. Juan fired twice and the shots slammed into the door frame and I shot at him once, but missed, and then I stuck the pistol in my belt, almost casual like, switched the AK-47 to my right hand, lifted it firing, bullets going all over the place, crazy like.

I hit a couple of the guys and one of the girls, and they did a kind of hop and a twist, like they were grooving at a party, and then there was blood everywhere and people were going down. I felt something hot in my side and I shot Hummy a bunch of times, and then I was walking, just straight out, not thinking about anything but killing, feeling the fire in my side, but not thinking much of it. I walked right through, whipping the weapon left and right, mowing flesh.

As I reached the far open door, I saw they were coming for me, maybe twenty guys, couple of the girls, but there were some holding back. The ones coming had weapons, all hand guns, and when they opened up the world went crazy and my ears went deaf and began to ring. And I don't remember it all, but the bullets cut all around me and one went through my left arm and it hurt like hell, and the next thing I know it's hanging at my side, and I got the AK-47 lifted, pushed up against my hip, and I'm rockin' and rollin' and bodies are jumping. I'm having a better day than they are. Probably because they couldn't hit an elephant in the ass at ten paces with a tossed bar stool, even spraying. I'm like the luckiest motherfucker that ever squatted to shit over a pair of shoes, cause except for that one hit, I'm doing good. It's like I was fucking charmed.

I saw my bullets jerk B.G. and Rhino around and take them apart, and a lot of the others, they went down too.

I started walking sideways, along the wall, and I came to the counter where the shoes used to be given out, slid behind that. I kept firing and their shots kept coming and the wood on the counter jumped and splintered and the shoe racks behind me came apart, and I wasn't hit again. I just kept pushing the AK-47 up against me, firing.

I was almost to the door, and I could see that the bodies were heaped. And there was that damn Juan, still alive, and I pulled the trigger on the AK-47 again, but it was empty, and I remembered that I had picked up another clip, but couldn't load it with only one hand working, so I dropped the AK-47 and pulled the pistol and fired one shot and didn't hit anyone, heard the lead bounce off a bowling ball, and then I was at the door. I ran out of there, my arm dangling at my side like a puppet that had lost a string.

∾

IT WAS COOL outside for a change and there was a thin rain blowing in my face as I ran. I felt a little dizzy, but for the most part things were all right, but the colors of the night, lit up by distant lights, were mostly shades of black and gray. I was glad there were no streetlights, because I got behind a parked car and dropped behind it and laid on my belly and looked under it and down the street at the bowling alley. As I was laying there, I felt the AK-47 clip sticking in my stomach, and I lifted up and pulled it out of my belt and left it on the concrete. I touched my pocket. The extra load for the automatic was gone. It must have fallen out of my pocket. I looked around under the car for it, and then I saw beneath the car that it was lying in the street between the car and the bowling alley. I hadn't stuck it in good, and it had gotten bumped out. I felt like an idiot.

After awhile the door opened a crack, and a head poked out, and then another, and then one other. They looked my direction first, then the other direction. I wondered how many were still in there. I had pretty much wiped out the crop of the gang, scared the shit out of the others. Only thing I hadn't done was blow up their meth lab, which was in a little house down the street from the bowling alley. There were some of the gang there, but, way I felt, they were going to get away. Maybe I'd come back and get them too, just for the hell of it. Kill them all and blow the place up and shit in the ashes.

I kept watching, and then I saw the heads move, and then the guys were out in the street. And then another guy showed, and then a girl. She had long black hair, and I even noted she had a good figure, and thought that was funny. Here I am, lying on the ground, people wanting to kill me, one of them that girl, and I'm taking note of her tits and ass.

They all had guns. Hand guns. I could see them moving them around in the dark. Altogether, there were five of them. Three of them broke off and went the opposite way, and then the other two, Juan, limping a little, and the girl, started my way. They saw the clip I had dropped, and Juan stopped and bent down and picked it up.

They looked back for the others, but they had long gone. At least it was just these two knew which direction I had gone.

It was all I could do to make myself move. The concrete felt good and cool. I lifted up on my hands and knees, and when I did, I could hear the sticky blood that had run out of me make a Velcro sound; it had dried enough to stick me to the cement. I realized then that I hadn't been as charmed as I thought. I had been hit a couple of times, but not anywhere too bad, or so I hoped. I did feel a little light headed.

I backed on hands and knees a few paces, then backed into an alley and hoped it wasn't a dead end. It wasn't. I went along it and tried not to breathe too heavy or too loud. I looked up. The sky was just a kind of slick glow. There were no lights where I was, but the city lights slicked the sky like that and gave it this gauzy look. I thought of where I had lived when Dad and me moved away from here. There you could see the sky and at night you could hear crickets and frogs and there were tall trees.

I went over a grating, and when I did steam came out of it like devil's breath, and I jumped a little. I went on and around a corner, and then I started feeling as if someone had opened up a spigot in my heel and the soul of me was running out of it.

I stopped and leaned against the alley wall and moved my shirt back and looked at where I had been hit in the side, realized it was a bad hit, worse than I thought. The other wounds weren't so bad, but they were all bleeding, and I felt as if there was something tunneling around inside of me.

I could hear Juan and that girl coming. I thought about running, but my body wasn't up for it. They knew where I was, and it was a matter of time before they caught up with me. I looked around, saw some garbage cans by some metal stairs. I made my way there and got behind the cans and eased over behind the stairs and watched between the garbage cans as Juan turned the corner, and then the girl.

They spread out, maybe trying to act like movies they'd seen, where the cops search rooms. But this was a big ass room, this wide spot in the alley, and when she went left, Juan came along the wall, and then he stopped as his arm brushed the bricks. He put out his hand and rubbed the wall, and I knew he had found my blood there.

He turned and looked toward the trashcans, and when he did, he saw me between those cans. I knew it. I could tell. I lifted the gun and fired and it hit him and he went down and his pistol skittered across the alley.

Bullets banged around the cans and along the stairs and a light went on somewhere above me, and the girl, panicking, fired at the lighted window. I heard glass crash and then someone smartly turned out the light. I stood up and kicked the trash cans over and came out blazing. I fired twice and both shots missed. She fired and hit me in the shoulder, and this one was solid, not just passing through. It knocked me down and I felt as if all the wind was out of me. I couldn't believe how hard I had been hit.

I lay on my back and she came toward me. She was smiling. She had a revolver. She pointed it at me. She straddled me and pulled the trigger. And it clicked empty. She had shot at me in the bowling alley, maybe one of her shots had hit me, but now, she was all used up.

I grinned and lifted the pistol and shot her in between the legs.

She seemed to jump backwards and then she hit the ground on her back, made a noise like someone trying to squeeze out a silent fart.

I could hardly get up, but I did. I staggered over to her and looked down at her. She looked young. Not a whole lot older than the girl I had punched.

"Shit," I said.

She quit moving, except for one leg that wiggled a moment, then quit.

I went over to Juan. He was breathing heavy. He had his hands on his belly. I got down on my knees by him.

I said, "That boy, whose feet you nailed to the floor. That was my brother. My father committed suicide over it. I don't like you or any of your gang. I'm glad you hurt bad."

He tried to say something, but he couldn't. All of his air was being used to stay alive.

"I just wanted you to know how much I hate you. You fucked up my life, and this sure fucks up yours. And I got Billy too. And the Headmaster, and a bunch of you fucks. You had a plastic Jesus in your pocket, I'd snap it in half. That's how much I hate you. How you feeling, Juan?"

Juan looked at me, and his mouth came open, like a fish on a dock, hoping for water.

"I could kill you," I said. "Make it stop hurting. But, I don't want to."

I stayed there on my knees until blood came out of his mouth and the smell of it and the shit in his pants became too strong for me to take. Then I stood up and looked at him. It was all I could do to stand up, and I should have moved on, maybe found a doctor. But I didn't want to miss a second of it.

I watched until he was dead and his eyes were as flat and lifeless as a teddy bear's.

I went away then, moving slow, but moving. I walked until I came to some lights, and down the way I could hear traffic, and I could see people. People who weren't in gangs. People with lives. People, many of which would live long and die of old age and have families. Stuff I wouldn't know about.

I leaned against a brick wall, under a street light. The first I had come to since leaving the bowling alley. I looked up and watched bugs swarm around the light. They didn't know they had short lives and didn't care. They just did what they did and had no thoughts about it.

I grinned at them.

I took the little girl's wallet out of my back pocket and opened it. It had five dollars in it. I looked through it and found her picture, and found a picture of her with a man, woman, and little boy. Her family, I figured. I found a little card behind a plastic window that had her address on it. It said: RETURN TO, and then there was the address. I knew that address, the general locale. It wasn't far from where I had lived as a kid, back when Dad owned the store and he and my brother worked there, and I hung out there from time to time. On that day my brother was murdered, set on fire, I had been at a theater down the street, watching a movie. It was a good movie, and now, because of my brother's death, I couldn't think of that movie without feeling a little sick, and I couldn't think of it now. I thought about the girl again, and that was almost as bad as thinking about my brother or my father.

I thought about her nose. I hoped she could fix it, or maybe it wasn't broken too badly and would heal all right. I thought about the guy whose knee I had taken out for the lack of payment to the Headmaster. I didn't really care about him. He was in bed with the skunks, so he got stink all over himself before I did anything to him. He had it coming. Maybe he didn't have it coming from me, not really, but he had it coming, and I didn't feel all that bad about him. I didn't feel bad about any of the gang. I just wished I had killed them all.

I read the address in the wallet again. I knew where that was. I started walking.

❧

I STUCK THE automatic under my shirt and went along the back streets as much as possible. When I got on a main street, people began to pull back from me, seeing all the blood, way my face looked. I saw it myself, reflected in a store window. I looked like a ghost who had seen a ghost. The shock was wearing off. I was really starting to hurt.

I probably didn't have long before the police got me, before people on the street called about this blood-covered guy.

I took a turn at the corner, and started walking as fast as I could. I felt as if most of what was left of me was turning to heat and going out the top of my head. I went along until I got to the back alleys, and then I darted in, and I went through them. I remembered these alleys like I had been here yesterday, though it had been a few years. I remembered them well because I had played here. I went down them and along them, and somewhere back behind me I heard sirens, wondered if they were for me.

I finally went down an alley so narrow I had to turn sideways to get down it. It opened up into a fairly well lit street. I got the girl's wallet out again and looked at the address. I was on the right street, and I memorized the number and put the wallet away and walked along the street until I found the number that fit the one on her little card in the wallet.

There was a series of stone steps that went up to a landing and there was a door there, and above it was the number. I climbed up to the top step, and that was about it. I sat down suddenly and leaned back so that my ass was on the stoop and my legs were hanging off on the top step. I could hardly feel that step. My legs seemed to be coming loose of me and sinking into something like quicksand. I had to take a look at them to make sure they were still attached. When I saw they were, I sort of laughed, because I couldn't feel them. I pulled myself up more with my hands and put my back at an angle against one of the concrete rails that lined the steps on both sides.

I took out the wallet and I put both my hands over it and put the wallet up against my stomach. I tried to put it some place where blood wouldn't get on it, but there wasn't any place. I realized now that the warm wetness I was feeling in the seat of my pants was blood running down from my wounds and into my underwear. I hated they would find me like that.

I sat there and thought about my dad and my brother and I thought about what my sensei had said about you can't correct what's done, and if you try, you won't feel any better. He was right. You can't correct what's been done. But I did feel better.

I felt bad about the girl though, but I felt good about all those dead fucks being dead. I felt real good.

I felt around in my shirt, and my hand was like a catcher's mitt trying to pick up a needle. I finally found my ballpoint and I opened the girl's wallet, which was bloody, and I pinched out the little card with her address on it, and I wrote the best I could: I'M SORRY. REALLY, I AM.

I laid the wallet on my knee, got out my own wallet. I had three hundred and twenty-five dollars in there. I put the money from my wallet in her wallet, along with her five. I turned and looked at the door. I didn't know if I could make it. There was a mailbox by the door, a black metal thing, and I wanted to get up and put the wallet in that, but I didn't know if I could.

I thought about it awhile, and finally I got some kind of strength, and pulled myself up along the concrete railing, and when I got up, it was like my legs and feet came back, and I made it to the mailbox, opened it and put her wallet in there with the card I had written on.

Then that was it. I fell down along the wall and lay on my face. I thought about all manner of things. I thought of my brother and my father, but the funny thing was I began to think about my sensei. I was on the mat and I was moving along the mat. And I was practicing in the air. Not traditional kata, because we didn't do that. But I was practicing, punching, kicking, swinging my elbows, jerking up my knees. It felt good, and I could see my sensei out of the corner of my eye. I couldn't make out if he was pleased or angry, but I was glad he was there.

The sirens grew louder.

I thought of bullets and fire, and a deep pit full of darkness. I wished I could see the stars.

CHARLIE THE
BARBER

CHARLIE RICHARDS, WHO thought of himself as a better than average barber, was lean and bright-eyed with a thin smile, his hair showing gray at the temples. He loved to cut hair and he loved that his daughter Mildred, Millie to most, worked with him. They were the only father and daughter barber team he knew of, and he was proud of that. He was also glad that she lived at home with him and her mother, Connie, at least for now.

Next year she was off to the big city, Dallas. Graduated high school a couple years back, hung around, cut hair, but now she was planning to attend some kind of beauty college where she could learn to cut women's hair as well. Planned to learn cosmetology too. Claimed when she finished schooling she could either fix a woman up for a night out, or spruce up a dead woman for a mortuary production. Charlie had no doubt that would be true. Millie learned quickly and was a hard worker.

Charlie snapped the towel loose from where it rested on his customer's neck, applied talc so liberally that particles floated in the air like an early morning mist. As the man stood up and unlimbered his wallet from his back pocket and paid his bill, Charlie called out, "Next."

Outside of the customer Millie was finishing up in her chair, there were only two others left. Mr. Weaver, a retired postal worker who looked as if he was born to be old, and a teenage boy, Billy Thompson, a young man known as a fine quarterback and a good kid.

As Charlie waited for his next customer to settle into the chair, Charlie glanced at Millie. She was tall and lean and pretty with dark hair and dark eyes, like her mother. She was hard at work on her customer's mop, an eleven year old boy reading a comic book and chewing a mouthful of bubble gum.

Outside the fall wind whistled. Leaves blew across from the park and rattled against the wide front window and the smaller windows behind the waiting chairs with a sound like someone wadding cellophane. It made Charlie feel nostalgic. It was that kind of day when he had his first date with Connie, many years before the war, back when he was a young barber and she worked as a secretary at a used car lot.

Their first date was a picnic in the park, but the fall leaves blew so furiously that day, they had to go to his barbershop to escape them. That shop had been smaller than the current one, a place he shared with a tire repair business. He had a corner, more or less, and he could hear the hydraulic car racks lifting and dropping, hoisting cars in and out of the pit where the tires were taken off, replaced, rotated.

In the corner of the shop, their hamburgers and colas resting on top of the magazine table, they ate, and finally, surprising to both of them, they had kissed. The moment their lips parted, they both knew. It was like a movie. Something like that happened, you didn't fight it. They had been inseparable ever since.

Except for the war.

He didn't like to think about the war. His quick smile went away then. It was better to not think on it too much.

Millie finished with the kid, and he stood up from the chair and fished a dollar from his pocket and paid her, then he was out, passing outside the big window of the shop like a wind-blown specter.

Charlie glanced at the clock. It was near five. He would cut Billy's hair, and Millie would cut Old Man Weaver's white ring of fuzz, and that would be it for the day.

Millie patted the back of her chair like a pet, said, "Mr. Weaver, you're next."

Old Man Weaver rose slowly from the waiting chair, placed the copy of *Life* he had been reading on the table, and moved toward her as if wading through drying cement. Charlie wished he would hurry, because they had a rule. You came in the door before five, they stayed to give you a hair cut. But at five they locked the door and pulled the window blind over the big window and closed the curtains over the smaller ones, and when they finished with any late arrivals, they left.

Charlie considered locking the door right then, but it was still a few minutes to five, and he wanted to keep his ritual. But at five on the dot he would wander over to the door and turn the sign and flick the lock.

He let his mind drift to the thought of a cold beer and then dinner. Connie was making pot roast tonight.

Billy came and sat in Charlie's chair. They exchanged a few pleasantries about football, and then Charlie went to work. Billy's hair was a little tricky, due to a front and back cow lick, but Charlie had enough practice now to make the cow licks lay flat. The trick was not to cut the licks too close. Did that, they stood up like spikes.

As for Old Man Weaver, his hair, though short, was actually trickier. Cut it too close he complained, didn't cut it enough, he complained. Sometimes, when you got it just right, he complained. Millie usually had better luck with the old man, so Charlie was glad he had gravitated to her chair.

Charlie touched the electric razor switch, and nothing happened. The clippers were dead as last July. He had used this Chic brand clipper so long, it had almost become a friend. It had sputtered and warned of its upcoming demise a few times recently, but now the inevitable had happened.

Charlie unplugged it, feeling as if he were unplugging a friend from an iron lung, and allowed it to check into that great barbershop in the sky, via the waste basket near his barber chair.

Charlie said, "Hold a moment, Billy."

Already Charlie was starting to sweat. He had to do something he dreaded, something he thought about correcting by changing where he kept his new equipment at the ready, but so far he hadn't. To do so was to admit something he didn't want to admit. To do so was to let the war and the past win.

Seemed silly when he thought about it, but not when he was confronted with it. He had to go to the back and open the storage closet door and go inside, reach on the top shelf for the new electric clippers. That wasn't the problem, it was the confined space. It was dark in there until he stepped inside and reached up and pulled the cord that activated the light. But even then, those walls seemed close and the light seemed dim and it felt like ages before he turned off the light and was out of there.

His walk to the storage room was his own personal Bataan Death March. When he arrived at the closed door, it seemed to him that he was willingly opening the door to hell. It was then that he told himself each time that he had to find shelf space in an open part of the shop, keep supplies out of the closet, and to hell with trying to beat this thing.

But he never made those changes. That would be giving up.

Charlie took a deep breath and felt the sweat on his forehead and palms bubble up and grease him.

I can do this, he told himself. It is not a hut on Palawan. It is not a tight grave.

Charlie opened the door and looked across the six foot length to the rows of shelves at the back. On the top shelf was the box that contained the clippers. He had the man who brought the supplies put them there, perhaps as a kind of test to himself. He couldn't really see them in the darkness of the closet, but he could visualize them and their location clearly.

In the prison camp, the shelter, as it was called, had been about the same size as the closet. It was dug into the side of the rocks, and part of it was made of wood. It was where he was kept with two other soldiers, a very tight living arrangement. There were other shelters and other prisoners, but that shelter was where he and his two companions were kept. It was bad then, but now that the war was over, the memory of it was worse; his mind wore it like a torture device.

One night the Japanese decided to rid the camp of prisoners. Orders from on high. They boarded up the narrow one way exit to the shelter and set it on fire. Smoke filled his lungs and heat licked at his flesh. He and the others had rushed the door, the only way out, and slammed against it with their shoulders, knocking it loose.

When he and his two companions were outside, there had been bayonets, and gasoline was tossed on them. He was able to dodge being lit on fire, but his companions did not. Their bodies were licked by orange tongues of fire that slavered up gasoline as well as flesh. Even now, if he closed his eyes, he could still see them, bright torches running wildly, falling down to be consumed by spirits of fire. The stench of their deaths was still in his nostrils.

Shelters were blazing. Men that had remained trapped inside the other shelters were screaming like women. Charlie tried to escape, but was bayoneted in the abdomen. The pain consumed him and he passed out. He awoke to darkness all around, the sound of scraping. He could barely breathe. Didn't have the strength to move. A great weight was resting on him. Gradually he realized his fate. They thought him dead and were burying him alive.

Then there was a call to dinner. He knew that call. He had heard it many times, and it was not for the prisoners. It was for his tormentors. When the soldiers got around to it, they would bring bowls of buggy rice cooked to the consistency of a loose bowel movement to the prisoners. Tonight, however, even that was finished; he and his fellow prisoners had been served their last meal.

When the dinner call came, the soldiers stopped burying him, tossed their shovels aside, and went away, assuming what they thought was a dead body would be there when they came back.

Charlie found that he could still breathe because the dirt was loose on his face, his nose and mouth were exposed to the air.

He managed to wiggle his head loose, opened his eyes.

It was still night. He had not been out long. It was darker than before, without the bright light of burning shelters and bodies. It was as if during his time unconscious, the night had fallen down on him like an avalanche. The soil was tight and damp against his body. His could only move his feet and hands a little. He wiggled them, flexed his fingers until they begin to come free of the dirt and he could sit up and scrape it off his lower body with his hands. He had not been buried deep, but another five minutes of shoveling and there would have been no escape.

As he came free from the grave, the pain in his abdomen intensified. He couldn't pull his legs loose. He bent forward and dug the dirt from around his legs. A hand rose up between his feet, the fingers spread, as if reaching for something. One of his comrades was lying across his legs. A dead comrade.

Charlie worked himself free. His wound and the exertion it took to free himself, sapped him, but he forced himself to crawl out of the grave. The dirt had actually filled his wound and stopped the bleeding. A silver lining.

Only strong enough to crawl, he reached the jungle, lay there for a while. He could hear the Japanese laughing and enjoying themselves back at the camp. Someone was singing. It was like when American soldiers told him how they enjoyed cutting trophies off Japanese soldiers, ears and noses, and sometimes genitals. War was not a friend to humankind. It changed you, even if you thought it didn't.

But he wasn't thinking about that then. Fear gave him strength to keep crawling. He crawled into a thickness of trees, headed toward where there would be rocks by the sea. He had only gone a few feet into the trees, when his hand landed on something. It was a boot and there was another boot, and legs. Charlie looked up, and looking down at him, was a Japanese soldier. The man had a rifle in his hand with a bayonet on it. He raised the rifle. There was a flash of gritted teeth, and then... Slowly he pulled the rifle away and stood with it clasped to his chest.

The soldier squatted on his haunches, put his face close to Charlie's lifted head. Charlie couldn't really see the soldier's features. It was too dark.

The man only studied him briefly, then rose and stepped aside. Charlie started crawling, expecting the bayonet, but that didn't happen. When Charlie had the courage to turn and look back, the soldier was still there, and he motioned with his hand, a waving motion, an invitation for Charlie to proceed, and then the soldier walked away, favoring a limp.

Charlie started crawling again. After a short time he stopped to lie on his belly and rest. It occurred to him later that the soldier may have been hiding from what had been going on in the camp, not wanting to be involved, probably in shock. Whatever his reasons, he had spared Charlie.

In time, Charlie managed to reach the rocks, even stand and stagger. There were the bodies of American soldiers in the rocks and along the shoreline. A number had made it this far only to be caught and killed, burned alive or bayoneted.

Charlie stayed in the rocks awhile, and it was at that point that he couldn't think about what had happened afterwards any longer. He had to jump over that memory and let his mind go to a day later when he was found by Filipino civilians who treated his wounds and helped him survive.

He was one of a very few who lived through the massacre at the internment camp of Palawan, but he had brought it home with him along with the darkness and confinement of the shelter and the grave.

And now he stood before the closet, its interior like a dark memory he had to enter into.

It's a closet, he told himself, but recognition of what it truly was turned into cold comfort when he had to go inside.

Way he went in there, every time, was he remembered before the war, when he was a young barber, the first head of hair he cut. It was a young boy that his mother brought in. The boy had long locks, and he was a fighter in the chair, oversized and strong for his age.

If it hadn't been his first official given haircut, he might have told them to walk, but he had to start somewhere, and why not some place difficult. So he concentrated on holding the boy's head firmly and talking to him softly, clipping away with the old fashioned squeeze clippers. Trying to cut the boy's hair was like conducting a bombing raid. He dove the clippers down when the kid quit moving, clipped, then waited until a new target presented itself. It took him an hour to cut the child's hair. From then on, even in war, when he needed to concentrate, he first focused on that unruly kid's noggin, a dive of the clippers, and then he took a deep breath and was ready for whatever was at hand. It was simple and silly and to some degree effective.

Charlie imagined the boy and opened the door to the dark closet, felt the walls move in close, the ceiling fall down, the floor rise up.

Entering the closet quickly, he grabbed the cord, turned on the light, but even with it brighter in there, it was for him bright like the first flames of the fire the soldiers lit up the shelter. He froze, and his nostrils filled with smoke and burning flesh.

Again, he thought of that kid, his first haircut. It gave him enough focus to reach the clippers off the shelf, pull the light cord... Oh hell, the horrid dark, and then he made for the light of the doorway, a finer light, and was out of there, almost at a run.

At home, at night, he had to sleep with the lamp on by his bed. Connie had grown accustomed to him rising up at night, saying, "Don't do it," over and over. Then she would touch him, and then she would hold him, and it would pass. For a time.

Back at his barber chair, Charlie plugged in the clippers and went to work.

Millie paused in cutting Old Man Weaver's hair, said, "Dad, are you hot?"

"What?" he said.

"You're sweating."

"Oh," Charlie said, reached up and wiped his forehead with the sleeve of his barber's coat. "I'm alright. It's warm in the back."

Millie nodded, then smiled, and that made a lot of things okay.

Charlie turned his attention back to Billy's hair, the clippers hummed pleasantly while he cut, and now again he paused them and used the scissors from his coat pocket to clip at the cow licks. The scissors worked better for that, keeping the licks even with the rest of the cut. When he felt he had the problem hair controlled, he returned the scissors to his pocket, picked up the clippers again, and went at it.

He and Billy talked about sports some more, Billy's family. Old Man Weaver and Millie talked about the weather, the tomato festival earlier that year, and about how Weaver's granddaughter had gone off to Tyler to teach high-school history. It was the usual barbershop experience, and Charlie enjoyed it.

Charlie was almost finished with Billy's hair when the bell over the door clanged, and two young men entered.

One was nice-looking in a street-tough kind of way, and the other wasn't so nice-looking. He had a face that looked as if it had been set on fire with a blow torch and the flames had been beat out with a garden rake.

Charlie could feel their attitude right away. It went before them like trucks pulling trailers. They sat in waiting chairs, reached magazines off the table, started thumbing through them. Now and again they looked up at Millie, and that bothered Charlie.

Charlie understood Millie was pretty. He understood that as a dad he was overprotective, and he knew nearly every male below the age of forty that came into the shop took note of her, and a lot of them above the age of forty. But these boys made him start to hurry Billy's cut. He almost decided to break a long-standing rule and tell them he was closing up and they had to go.

Old Man Weaver was finished. He climbed down from his chair, paid up and went out. After he was gone, Millie turned the sign on the door from OPEN to CLOSED.

She walked to the big window and looked out. "You fellows walked here?" she said, turning to look at them.

"Yeah," said Inflamed-face. "We like to walk."

"Walking's good for you," said Nice-looking. "I read that in a magazine, maybe in a barbershop. I forget."

"I don't recognize either of you," she said.

"Visiting relatives," said Nice-looking.

"Who's would that be?" Billy said.

"Don't be nosey," said Nice-looking.

"Sorry," Billy said. "Didn't mean nothing by it."

"Don't mean we didn't take something from it, though, does it," said Inflamed-face.

"Let's stay civil," Charlie said. "It was an innocent question."

"Yeah, that's right," said Inflamed-face, "civil. That's how we want to be. Civil."

Millie went back to her chair, said, "Who's next?"

"That will be me," said Nice-looking.

"I got to let him cut my hair?" Inflamed-face said, "and you get the good-looking girl?"

"Get what you deserve in life," said Nice-looking.

Nice-looking put the magazine on the table and climbed into Millie's chair.

"How would you like it?" she said.

"Like it is, only shorter."

Millie went to work. Charlie continued to cut hair, but he checked on Inflamed-face from time to time, glanced over at pretty boy in Millie's chair.

"Barbers, they do right smart business in a small town, don't they?" Inflamed-face said.

"We do all right," Charlie said.

"I'm thinking you might do better than that. Bet you bring in plenty. Men got to get their hair cut to stay respectable, don't they? You like them respectable, don't you, Dad?"

Charlie paused the clippers, looked at the one with the wrecked face. "Let me explain this where you understand it. Don't call me Dad, and leave my shop. Both of you. I don't like the way you talk."

"Well, that's all right, because we don't like the way you talk," said Inflamed-face, and he didn't move. Nice-looking stayed in Millie's barber chair.

"Want me to go with my hair partly cut?" said Nice-looking. "I can't do that."

"Yeah, you can," Charlie said.

Millie had ceased to run the clippers and had stepped back from the chair. Nice-looking didn't get up. He said, "Tommy, lock the door."

Inflamed-face, Tommy, stood up and locked the door. He went over to the big window and pulled down the blind. He started for the smaller windows.

"What the hell do you think you're doing?" Charlie said.

"We're helping you close up," Nice-looking said. "Finish the haircut, doll."

"You're leaving," Charlie said. "Buy yourself some clippers and do it yourself."

"I could do that," Nice-looking said, "but I won't."

Nice-looking stood up from the barber chair and opened his jacket. There was a .45 automatic in his waistband, a military pistol.

"What's this all about?" Charlie said.

"Easy, Dad," Millie said.

"Yeah," Inflamed-face said. "Easy, Dad."

"You got some money here, and we need it," Nice-looking said. "I think that's the best way to stuff it in a nut shell, though sometimes I like to talk and couldn't put it in a bushel basket. Today, though, I'm feeling less talky. Here's so you rubes will understand us. We'd like your money. We'll take the money, and we'll hole up here for awhile."

Tommy laughed.

Nice-looking eased the pistol out of his waistband and held it alongside his leg, tapping his thigh gently with the barrel. "You're all right with that, aren't you...Dad?"

"Take the money and go," Charlie said. "Take it all, but leave."

"Naw," said Nice-looking, "we kind of got a situation on our hands. Made a run at the bank here. Didn't work out so good. Cop came in while the gal was handing me the money, someone yelled. I had to shoot the cop, and Tommy here had to shoot the one who yelled."

"Didn't have to shoot anyone after you killed the cop," Tommy said. "Just wanted to."

"I stand corrected," Nice-looking said. "Okay. Here's how we start. Give us the money, Dad. Now."

"And you," Tommy said, pointing at Billy. "You got some money, don't you?"

"Enough for a haircut," Billy said.

Tommy grinned. "Like the old lady who peed in the ocean said, every little bit helps."

Billy stood up and fished in his front pocket and came up with a few dollar bills. Tommy came over and took them. "Hell, you got enough for a haircut and a shave. If you shaved. Go over there and sit in a chair and be still. You get nervous, we'll shoot you and tell God you died."

Billy went over and sat in one of the customer chairs.

"Now you, doll," Nice-looking said. "Finish cutting my hair. And you, Dad, you sit in the barber chair and be nice, or we won't be nice. Dig? Same goes for you, what is it, Billy?"

Charlie moved around to the front of the chair and sat in it. He could see Billy in the chair across the way. Billy was fuming. Charlie feared he might do something silly.

"I'm thinking I'll give you a haircut," Tommy said to Charlie, and wandered behind the chair where Charlie sat. "Little off the top first, then maybe I'll part your hair with a bullet. I got a gun too, Dad."

Tommy turned his attention to Millie, standing with the clippers in hand. Nice-looking had climbed back in the chair. "And you, girlie," Tommy said. "We might do some hair parting of a different kind with you."

"Leave her alone," Charlie said, and he moved to come out of the chair.

Tommy slapped Charlie over the ear. Charlie's head rang like a bell. "You shut up, Dad, unless you want to get the party started."

"Let her and the boy go," Charlie said. "Keep me. They won't say a word."

Tommy slapped him over the ear again. Charlie winced.

"Like we believe that," Nice-looking said, leaning back in the chair, shifting into a comfortable spot, resting the gun on his knee. "No one leaves. Not until we leave. Besides, you people make nice company, don't they, Tommy?"

"Damn nice company," Tommy said. "I think girlie could be nicer company than these two, though."

Billy started to rise out of his chair, Charlie lifted a hand off his knee and patted the air. Billy stopped trying to rise up.

"That'a boy," Tommy said. "You get excited, want to play the hero, you'll get dead."

Billy's face turned bright red, but he kept his seat.

Nice-looking turned in the barber chair and looked at Millie.

"You don't look like any barber I ever had," he said. "Look here, girlie. I'm going to need you to say a word or two. Not too much, but you can say something."

"Something," Millie said.

"Oh, a smart ass," Tommy said. "We can fix that."

"Naw, it's alright," Nice-looking said. "I like them a little feisty. It's more fun to bring them down. The higher something is, more the fun to watch it fall. You got a purse, doll?"

Millie nodded.

"I want to hear you say it."

"Yes. I have a purse."

"That's good. You got any money in it?"

"A few dollars."

"Tell them what you think about that again, Tommy."

"Like the old lady that peed in the ocean," Tommy said. "Every little bit counts."

"That's your cue, doll," Nice-looking said. "Give me your purse."

Millie turned and reached under a shelf and brought it out. Tommy came over and took it, as he did, he ran his hand over her hand. Millie recoiled.

"Ah now, sweet girlie, I'm not so bad," Tommy said.

"Yes he is," Nice-looking said. "He's bad."

Tommy took Millie's chin in his hand and said, "I think you ought to give me a kiss."

Tommy snickered, let her go, went back to stand behind Charlie. He began looking through the purse. After a few minutes he found a small wallet. He dropped the purse and opened the wallet. He took out some bills and put those in his pocket, tossed the wallet on the floor with the purse.

"Where's the barbershop money?" Tommy said, leaning over Charlie's shoulder.

"Behind you, in the shelf, a cigar box," Charlie said.

"No cash register?" Tommy said.

"No," Charlie said.

"You see a cash register, Tommy?" Nice-looking said.

"No."

"Then what's the point in asking?"

Tommy shrugged, found the cigar box, opened it, thumbed through it. "What, a hundred dollars, some change? You might as well take Green Stamps."

"That's all we have," Charlie said.

"What's in the back?" Tommy said.

"Barber supplies, bathroom, back door and the parking lot."

"Money?"

"No," Charlie said.

"Had to leave our car behind," Nice-looking said. "Or someone's car. We stole it. Now we got to have another one, so that one in the back I saw, that yours?"

Charlie nodded.

"We'll be taking it," Nice-looking said. "Having the keys is better than hotwiring some car. Neither of us are too good at it. Give me the keys."

"There on that hook by the front door," Charlie said.

"Tommy," Nice-looking said, "get those keys."

Tommy got them, gave them to Nice-looking who was holding out his hand. Nice-looking shoved the keys into his coat pocket.

"Finish my hair, doll," Nice-looking said.

Millie lifted the clippers and began to cut. Her hands trembled slightly.

❧

WHEN MILLIE FINISHED cutting Nice-looking's hair, he climbed out of the chair, looked in the mirror. He went over to the shelf in front of the mirror, found a comb and a bottle of red hair oil. He dripped a bit of oil into his palm, slicked his hair back with it, combed it.

"We could just lay low here awhile," Tommy said.

Nice-looking nodded. "We could, but they don't go home, and we're here, someone might come looking for them."

"Hadn't thought of that," Tommy said.

"Ask me if I'm surprised."

Tommy's forehead wrinkled. "You don't have to talk that way."

"I don't have to is right," Nice-looking said. "Now, we're going to need the three of you to go in the back."

Charlie and Billy stood up from their seats, and Millie started to follow.

As Millie passed and came up close to Charlie, Tommy said, "Honey, I'm going to need to pinch that butt. I been wanting to do that since we got here."

Tommy reached out to pinch her, and when he did Charlie stepped back and hit him in the face with an elbow. It was a sharp blow and Tommy staggered, his nose spouting blood.

Nice-looking moved quickly, slammed the gun barrel into the side of Charlie's head. It was a good blow, but Charlie only moved a little. Nice-looking seemed surprised by that. He started to hit Charlie again, but now Tommy was there, and he had drawn a small revolver from inside his coat. He said, "Let me do it."

"Alright," Nice-looking said.

Tommy brought the revolver around to hit Charlie, and when he did, Billy grabbed Tommy's wrist, yelled, "Stop it."

Tommy jerked his hand free, pointed the revolver.

Nice-looking said, "Don't make noise unless you got to."

"I got to," Tommy said.

"No, you don't," Nice-looking said.

"Okay," Tommy said, and stuck the pistol in his waistband, reached into his pants pocket, pulled out a knife, and clicked it open.

Before Billy could move, Tommy stabbed him in the gut. Billy fell back against the barber chair. Charlie grabbed him, pulled Billy away from Tommy, stepped in between them.

Billy sagged to the floor. Blood leaked out of him like spilled motor oil.

"Better move, cause I'm not finished, and I can cut you too, old man," Tommy said.

"I been cut," Charlie said.

"That's enough," Nice-looking said. "Got time for that later, we want it. Get them in the back. Might want them for hostages, and if we do, it's best they're alive. Except Billy there. I don't want him. He don't look so good, and he's wet. We'd just be dumping him beside the road somewhere, have to clean up after him."

"Cowards," Millie said. "You sorry cowards." Her body shook.

"Easy, baby," Charlie said.

"Yeah," Nice-looking said. "Easy, baby."

"In the back, now, and get that son-of-a-bitch off the floor, or I'll finish him here," Tommy said.

Charlie bent down, slipped his arm under Billy's arm, lifted him up. "Sorry, son," Charlie said in his ear.

"I ain't," Billy said, but he had turned pale and his face was beaded with sweat.

Charlie grabbed the barber towel off the back of his chair, folded it and pushed it against Billy's wound. "Hold it there, son, press tight."

Billy pressed on the towel. When he did, he groaned. The towel began to turn red.

Millie came around and got on the other side of Billy, and they helped him walk to the back.

🌾

"IT'S NOT SO bad," Billy said, as they went.

"Good," Charlie said, but from experience, he knew Billy was wrong. A stab like that felt like a punch in the gut at first, but then it felt like the fires of hell blazing through your belly. Pain would come, and Billy was leaking a lot of blood; his life was running out of him like water down a drain.

"It'll be okay, Billy," Millie said.

When they got to the rear of the shop, Nice-looking went to the back door and cracked it open. He looked out for a short time then eased the door shut.

"There's a park back there," Nice-looking said. "There's a lot of people out there. Go out with them, someone might look and know better."

"What now?" Tommy said.

"Billy there, he isn't going, that's for sure. Put them in that closet, let me think on it."

A great shadow moved inside of Charlie. Of all the damn things, a confined space. It was one thing to will himself to grab clippers off a top shelf, but to be closed in, that was beyond what he could manage.

Charlie glanced at Millie. Her eyes were wide, her lips tight and thin. He knew that look. He had seen it on the face of soldiers about to enter into battle; he had seen it every day on the faces of his fellow prisoners.

Tommy got a chair from the front of the shop while Nice-looking pointed his gun and a smile at them. Tommy brought a customer chair in, placed it by the closet, opened the closet door. "All of you, get inside."

"Dad," Millie said.

Charlie hadn't moved. He still had one arm around Billy, Millie on the other side.

"Inside, I said."

With more will than Charlie thought he possessed, he began to trudge toward the dark opening.

I'll be alright with the light on, he told himself. It won't be good, but it won't be as bad. As long as I have a light, that will make it better.

At the doorway, looking into the darkness, Charlie almost broke and ran, but he couldn't do that. He couldn't. Not with Millie and Billy here. He had to go inside. As they entered the closet, he reached up quickly, pulled the cord and turned on the overhead light. They eased Billy to the ground with his back against a shelf.

"No," Tommy said, and he entered into the closet, hopped up and broke the light with his pistol. "Let's keep it dark. And you, girlie, we get ready, we'll take you with us. We can have a party somewhere."

Tommy stepped back, framed by the light of the outside room, and closed the door, plunging them in the darkness. Then they heard Tommy scraping the chair across the floor, sticking it under the doorknob to hold them in.

Charlie took a deep breath. All he could do was sit on the floor of the closet and tremble. He knew he was in the closet, but he felt he was in the grave.

Why can't I move, he thought? Why can't I do something? I did something then. Why can't I now?

Because you know how it could end, for you and Millie and Billy, but you know too it will end that way anyway. You know what you did back then, and if you let yourself loose, you may do what you did before, and that's not how you want to be. Not like that. Never like that.

"Dad?" Millie said.

She touched his arm. He was embarrassed that she would feel it trembling, and that he was already so beaded with sweat his clothes were wet.

"What do we do, Dad?"

He thought about that first haircut again, but that still wasn't working. That worked when he knew he could leave, but now the dirt seemed to press against him, and if he broke from the grave, it would be dark, and there was the woods, the soldier and the rocks, and then there was what he had done.

Charlie told himself, you got to stop worrying about what you did, think about that thing you did instead, let it come out, let that rage rush to the surface like a missile. He could hear the soldiers talking outside of the shelter. No. Not the shelter. It was the thugs, and they were talking outside of the closet. Just a damn closet, not a shelter, not a grave.

"I go outside with the girl," Charlie heard Nice-looking say. "We go cool, and she drives the car around front and we pick you up there."

"I don't know," Tommy said.

"You don't know what?"

"What if you keep going?"

"Why would I do that? You got the money in your pocket, right?"

"Yeah, but what if you just kept going anyway. You and her. You could have some fun with her, dump her somewhere, keep driving. And here I'd be."

"I wouldn't do that to you, Tommy."

"Wouldn't you?" Tommy said.

Then they must have moved across the room, because all of a sudden, they couldn't hear them anymore.

Inside the closet, Charlie felt Millie push up against him, grab his arm and hold it. "Oh, Dad. What if they take me?"

"It'll be okay," Charlie said. A kind of cool had settled over him, and it made the sweat on his body turn cold. He remembered something. The scissors in his barber coat. He reached and took them out.

And then he let himself remember how it was, how he had crawled and then hid in the rocks. The part he wouldn't let himself think about before, he thought about now. It was the part about where the soldier who had let him go, came back later, maybe an hour later. Charlie had reached the rocks by then and he could hear the pounding of the surf and through a split in the rocks he could see other rock heaps and the sand on the beach, and it was all bathed silver by the moonlight.

There was a soldier with rifle and bayonet walking along the beach, looking left and right, crouched a little. The soldier had a limp like the one that had let him go. He had no doubt it was the same man.

Charlie didn't know if the soldier had been sent to look for stragglers, or if he had thought about what he had done, letting a prisoner go, felt bad for it, and had come to finish Charlie off.

A rage swelled up in Charlie, and though his wound was bad, he felt strong then. The dirt in the wound had lessened the flow of blood and clotted it, and Charlie was touched with madness. It was like a crawling thing inside of him; a den of twisting, poisonous reptiles. He had picked up a rock then. It was heavy and one end was a little sharp, and he could hold it firmly in his hand.

The soldier worked his way among the rocks, holding his bayonet tipped rifle at the ready. The moonlight danced on the blade. The soldier passed the split in the rocks where Charlie hid in shadow, and before the soldier could look his way, Charlie sprang.

Charlie had felt in that moment like a panther. He landed on the soldier, knocked him to the ground. The soldier squeaked like a rat. The rock went up and the rock came down. A wet warmness splashed against Charlie. Some of it splashed into his mouth, and it was hot and coppery, and it tasted like vengeance, and the rock went up and the rock came down, and there was a sound like someone stepping on egg shells after awhile, but still the rock went up and the rock came down.

Straddling that soldier, the one who had let him go, all he could think about then was the months of cruelty, the beatings, the starving, the fires and bayonets. The rock went up and the rock went down.

When Charlie paused from exhaustion, the soldier no longer had a head. It was a puddle of blood mixed with sand and bone fragments. The light of the moon had changed, and the shadows were different, and the shadows covered Charlie and the dead soldier. Charlie realized he had been striking the soldier for a long time. He could hardly move, he was so exhausted. In that moment Charlie knew what was inside of him, and it had gone on beyond the need to kill the man. It had turned into the same kind of wicked vengeance as the American soldiers he knew who had cut pieces off dead Japanese soldiers and kept them as souvenirs, or who mutilated bodies, or enjoyed burning men with flamethrowers. The same sort of men he had been captured by. The same kind of man he had become.

Charlie sprang up and rushed the closet door. There was a jar to his shoulder, and he was bounced back, but he went at it again, and this time he heard the chair scrape and go scuttling along the floor. Charlie let what was inside of him come out in full, the thing he feared and had tamped down after that time with the soldier in the rocks. The door sprang open as the hinges creaked out of the wall. Charlie stumbled out into the light with the scissors clutched in his fist, slamming into something, and that something was Tommy.

Charlie hit him like an express train. Tommy went back and tripped over the chair Charlie had dislodged, smacked his head hard on the floor, and his gun came loose from his hand and went skittering across the tile floor.

Nice-looking, standing near the back door, panicked, fired his gun. The shot missed Charlie, slammed into the wall, but Charlie felt the bullet ruffle his hair. Nice-looking was trying to fire again, but the gun was jammed, and he was struggling with it, and Charlie was coming, the scissors raised.

Nice-looking let out a noise that reminded Charlie of the soldier that night, and then Charlie was on him.

The scissors flashed (the rock went up, the rock went down) and there was a scream, and at first he thought it was Nice-looking, but then realized it was him, and that what was coming out of him was pure rage. Blood spattered against his face, and for a moment he was in those rocks, and then heard Millie scream, and he was sure this time it was her, not him.

"Dad, don't, please don't," she said, and her voice broke through the roar in his ears. He sagged slightly. The haze in front of his eyes faded.

Looking down at Nice-looking, who he was straddling, his hand raised with the bloody scissors in his fist, he saw that he had stabbed Nice-looking through the cheek, and had struck him in the shoulder and chest. He could see the swelling red spots there, leaking through Nice-looking's shirt and jacket, streaming down his face and onto the floor. Nice-looking was crying like a child.

When Charlie looked back over his shoulder, he saw that Millie had picked up Tommy's revolver, and was pointing it at him. Tommy was in a heap on the floor, but he was starting to stir.

Charlie stood up. He put the scissors in his barber coat pocket, picked up Nice-looking's gun where it lay next to him on the floor. He saw the problem, worked with it briefly, cleared the chamber. It was the same kind of gun he had carried in the war.

He pointed the gun at Nice-looking, stepped back where he could see both of the men. "Don't get up, punk," he said to Nice-looking. "And you, Tommy, get over here and sit down beside him. You can hold hands if you like."

"I'm hurt," Nice-looking said, and he whimpered after saying it, like a mistreated dog.

"Yeah, you are," Charlie said. "But believe me, if not for Millie, you'd be dead."

And he would have, and worse. Charlie would have let what was inside of him keep coming out, like that time with the soldier in the rocks, but Millie's voice had cut through it all, and even the burning need to kill had been defeated by that small but wonderful thing. His daughter's voice.

I didn't kill because I didn't need to, Charlie thought. I am human. I am a husband and a father. I gained control. That was war and that was then and this is now.

Tommy shuffled over, still looking dazed. He sat on the floor by Nice-Looking. He didn't look up to see that Charlie was smiling at him.

Charlie took a deep breath. The demons were still there, but they were smaller now, and maybe in time, he could defeat them, or at least make them so small as to no longer matter. He wasn't fixed, and maybe never would be, but he was better and felt as good as he had felt in a long time.

"Millie, darling," Charlie said, pointing the gun at the pair on the floor. "Go up and call some law, and tell them to send an ambulance for Billy. Everyone lives today."

DEAD
CAR

STRUCTURE TYPE: JUNKYARD
LOCATION: GLADEWATER, TEXAS
LAT./ LONG: 32.5520° N, 94.9334° W
BUILT: CIRCA 1963
ELEVATION: 380 FT. (116 M.)
WRITTEN BY: JOE R. LANSDALE

THE CHEVROLET SAT in the junkyard. It was a wad of blue metal with silver scrapes, and the windshield was gone and the side windows were webbed with safety-glass cracks. The steering wheel had been bent on both sides. There was still blood on the seats. The sun was going down so the blood looked like dark drops of a soul dripped loose from its hosts.

Bill and Janey arrived. Bill touched the car, bent down and looked inside.

"What a mess," Janey said.

"Yeah."

"Way it hit that tree, there was no chance."

"None at all," Bill said. "We were lucky."

"We have to convince them for sure, tonight."

"I know. We've been careful, but now, we need to be a bit more forceful."

"Stay kind," she said. "It has to be hard."

"Of course," he said. "It should be about time."

Janey checked her watch, then turned her head to see the other couple had arrived at the trunk of the car and were standing there.

Jim was tall and handsome, wearing his cocky smile like an ornament. Claire was as pretty as the feel of nostalgia. Her hair was silver as the moon.

"Man, that looks bad," Jim said.

"It is," Janey said.

"What was it, last night it happened? I've been a bit confused since the wreck. It's like things aren't quite yet in focus."

"It's been four days," Janey said.

"Go out for a ride, something goes that wrong. I never considered such. All that booze we had in us. Stupid of us."

"We were fools," Claire said. "We could have all been killed."

"That's right," Janey said.

"But we weren't," Claire said.

"I was driving," Bill said. "It was my fault."

"What ends well, ends well," Jim said. "We all learned a lesson."

"What happened to you guys after the wreck?" Bill said.

"What do you mean?" Claire said.

"After the wreck. Where did you guys go?"

"Home," Jim said. "We went home."

"You went off in an ambulance," Janey said. "Same as us."

"Yeah," Jim said.

"And then what?"

"Went home," Jim said.

"What did you do when you got home?" Bill asked.

"Well..." Jim paused. "That's funny. I don't remember exactly. I think I had a mild concussion. Still do, I guess. Can't quite put it all together."

"Think a moment. What did you do when you woke up?" Bill said.

"I guess I just got up."

"But you don't remember exactly?" Janey said.

"Must have hit my head harder than I thought."

"Must have," Janey said. "Claire, what did you do after the wreck?"

"I don't remember either."

"There's a reason," Bill said. "I want you to really listen to us this time. Neither of you made it."

"Made what?"

Neither Bill nor Janey responded. They let their comment float about.

"What do you mean?" Jim said. "Made what? You're making me nervous. Made what?"

"You're here, all right, but you're not here."

"Sort of double talk is that?" Jim said.

"Last place you were, when you were alive, was this car," Bill said.

"Alive?" Jim said.

"You keep coming back here, every night," Bill said. "You and Claire."

"But we're talking to you," Jim said. "We're looking right at you. Don't be daft."

"Yes, you are," Janey said. "We see you, me and Bill. Because you were with us. In the wreck. We came here next night after the wreck, saw the car out of curiosity, and you two showed up. Right on time, at nightfall. We could tell right away... That you weren't right."

"I don't accept that," Claire said. "That's ridiculous."

"It doesn't matter what you accept," Bill said. "You haven't let go yet. Haven't accepted it. We first saw you, we thought you were alive, and then we saw you weren't."

"I don't understand," Claire said.

"I feel plenty alive," Jim said.

"Do you?" Janey asked. "We just want you to let go, find peace. Quit coming back nightly to look at the car. We're going to quit coming to see you, so, it'll just be the two of you showing up here looking inside the car until you decide to let go. We want to help, but we can't keep doing this. We truly are sorry."

"Look inside the car, at the backseat," Bill said. "That blood on the seat covers, that belongs to the two of you."

Realization landed on Claire like a grand piano. "It's true. I know it now. It's true."

She held out her hands and looked at them.

"The starlight shines through them," she said. "I read somewhere we're all part of the stars."

"That's right," Bill said.

Jim felt the weight of the truth as well. He said, "What do we do?"

"Don't know exactly," Bill said. "You could climb in the car, sit there, close your eyes, and maybe it will come. Whatever it is. I think you just did the hard part. Accepted that you're not living anymore."

"I'm afraid," Claire said.

"I'm thinking it'll be easy," Janey said. "You're already dead. Past pain. My guess is you'll just slip away."

"And if we don't?" Jim said.

"I don't know," Janey said.

"I remember now," Claire said. "I never went home. I was awake in the ambulance a little, and then I wasn't. Next thing I remember, we came out here."

"Yeah," Jim said. "I remember the hospital though, and then I felt sleepy. Next thing I know, we were together, coming here."

"And you have been coming for some time," Janey said. "You come, and then before daylight you walk off and disappear."

"To where?" Claire said.

"Limbo, maybe," Janey said. "I don't know. Some place that holds you until you decide to let go."

Jim reached out and touched the car trunk. He pushed and his hand went right through it. He pulled it back.

Jim walked around and looked inside the car through the back window, then he bent forward and sat down inside on the back seat by sliding right through the door. Claire followed, sat beside him. They held hands.

"She feels so solid," Jim said.

"On your plane, she is," Bill said.

"So, this is it," Jim said.

"I feel it," Claire said.

Bill and Janey watched as Jim and Claire slowly faded away like morning mist on a warming pond.

"They've accepted," Bill said. "They're gone."

"I'm glad," Janey said. "Now we can go home."

They started away from there, but when they got to the edge of the wrecking yard, near the gate, they paused.

"Strangely," Janey said. "I don't know where to go."

"Home."

"I can't seem to do that."

They stood for a long moment. The cosmos clicked. The stars seemed different.

"I can see the moonlight through you," Bill said. "I know now I always could."

Janey said, "The four of us. We all…"

She let that hang as if on a hook.

"We thought we came to help Jim and Claire pass over," Bill said, "but I don't remember anything but this place after the wreck. I saw the tree. Threw my hands in front of my face, and then we were here, and Jim and Claire came up."

"We found a reason to be here that made more sense than the truth. We hadn't accepted it either."

Bill didn't answer. Starlight and moonlight crawled through the air. Bill took her hand. They turned and went back to the car and climbed in the front seat and held hands. They looked through where the windshield had been.

"I'd been drinking," Bill said.

"We all had."

"I swerved for a shadow in the road. Something that wasn't really there. And there was the tree."

"It doesn't matter anymore."

They sat in silence, then the cosmos clicked again. They slowly faded, leaving silver moonlight lying on the seat.

The car motor hummed soft and distant. The car remained, but a misty shape that looked like the car started to move away from it, out across the wrecking yard, passing through the tin fence that surrounded the yard, down the hill and onto the highway, gliding like a bird on an air current.

Back in the junkyard, some of the cars hummed and shimmered, waiting for the return of those who had died in them, those who still wandered. The rest of the cars were just cars and had not housed the dead or dying. The light of the moon and the stars lay flat against them.

The spectral Chevy that carried Bill and Janey, Jim and Claire, rolled along. Then it became thin and pale. Finally, it was an outline, and in short time, a shadow of a shadow.

And then it was gone.

THE SENIOR GIRLS
BAYONET DRILL TEAM

THE BUS RIDE can be all right, if everyone talks and cuts up, sings the school fight song, and keeps a positive attitude. It keeps your mind off what's to come. Oh, you don't want to not think about it at all, or you won't be ready, you won't have your grit built up. You need that, but you can't think about it all the time, or you start to worry too much.

You got to believe all the training and team preparation will carry you through, even if sometimes it doesn't. I started in Junior High, so I'm an old pro now. This is my last year on the team, and my last event, and if I'm careful, and maybe a little lucky, I'll graduate and move on. It's all about the survivors.

I was thinking about Ronnie. She was full of life and energy and as good as any of us, but she's not with us anymore. She got replaced by a new girl that isn't fit to tie Ronnie's war shoes, which her parents bronzed and keep in their living room on a table next to the ashes of Ronnie's pet shih tzu. I saw the shoes there during the memorial. The dog had been there for at least three years before Ronnie died. It bit me once. Maybe that's why it died. Poisoned. I remembered too that it slept a lot and snored in little stutters, like an old lawn mower starting.

Ronnie has a gold plaque on the wall back at the gym, along-side some others, and if you were to break that plaque apart, behind it you'd find a little slot, and in that slot is her bayonet and her ashes in an urn. I guess that's something. Her name is on the plaque, of course. Her years on the team, and her death year is listed too.

There have been a lot of plaques put in the gym over the years, but it still feels special and sacred to see them. You kind of want to end up there when you're feeling the passion, and the rest of the time that's just what you don't want.

Ronnie also has a nice photo of her in her uniform, holding her bayonet, over in Cumshaw Hall, which is named after the girl they think was the greatest player of all, Margret Cumshaw. Cumshaw Hall is also known as the Hall of Fame.

To be in both spots is unique, so I guess Ronnie has that going for her, though it occurs to me more than now and again, that she hasn't any idea that this is so. I'm not one that believes in the big stadium in the sky. I figure dead is dead, but because of that, I guess you got to look at the honor of it all and know it matters. Without that plaque, photo, ten years from now, who's to know she existed at all?

Sometimes, though, the bus ride can be a pain in the ass, and not just because you might get your mind on what's to come and not be able to lose your thoughts in talk and such, but as of late, we got to put up with Clarisse.

Clarisse thinks she's something swell, but she's not the only one with scars, and she's not the only one who's killed someone. And though she sometimes acts like it, she's not the team captain. Not legitimately, anyway.

It's gotten so it's a chore to ride with her on the bus to a game. She never shuts up, and all she talks about is herself. She acts like we need a blow-by-blow of her achievements, like the rest of us weren't there to perform as well. Like we didn't see what she did.

She remembers her own deeds perfectly, but the rest of us, well, she finds it hard to remember where we were and what we did, and how there have been a few of us that haven't come back. She scoots over the detail about how our teammates' bodies, as is the rule of the game, become the property of the other team if we aren't able to rescue them before the buzzer. You'd think she saved everyone, to hear her rattle on. She hasn't. We haven't.

We managed a save with Ronnie's body, but we've lost a few. That's tough to think about. The whole ritual when you lose a team member to the other side. The ceremony of the body being hooked up to a harness that the other team takes hold of so they can drag the body around the playing field three or four times, like it's Hector being pulled about the walls of Troy by Achilles in his chariot. And then there's the whole thing of the other team hacking up the body with bayonets when the dragging is done, having to stand there and watch and salute those bastards. That happens, the dead teammate still gets a plaque, but there's nothing behind it but bricks.

When we end up dragging one of theirs and hacking on it, well, I enjoy that part immensely. I put my all into it and think of teammates we've lost. We yell their names as we pull and then hack.

Thing was, Clarisse's bullshit wasn't boosting me up, it was bringing me down, cause all I could think about were the dead comrades and how it could be me, and here it was my last game, and all I had to do was make it through this one and I was graduating and home free.

A number of us were in that position, on the edge of graduation. I think it made half the team solemn. Some of the girls don't want it to end. Me, I can't wait to get out. There's a saying in the squad. First game. Last game. They're the ones that are most likely to get you killed.

First time out you're too full of piss and vinegar to be as cautious as you should be, last time out you're overly cautious, and that could end up just as bad.

Clarisse thinks she's immortal and can do no wrong, but sometimes you go left when you should go right, or the girl on the other team is stronger or swifter than you. Things can change in a heartbeat.

Clarisse, for all her skill, hasn't learned that. For her, every day is Clarisse Day, even though that was just one special day of recognition she got some six months back. It was on account of her having a wonderful moment on the field, so wonderful she was honored with a parade and flowers and one of the boys from the bus repair pool; the usual ritual. Me, I have always played well, and I'm what they call dependable. But I've never had my own day, a parade, flowers, and a boy toy. I've never had that honor. That's okay. I used to think about it, but now the only honor I want is to graduate and not embarrass my team in the process, try to make sure no one gets killed on my side of the field. Especially me.

We may be the state champions, but the position can change in one game. More experienced players you lose on the team, through graduation or death, less likely you'll make State Championship. You can train new girls, bring up the bench team. But it's not the same. They haven't been working together with us the same way. They don't move as one, the way the rest

of us do. They're lumps in the gravy. They would need to survive several games before they were like a part of us.

Of course, listening to Clarisse you'd think she was the team
all by herself. I've heard of some teams who would leave one
of their members to the blades, for whatever reason. Maybe
haughty teammates not unlike Clarisse. But no matter how
annoying she is, that's not the way we play. That's not teamwork. We stick with her, like her or not. She's a hell of a player,
but she's not the official team captain. But with Jane in the
hospital they've given her the team for a while, so I guess, like it
or not, she does have that position, but I just can't quite see her
that way, as a true leader.

Our coach is around, of course, but she rides in a separate
car when we go on a trip to a game. She says us having to deal
with one another forces comradery. But I think the coach just
likes to ride in a car and not hear our bullshit.

She's had a lot of winning teams, but this year, I figure she's
done. She knows we know our stuff, and there's not much she
can do. Just have us run our drills and give us a pep talk now
and again. She was a great champion before she was a famous
coach. She has fifty kills to her credit. Only Margret Cumshaw
and Ronnie have more than that. But for all practical purposes,
she's out of the picture.

"Thing you got to remember," Clarisse said, turning in the
bus seat, looking back at us, "is you can't hesitate. Can't do like
Millicent last time out. You have the moment, you take it."

Hearing my name mentioned made my ears burn. I hadn't
hesitated. Things went a little wrong is all, and in the end, no
one died and we won easily.

"Yeah. We know how it works," Bundy says.

Clarisse gave Bundy a glance, but it wasn't a strong one. We all knew Bundy was vital to our success. Clarisse was too, but nobody liked her the way they liked Bundy, though Bundy can connive a little herself, always wanted to be a team captain, end up a coach.

Bundy was one of our corners. She made things look easy. She wasn't fast like me or some of the other girls, but she was strong and taller than the rest. She had taken on two at a time more than once, and won, leaving them dead in her wake. She had her own parade day, twice, and she also had the scars across her cheeks and chin to prove her moments under the lights. Everyone said it made her look like a warrior, and that's true, but they were still scars. Bundy had been pretty once.

Me, I've done okay in that department. I have a scar on my left side, just below the rib cage, some small ones here and there, but I've come out all right, so far. At least I got both eyes. Bundy has a black pirate patch over her left one.

"I'm merely doing my job," Clarisse says.

"Sounds to me like you're trying to do all our jobs," I say, and that sets her off a little, but not in words. She just gives me the look. That burning look she usually saves for when we're on the field, the one she has for the girls on the other team. It's the look she wanted to give Bundy but didn't, so I'm getting it double-time.

"As team captain," Clarisse says, "I—"

"Temporary team captain," I say.

Now that look from her was stronger. Me and her, we've always rubbed each other the wrong way, even back when we were in grade school, when we first started training with wooden bayonets and swatting dummies full of candy at each other's birthday parties.

The dummies were always dressed up in drill team colors from other schools. It was a way of starting to think right about what we wanted to grow up and become. Me and her, we made the team, way we dreamed we would, and though we were a bit at each other all through school, we mostly got along. Guess you could say more than that. That we were close, like competitive sisters. Lately it was nothing but snide remarks and go-to-hell stares, grins like sharks. Only thing that held us together was the team.

"Just think," says the new girl, Remington, sitting beside me, fidgety, "tonight, all over the country, stadiums will light up, and teams will go inside, and the crowds will grow, and we'll play beneath the lights."

I turn to look at her. "The lights will go up and the teams will march out and look up into the crowd, and you'll be sitting on the bench, maybe getting us some water when we change out."

"Yeah, I guess so," Remington says, turning red, making me feel a bit like an asshole.

Remington was a little thing, just barely made the team, but the roster was thin for new troops this year, so she was the best of the worst. "But I'm on the team. That means something, doesn't it?"

"Sure," I say. "We all start that way, asses on the bench. But eventually you'll get your shot. You'll be all right."

I didn't really think that. I figured first time she was on the field, after she got through the performance, the ritual, she'd hit the turf running and end up with a bayonet through her throat. I'd seen it happen more than once. The real Rah-rahs, as I called them, often didn't make it out of their first game without being badly wounded or dead, sometimes carried away by the other team for that drag and hack business.

I told myself, she got in the game, she went down, I'd do my best to save her body from the other side, but I'd only go so far. I didn't know her like I knew the others. The loss wouldn't be the same. I kind of felt the same way about Clarisse, and we were long time teammates, but at some point, you draw the line on risk. And tonight, I had drawn that line.

If I lived to get on the bus to go home, I would have had all I ever wanted of red, wet grass and cheering crowds. I could probably get an endorsement deal or two if I played my cards right.

But when I, if I, stepped off that field tonight, from that point on I was a happily bored civilian.

"All I ever wanted to be," says Remington, "is on the team, to wear the white and purple."

"You haven't made it yet," I say. "You have on the colors, and you can say you're on the team, but until you're on the field facing those who want to stab you, and you need to stab them, and you've played through, then you can truly say you're one of us. Not before."

She practically glowed there in the thin inner lights of the bus. "I'll get there."

Maybe.

"It's about our school," she says. "It's about our tribe, isn't it? Nothing really matters but our group, right or wrong."

I thought the problem was just that. The way the tribe takes over logic. The way other girls on other teams are the same. Them against us, us against them. But I say what I was expected to say, what I had to say, "Yeah, sure, girl. That's it."

The bus slowed at a light, adjusted with a whining sound which meant it might need some overhaul or something, and then it moved forward again without dying or going to pieces. It just might get us there.

I thought of something my mother said, that they used to have an actual driver up there, in the seat, and it was always a cranky old fart. She said she missed cars and buses that you drove, but me, I can't imagine such a thing. I was cranky enough tonight without having a cranky bus driver. I looked at Clarisse sitting up front, and I'm thinking there was a time when we gave our dolls swords, and each held one and made them fight one another. We got our fingers banged a lot. Lot of girls that wanted to make the team did that, but I didn't know any started as early as we did. We would sleep over at my house, or me at hers, and we'd talk. I couldn't figure it sometimes. How we went from what we were then to what we were now. It's like someone had cast a spell on us. We had a whole new set of friends outside the team, and now me and her only talked when we had to, when we needed to for the games.

Sometimes it hurt me to think about what had been.

I looked out the window as we passed a field full of corn. There were lights in the field, and you could see the corn standing high, and beyond the field it was as dark as the space between the stars. I remembered once my mother, who had been quite a team champion herself, told me that when people came here, that was the part that was terraformed first. That very spot.

"Once, it was barren, and there was a dome," she said. "Right there is the heart of our beginning."

That was hard to imagine.

"Remington." It was Clarisse's voice cutting through my moment of silence, and I had so been enjoying it. "I think we might pull you off the bench tonight, you know, let you play first, be up front to feel things out."

"What the hell," I say. "She doesn't know her ass from her elbow."

"She's got about three seconds after they blow the whistle," Bundy says. "Then her dead ass will be taking a tour around the arena."

"Two seconds," I say.

"She's been trained," Clarisse says.

"That's right," Remington says. "I'm on the team. I'm honored to have the chance, Captain."

"Temporary Captain," I say.

"Temporary or not," Remington says, "that's the same thing, though. Right?"

Remington's saying that made my face flush. I hoped that didn't show in the poor light. It took me a long moment to say it, but I did. "Right."

I made a point then of deciding not to get to know Remington at all, because tonight would be her last night. I knew what Clarisse was doing. She was going to use someone we weren't close to for probing the team, seeing how good they were, how long it took them to put Remington down. It was a mean sort of gesture, to put her at the front, like she was important to the team, but what she was, was expendable.

I could practically feel Remington vibrate beside me. In a few hours there wouldn't be any more vibrating. It would be over for her, and we might learn something from her death about the other team, which admittedly was a team that changed up their game plans. They had a lot of solid, long term members, and they were without a doubt the toughest we had ever faced. I had seen some of the film made of their games, and it was chilling. They had an amazing defense and an even more amazing offense. When they left the field, it was always wet with the blood of the other team.

"I'm going to make all of you proud," Remington says.

"Of course you are," Bundy says, and all the other girls said something like that out loud. They were supposed to. I didn't say a damn thing. It might cost me some extra laps at the gym, Clarisse wanted to push it, tell the coach, but the thing was, I was done after tonight. I got home, I only had one more week on the team, and that was all ceremonial until the graduation honors. I could run a few laps. I could do extra sit-ups or any other exercise that was asked of me. But tonight, I wasn't going to give Clarisse the satisfaction of agreeing with Remington's sacrifice. Poor Remington. She thought she was going to be a hero, not a corpse.

"Should I attack right off?" Remington says.

I didn't answer her. I didn't say anything. She said a few more things out loud, but I wasn't paying any attention any more. I was sitting there looking out at the landscape, flooded white by the moonlight.

WHEN WE GOT to the café where we always stopped, Clarisse stood by the door of the bus, and as the team came out she reminded us not to eat heavy, the way Jane always did, like we needed to be reminded.

As I started past her, she called my name, says, "I need to speak to you privately."

I took a deep breath and let it out and stood off to the side and let the others pass as they headed into the café.

When it was just me and her, I say, "What?"

"You're supposed to be an example. Keep the new girl up, not try and bring her down."

"She'll go down all right," I say. "She's got about as much chance as a rabbit in a dog's cage."

"She has her training. We were all newbies once, and we all took our chances."

"We were better than her."

"That's how we remember it."

"That's how it was. And why aren't you talking to Bundy? Why didn't you pull her aside?"

"Because you're a Point, like me, like Jane. There has to be a third point, and with Jane out, she's the only one with the jets to play that position."

"Remington's no Jane. She's no anybody. And besides, you don't start the new ones off on Point first game out. Pull Bundy up."

"She's not fast enough. She's better where she is. Remington is fast, I've noticed that at workouts."

"Yeah. All right."

I knew it was a done deal. Clarisse was, much as I hated to admit it, the team captain. Unless the coach decided to override her, Remington would have her two seconds. And then she'd eat dirt.

"You protect the ones who have experience," Clarisse says. "That's how we win, with the regulars."

I quit talking to her then, went inside the café.

There was music playing and I could smell food cooking. I ordered a hamburger, one of the small ones and a side salad. Remington came over and slid into the seat across from me.

"I'm so excited," she says.

"Save some of that," I say. "Tame it, use it."

I don't know why I even bothered. She was a goner.

She chattered on about this and that, about the team, and finally our food came, and still she chattered. I ate slowly, way you need to, and when Remington wasn't chattering, she ate quickly, the way you're not supposed to.

"I know you don't think I'm ready, but I am."

"I know you're not ready."

"I believe in the team."

"That's nice."

"Don't you?"

"Sure," I say, but I wasn't certain. Did I?

Clarisse had already eaten, something small and mostly vegetables, I figured. She always looked great, played great. She came down the aisle of the café, walking between the rows of tables, saying, "Everyone. This is the championship game. This one counts more than any of the others counted. We have to—"

"They all counted," I say, the words jumping out of my mouth. "Ronnie's game counted, didn't it?"

"Of course. That's not what I meant."

"I am so tired of your yacking and trying to act like you're some kind of hot stuff. Why don't you shut up and sit down and just do your part later?"

"You're jealous, aren't you?" she says, glaring at me. "You wanted to have a day dedicated to you, and you didn't. Didn't earn one. And you thought you might actually take Jane's place while she was out. Be team captain instead of me."

"You don't know anything," I say, but I was thinking, yep, that's about it. That and the fact that I was tired of the whole thing, tired of dreaming about the final dark, the possible pain. I have nightmares about being dragged around the inner stadium with my dress hiked up and my ass hanging out, flapping along like Clarisse's tongue.

"I'm the team captain," Clarisse says, "like it or not."

"I don't like it much," I say.

Everyone looked from my face to Clarisse's, except Bundy. She says, "This can be settled."

"It can," I say. "The old way it used to be settled."

"We don't do that anymore," Clarisse says.

"You mean you don't want to do it that way," I say.

"You and me, we been friends a long time."

"No, we were friends a long time ago. This whole team captain thing, it can be solved, way Bundy says. It's in the rule book."

Bundy eyed Clarisse, says, "Think she's got you there, Captain."

"Very well," Clarisse says. "This is a bad time for it. Game night. But yeah, I'll give you your satisfaction."

She touched the bayonet strapped to her hip.

That's when Lady Red, owner of the café, her hair dyed red as a beet, drags all three hundred pounds of herself out from behind the counter, wags a finger at us. "You know the rules for any squabbles, fist or bayonets, or just bad language. Take it outside. One of you gets killed, you'll bleed in the parking lot, not on my floor."

"There's no need for this," Remington says. "All for one, and one for all."

"Shut up, Remington," I say.

❧

THE LOT WAS lit with lights and moonlight. It wasn't as bright as the stadium would be, but it was pretty good. We could see how to kill one another, that was for sure.

We spaced off, ten feet between us, our bayonets drawn, the edges of them winking light. Clarisse stood with her legs a little wider than shoulder width, standing to the side, the bayonet in her forward hand, not the back one, way you should hold it if you knew something. We both knew something, but I got to thinking there might be a reason she was team captain, not me, because earlier she had hit it on the head. I wanted that place, thought I deserved it, and Clarisse had always won out over me, in everything. She got the best body and face to begin with, born that way, and she had better clothes and they fit her the way the same clothes would never have fit me, even if my parents had the money to buy them, and she got all the boys, and twice she got my boyfriends, and all she had to do was walk by and smile, and it was a done deal.

I had dreams where she died, and I never knew how I felt about them. Was I happy or sad? I awoke with tears on my face but a happy heart.

"You've always been jealous of me," Clarisse says, like she's been reading my mind.

"You don't know everything," I say, but right then I'm thinking, yeah, well, she knows a lot, and she probably was a pretty good team captain, and she just might kill me tonight, or wound me bad. I didn't have the team to work with against her. I had me and she had her, and that was it.

Thing was, to save face, I had to do it now, and I thought, maybe I'll wound her good enough, or maybe she'll wound me good enough I won't have to go in with the team tonight. I'll be through.

I swallowed and eased forward and she eased toward me.

"Touch off," she says, and though this isn't a game, just a fight, I do it, reach out and tip my blade against hers. They make a clinking sound, and then we both move back one step, like we would in a game, and start to circle one another.

"This isn't teamwork," Remington says, stepping out of the circle of girls around us, saying that like it might not occur to us that it wasn't.

It's then, that just beyond Clarisse, as we're circling, I see Bundy's scarred face there in the light, her one eye and her black patch on the other, and she's lit up like she's just had an orgasm, first communion, and a ticket to heaven.

Oh yeah, I'm thinking. We do this, I kill Clarisse, or she kills me, or we just get injured bad, neither of us may be able to be team captain, and next in line is Bundy. Wouldn't be a lot of discussion on that, not tonight, when it's the last game and there's no time to rethink things. Bundy ends up captain tonight, and we win the game, she goes out a hero, gets another parade. Me and Clarisse get some hospital time, and maybe the game's lost because we're not there.

Was that why Bundy was so eager to have us fight?

Was I trying to find excuses to dodge out?

Now Clarisse was easing closer, using the fake step, where you drop your back leg behind you, but your front stays where it was, gives the impression she's moving away, might make you think you can get her on the retreat, but it's just a trick.

I knew all her tricks, and she knew mine.

"We're a team," Remington said. It sounded like her voice had been sent to her via wounded carrier pigeon, like it didn't really want to be there.

"Hush," Bundy says to Remington.

But that's when Remington began to sing our fight song, and damn, her voice was good. It rose up and filled the air and it almost seemed as if the lights got brighter, and if that wasn't enough, some of the other girls started to sing. They tightened the circle around us, and the singing got louder. I could feel tears in my eyes, and then one of those tears escaped and streamed down my face, and the other tears, like lemmings, followed.

"And they called to the crowd, and the crowd called death, and the bayonets came down," they sang, and then the chorus, "Came down, came down, like a mountain, came down."

For whatever reason, that chorus always got me, and it had me then, and I think to myself, get it together, lose the emotion, or Clarisse has got you.

But that's when I see Clarisse's face in the light, and it looks like she's just sucked a lemon. The war paint she wears was running over her cheeks, her face was wet. Her bottom lip was trembling.

All of a sudden, she lowers the bayonet to her side and starts to sing, and then I lower my bayonet, and I start to sing, and coming in late, but clear and strong, Bundy begins to sing.

Everyone of the girls is singing now, and just as loud as they can.

Me and Clarisse spin our bayonets into our sheaths in unison, like one of our drills, and we smile at each other, and we keep singing, and when we come to the end of the song we embrace.

Remington says then, "We got time for a cup of coffee. One cup is good for you in a game, coach told me that, but two, that's too many."

I went over and put my arm around Remington, and then Clarisse did the same thing from the other side, and we walked Remington back into the café, the team following.

❦

ON THE BUS, me and Clarisse sat together, up front of everyone else, and were mostly silent in the dark, but when we were maybe like, five miles out, she says, "Do you remember when we were little, how we used to make our dolls fight?"

"Sure," I say. "I remember," not telling her I was thinking just that thing earlier tonight.

"We were close then," she says, "and I always have felt close to you, even when we weren't getting along."

"Me too, I guess."

"I was always jealous of you, Millicent."

"Say you were?"

"You were smart, and could see things quick, and I got to tell you, I maybe overdo a bit when I'm around you, cause I'm thinking whatever I'm doing, you could do as well or better. I don't like to admit that, but I'm admitting it now."

"Yeah, well, you got your stuff too. I never had your looks, your style."

"You say. I mean, you know, you could push your hair back a little more, show your face. You got a good profile, girl."

"Yeah?"

"But mostly you're smart. You're smart, and you'll probably stay smart. No one stays pretty, not in the way they think. My mama told me that."

"She's damn pretty."

"Yeah, but you should see pictures of her when she was younger. She was beyond pretty."

I let that soak in, her compliments, and then I say, "Remington, I don't know. Front lines. I mean, it's your call. She is quick, damn quick, and eager, but I'm thinking maybe you put her in at the back, first round, then move her to the front later, second or third round, third would be best, and by then she's got a feel, isn't quite so eager she's rushing into something she doesn't understand."

Clarisse nodded. "Coach told me, said, you're the captain, but someone has a suggestion, listen to it, and you like it, do it, you don't, don't do it, but whatever happens it's on your head."

"That's a heavy responsibility."

"Listen here, girl. Let me be completely honest. I wanted Remington up front, because I didn't want you up front. You're great. You can play the spot, you know you can, and you do, but, I figured tonight, we might both go home, and then, we might can, you know, be friends again."

"I'd like that, but I don't want Remington to die for it. And besides, you need me up front with you. Like always."

Well, then we could see the stadium lights, they were pointed out from the stadium toward the sky. A moment later we could see the big open gate that led inside. The bus went in, and then it stopped and we got out.

Clarisse tries to get everyone's attention, but there's too much excitement. Championship game, you know.

"Hey, listen up," I say, and I say it like I mean it. "Captain has something to say."

Everyone goes silent and we huddle around, and Clarisse says, "Remington, you'll play at the back first round, maybe through the second. Then, everything looks good, we'll move you up."

"Yes, Captain," Remington says, and if she looked disappointed, I couldn't tell it.

Clarisse gave us a few more instructions, stuff we already knew, but it's all right to hear it again, to keep sharp.

Then we marched in formation toward the big opening that led onto the field. It was dark in the tunnel and we stopped right at the opening that led onto the field, and looked out. There was some light on the field, but only at the far end, where the other team stood waiting. Being that they were the challenging team, they got to come out first, get hit with their lights.

Clarisse says what we always say before we step onto the field. "We know not what comes."

We chant the same words once, softly, and then Clarisse says, "Remington, lead off with it."

Remington starts to sing our fight song, and then we all start to sing. Bundy slaps Clarisse on the back, and out we go, marching onto the field.

Hearing our voices, our school band starts to play up in the stands, a little heavy on the drums, but good on the horns, and then everyone from our school, parents, students, teachers and so on, they start to sing too, and then the stadium lights flare on us.

We look up and see our supporters standing up, singing, smiling down at us, and we march confidently onto the field, still singing.

DEAD MAN'S
CURVE

I CAN'T BUILD THEM and I can't fix them. That's what my brother Tommy does, and he does it well. He could make a lawn mower outrun a flathead Ford, but if I'm short in the mechanic department, I sure can drive them. No brag, just fact.

That's what Tommy was trying to explain to Matt.

"She may be a girl," Tommy said, "but she can drive."

"May be a girl?" I said. "What the hell is that?"

"You know what I mean," Tommy said, glancing back at me.

I knew what he meant all right.

Matt leaned on the hood of his Pontiac GTO and studied me, his hands thrust into his blue jean pockets. I thought he was taking a bit long for the evaluation. His friend Duane stood nearby. He looked amused.

"She looks all right, and she'll make someone a good wife, but drive?" he said.

"Goddamn you," I said.

"Okay," Matt said, "she might not make someone a good wife either."

"You scared a girl will beat you?" I said.

Duane snickered. Matt didn't say anything, but even in the dying light, I could tell he didn't like that. Duane wasn't quite the asshole Matt was, but my rule of thumb is simple. You're an asshole until you prove otherwise. It's just that right then I took Matt to be the bigger asshole of the two.

Matt studied me again. Now I was doing the leaning, my blue-jeaned butt against the apple-red Dodge Charger. I cocked a foot against the bumper so that my knee was up high, in what I thought was a cool-looking position. I stuck a finger into the pocket of my blue jeans like I might have money in it. And I did.

I gave Matt what I thought was my movie star smile and tried to look as smug as a duck with a June bug. The Charger I was leaning on was Tommy's, being bought and paid for by part-time work. It might as well have been mine. It liked me best. Tommy drove it, shifted gears, it sounded like someone was trying to beat a cat to death with a logging chain, but when I drove it, it purred like a tiger cub and ran like a cheetah with its ass on fire.

"Are all the girls from Texas like this one?" Matt said.

"Well, they got their similarities," Tommy said, "but Janey is a little bit special."

"You Yankees afraid I might blow your asses in the trees?" I said.

Matt turned and looked down the road. The sun was dropping down at the end of it, seeming to melt into the earth like a heated snow cone. It looked like a northern sun to me, not a Texas one. The one in Texas was a whole hell of a lot brighter and warmer. The air here, even on the edge of summer, was nippy.

"All right," Matt said. "She can race me."

"Why thank you, Mister Matt," I said. "You're quite the sport."

"Don't push it," Matt said.

"You don't race me, who else you going to race?" I said. "No one else is here."

"I thought I was going to take money from Tommy, not some cute girl who likes to hang on to a stick shift."

"Oh, you'll never know what I like to hang on to, Matthew," I said.

He gave me a sour look.

"What I got is this," and I reached in my jean pocket and pulled out a wad of bills that would have choked a horse and made its stablemate cough.

"This here, Matthew, is two hundred dollars. You ever ran for two hundred dollars?"

"I've ran for more than twice that much. And I won."

"Then you can sure run for two hundred."

"Hate to take your makeup money, baby."

"Just show your dough," I said.

Matt turned to Duane, said, "Hey, I'm short about a hundred and forty."

"Damn," Duane said. "Might as well ask for the whole enchilada."

"Come on, man. Help me out."

Duane removed his billfold from his hip pocket and peeled some bills out of it with all the enthusiasm of a man removing layers of skin from his forehead with a pair of tweezers.

"You lose, you owe me double," Duane said, and gave it to him.

"Man," Matt said, "double?"

"You're the one so all-fired certain," Duane said.

"All right," Matt said. "All right. Let's fire 'em up. See who makes those hard left turns."

"What hard left turns?" Tommy asked.

"Couple of them," Duane said.

"First one, it's not so bad," Matt said, "but then the road gets so narrow another coat of paint and you're rubbing the bark off the trees. Got a ways to go then, but there's another curve, down by the old quarry. Dead Man's Curve. Take that one too quick you'll find yourself airborne, sailing over the rim. Drop don't kill you, you drown."

"It's like a lake," Duane said.

"After that, if you make that curve, because I know I will, we'll end it at the hospital parking lot," Matt said.

"Hospital?" Tommy said.

"What are you, a fucking parrot?" Matt said. "Yeah, the hospital. Just beyond it is the city morgue. We can end it there if you prefer."

"Hospital is fine," Tommy said.

"Bunch of dead old folks in the morgue right now," Duane said, "some kind of convention, they all got sick at the hotel. Bet twenty of them died. Hospital has a bunch of sick ones packed in, some in bad shape, probably buying a ticket for the morgue right now."

"Read about it," I said. "Some kind of mold in the ventilation system, I think."

"Who knows?" Duane said. "All that's certain is that stuff is killing them and packing them in the dead house."

"Let's talk about racing," Matt said. "That's what we're here for."

"Cops?" Tommy said.

"No worries there," Matt said. "Law rarely comes out here."

"What if you're wrong, and they're sitting around the corner?" I said.

"Well, girly, we get a ticket. You up for it, or are you just going to stand there trying to look good?"

"Oh, Matt, honey," I said, "I have no need to try."

🙠

AS I SETTLED in behind the wheel, and Tommy sat beside me, I had a small faint feeling that I might have mouthed myself out of some money. I had enough confidence to loan some of it out, but I was uncertain about those sharp curves. If I had driven them once before, that would be different. But when we agreed to meet Matt and Duane on the road, we didn't know the route. That was a bit of a mistake, and it was too late now. Matt was revving his engine.

"You sure about this?" Tommy said.

I lied a little. "I was born sure."

"I was there," Tommy said. "I don't know how certain you were then."

"You were at Grandma's house playing with building blocks or some such shit," I said.

"That's true," he said.

He was the older sibling by three years, but most of the time it seemed the other way around.

Matthew revved his engine some more, then pulled his Pontiac to the right side of the road. I was on the left, of course. We hadn't seen a car yet, and we'd been there talking and wheedling about who drove against who for half an hour. I think Matt was afraid of me and wanted Tommy to be his opponent. I had a bit of a reputation.

"You know he's got more under the hood than came with it," Tommy said.

"So does this one," I said.

"But I don't know if he's got more or less."

"You wanted me to race him," I said. "That's how you find out who's got more or less, who's the best driver. Have I ever let you down?"

"Twice."

"Blew a tire once, bad carburetor the time after. Tonight, everything under the hood is as fresh as a baby's first fart."

"You know, half that money in your pocket is mine."

"The die is cast, brother mine. Grab your ass and grit your teeth."

Matt rolled down his window, and Tommy rolled down his.

"What we do," said Matt, "is I count to three, or you can do it, no matter, but count to three, and on three we go for it. And watch those curves. Something happens to you, we just go home and have a hot chocolate like it never happened."

"Quit talking, and start counting," I said.

"One," said Matt, and when he got to three you could hear those motors roar, hear those tires scream for mercy. We both blew out of there like rockets to Mars.

Let me tell you, there's nothing like it. The car leaps, and then it grabs the road, and then it doesn't feel like there is a road, just you and the machine floating on air.

Glanced to my right, saw that Matt and I were neck and neck. He had his teeth clenched, his window still down. That was a mistake. It gathered up air that way, pushed it to the back insides of the car, lay there like a weight. Tommy knew that, and he had rolled up his window to streamline us.

Let me tell you, that first curve came up fast, and we had to make it together, and the road, just as you made the curve, grew narrow, and then there was another problem.

The road was full of people.

There were at least twenty, men and women, and one of the men wasn't wearing any drawers. He had it all flapping out. The rest wore hospital gowns. They stretched across the road in a thin line, seemed drunk the way they staggered, and that was all I could tell in that moment when they suddenly appeared, dipped in moonlight as pale as Communion wafers. Even the one black lady seemed pale.

I fought the wheel and tried to avoid them, but they were straight across the road and there really wasn't anywhere to go. On the left were trees, on the right was Matt's car. I veered as far left as I could, and fortunately, two of them on the left wandered right, and I missed them, but I'm sure I made enough breeze to blow up their gowns. My car threw up gravel, a bit of forest dirt, and then I spun beyond them like a top, turned the wheel in the direction of the skid and righted myself onto the road again. In my rearview mirror I saw Matt hit a couple of them staggering in front of his car. It was a hard, loud smack. They went flying like Mighty Mouse.

Matt was braking, and it made his car scream like a panther. It slid sideways, almost up to where we sat in the road, and then it stopped, rocking like it had palsy.

Duane rushed out of the car on his side, started running toward the people lying in the road, the ones wandering about.

"You okay?" he said.

Me and Tommy were out of our car too, wandering back to Matt, who opened his door and jumped out, stumbled a little.

"I didn't see them," he said. "They were just there."

That's when the two lying in the road tried to get up. One of them, a woman, managed it, but stood with her head dangling to the side, like it was held there by a thin string. Something like that, that kind of injury, you don't expect people to be walking around. The other, an old man, his legs smashed, pulled himself forward with his hands, his fingernails scratching along on the blacktop. His legs as useless as mop strands.

The others closed around Duane, and then, as if he had been lowered into a pool of piranha, they swarmed him. They could move pretty fast when they wanted to. They grabbed Duane.

I could understand they were angry, and had reason. We were irresponsible jerks driving too fast on a narrow road—

And then they began to eat Duane.

The one crawling had him by the ankle and was biting through his pants legs, gnawing at his high-top boots, and the others were all over him, biting and pulling at him. I saw the black woman bite his ear and rip it off.

Duane screamed. I started toward him, but Tommy, who had come around on my side of the car, grabbed me and pulled me back.

I could see more clearly now, but somehow, what I was seeing was too strange to be real. Yet, there I was, standing next to Tommy on a moonlit road, far from where we grew up, watching a mass of people bite and gnaw at Duane.

Duane screamed. Blood flew. Teeth snapped. They took him down. I could see naked asses through the hospital gown slits as the crazed crowd bent over him and began to rip at him with their hands and pull guts from his belly, lifting them to their mouths as if they were huge strands of spaghetti coated in marinara sauce.

I could see too that some of those people had awful bite marks on them, like they had just escaped a pack of wild dogs. And the other thing was, well, they all looked dead. There was no spark in their eyes and they moved like puppets. And those two Matt had hit with his car, there was no way they should have survived, but they were going at poor Duane like he was a buffet.

I ran around to the trunk, stuck the key in there, popped it, and pulled out the tire iron.

"No," Tommy said, but it was too late. I was weighing in. Those people were murderers, and they were killing...well, had killed, Duane. His body steamed in the cool air where he had been ripped open. One of those things was pounding Duane's head with its fists, cracking it apart like a giant walnut. Brains oozed and hands tore at the break in his skull. Brain matter was snatched and eaten.

My hits were good ones. I turned my tire iron blows to their heads. If I hit their heads hard enough, they went down and didn't get up. Otherwise, I didn't hit the head, they just kept coming. None of it made any sense, but I knew I hated those things, and I was proving it. I knew too, without having to really think about it, they were all dead and I was making some of them deader.

There were a lot of them, and then there were more. Tommy grabbed me, was pulling me back toward the car. Matt climbed into his GTO, woke the engine, and roared around us, nearly clipping us in the process.

"Look," Tommy said.

I was no longer swinging the tire iron or struggling, so I looked. There were more of them coming down the hill, out of the woods. Some of them looked to be little more than skeletal structure with a thin parchment of skin stretched over them. Many were naked.

"In the car," Tommy said.

The ones who had been snacking on Duane were close to us now, and I had no more than closed the car door, Tommy slipping in on the other side, when those things began to beat on the door glass. I fired up the engine, gunned it, hit one in front of the hood and sent it flying backwards into the road, and then I ran over it.

We drove on, had to stop once and pull a small tree out of the road. It had taken that moment in time to fall and block our path. It took some work, but thank goodness it wasn't too big a tree and those things weren't around.

Some time later we saw Matt's car. He had skidded out and hit a tree. Driver's side door was open, but he wasn't in view.

Eventually we came to Dead Man's Curve, and since we had outdistanced those things by quite a bit, we were going slow and made the curve easy, but I was glad I hadn't been racing. That curve, let me tell you, it was a bitch. I saw off to our right that the earth fell off into a man-made cut about the size of the largest moon crater, and it was full of still water. The old rock quarry. It stretched for a great distance, and across the way I could see the straight-up wall on the other side, slick and snot-shiny in the moonlight.

That's when we came to more of those things, wandering across the road, and there was a driveway on the left, and I took it. I thought about smashing through those things, whatever the hell they were, but they were too thick, and if I wrecked the car we'd be out here with them, just me and Tommy fighting for our lives with a tire iron and wishful thinking.

Still, didn't mean the driveway was a good idea. It was a reflex move. It was a long straight shot on concrete, and in the rearview mirror I could see those things lumbering after us. The drive ended at a nice farmhouse. Out beside it was a large barn. Behind a long white-board fence on the left was a lot of pasture.

As we drove onto the looping driveway in front of the house, I saw the front door to the place was open, and wandering out of it were two of those things. The yard was full of them. Not all of them were wearing hospital gowns or were naked. Some were fully dressed. Young and old. No doubt they were like the others, way their bodies jerked, way their heads rolled from side to side and their eyes seemed to look off in one direction or another, not latching right on you. Some of them were bloody, fresher.

"Damn," said Tommy.

"Double damn," I said. It was something we almost always said when one said damn, or hell. Double damn. Double hell. This time it was not pure fun and hyperbole. It was accurate.

I glanced toward the barn, saw a woman there. She had pushed one of the two wide doors open, probably hearing us roar up, and was waving for us to come that way. Then I saw Matt appear, grab her by the arm and jerk her back.

I gunned it. There was a gravel drive from house to barn, and I went that way fast as a bullet. When we got in front of the barn, Matt was struggling with the woman, had her bent back and was flinging a fist into her face, time and again, until she fell down.

The tire iron was in the seat beside me. I got out of the car with it. Matt tried to grab the open door and close it. I leapt forward, swung the tire iron, hit his arm through the crack in the doors, made him scream and stumble back. Tommy had slipped to the driver's seat, and he tooled the car inside as I pushed both doors wide. Up at the house I could see dead people wandering around in the yard, starting to trudge toward the barn.

When Tommy had our ride inside, I closed the doors. Tommy got out and helped me put a large and heavy wooden slat between two metal supports, barring the doors soundly.

That was done, I took a moment to kick Matt in the head. Within seconds the barn doors began to rattle, and you could hear those things moaning on the other side of it. The noise they made caused me to feel like my panties were crawling up my ass like a spider.

Tommy was helping the woman up, and he sat her on a bale of hay. A boy came out of the dark, ran over to her. She hugged him to her. Three more children, a couple of boys and a girl, eased out of the shadows too. The girl looked to be the oldest, but she wasn't more than twelve, if she was that old. They didn't go far. The boys were wandering about more than moving forward, and the girl seemed frozen, as if her feet had been stuck down in a tub filled with cold water and held there until the water turned to ice.

"You damn near broke my arm," Matt said. "And that kick cracked my jaw. I can feel it."

"Why thank you," I said.

"Bitch," Matt said.

"My middle name," I said.

"He was trying to force us out," said the lady, who held a hand to her battered eye.

"It's survival of the fittest," Matt said.

"You're not that fit," Tommy said. "A girl whipped your ass."

"You say that like it's a bad thing," I said.

"You sons of bitches," Matt said. "A woman, some brats, and one of them a retard, what the hell?"

"And you such a sterling member of society," Tommy said.

There were electric lights burning inside the barn. It was a class thing with front and back double doors, lots of hay. A tractor with a trailer fastened to it was parked near the back door. Two of the horse stalls had horses in them. A sorrel and a paint. I liked horses. Me and Tommy used to ride all the time at summer camp. That was before our parents split up.

I went over and took a look at the lady's eye. She was pretty bedraggled. She looked to be in her sixties, solid and sun-coated, time-worn. There was a toughness about her. The boy she had her arm around was obviously disabled. Must have been thirteen or fourteen, oldest of the children. I could tell he was disabled because of the way he looked. He had a sweet and innocent appearance that most of us lose about the time we realize the shit in our diapers stinks.

"My grandchildren," the lady said.

"What's happened?" I said.

She shook her head, tears streamed down her face. All of the children had come over now and were sitting on the bale of hay with her, close to her like a cluster of grapes.

"I don't know exactly," she said. "But those people, they're dead. You can tell."

"I'll say," I said. "But again, why?"

She shook her head. "Can't say. No idea. I have my daughter's kids with me. One of them left the front door open. I went to close it, and the yard was full of them. Kids were playing outside in the moonlight, and I saw those things coming up on them. I yelled at them and then, for whatever reason, we all broke toward the barn. We got here just as that asshole," she pointed at Matt, "showed up. He was trying to barricade himself in the barn. I struggled with him so the kids could get inside. I saw you pull up, and I wanted to help you, but he started fighting with me. He wanted to leave you out there, with those things. He wanted us out there too, to keep them busy, I guess. So they'd forget about him."

As if to emphasize that, the barn doors on both ends rattled like giant dice.

"I can't believe it," she said. "I keep trying to figure it. What brings people back from the dead? Old Man Turner was with them, and he died yesterday. He was in the morgue. I knew him well. He was ninety years old if he was a day."

"Did you recognize others?" Tommy said.

"I did. Friends. Neighbors."

"How far is the town from here?" I said.

"We're practically in it. Town's not far from the hospital and the morgue. Couple miles maybe."

Tommy looked at me, said, "They could be all over town as well."

I said to the woman, "People out there, recognize any from town?"

"Don't know everyone in town, of course," the lady said. "But it's not that big. Everyone I recognized was from out here, houses nearby, but there were plenty I didn't know one way or another. They could have been from town, I suppose."

"Or the morgue and the hospital," Tommy said.

"Way some of them are dressed, sure," said the woman.

Matt started to get up.

"Lie down," I said, and lifted the tire iron.

He stayed where he was, said, "What we do is we stick the woman and the kids out there, get those things busy on them, and then we make a break for it. Drive out of here."

"So now you and me and Tommy are a team," I said.

"Please don't," the lady said.

"Of course not," Tommy said. "Don't you worry about that."

"You can't think the old way," Matt said. "You got to think about how it is now. This could be happening all over."

"Just stay there and shut up," I said.

"You need to think of yourself," Matt said. "You don't even know these people."

"Can't say I actually know you," I said. "And what little I do know of you, I don't like."

"We're racers. We go fast and live fast, and we survive. We know how to take a curve."

"You don't," Tommy said. "You smacked your car into a tree. Hell, it was a straightaway. Unfortunately, you survived. My guess is you're part cockroach, and the rest of you is all asshole."

"They are our way out," Matt said, nodding toward the woman and her grandchildren.

"I said shut up." I slapped the tire iron in my open palm and Matt went silent.

I turned to the woman. "Does the tractor run?"

"Yes. But it doesn't have a lot of speed, more if you drop the trailer."

"We want to keep the trailer," I said.

Tommy said, "What are we talking about here?"

I turned and looked at Matt lying there on the ground. He had abandoned us back on the road, and then he had tried to lock us out, and now he wanted us to take him and leave these people to their fate.

The barn doors rattled.

"Ma'am," I said, "would you and the children go to the back of the barn, over behind the horse stalls? Stay there for a bit. And you might want to cover your ears."

They didn't stir.

"Now," I said.

They moved then, quickly. When I saw they were behind the back stall, out of sight, I walked over to Matt. He saw it in my eyes. He tried to get up and make a break for it. But it was too late. I think the first swing of the tire iron killed him. I can't be sure. It knocked him down and out, that's for sure. And if it didn't kill him, the other blows did.

I hit him a lot.

ME AND TOMMY fastened Matt to the back bumper of the Charger with baling wire, several strands. I felt like Achilles tying Hector to the back of his chariot.

The woman and her grandchildren came back into view. I was covered in blood and I was shaking. But there was nothing for it. They would see what they saw. Therapy was in their future. If they had a future.

"What's going to happen," I said, "is Tommy is going to open the door, and I'm driving out. I could try and stuff you all in the car, but if they're thick on the road, well, you can only get so far, even in a car. But Tommy here, once I'm out there, once they get after Matt's body, which I think they will, you guys will go out the back with the tractor and trailer. Head toward town. Maybe it's safe there. Just sit quietly and ready to go until I can give them a whiff of this guy, let them smell the blood."

"I can't let you do that," Tommy said.

"Yes, you can. You have to. I'm going to be the Pied Piper, but it's going to be my car engine and the smell of this dead bastard that're going to lead the rats away. You and the family go out the back."

The woman came up closer, stared down at what was left of Matt's head. I had hit so many times you could have slipped his head through a mail slot.

"You're going to go the opposite way I go," I said. "You might come across some of those things, so you'll need to take something to fight with. I see farm tools on the wall, that pitch-fork, the hoe, things like that. It's not a perfect plan, but we can't wait here in the barn until we eat the horses. Two horses might last a while, but not forever."

"Grandma," said the granddaughter, who had started to cry. "We can't eat the horses."

"Of course not," the woman said, but the look in her eyes made it clear to me she knew they would have to if they stayed, and probably raw.

"You let the horses out of their stalls, let them run. What you do is you drive that tractor to town, pulling Tommy here and the kids on the trailer. He can help you fight if you run into more of those things. It's the only choice."

TOMMY HELPED ME lift off the door barrier. When we dropped it, I ran and got in the car. Tommy pulled one of the barn doors open slightly, then darted back to the tractor. The lady had already started it. The kids were on the trailer. Everyone had a farm implement. That was a little like giving everyone switches to fight a bear, but it was all they had.

I could hear the things outside not only the front door, but the back door as well. This was going to be tricky.

When that unlatched front door was shoved wide open by those monsters, I turned on the headlights, startling them, put my foot on the gas and made the engine roar. I popped the clutch and jerked the car into gear. It leapt, knocking several of those things back. I let the car bunny hop a little, and die. They were smelling Matt back there, and they all went for him. It was like someone had rung the dinner bell. They had started crawling over the car too, pounding on the window glass, as if I was a pie on display and they wanted it.

I started up the car again, eased forward, but not too fast. Enough I was able to break free of them, and yet keep them interested in Matt, the hot lunch.

I drove around the barn. There was a well-worn path, and the car went smoothly. When I had driven around a couple of times, the car was covered in those things. I could hardly see out the windshield, they were gathered on it so thick. The back way was open.

I didn't want them to eat all my bait, so I drove faster, onto the drive. I reached the road, and they were still with me. I heard the back glass crack from the pounding the clingers were giving it with their fists. I glanced in the rearview mirror. The back window still held, but it was starred and lined with breaks.

If Tommy was lucky, they would have the tractor going now, following slightly behind, turning the opposite direction toward town. Maybe all the things were following me. Maybe Tommy, that woman and her grandkids, would do all right.

The moon had brightened up the road as the night had worn on. It was like having your own night-light. I decided it was time to pick it up a little, make it hard for the things to keep clinging to the car. As I increased speed, they peeled off the Charger like dead skin.

I sped up enough to get ahead of them, but not so much they couldn't see me. They kept following.

I wondered how much was left of Matt. Way I had him fastened on back there, I couldn't see him in the rearview. That was probably best. I had killed him in cold blood, and now I was feeding him to those things. Was I any better than him, choosing to do such a thing?

I thought on that for a short time, came to a conclusion.

Yeah. I was.

❧

I KEPT TEASING those things with the body, speeding and slowing. I checked the gas. Low. When I glanced up from the gauge I checked the rearview mirror. The road behind me was a wall of those things.

And then I saw him. He was on horseback. He was carrying something shiny and swinging it as he rode through the mass, surprising them, smashing heads, sending them sprawling.

It was Tommy playing cowboy. He had saddled up one of the horses and was riding it through the drooling crowd toward me. When he burst out in front of that bunch, I slowed to a stop.

Tommy rode up to the passenger door, swung off the horse. I leaned across the seat and opened the door. Tommy dropped what he had been carrying into the seat—a lawn-mower blade. He unsaddled the horse, dropped the saddle in the road, peeled off the bridle, and slapped the horse on the ass. It went off the road and up through the trees and out of sight, a flock of ghouls pursuing at a considerably slower pace.

"Good luck, noble steed," Tommy said.

He jerked the door open and climbed onto the seat, placing the lawn-mower blade in his lap.

I turned and looked back. Those things were almost to us. I clutched and geared and we started rolling.

"What the hell?" I said.

"What the double hell, you mean. The lady is driving the tractor, taking the kids into town. I saddled a horse and rode along with them. When I figured they were doing good, because we didn't see any of those things, I turned around and came after you. I always had that in my head."

"You're a good brother, Tommy. I never thought you were before."

Tommy laughed.

As we came around a patch of trees we saw the road had quite a few of those things in it. I put the pedal to the metal and knocked a couple aside, crunched one under the wheel. Now I was gaining speed. I glanced at the gas gauge. Before long we'd be walking, and that wouldn't be good. I only had one head-light now, the left one. The other one had been broken in my collision with those things. Bless the moonlight.

I was picking up speed.

"Buckle up. We're going to straighten out the curve."

"Damn, girl."

"Double damn," I said.

Tommy reached across me, got my seat belt and strapped it over my lap, and then he buckled his own.

I was hot on the straightaway now, and Dead Man's Curve was coming up, but I wasn't slowing. I could see those things in the faint light from the left head-beam. They were coming down the wooded hill on our right. A better-dressed group than before. Probably from farmhouses that had been attacked, survivors who had not been consumed. It was clear that being bitten made you like the others. You died and came back. Hungry.

"We're going to overshoot the curve, out into the quarry," I said.

"Big drop, sis. Full of water. You know that, right?"

"You can swim."

"Only if the fall doesn't kill us, and then, swim where?"

"To the other side."

"Walls are slick."

"Maybe there's a way up."

"Maybe?"

"We're short on options. Roll down your window. Water pressure may not let you later."

Tommy frantically rolled down his window, and I did the same.

Now the curve was ahead, and when I made it those things were in the road. I clipped a few of them, and long past when I should have turned the wheel, I kept going, wearing a few of those monsters on the windshield. I put my foot through the floor, and we went sailing off the edge of Dead Man's Curve.

There were bits of tree limbs and brush growing out of the side of the quarry, and we shot out over it. Limbs and brush scratched the bottom of the Charger like a pissed-off cat. Out of instinct I looked in the rearview and saw what was left of Matt floating up in the air on that baling wire, coming apart in pieces that were sailing backwards in the draft like wet confetti.

Way, way out that car sailed, and in the moonlight I saw the wall of the quarry on the other side. It looked slick and straight up. The Charger dipped and the car was an angular shadow shooting toward where the moon floated in the water like a target. The water looked as firm as a giant piece of sheet metal.

The air whistled in the windows. The back glass of the car, already cracked and pressured by the wind, shattered into a mass of moon-colored stars and was gone.

We smacked the water.

I don't know exactly what happened after that. I guess the impact knocked me out. My head may have bounced off the steering wheel. The water eventually brought me around. I didn't know where I was right away, but the water went in my mouth and nose and I finally realized I was drowning. I felt out for Tommy, but he wasn't there. I reached for my seat belt. There wasn't any. I came to understand I had somehow gotten out of the car, that I was free and floating, twisting around underwater like a strand of weed. I couldn't remember how I got out.

Then something had me. I was pulled up and out of the water, gasping for breath, sputtering and spitting. Tommy was holding on to me. We were moving our feet to stay afloat.

"You all right, sis?"

"You saved me," I said.

"Yep. Started to leave you, but then I remembered you win all the races. That's too good a money to throw away."

I thought about that fine Dodge Charger, down below in the deep dark wet. What a waste.

Those things, maybe half a dozen were in the water, having grabbed at the car, or having run off the cliff after us. They weren't close and they weren't swimming. They bobbed a little and sank like anvils.

I was coming back to myself by then.

"What now?" Tommy said. "So far, I'm not crazy about your plan."

"We swim together," I said, "then we take turns with one swimming, the other hanging on. Then we go back to swimming separate. We take our time, do that until we get to the other side."

"It's a long ways," Tommy said. "I already feel like I was eaten by a wolf and shit off a cliff."

I looked at the far quarry wall. It was a lot more distant than it had seemed from above.

"And the walls are high and slick as glass," he said. "What do we do if we get there? Levitate?"

"If we have to."

We started seriously swimming, first side by side, and then I put an arm around Tommy's neck and he swam. Then we switched and he held my neck. I was the stronger swimmer by far. When I looked around after what had seemed like forever, I couldn't tell that we had covered much distance at all. But I thought I saw a trail going up the far wall, and then the moon was shadowed by clouds and the shadows lay on the quarry wall like a curtain. I couldn't be sure if I had seen a trail or not.

Maybe the moon would break the clouds apart and I would see the trail again. If it was there, and I hoped like hell it was, I thought we might just make it.

FILLING
STATION

IT WAS AN old filling station. It was set off the road and the only reason I went there was because I really had to pee, and it was the only station I had seen signs for in a while. The signs were old and hand painted, and they had big faded red arrows on them that directed me to the place.

The station had once been on a main highway, but they built the Interstate through, and that put it out of the way. But somehow, it had hung on.

The station was grimy, with dust and bugs that had blown against the outside glass, which was long and wide. You could see through all the grime, but not clearly. The light behind the glass was dim, as if seen from a distance, even though I was close.

There were two pumps outside, and they were really old. There wasn't any business about putting your charge card in them and running the gas yourself. I could tell that just by looking at them.

You had to go inside to pay before the gas was turned on. But I didn't want gas. I wanted to pee. I parked over by the restroom and when I got out I saw on the restroom door a sign that said you had to ask for the key.

I quick-walked to the station's front door, which was an old, wooden affair that creaked open with a rusty hinge sound. There was a stringy guy in a gray cap behind the cash register, and on the counter next to the register were large smudgy glass jars of pickled eggs, pickled pig's feet, some big dill pickles in brine, as well as something suspicious in a jar full of yellow liquid. There was a pair of tongs lying on a cracked saucer, in case you wanted to screw off the lid of one of the jars and pull something out.

There were the usual odds and ends elsewhere. Chips, beef jerky, air-fresheners, and the like. Some of it looked too old to still be for sale. Some of the candies and chips had names I hadn't seen in ages and thought were long out of business.

On the wall behind the man was a boar's head. It was moth-eaten and one of the tusks was missing.

I asked about the restroom key. He took his time to answer. He had one of those voices that sounded as if it weren't used often and had corroded.

"You got to buy something."

"All right," I said. "I'll have a pack of gum."

"Needs to be more than gum."

"All right, then, how about a bag of chips and a package of gum?"

I got those items and paid for them and he gave me the restroom key, which was attached by a chain to a narrow board a foot long and as thick as my wrist.

"Door locks behind you," he said. "You won't need it coming out, but bring it back."

I told him I'd return for my goods after I finished up, went out, and walked around to where the restroom was.

When I used the key and entered, I heard the door lock behind me. I flicked on the light, which was one bulb in the center of the ceiling. It hummed to life, but was hazy and gave off a urine-like color. I decided the station fellow might not think the restroom was public, but it looked as if it were quite public, because it stank of urine and feces and the little white mint in the urinal had turned as yellow as a canary. The smell that rose up from it was stifling. Beneath the urinal was a crusty dark stain. The last time this place had been clean was when it was built.

I decided I ought to do more than pee. I ought to go the whole hog, as much as I hated to in a hole like that. I went into the toilet, closed the door, tried to lock it, but the lock was poor, so you were really on a kind of honor system. If someone pushed it from the outside, the stall door would easily fly open.

By this time, I was glad to see there was paper on a roller, and that the seat wasn't too nasty looking, though there was a dark stain inside the porcelain bowl that made me gag a little. And, like the urinal, it was odiferous.

I used some toilet paper to wipe the seat off, placed the board and key on the back of the toilet tank, let down my pants, managed to sit down on the toilet to do my business, and that's when I heard the door open and someone come in.

I couldn't see who it was, but I could hear them, and they were next to the toilet stall, at that horrid urinal. I could hear them peeing.

"I showed him," said a man's voice, and for a moment I thought he might be speaking to me.

I decided not to respond, but tried to do what I had come to do as quickly as I could.

"I showed him. I showed him all right. But, oh, so much blood. And the guts steaming. Nice. Real nice."

I wondered if he was talking about a deer. It was hunting season. But who was he talking to? Had someone come inside with him, and if so, why weren't they speaking back?

There was a long moment of silence, and then I heard, "I cut him a lot. I wanted to meet some place nice, not here. I sure cut him, though. I should never have picked him up. I should never have. Jesus, why do I keep coming back here?"

There was a pause, as if waiting for an answer.

"He was like all the others. Just wouldn't listen. And I had to cut him. I had to cook him. I had to eat him."

I was finished doing what I had come to do by this time. I used the toilet paper, stood, and quietly pulled up and fastened my pants.

My skin was cold and there were goose bumps on my arms and on the back of my neck.

"You would know how to act, wouldn't you?" said the voice.

I caught my breath. Was he speaking to me?

The man had moved. I couldn't see him, but I could hear a bit of shuffling from the urinal to the door of the stall. I looked at the crack between the door and the stall, but couldn't see anyone. The door was a partial door so you could see feet underneath it, if you bent down to look, but I wasn't about to bend down and look with him that close. I clenched my fist in case he should push the door and come through.

The stall door moved ever so slightly.

"Not everyone has to die. Sometimes, it's good."

There was movement again, and I had the distinct feeling the man had stepped away from the stall. I stood there with my fist clenched for a long time. I didn't hear the outside bathroom door open, but I didn't hear him roaming around in there anymore either.

I decided I couldn't just stay in this stinky stall and wait and see what he was up to. Maybe he had gone out, and I hadn't heard him leave.

I inched close to the stall door, and though my skin tingled with fear, I put my eye to the crack and looked out. I couldn't see anyone from that angle. I stepped back and bent down and looked under the stall, where the urinal was, but I couldn't see feet.

I remembered then I had put the key and board on the back of the toilet tank lid. I picked it up. It was heavy. It would make a good weapon.

I took a deep breath and came out of the stall with the board cocked over my shoulder. I didn't see anyone. Now I was too frightened to go outside. I had the board, but opening the door and finding someone waiting out there was a horrible thing to contemplate.

Eventually, I built up my courage enough to open the door and look out at the night.

No one was outside. As I was standing there, the water at the sink came on. It startled me. I glanced back. Water was running full force from the faucet. It didn't look like the sort of faucet that was set off by movement. It was one of those old turn it on and off with your hand affairs. But how had it come on?

I took a breath. Decided it was obvious. It was as flawed as this entire bathroom. Somehow the handle had slipped and the water came on. It wasn't an entirely satisfying solution, but I went with it.

A moment later, the water shut off. That really troubled me. I went out.

I let the door close behind me without bothering with cutting off the light. I walked away with the board still in my hand. I went out and stood by my car. There was no one around. It was warmer out there and the air was certainly fresher.

Had it been the station owner? And if so, what the hell was he talking about? Was he messing with me? Was it someone confessing something terrible to himself, someone who noticed I was in there, then asked me how I would act if I were with him?

And that's when I heard a noise behind the closed bathroom door, and then the voice.

"I need someone else. I really do."

The bathroom door cracked open slightly. I could feel cold air slipping out from inside, along with the stink.

"Come back in," the voice said.

I got in my car, started it, backed up, and rolled away from there. I looked in my rearview mirror.

The bathroom door was open wider now. I could see a shadow pinned against the light from inside? Then the door opened even more and the shadow slipped out and rushed toward the rear of my car.

A somewhat human shape grabbed at the back of the car, found purchase and clung there, crawling up to the rear windshield.

At that moment, behind the car, the wedge of light the open bathroom door had provided went away as the door closed by itself and the shadowy shape clinging to the rear windshield blended with the night.

The light that had been on inside the main section of the grimy filling station was dark. My view of the station in my rearview mirror receded as I pressed my foot on the accelerator.

I drove onto the Interstate. There were lots of street lights along the way and lots of cars, and they made me feel better.

Few hours later I had the urge to stop for another bathroom break, and even though there were now plenty of brightly lit and modern stations just off the four-lane highway, I didn't stop. I held it.

At some point I realized I hadn't picked up the items I had bought at the station, and the bathroom key on the chain fastened to the board was on the seat beside me. I also remembered the bathroom door had locked behind me when I entered, so how had someone come in?

I rolled down my window to throw out the board and key. The wind that blew in was dark and foul and icy cold.

THE HOODOO MAN AND THE
MIDNIGHT TRAIN

THERE'S PEOPLE DON'T believe in booger stories, as my grandma used to call them, but that don't mean there isn't strange stuff out there in them dark woods, or for that matter on the streets in town, out there on a buggy ride down to the river for a picnic, or coming through the woods spitting black smoke and carrying hell and damnation with it.

Thing is, once you know the world has a sliced sky from which things leak, well, you can't never lay down at night without your protections.

I work in a gun shop and I live there too, but it isn't just any gun shop. Zachary, who prefers to be called Zach, repairs and even makes guns, but he's got another kind of job that don't always pay and sometimes does, depending. But it's a job he will take on either way in the end. If he tries to bicker and fails to get some money out of the deal, he just sighs and goes on with it.

Zach had owed a hundred good deeds on account of a bad thing he did, and on the day the old man came in, his black skin graying, his black suit graying as well, thinning too, a wide brimmed black hat on his head with a white feather in it, I seen Zach perk up. Zach had done ninety-nine good deeds and still owed one more. That was the only way he could get rid of the baggage. He thought that old man might be the last deed needed for him to get shed of his little problem.

Now, when I say good deeds, I don't mean help an old lady across the street so she don't get run over by wild horses. A thing like that is damn sure a nice thing to do, but it don't go on the ledger, so to speak. It's got to be bigger than that. Something real special.

I guess Zach's around fifty or so, though I have heard people comment on how he seems to stay at an age and not move away from it. Zach is a stout man with a gleam in his eye, and his skin is dark as the bottom of a well, and always shiny, like he just ran a race in the hot sunshine. He's always bent forward a little, like he's considering tying his shoe. If he wore shoes.

Zach not only makes and repairs guns, he can shoot them right smart as well, has a fast draw. And then, of course, there are all the magic books and talismans. He knows that stuff. That's his side business, and all the business he does he does well.

I was sold to him when I was young by my folks who didn't want me. They were going through town with a traveling medicine wagon. They sold a few bottles of this and that. All of which my mama made, and nearly all of them a mixture of water and whisky and berry juice, but nothing that would do anything for you but make you slightly drunk and loosen your bowels.

Cure-all my folks called it, but it didn't cure much. I didn't miss them any. My pa beat me and Mama didn't love me enough to even hit me. I don't know it for a fact, but I heard they was hung from an oak tree for selling something that made a child get sick and die. Mama probably put the wrong berry juice in a bottle, or some such when she was drunk. She could be a bad drunk. It was the parents of that child and some townsfolks that did them in. It wasn't the law, but it was justice, no doubt.

Zach had been good to me. He was teaching me a trade, two trades, like he had. I got three meals a day and I had a bed in the back of the shop. It was set on top of a pentagram, surrounded by all the protections Zach had made for me. Blue bottles full of dead flies and horny-toad guts, crosses, silver doodads, and a salt circle around the inner circle of chalk that made up the outside part of the pentagram.

Early on, I wondered if there was any sense to all that stuff, until I woke up and seen sitting there in the dark, all around that chalk and salt circle, a series of squatting toad-like things. It was frightening, but I knew then that it was the circle and all that other stuff that kept them out. During the day I didn't have to worry, Zach told me, but at night, I wanted something like water or a good book to read, a fresh candle for my night table, I needed to bring it in before the dark got deep and the clock beat twelve. Straight-up midnight was the time the demon door opened and the things came out in search of those that were involved in the hoodoo.

I told Zach I didn't never have to do that before he took me in, and he said, "I know, but them demons want me, and now they want you, or anything to do with me and you. You want a girlfriend, have your fun, but don't never fall in love, cause you can't have it, not really. You love someone, you're bringing them into something slimy and dangerous, and once in the life, it takes something really special and goddamn biblical to get out of it." He said there were days when he hated having pulled me into all these dark shenanigans.

I told him I was glad to have been rescued, and that Mama and Pa were a lot worse than the demons, because wasn't no spells and diagrams that could keep them out, and besides, he had educated me some. I could read and write and do my ciphers, and I was learning the gunsmith trade as well as that other trade of his.

I know I'm wandering, but I think for you to understand it better, you got to know Zach's circumstances, about them good deeds. You see, I was good deed number fourteen of the one hundred he owed. I've seen him do all the others up to where he is now. I helped him do quite a few.

He told me once that he had gotten as far as ninety-eight good deeds once, then messed up by doing something bad, and had to start over, and when he did, the baggage got heavier. When I say baggage, I ain't talking about no grip, or a tow sack full of possibles.

In the back of the shop there's a long hallway, and off the hallway are two rooms, one on the left, one on the right. I'm off to the left, and Zach is off to the right. But at the end of the hallway hanging on the wall is a big old mirror made of silver and it's shiny as a baby's ass all greased with lotion. The mirror is framed in hawthorn wood painted red with hog's blood and grave clay, and the painted wood is treated with hoss apple juice.

When Zach enters the hall, even if the light is bad, you can see him and me in the mirror, but you can also see the baggage, and no matter how many times I see it, even expecting it, it gets to me, makes my bones tremble inside of me like an old house rotting its lumber.

It looks a little like an old woman, and she's got her arms around Zach's neck, and her legs wrapped around his middle, and her head rises just above Zach's. Her face is long and she has a possum jaw, with a lot of jagged teeth in it, and once a month she smells so bad Zach can hardly stand it. Just once a month, and on that day he doesn't work, just rides off in the country and lives with the stink, which when the morning breaks and the sun gets warm, goes away, like a visiting in-law you don't care for.

He can do whatever he would do without her on his back, but she's there, in dark spirit he says, and he can feel her arms around his neck and her legs and feet around his waist, and he can always feel her hot breath on the back of his neck, and on that stink day, he says it's the breath that nearly kills him, cause it reeks like a feed lot for cattle. She's his baggage for killing a child to save his own. Both children died, his and the one he sacrificed to the dark ones. I don't know much more than that, but let me ask you, would you kill a child to save your own? You can bet my folks wouldn't have done a thing to save me or any other child either. They sold me for thirty dollars and was glad to get shed of me.

❱

I WAS TELLING you about the man that came in, all dressed in fading black, and the first thing he sees is me, working on some leather, designing a holster for a pistol, using the pattern laid out for me by Zach.

I didn't really need the pattern anymore, but I liked to keep it near, just as a way of feeling like I always had it in case I needed it. Working on the guns, well, that's a different story, especially some of the guns Zach worked on, and certainly the ones he made to his own design. I liked him nearby to make sure I was doing that kind of business right.

"Boy," the old man says, "maybe you ought to leave the room. I got to talk to this man here."

"He doesn't leave the room," Zach said, his hands on the glass top counter that held a number of Colts and Remington pistols. "He's my apprentice. Name is James."

"What is he? A high yella?"

"I suppose you could call him that. I call him James."

The man nodded. "All right then, but I got the kind of business to talk about that you pull out of a deep dark sack."

"I understand that kind of business, and so does the boy."

The old man nodded again.

"I been trying to find someone for years to help me do what I got to do, cause there's someone stolen and riding a kind of train that don't never let a passenger off. They say you're the man I need. A hoodoo man."

"Go on," Zach said.

"I heard rumor of you from an old man out in West Texas. Thing is, the whole thing that happened to me happened here in this very town, and now I'm back in it. I find that strange, that I didn't know you were here all along."

"Fate makes circles," Zach said. "I keep a low profile on the hoodoo business, and you got to be in the hoodoo to know who I am and where I am. In the hoodoo like you. But, I don't work for free."

The man came closer to the counter and opened his coat and took out a small bag and set it on the counter in front of Zach, said, "That there is silver dust. It's what I can pay you. It's worth a lot."

Zach pulled the drawstring loose and pinched some of the dust and worked it with his thumb and forefinger, and let it fall back in the bag.

"All right," Zach said. "Tell me about it."

❧

ZACH LOCKED THE door and turned the sign to CLOSED, and we went into the back room and sat at the table where me and him eat. I got out the bottle and poured them both little glasses full of a dark whisky.

They took their sips and I sat silent, and then the wrecked old man said, "Some years ago, right here in this town, I made a mistake. I wanted to be rich and powerful, and, well, there was a woman, and she was a fine-looking woman, dark, dark skin, with a heart like a lump of coal. Name was Consuela. Skin like black velvet, long-legged and high-breasted, but she had a gleam in her eye that made you weak."

"I know who Consuela was," Zach said. "We had what you might call a rivalry. Before her house burned down with her in it."

"Again, I had no idea there were two hoodoo masters in town."

"You don't really master the hoodoo. It masters you."

"True enough. Consuela had me do things for her, bad things. I stole and killed for her. She had spells, you see, and she needed certain things and certain events to make those spells happen. Items and sacrifice. She used them spells to help me along with money and for a long time magnificent health. She owned my pecker, owned my soul. I dressed nice, had money in my wallet and fine clothes, of which these I'm wearing are remnants, but there were restrictions and prices to pay. One was, she kept me in her sight. Didn't want me to let on what I knew, I suppose, but mostly she kept me like a pet. All that I was missing was a collar and a bowl on the floor.

"Got so the only time I could get away from her was when I was on one of her errands. It's hard for me to talk about those errands, because sometimes they were bad errands. Really bad. I really don't want to talk about that.

"Then come a day I'm on my own at night, and I'd done a thing so bad I was sick, and I couldn't make myself go back to Consuela, not right then. I went to the café just to have some place to go where the light was bright and the voices in the room weren't demonic whispers.

"There was this young woman worked at the café. She was petite, soft-looking as a puppy, skin the color of coffee with a splash of cream. Not as wildly beautiful as Consuela, but she was certainly pretty. I went there every chance I got, just to be in the warmth and the light, to smell fresh coffee and frying eggs and bacon. But mostly, I went there for her.

"When things were slow in the café, she would pause and talk to me. I learned she lost her parents to a fever, lost everyone she ever loved in one way or another, and yet, she was cheerful, positive, and I could feel the meanness I had in me, that Consuela had encouraged, easing out of me, like a snake going away from the chicken house.

"Her name was Jenny. She liked a simple life, and I decided I could like one too. I had to get rid of Consuela. I figured best way to break her hold on me was to kill her. I thought I was most likely able to do that when she slept. You see, at night we slept in a bed inside a circle drawn on the floor, with diagrams—"

"We know all about that," Zach said.

"Why I come to you. You got a reputation for knowing your business. When Consuela was asleep, and I was lying in the bed next to her, I eased over to the side of the bed and pulled the hammer out from under it, where I had placed it earlier in the day, and hit her in the head. She could keep those demons out, but she couldn't keep me out. I hit her and hit her until her skull and wicked brain were nothing but a splash on the sheets. And these demons that were all around us, they cackled.

"I waited until morning, when the cock crowed and the demons around the bed became mist and wafted away. I got out of bed and fell to my knees, weak from fear and guilt and excitement. I'd broken the hold she had on me. I cleaned myself up and waited until Jenny was at work. I was thinking me and her could go away together. It might take some time to convince her, but I was determined. That's how much I loved her. You seem perturbed."

The old man had noticed that Zach's expression had changed and that he had cupped his hands together and let them rest on his chest. He seemed to be holding something inside of himself.

"You're blaming Consuela for the very things you wanted," Zach said. "She didn't make you do nothing. You did bad things on your own to get money and power, and now you want to lay it at her feet, justify what you done. You weren't under any kind of spell, because if you were, you wouldn't have been able to plan killing her, or even want to."

The old man nodded slowly, the feather on his hat bobbing like a big white finger. "Yeah. I can't disagree with that. That doesn't change the fact that she was evil and killing her was a good thing. Shall I go on with my story?"

Zach nodded.

"When morning came, I felt weak. It wasn't like I had slept. I ended up going into the front room to lay down on a pallet. Woke up and it was near dark, checked the big clock in the hall. It wasn't long before midnight. That's how much what I had done had taken out of me. I had slept the entire day and part of the night away.

"I realized, of course, that the demons would soon be out. I had to get back in that bed with Consuela's corpse so I could be protected by the charms and the pentagram. I was in the hoodoo life, a minor hoodoo man, but minor or major, the results would have been the same. These days I make my own pentagram and lay out the protection. It's second nature now. But right then, I didn't have the time. Not that I slept that much with her body in the bed, and after me sleeping all day, I was wide awake. The sheets were bloodstained, her brains splattered about, all of it beginning to stink. And I swear, her dead body twitched in the bed all of the night.

"Still, next morning, I was felt happy, just as free and happy as I could be. I cleaned up, fixed me some food, and then I began to feel like I was carrying something heavy on my back."

"You're toting the baggage," Zach said.

The old man nodded.

"I can see its reflection in pools of clear water, and in things that are silver. It looks a little like Consuela. In one way it's heavy, and in another it's not."

"Your baggage is different from mine, but it's still baggage," Zach said. "And it's soul weight, not weight by the pound."

"I know that now, but that day and that night, I was figuring it out, consulting the tomes Consuela had, the books she never let me look in, only allowing me to read the pages she chose, teaching me little spells and having me run her errands, but never teaching me the big things.

"I boarded up the room where Consuela lay, took all the protections into the front room and drew a new pentagram and set myself a fresh pallet inside of it. Next night I could hear a lot of pounding and ripping in that other room. The demons were having their way with her body. Doing whatever they do. That night I started going back to the café to see Jenny."

"You had killed a woman with a hammer, and you went to courting?"

"Consuela was a monster. I had rid the world of her. I wanted a new life, a better one. One without murder and spells. Is that so bad?"

Zach didn't reply, but he sighed heavily.

"After a couple weeks and a lot of sweet talk, I convinced her to walk with me down by the river. She brought a blanket, and we sat on it and looked out at the water. Soon we were kissing, and then we did what men and women do. We hadn't no more than made love, than I felt that baggage on my back grow heavy. I had a moment of joy, and that seemed to make the baggage grow heavy.

"We hadn't no more than gotten dressed than I heard it. A little toot at first, then a long low whistle coming from the north, heading in our direction. Jenny heard it too, said, 'There aren't any trains near here.'

"But there was. We could hear it, and then we could see its smoke rising up above the forest, floating into the moonlight. It was coming closer. The whistle grew louder, the smoke grew thicker, and my courage grew smaller. I didn't know it right then, but I know it now. It was the Midnight Train."

I saw Zach stiffen.

"Then we saw the tracks. One moment they weren't there, then they were. Not on any bridge mind you, they lay right on the water, and ended at our feet. There was a split in the woods and the split was shiny like a polished coin, and then we could see the train. It had one big ole red light in front and the smoke it was puffing had turned thick and dark. We were frozen to the spot. It looked as if that train was going to run right over us, and wasn't a thing we could do about it.

"Jenny took my arm and squeezed it. Instinctively we knew there wasn't any reason to run. It would catch us. The train stopped. No metal screeching, no sliding. The engine stopped right where the tracks ended. There was a hiss of stinking steam and the cool air crackled against the hot engine.

"Then a door on the side of the train opened up, and some steps was rolled out. A little creature so white you'd have thought it was made of snow, bounced down the steps and landed on the ground and looked at me and Jenny. It looked like a huge white frog, but kind of human too. Its mouth cracked wide, and it was toothless, all pink gums, showing bright in the moonlight.

"Then another one of them toads hopped down. This one was black as a raven's wing, and it had a mouthful of shiny teeth, pointed and long. It looked like it could have chewed its way through an angle of iron.

"Then both them things turned their heads and looked up at the open doorway, like they were scared. First there was a boot, hanging in mid-air. Blood-red, and tipped at the toes with shadow. Then there was a leg stick in the boot, clothed in white pants with thin black stripes. As the boot put a heel on the top step, another boot and leg appeared, and the owner of the boots and pants stepped into view, ducking his head to come out of that door on the train. He wore a big white hat with a thin black band around it. He was eight foot tall if he was an inch. I could feel that burden on my back swell and grow heavy on my soul.

"This tall man, pale of face with the corners of his mouth upturned, like he might break into a smile, came to stand on the ground by the train, the toad-things on either side of him. He looked at us. His eyes were dead-looking. You could barely see his moonlit pupils through the milky covering over them, but now and then in that rich moonlight, you could see red shadows move in the whites of those big, dead eyes. He had on a long white duster and his hands were big and his fingers long and many-knuckled. He lifted one hand, extended a finger and pointed right at Jenny. Then he turned his hand over and wiggled his finger for her to come to him. Jenny clutched my arm harder, and the tall man smiled. It was a smile where the edges of his lips slid up to touch his earlobes, widening so that I could see some blocky white teeth like tombstones and a thin, forked pink tongue that licked at the air like a snake.

"The train had come for Jenny, but the taking of her was to punish me for what I had done to Consuela. Her hex reached out beyond her death to make sure I stayed unhappy.

"Jenny says, 'Pray. Pray to Jesus.' But I knew there wasn't any Jesus that could help us. That's when the tall, white man pushed that duster back with his long-fingered hands and I could see on his hips, in snow-white holsters, two big ole pistols. He kept that horrible smile on his face, linked his fingers, flexed, popped them so loud, both me and Jenny jumped. He pointed at Jenny again and nodded toward the train.

"Now the windows, which had been foggy, cleared, and what I saw through them windows I can't explain. It was full of passengers and they were screaming and howling, had their faces pressed against the windows. They looked as if they had been boiled, fried, and generally shit on. I looked at the tall man and he cocked his hands above his guns, and though I was wearing a pistol, and wasn't a bad hand with a gun, I knew right then I couldn't beat him, and if I could, my bullets wouldn't do a thing to him. It was obvious to me that I either had to draw and lose, or give up Jenny.

"I can't tell you how ashamed I am, which is why I have come to you, to repair as best I can what I did. I put my hand on Jenny's back and pushed her toward him, said, 'Take her.'

"Jenny stumbled forward, looked back at me. I can still see her face, the expression of betrayal. Not long before I had held her in my arms and we had made love, and now I was passing her on to an eternity of torment. She didn't say anything. Not a word, didn't make a sound. Don't think she could. The hopping men came and grabbed her arms, lifted her and carried her onto that horrible train. And then I heard her scream. It was a scream that made the short hairs on my neck stand up, made the goosebumps on my arms ripple and my stomach rumble with fear.

"That tall man, he got on the train too, and the steps went up with a snap. He leaned out from the door, and he cackled at me, and the sound of it was like having your flesh cut open with a crosscut saw. The train coughed smoke, and when it did an open space near the engine lit up with a white light.

I could see inside that gap, and the Engineer was there with his oversized engineer hat and baggy coveralls. He was little more than bones stretched over wet, dark flesh, and he and the Fireman, I suppose the other man would be called that, were feeding screaming, struggling bodies bound up in guts and skin and long weaves of hair, straight into the blazing fire box. When they went in you could hear them scream, and then their screams became as one and turned into the sound of the train's whistle. The train coughed and it began to back up, and then in no way I can explain, I was no longer looking at the engine, but at the caboose. Away that train went along those tracks, and as it went the tracks disappeared behind it. The woods swallowed the train, but for a moment I could hear it toot its whistle and I could see smoke above the tree line. Then the whistle stopped screaming and the smoke was gone. There was only the moonlight tipping the trees with hats of silver.

"Everything outside that bubble we had been in, set itself free. You could feel it in the wind and in the way the trees weaved a bit in the breeze. Where before the world was silent, you could now hear night birds sing, frogs bleat and crickets chirp.

"The train was gone and Jenny was gone, and there I stood, the weight on my back heavier than even moments before. A coward in moonlight and shadow.

"I ran away quick, didn't go back down there, next day or the day after. Didn't want the train to come back. I had Consuela's books of magic, some she had written herself in her own crabbed handwriting. Heavy of heart, and heavier of soul, I began to read them carefully. I started thinking maybe I could get Jenny off that train, get that burden off my back. But if the answer was in those books, I didn't find it.

"I decided I had to search out someone who could help me, not knowing the very person who could was right here in this town, near where it all happened. I packed up my goods and Consuela's books and all her money, which was considerable, loaded it all in a wagon drawn by two strong horses. I quested for years, looking for help, and now, here I am, looking at you, asking you to help me for a bag of silver. I'm getting old now, and if I die with this thing on my back, well, no telling where I'll end up, but I know this much, it isn't good. And Jenny's on that train, and it's all my fault."

♊

WHEN THE STORY was finished, we all sat there quietly.

It was the old man that broke the ice.

"Will you assist me? Help me rescue Jenny?"

Zach pooched his lips the way he does when he's thinking hard on something. He let the old man's question hang in the air awhile. Finally, he spoke.

"Go back to wherever you're staying, and let me marinate on this thing. Come see me tomorrow when the sun's dying, and I'll tell you what I will or will not do. But let me explain to you what you're up against. It's not just the Midnight Train, but the Dueling Man and his minions you got to deal with. And let me tell you, the Dueling Man is made up of more bad deeds than either of us have seen. He works for the Engineer. He could go bear hunting with harsh language and wipe his ass with an angry badger, and that doesn't even begin to explain what he is and how he is. Go away for now."

That old man got up slow, like he had to build himself bone by bone to stand up, and then he dragged out of there like there was a ball and chain on his foot.

I looked at Zach. "Well?"

"I don't know. He's blaming this Consuela for everything he's ever done, and he mentioned murder as some of the things he done. I'm thinking he did it for himself as well, that he earned his burden more than Consuela gave it to him. Her death was just the final act that put that weight on his soul."

"But what about Jenny?" I said.

Zach didn't answer.

❧

THAT DAY I did all the work that was to be done, except some fine touchups on a gun being made for a gambling man. It was going to have some etchings on the hilt, and Zach had to do that. He had the talent and he had the steady hand.

Zach sat in the hallway in a padded chair in front of the long mirror and looked at himself and that baggage on his back. He had a stand by his chair, and had a lamp on it and some hoodoo books. I looked in on him a couple times, brought him a cup of coffee and a piece of ham and bread about noon. He took it from me without comment, continued to look at himself and his baggage in the mirror. The thing in the mirror looked at me, and when it did it made me feel cold from the top of my head all the way down to the heels of my feet. I got out of there pretty quick, left Zach to his considerations.

It was late afternoon of the next day when the bell over the door clanked and the old man came in and walked over to me.

I got up and told Zach he had arrived. Zach sighed deep, rose and followed me into the main part of the shop.

"Your decision? "said the old man.

"I've studied on it. I have to build you a gun, a special gun to use against the Dueling Man. I'll have to make some special ammunition for you too. Come back in a week's time, and I'll have it ready."

The old man tipped his hat and went away. Zach looked at me. "This is going to require a lot of black coffee."

THE DAYS PASSED by so slow you would have thought they was crippled.

I did the work Zach asked me to do, as well as kept making coffee, because once he got started on that gun he didn't sleep much, and with all that coffee, how could he?

Among the jobs I did for him was pack some powder and a specific shot inside the casings for the pistol ammunition. Those were big old bullets when they were finished. Fifty calibers, and for a pistol! But here's the odd thing, they was as light as if they was made of air and a prayer.

Zach had some metal to use for making pistols and such, but this metal he had he got out of an old trunk in the back, and the long barrel of the pistol was made of a steel so blue it made a clear spring day look dull. You could see your reflection in it. Zach looked into it with me, and I could see the baggage on his back, that horrible face. That told me there was silver in the bluing. That barrel was light in a similar way as the ammunition. The hilt was made of hawthorn wood, painted black with

414

a paint made of ashes and drops of frog blood and glue. When the gun was finished, it looked right smart the way it gleamed in the sunlight coming through the window.

Zach let me handle it. It was the best-balanced pistol I had ever held, single action, cause Zach said it was a more steady shot when cocked and aimed.

I gave Zach the holster I had been working on, made of gold-dyed leather, the dye some concoction of Zach's. He heated an iron in the fire from the wood stove and burned designs into the leather. Those designs were swirls and little figures that Zach said were spells and such. I took his word for it.

He loaded the gun, shoved it in the holster, had me put it away. When I carried it to place inside the trunk where he kept his most important stuff, that gun seemed alive in my hand. I thought I could hear it whisper.

Zach had finished his work two days early, and when he was done, he went to bed and stayed there through dark and light without waking for two whole days.

COME THE MORNING of the day the old man was to come, Zach got up and had me heat some water and fill a number-ten tub. He stripped down and got in it and soaked in a lot of soapy suds.

When he finished bathing, he got dressed. Put on black pants and a black shirt and a black hat with linked silver Conchos for a hat band. He wore a bolo tie with black strings and silver tips, and the clutch of the tie was silver and in the shape of a scorpion. He pulled on black boots fresh polished, with silver-tip toes. He had me fetch the holster and pistol. I brought it to him and he sat behind the counter on a stool and read a dime novel while waiting for the old man to come. He had me pull down the shades and lock the door and turn the sign to say CLOSED.

We sat there all day, Zach reading dime novels, and sometimes reading from the big hoodoo books he had, or from clutches of loose notes.

It was nearly dark when there was a tap on the door. I looked at Zach, and he nodded. I opened the door to the sound of the overhead bell clanging. It was the old man, dressed as he always was, like Zach, in black, except for that tall white feather. He was bent over more than before and walked like his feet was tied together. He was old the day he first came into the shop, but today he was much older.

"I have the gun," Zach said.

Zach lifted the holstered pistol up and put it on the counter. The pistol had the smell of gun oil about it, but there was something else, a tinge of something long dead; just a whiff, but it was there.

The old man spoke, sweat popping out all over his face. "I want to get Jenny off that train, but I've gotten old, and I'm not that good a gun hand anymore. I appreciate the gun, and I'm sure it's worth all the dust I paid you... But can I ask you to handle it? To be my surrogate?"

Zach smiled, and made a kind of gurgle that might have been a laugh, said, "I expected just this. I can tell a man that wants to do something he's afraid to do and wants someone else to do it for him the moment I talk to them."

"If I were younger—"

"When you were younger you let the Dueling Man take Jenny. You killed a woman, who though she may have had it coming, you were in the deep hoodoo before. The power, the money, the black magic. I know what kind of draw Consuela had. I was in her arms once. Does that surprise you? Her price was too high for me. But not you. Then you wanted out, and you wanted something clean and innocent to make you feel clean, so you took up with Jenny and let the doo-doo from the hoodoo rub off on her."

"I was young then."

"We all been young," Zach said. "But, that's not enough of an excuse. Not for what you said you done. You got guilt on you, and shame, and that's at least a good thing. It's the only reason I'm helping you. You feel remorse for what you've done and have thought about it for years. As for Jenny, I don't know her, but she's an innocent soul, and I want to get her off that train. So, let's cut the bull and get down to brass tacks and good ammunition."

Zach looked at me, "I'm going to have to depend on you for something, son. And it's a big thing."

"Just tell me what you want," I said, and I sounded a lot braver than what I felt, having heard about the Dueling Man and the Midnight Train.

"If and when I dispatch the Dueling Man, there will be the two demons. The froglike things he's been talking about. I'll try to deal with them. Meantime, you gather up all the courage you have, because it will take it, and you get on that train and you yell, 'Miss Jenny, I'm a hoodoo man and I've come for you.'"

"But I'm not a hoodoo man," I said.

"Yes, you are. You've worked for me, and I'm going to put a spell in your pocket. It's not a strong one. There ain't much in the way of strong when it comes to the Midnight Train, cause you might have to face the Engineer. He gets you, all bets are off. Your ass is good and got. The good thing though is the Engineer lets the others handle the bad business most of the time, but if he should decide to handle it himself, you get off that train quick as you can.

"That little spell I'll put in your pocket, it'll make it so if someone on the train tries to grab you, they'll not be able to. But it's not a long-lasting spell. Some of those on the train will be wailing and begging for you to take them with you. You won't have the ability to take anyone off the train except the one you call out to. When you call out for Jenny, she'll come to you. She may not look just right. In fact, she will look terrible. You take her hand, and that will give her the protection you got. But that sucks on the protective spell, and you'll have even less time than before.

"Get her and you run for the door, any door that'll get you off that train. Even if it's moving, you jump, you jump as hard and far as you can, and have Jenny jump with you. She gets off the train, she'll be the Jenny that was put on that train all those many years ago.

"Course, if I can't beat the Dueling Man, then you run like your ass is on fire and don't never even think for a moment about getting on that train. I'll be done for, me and my baggage will get on that train and we'll ride and ride and ride. We succeed, then I'm free of my baggage."

"What about me," the old man said, "will I be free?"

"That remains to be seen," Zach said. "I don't like you. I got nothing for you except to help Miss Jenny. Where she is, that's on you. And just to make myself understood, if you get out there and decide to run, like you did before, I'll shoot you.

That way, with the baggage you got, I can assure you of a long train ride."

"Should I actually go with you?" the old man said. "Maybe, being old like I am, decrepit, I ought to stay here until you get back. I might make things worse."

Zach laughed loud enough to tremble the rafters.

"Oh no you don't. You're going."

WE HAD SOME ham and bread and Zach let the old man take a shot of whisky, but Zach didn't have none. He had coffee instead, and when he finished with it, he said, "We'll go down early and take the lay of the land. I suggest we go to the place where you and Jenny encountered the train. Might as well make this whole thing full circle."

We played some cards as the night grew rich, and then we packed up some folding stools and a basket with more of that damn ham and bread in it. Zach went and wrapped his mirror in a black cloth and brought it out and put it with the other stuff.

"What you need that for?" the old man asked.

"I hope it'll give me an edge."

We didn't bother with horses. It wasn't that far away, and Zach said if we all got killed, or worse, taken on the train, we didn't want to leave the horses out there all alone.

That kind of talk made me nervous.

Zach had the old man carry the basket of ham and bread. I had the folding stools under my arm, and Zach carried the cloth-covered mirror, which is a really light tote. He, of course, wore the big gun on his hip.

It wasn't a long walk. You were in town one moment, and then you weren't. Before you knew it, you was traveling along a moonlit trail in the woods, on down to the river. You could hear it gurgling before you could see it.

When we got to the river, Zach said to the old man, "Where were you when the train came?"

"Almost right here. Maybe a little closer to the river."

It was a full-moon night and it was near bright as day, and the moon's reflection in the water made it look as if it was floating on the river. The water and the trees looked to be frosted.

Zach got out his big turnip watch and popped the cover on it and looked at the time in the silver moonlight.

"We are two hours ahead of time. Good."

I unfolded the stools as Zach set the mirror so that it stood upright, but with the cloth still over it. The old man placed the basket on the ground and sat down heavily on one of the stools.

I won't lie to you. I was as nervous as a long-tailed cat in a room full of rocking chairs, and the old man, well, I think he was starting to wish maybe all those years he shouldn't have been planning to come back here and set Jenny free. And maybe it wasn't so much about Jenny, as it was getting rid of the baggage before he died. I figured that was what his lookout was for. Get her off that train and lose that baggage.

Zach gave me a little bag and told me to put it in my pocket, that it was my protection. I took it and did just that, but I'll tell you, the idea that there might be anything in that little bag that would spare me from what was on that train was hard to grasp.

"What about me?" the old man said.

"You don't get a bag," Zach said. "You got to depend on me."

Zach ate some more of the ham and bread, but me, I was too nervous to eat, and so was the old man. We sat there watching the river, the woods, and the big ole moon, waiting for the tick of midnight, which came slow. The minutes weren't in any hurry that night, and seemed each of them was an hour long.

Finally, Zach got out his watch again, looked at it, said, "Won't be long now."

Short time after he said that the air turned chill and we heard a kind of chugging, a long way off, but the sound was growing closer. There was a long high lonesome whistle and a series of toots. It sounded like a train, and at the same time it didn't.

Black smoke appeared above the moon-tipped trees and a rolling white mist moved between the trees and blew over the river. When the mist faded there were tracks lying right on top of the river, and running on through a gauzy silver split in the woods. Then, here come that train. You could see the cow catcher in front, black and shiny as Cain's sin, and the one big light of the train was like a burning red eye. The whistle blew long and hard, and the air went still as an oil painting, and there was a bright cold glow around us for some distance, and outside of that glow I could see bats frozen in flight. Time had stopped out there, but we were inside the spell of the train and what it carried.

The train chugged on across the river, and the engine passed us close enough that the wind from it blew off the old man's hat. He didn't try to chase it down. He may not have even known he'd lost it, so intent was he on that strange, black train.

The train stopped with part of it on the tracks stretching across the river, but with a lot of it on the river bank. The engine was right next to us. You could hear the train crackle as the hot engine was being cooled by the air. We was still on our stools, but now we stood up, and I could see that the old man was trembling like a naked man in a snowstorm. Zach seemed remarkably calm. He pushed his coat back so that the hilt of the hoodoo gun showed. He took a deep breath.

Then came a snapping sound, like a big bone breaking, and a door on the side of the train sprang open. Down came some steps. They just flopped right out of the train and expanded, with the bottom step lying flat out on the ground.

Something moved inside the doorway, and then it leaped out, not bothering with the steps. It was a kind of black frog, I think, and yet, it looked somewhat like a man, bent low and held up by its squatty legs. Its hands were in front of it, and the thing was rubbing them together like a fat man ready for lunch. It had a mouthful of long, sharp teeth.

Another one of those things sprang into view, pale and larger than the other, more upright. It didn't have no teeth at all, just pink gums the way the old man had described them.

A boot stuck out of the doorway, rested heavy on the top step. A leg grew up from the boot, and then another boot came out of the train, and a leg grew up inside of that, and then above the legs the air darkened and took the shape of a man dressed all in white, except for black stripes on his pants. He wore a snow-white hat and had on a long white duster. He smiled. It was how the old man had described. The tops of his lips nearly touched his ears, and that mouth was like an open doorway to somewhere you didn't want to go. It was filled with teeth that made you think of murder and cannibals. The man's eyes—if it was a man—had a dead look, but in the whites of his eyes were little red shadows.

They flickered and crawled. His forked tongue lashed out and whipped back inside his mouth like a snake discovering the weather was bad.

It was the Dueling Man, of course.

The Dueling Man turned his head from side to side, as if trying to figure us, and then he pushed his duster back on both sides, and you could see his guns, and they were just as the old man had described them.

Zach stepped so that he was centered with the man, and when he did he said, "Move the mirror up beside me, son. Now!"

I did just that. The mirror was so light and easy to handle I managed it in instants.

The Dueling Man's expression hadn't changed. He wiggled his long fingers and the whites of his eyes were no longer white with red shadows flicking around the edges. They had turned completely blood-red. The frog-things squatted on either side of him.

"Take the cloth off the mirror," Zach said.

I whipped it off, and when I did, the Dueling Man's head pivoted slightly to take in his reflection in that silver mirror. I looked at that reflection. It was of a handsome man in the Dueling Man's clothes, not nearly as tall, normal teeth. Squatting beside him was a sad-looking naked man on one side, and an even sadder-looking naked woman on the other side of him. Tears fat as raindrops began to run down their faces.

I glanced at them, back to the mirror. The handsome reflection of the Dueling Man drooped and he rested his hands on the hilts of his pistols like he was all worn out. He sagged inside his duster and white clothes. His unique boots looked worn and scuffed, and as I watched his white suit frayed and became covered in dust that made the cloth gray. The brim of his hat lost its snap and wilted.

The wide, ear-licking smile on the Dueling Man's face closed slowly, and he just stood there, looking at his reflection in the mirror, thinking on who he had been before he became a slave to the train and the Engineer. I felt sure that's what the reflection was. Who he had been.

In that instant, Zach drew.

It was a cheater's way to do it, but it was still the right way to do it. The Dueling Man, distracted by who he once was, hesitated, and that's when Zach's pistol cracked. A hole about the size of the tip of my thumb spotted him between the eyes and you could hear what had been in his head splattering out behind him.

His long legs wiggled and then they collapsed inside his boots and all of him, clothes and flesh, went into those boots and the white hat fell down on top.

The demons came for Zach.

The old man looked as if he might run. "Hold up," I said.

"I got him," Zach said, and even as those demons rushed forward, he whipped the gun over his shoulder and shot the old man right in the chest, without even looking.

The old man crumpled, ended up on his knees. He held his hand to his chest and fell forward, his face in the dirt.

"Consider that an extra good deed," Zach said as he shot one of the demons solid in the head, and then shot the other. It was all so fast and so calm you would have thought Zach wasn't doing nothing more than out target shooting.

The demons collapsed onto the river bank and the next instant they were gone to dust. The train fired up and I bolted for the steps, hit them with a leap and was inside the train just as the steps clapped up behind me and the door slammed shut.

The train's corridor ran left and right. I could see all the way up to the open engine, and I could see the Engineer with his big engineer's hat on and his dirty overalls, his flesh all taut, the bones in his face breaking through in spots. I swear he had an extra set of arms that lifted up out of his overalls. He and the Fireman, who was short and stout and dark from soot, sweat-licked from the fire in the engine, were loading gut-wrapped bodies into the fire.

They stared at me, but neither moved toward me. They kept loading those bodies, working to get that train to run. If it did, and I couldn't get off before my protection went thin, then I would be trapped.

I took a deep breath and turned in the other direction, started through the cars. The seats were full and the people in them, if you can call them that, were coming out of them. They were blistered and scarred and their hair was in patches. They all reached out for me, but soon as they touched me the spell in my pocket coated them with fire.

They leapt back and the flames went away. I moved on through the box car, yelling, "Miss Jenny, I am a hoodoo man, and I've come for you."

A man and a woman stood up from a seat and moved into the aisle in front of me. At first, they were just two scab covered monsters, like all the rest, and then one of them called my name and I knew immediately who they were.

My mother and father. I won't lie to you, hate them as I did, I was sad to think of where they ended up. Somewhere along the line they'd gotten in the hoodoo and when they was killed, they took the train ride. I felt my heart melt. But pretty soon it was solid again. What they wanted wasn't me, it was a way off that train. Zach was my family. Not them.

By then the train was chugging and moving and rocking, and it was hot in there. It was as if the heat was lessened by that charm in my pocket, but I could feel it pushing at the air around me. I was starting to grow weak.

I kind of closed my eyes and forced myself between my mother and father, remembering how my father had beat me with a strop and my mother had cheered him on. They reached out to touch me as I passed, and their hands flamed. They screamed and stepped back into their row.

"Miss Jenny!" I called out again and again.

Then, as I entered the next boxcar, a little figure came out of one of the seats and staggered toward me. I could see that she was female, but her boiled skin flapped off her face and her neck was broken so that her head was on her shoulder. She was naked, but it wasn't an exciting kind of naked. It was the kind that made your stomach churn and your brain deny.

She said to me in a voice that bubbled as if she was swallowing lava, "I am Jenny."

I hesitated, but finally stuck out my hand. She took it. No flames came off of me and jumped on her. It was Jenny all right. I turned and started pulling her after me as I ran back through the box cars.

We hadn't gone far when I seen the old man that had hired Zach. He had been hoodooed onto the train, and his baggage was full grown now, weighting him down so much he was nearly bent double. He lifted an eye and looked up at me. The baggage, a filthy old woman that I knew was Consuela, grinned rotten teeth at me.

"Help me," he said.

"You earned your place," I said, and pushed by him and the thing on his back, yanked at Jenny's hand. I glanced back at her, saw her head was straight now and the flesh on her face was flapping back into place and her skin was turning to its former coffee and cream color that the old man had described.

We came to the doorway and the steps. I opened the door with my free hand, kicked the steps out.

When I looked up the Engineer was hustling from his place up front, coming along the floor like a spider, using those extra arms to launch him forward. His engineer hat tilted to one side, but it stayed on his head.

Behind him, in the engine room the Fireman's face turned soft and he yelled in a voice that coughed out in smoke. "Run. Run for all you're worth."

There wasn't really anyplace to run, but there was the open door now and the night outside, the moonlight.

I said to Jenny, "Jump."

I pushed Jenny in front of me and gave her a bit of a push, and she jumped. I stepped onto the top step, coiled my legs and leaped, just as the Engineer grabbed my boot, and it come off in his hand.

I went tumbling, and it was like I'd never stop. Down a grassy hill and into a wad of briars and brush. I hit something hard then and I was out.

WHEN I AWOKE my head was in Jenny's lap. She was put back together, so to speak. Her features were smooth and beautiful, and her skin looked like chocolate there in the moonlight. She was stroking my forehead. Tears were running down her cheeks.

"You got me off that awful train, away from that awful place."

I sat up slowly and looked around. There wasn't no train tracks and no train, and I had no idea where we was.

After I got to my feet and looked around, placed the moon, which was beginning to slide down behind the trees, I knew the direction to go. I was all cut up from the briars and such, but Jenny had pulled me out of them, and wiped me off with the folds of her dress, staining it with my blood. I had nothing worse than a missing boot and a slight limp that was going away even as we walked. Jenny had hit ahead of the briars and wasn't cut up at all. Her blue dress was ripped a little and there were pieces of weeds and cockleburs in her hair, but she looked fine.

We finally managed to get to where Zach was. He had covered the mirror and was sitting on one of the stools eating some ham and bread.

Except for the Dueling Man's boots and his hat on top of them, there was nothing left of him. The body of the old man was there, but I knew his soul was on that train with his baggage, riding on and on for a bleak eternity. And I knew too, from the way Zach was smiling, his baggage was gone.

"Hello there," Zach said.

๑

JENNY STAYED ON with us, which suited me fine. She didn't have any connection to her old life. The café she had worked at and the people there were long gone. I found me and her kind of suited one another.

Since I didn't have no baggage on me, I felt I could have a life, a relationship, not like before when I was linked to Zach. You see, after that night I was done with the hoodoo in any shape or form.

I quit working at the gun shop too. Zach insisted. He wrapped the hoodoo gun up and put it away.

Me and Jenny was hitched by the Justice of the Peace, got a place of our own. In our little home, no demons came out after midnight, and I could get up and have a glass of water or go to the outhouse anytime I pleased.

One day, when I went to visit Zach, just to see how he was, not to get involved in anything, he and everything in the shop was gone.

A man down at the livery told me Zach bought a wagon, hitched his horses to them, and that was the last he had seen of him. But Zach had left me something, figuring I'd come to the livery to ask about him, since a wagon would have to be rented or purchased to haul off all that was in the shop.

What Zach left me was a wooden box.

"It don't have no key," said the man at the livery.

I took it home and used a chisel to pry it open. Inside was the bag of silver the old man had given Zach. In the bottom of the box was a note.

SO YOU AND JENNY DON'T HAVE TO WORRY NONE.

Well, so far, me and Jenny don't have no worries, but now and again I think about Zach and wonder where he is, and if he's still gunsmithing, or if he might be back heavy in the hoo-doo business again.

STORY NOTES

THE HUNGRY SNOW

THIS STORY CAME in the wake of *The Hoodoo Man and the Midnight Train*.

I was certain I was through with Weird Westerns until I wrote *Midnight Train*, and suddenly I was full of ideas.

I didn't write this right away, but the premise was there in my head. Wendigo. Mountains. A Donner Party-like situation.

It wasn't until the publisher and editor Jarod Barbee at *Death's Head Press* came calling for me to do a long story for a chapbook that I was motivated enough to write it.

I wrote it like I was on fire. It was so much fun, and did quite well for Jarod, and I'm glad. It stars my character the Reverend, and it has given me an interest in writing more Weird Westerns, though my lead character from *Midnight Train* might be more likely, as I have given the Reverend a number of trails to pursue, and have only given the Hoodoo Man one, so far.

Both characters have a lot of adventures to reveal. The question is, will I live long enough to reveal them all? Unlikely, because the stories keep coming. That's the way a writer wants it. More tales to write than they can ever produce in a lifetime.

THE SECOND FLOOR OF THE CHRISTMAS HOTEL

I'VE ALWAYS LIKED a variety of horror tales, and old-style ghost stories are one of the things I grew up on and devoured. I'm not a believer in ghosts, actually, or the supernatural for that matter, but I do love the fantasy and creep factor of it. I can put myself into that belief system during the duration of a story if it invites me in comfortably enough.

Early on I wrote a number of very graphic stories, and I loved doing that as well, but that didn't negate my interest in other variations of horrors and creepy suspense. If you split hairs, horror is something in-your-face, and terror is suspense and the creeps, though to me a horror story can be some of those things, or all those things at once. Depends.

This is one of my creepers. I liked the idea of ghostly retribution, as well as a Christmas ghost story, and this one jumped out. It has elements of creepy suspense as well as outright horror.

A great time to read this one would be on Christmas, best at night when things are quiet and even the mice are tucked in for the night.

THE DARK THING

I WROTE THIS one for *Fangoria Magazine*, and there's not really a lot to say about it. It's kind of an old-fashioned Weird Tales type of story.

Unsurprisingly, it has to do with dark things and dark incidents. My son Keith and I started adapting it for a short film, but it never quite happened. We gave up because our target market, which shall go unnamed, seemed to be struggling with finances, and we became suspicious that it wasn't worth the candle.

Time proved it wasn't.

But the story exists, and here it is.

BIRD

NOW AND AGAIN, I return to my early short-short story writing, as we used to call them.

Flash fiction is the current name for these sorts of stories. This one came to me in an explosion that generated several other stories, all of them brief.

There is nothing really to say about it. It is self-evident.

I will add it appeared in the short-lived *Full Bleed* series, and it was illustrated by my buddy Tim Truman. That's always a plus.

THE MOUSE AND THE ELEPHANT

THIS ONE IS what you might call a dark fable. It is influenced by Aesop's tales which I read as a kid, as well as Fractured Fairy Tales, a great animated cartoon that was part of *The Adventures of Rocky and Bullwinkle* TV show. That's really all that needs to be said about this one.

THE SKULL COLLECTOR

LARRY BLOCK IS to blame.

He edited an anthology titled *Collectibles*, which was about, you guessed it, collectibles and collectors.

I felt a simple story about two women who acted as adventurers would be fun, and this popped out. I also like the connection to the Old West, and a very interesting woman who has been lost to history.

I was able to apply my love for the old pulp detective adventures with my interest in the Old West, and collectors of odd items.

Thanks again, Larry. Not only have you allowed me to write a variety of different stories for you, they are some of my best.

CAMEL

ALL THE SILLY crap going on with the right-wingers about immigrants is the source of this story.

I have always liked bringing animals into my stories as anthropomorphic beings. Stories where I have done this are peppered throughout my catalogue. I think I saw too many cartoons growing up.

Whatever the source, this is one of those tales, and fits in with "Monkey's Uncle" and "The Mouse and the Elephant" here. Outside of this collection there are others, including one about a forest ranger-style bear that you wouldn't want to meet in real life, and one about a poor guy who ends up taking a job as the local fire dog. But those tales are found elsewhere.

This one is found here.

SNAPSHOT

KASEY LANSDALE, MY daughter, and I wrote this for an anthology, and the idea was it was supposed to be a story that fit the horror tropes of the eighties. The influences being more film than prose, I believe. We did it. In my view it owes as much to the horror films of the seventies as to the eighties, but the bottom line is we had fun writing it.

Side note. My daughter isn't old enough to remember the eighties.

Kasey and my son, Keith, have become somewhat frequent collaborators with me, and it's fun to work with them. We all did one story together when they were quite young, "The Companion" and it was adapted for the *Creepshow* revival on *Shudder*, adapted by Matt Venne.

As another side note, my wife and I have also collaborated on stories and an anthology.

This one came pretty easy, I think, though Kasey might have a different view. I wrote a bit. She wrote a bit. And then we each took turns polishing.

SWEET POTATO

ONCE UPON A time, back in the seventies, my wife Karen and I wanted to grow a sweet potato crop. I plowed with a mule back then, and for a couple years we made a living as small-scale organic farmers.

We raised nearly everything we ate. I decided to rent some land and raise a big sweet-potato crop to supplement our goat milk (we had a small goat dairy), vegetables and meat. We sold some of our vegetables to a health-food store. I also worked for others in the rose fields, and from time to time picked peas, beans, tomatoes, etc.

The sweet potatoes were to be our big cash crop. I rented several acres up the road from us, and with the help of a friend driving a truck with my plow and accouterments in the back, I rode the mule to the acres we had rented, and put out sweet potato slips.

It was a scorching hot summer, and there was no water source outside of rain, which would usually have been enough.

What sweet potato slips that didn't die a natural death that summer, gleefully committed suicide.

It pretty much ruined us, with the cost of slips and rented land and hauled water.

Ruined us as far as small-scale farming went. But that's another story.

But those sweet potatoes, a favorite food of mine, stirred ideas about a novel called Tater Barons. It had to do with sweet potato cults, lost pyramids, and other nefarious goings-on based around sweet potatoes. The novel didn't happen.

Later, I envisioned it as a straight novel involving someone trying to grow a sweet-potato crop, but being thwarted by a terrible summer. Sound familiar?

It was supposed to be humorous.

It didn't get written either. But when Ellen Datlow asked me for a story for an anthology, this popped up. I guess it will have to do, and Tater Barons will remain unwritten.

I like this story quite a bit. I think it's odd, a bit creepy, and a lot of fun.

So, bake a sweet potato, slather it with butter and cinnamon, grab a cup of coffee and this collection, and between bites, without dripping butter on the pages, enjoy.

HATS

I DID THIS as a wake-up exercise. I thought it was fun and for some reason sent it to Jonathan Maberry, a good writer, editor and friend. He may have thought it was a submission to *Weird Tales*. I had just written it and sent it to him, and maybe in the back of my mind that's exactly what it was. I actually have no idea why I sent it to him. Guess I just wanted someone to see it.

He liked it. He bought it. And it appeared in *Weird Tales*, and I'm happy with that.

This is in the vein of the weird shop on the corner subset of stories. The shop that appears in a place where it wasn't before, allows someone to enter, and then goes away when they leave, having left them with some sort of experience, that generally in these stories isn't good.

I've read a number of stories with this general premise. "The Magic Shop" by H.G. Wells comes immediately to mind. I've seen the premise played with in film, TV shows, comics and radio shows. I took my own crack at the idea here.

MONKEY'S UNCLE

I THINK I got this idea from all the fraud emails or phone calls I receive. I thought it would be funny if a monkey had found some sort of genetic structure between himself and a human on a site like Ancestry.com. Only he is a highly developed monkey due to scientific meddling. I thought, what if he wanted to make contact with a relative, as the DNA can connect to where he and his common ancestor share genetic background. It's a ridiculous concept, of course, and science will have to forgive me, but I have fun with a lot of ridiculous concepts. This is one result.

JULIET UNCHAINED

THIS WAS WRITTEN for an Italian publisher, and the idea was it had to be some new look at Juliet from Shakespeare's *Romeo and Juliet*.

When I was young, I really loved that play. It was romantic, and so was I. At least in thought.

Later, I read it and thought, what a couple of dumbasses.

Still, it's beautifully written and cleverly conceived, and has been the inspiration for so many other stories, books, films, etc. The boy could write.

I wrote this one as a kind of response to my different feelings about *Romeo and Juliet*.

THE BRIGHT CITY HIGH ON THE HILL

I WAS ASKED to write a story for *Ferrari Magazine*, and the idea was a Ferrari had to appear in the story, and the car had to be treated well. It couldn't run over people or be put in a bad light.

That was okay with me. I wanted to write what might be considered a love story, or the beginnings of one.

Once upon a time my wife and I went to Italy (we have been many times) to be part of a documentary. The idea was the South of the U.S., and the southern part of Italy. What was alike, what was different.

It was great fun and greatly tiring.

There is a beautiful little village in Italy (and there are many) atop a hill near the sea, called Monte Sant'Angelo. It is white in the sun and cool in the dark, the walls of buildings like tombstones. Down below is the sea, and there are lights from ships, and observationally, if not literally, the place appears to be right out of a fairy tale.

Arthur Miller once wrote a story about the village, and it's said that he visited there with Marilyn Monroe, though her presence there might be myth.

Ferrari Magazine may have expected a crime piece from me as I am known in Italy for crime writing, though the instructions were to write anything I wanted to do. This is what I wanted to do.

ROOM FOR ONE MORE

THE VERY GOOD writer Michael Koryta asked me for a story for an anthology he was editing about strangers coming into a town.

I wanted to do something short and not too sweet. I was in a Robert Bloch kind of mood, seasoned with Jim Thompson and Fredric Brown.

This dark little snapper practically leaped out.

SHRINKAGE

AS THE WORLD grows smaller, as technology develops, we can feel overwhelmed by more people, more of this, and more of that. We can feel pressured from all sides, trapped between a squeezing universe and an invasion of privacy.

That is the catalyst for this.

It appeared in the short-lived but very cool magazine anthology *Full Bleed*, edited by Dirk Wood. I was in all of the issues. I wasn't surprised when it ended. It was cool, but the market for a "magazine" this varied wasn't there.

Too bad.

They were lovely hardback "magazines."

I loved how the editor, Dirk Wood, trusted me and gave me free rein to write what I wanted.

I guess you could call this one a fable.

ON THE MUDDY BANKS OF THE OLD SABINE

ANDY DAVIDSON HAD a gig as a guest editor for the *Southwest Review* Halloween issue, and asked me for a story. I wrote a horror/crime story. It is also a parody without that being its entire purpose. I'm not crazy about parody, but find some stories I write fit that label to some extent, and this is one of them.

It parodies literary, horror, and crime genres. It is also a kind of "poem." Depending on one's definition of poems.

And that's not all, folks. It is also a series of little short pieces that stand alone, but collected make up a complete story.

It came quick, and came out pretty damn dark.

THE DEGREE

WE ARE BACK to Lawrence Block and one of his anthologies that had to do with the institutions of higher learning.

I immediately had an idea, but was uncertain how well it would fit. I wrote it in one sitting, but didn't get around to the polish for a while.

I don't do the classic idea of multiple drafts. I write one, then a polish. But, every day as I write, I stop and redraft, and generally the next morning reread what was written and touch it up. When I finish the work I give it a polish, which is not a draft. I'm not stuck to that way of working. I would change if needed, but I learned years earlier that multiple drafts did not help me, and in fact, confused the story and bored me. This way works for me, so I've stuck to it.

Usually, I do that polish immediately, or maybe a day or two later. The deadline was not looming, so I put it aside, got distracted, and didn't return to it for quite some time.

When I revisited it, I liked it. It was a short one, the kind of story they now call flash fiction and once called short-short stories, which sounded to me like a story attempting to be sexy.

I love that sort of fiction, and overall, prefer shorter fiction to novels, though I enjoy reading and writing both. But if I was forced to pick one mode of writing and could have only that one, I'd pick short stories.

"The Degree" was somewhat inspired by being around academics. I never was one, as I don't have a degree, but I was for several years Writer in Residence at Stephen F. Austin State University. I loved teaching, but I loved writing more, and the overlap in time wasn't worth the payment or the satisfaction compared to my first love, writing. Also, I hate grading papers.

The people there were nice to me. I had good students who truly wanted to learn about writing, for the most part anyway. I don't think it was a hard class, but I meant business. I wanted effort from all the would-be writers and those who had planned to coast through as well.

I attended one Faculty meeting. Literally, people were crying, sniping, and generally letting their egos run amok. Many of them had never done anything outside of academics, and there were a few that felt that since I didn't have a degree, what right did I have teaching writing?

A long career in writing, stacks of books, stories, articles, a variety of literary awards, international publication, film, TV, animation, and so on, at least in my mind, seemed to be solid justification for teaching about writing. More so than a handful of literary magazine articles on the real meaning of Moby Dick's asshole in the sunlight.

Also, the political climate was at an all-time high of purposeful stupidity when I wrote this, and that's saying something. I fear we are in for more of the ignorant, and happily stupid, ruling over the masses in a dictatorial manner while crying out about the freedom they don't really believe in. And while I'm at it, I find the recent Woke Movement better in theory than in practice. Raising awareness, changing minds is one thing, telling folks the words they should use and the way they should use them, and so on, is no different than the anti-woke folks who want to tell you not to believe those things. I am not your monkey. I don't have to choose a group, though I may choose a side, but that side may be one that doesn't entirely fit with the others. I think it's interesting that the right wing wants to ban books like *To Kill a Mockingbird* for suggesting the South is a racist culture, and the left wants to ban it because they are offended by certain words, and lack the ability to consider context, the overall meaning and purpose of the book.

And for those who say, yes, but it's written from a white person's perspective, I say yes, it is. And it's necessary for white people to have an entry into understanding racism from their own lives, before they can understand it from the Black point of view; which they may never fully be able to do, but should try. It's also a book that many Black readers love as much as white. Same with Mark Twain's *Huckleberry Finn*. Writing is supposed to be willing to be offensive and in-your-face. Reading both of those books as a kid changed my perspective. I grew up in the South, but those books made racism hit home and caused me to realize the injustice going on around me. Before that, it was just how it was, and I didn't know enough, was too young to understand and challenge it.

Later, Ralph Ellison showed me more. Iceberg Slim showed me more. James Baldwin, Chester Himes, one of my all-time favorite writers.

A long intro for a short story, but not only is it a story about bizarre and dark things, it is kind of a warning. I don't know how good I am at warning you the assholes are not only coming, but are already here, but that is the point.

We are tottering on the edge of democratic principles, tottering toward a deep, dark pit, and the pit contains the hungry absolutist. This story contains those thoughts. It's satire, but satire is about reality, isn't it?

RED BILLIE

AGAIN, LARRY BLOCK was editing an anthology, and I wrote this one for it.

I think it's about a number of things, but it's mostly just a cool story about a strange being that changes things in a small town, and worldwide. Perhaps, universe-wide.

I love small town and country stories, because that's how I grew up. This one took a while to write. I write pretty fast most of the time, and the ideas come easy, but I believe the reason this took so long was I was exhausted.

I think it was Covid. My wife and I were in China, and she became pretty crazy sick, and I felt tired beyond reason. We toughed out the trip, and it was wonderful despite her illness and my exhaustion. The Great Wall, the Forbidden City, the Terracotta Warriors, Panda Bears, too much food. But when we returned home, we were both beyond exhausted. I felt as if some kind of soul spider had latched onto me and was sucking out my very essence. I felt as if I had aged ten years overnight. It clung for weeks, and then months, occasionally washing away, then coming back as if on the tide.

I thought, is this about getting old?

Well, I was sixty-nine, but I had felt fine before going, and then I didn't. Same for Karen.

And then it was announced there was a dangerous disease going around called Covid. Its source was China.

When vaccines were available, we were one of the first, and later we got the booster. I've never understood the vaccine controversy. It prevents disease. Not perfectly, but perfect enough. We lost friends and family who were not vaccinated, and nearly lost others. Turning a health problem into politics is as stupid as putting your arm in a lion's cage to see if it will bite.

Bottom line is, this story took me longer than usual. I had been working on it before Larry asked for a story. It was one of those that woke me up in the night with imagery more than story. The story part came to me a little more slowly. Writing it first required I fan the brain fog away, start early, and be content with a little bit of story at a time. I also did something I don't normally do. I asked my friend Lewis Shiner, a super writer, to look at it. He told me what I knew, but it was good to hear. I was having so much brain fog and exhaustion I didn't quite trust myself.

Most of my energy has returned, and that's good, but I wouldn't wish the kind of exhaustion I experienced for almost three months on anyone. My wife was exhausted, had fever, aches, pains, confusion, you name it.

We survived.

And, I think the story turned out well.

GORILLAS IN THE YARD

ANOTHER OF THOSE that doesn't need a lot said about it, but I will say this, it is at heart a story about how we don't always know ourselves, or we are unwilling to confront ourselves. We can self-delude, and then in rare moments the hot-shower fog will blow away, and we'll look in the mirror and see ourselves for who we really are.

Sometimes we will be reasonably pleased. Other times, it can be disconcerting.

BULLETS AND FIRE

THIS WAS WRITTEN for a magazine, *Savage Kick*. They wanted hardcore stories. I wrote this one. It's a revenge tale, and a savage one, as the title of the magazine suggests.

It has a character who is fond of using the word "and" instead of commas. I felt it was how he would think and talk. His thoughts were coming so fast he just kept linking one thought to the next.

Some might think these aspects of the story are run on sentences. No, they're not. They make sense and are meant to be that way. Genre fiction gets to experiment and play same as literary fiction, you know. You won't put my baby in the corner.

Sorry.

Action packed, dark, violent, a bit strange.

CHARLIE THE BARBER

WHEN I WAS nine or ten, I discovered my mother had an entire mass of magazines she had collected and hung on to, among them *Saturday Evening Post*, *Look*, *Life*, *National Geographic*, and others. I was excited beyond reason, and dove into their dusty piles.

Ray Bradbury, Kurt Vonnegut, and I believe it was *Look Magazine* that contained *The Old Man and the Sea*. I remember, as a kid, being disappointed that in *The Old Man and the Sea*, Santiago didn't get the fish and I felt he should have. Later, when I re-read it, I knew it was better for the story that he did not. A ten- or eleven-year-old mind versus an older one. I love the younger one, but things don't always come out the way you want. That's a tough lesson. That and learning that life isn't fair.

I read in this mass of magazines stories about Alexander Botts, the World's Greatest Tractor Salesman, and so on, westerns, humor, you name it. Those were the days when you never knew what you were going to find. I find that sort of thing invigorating.

My mother also had volumes of *Alfred Hitchcock* anthologies, and some of *Ellery Queen*. I read all of those, and the old magazines had grittier stories than later editions, though they were always less gritty than the hardboiled school. I like the hardboiled school far better, but now and then I pull out those old anthologies. I used them to teach me how to construct stories, and not just crime or mystery stories.

There was a tone to those stories in those old magazines and in the later Hitchcock anthologies that has for the most part vanished. I suppose you could call it an after-World War II tone. That says something and really means nothing, but I know that tone when I encounter it. I liked that tone. I like Norman Rockwell paintings as well.

I had previously written stories for Larry Block, and now he was asking us to pick an artist and write a story based on a chosen painting. I had in my mind an old Rockwell painting, perhaps it was for the *Saturday Evening Post*, about a kid getting a first haircut. At least that's the way I remembered it. I finally located it, though it wasn't quite what I remembered. It was fantastic. A side note, in the ARC version they printed the wrong painting, a beauty shop painting. They got it right in the actual anthology, however.

I wanted to capture the tone of the old *Saturday Evening Post* stories, the paintings of Norman Rockwell, while maintaining a somewhat modern view.

This is the result. Another of my favorites. Larry seems to bring out the best in me. He says he's retired from editing anthologies, as it is a lot of work, and as a sometime anthologist, I agree, but I say, "Larry, don't do it!"

DEAD CAR

THIS WAS A story for an anthology edited by Eric J. Guignard and Charlatan Bardot.

The idea was it was part of a book like those you find in gift stores that talk about supposed strange and paranormal events.

Each story was an entry from a different part of the United States.

I ended up with East Texas.

Honk, honk.

THE SENIOR GIRLS BAYONET DRILL TEAM

THIS STORY CAME to me in the late nineties, and I wrote a large portion of it. I then accidently deleted the entire thing. I was learning how to operate a computer. I was late to the whole gig, having used a typewriter for years. I learned slowly and lost a lot of material in the process.

It was to be a longer story then, going into greater detail, and it was vulgar and mean and interesting. But after losing it to the wilds of computer land, I didn't have the heart to go back to it. I had lost a few stories and novel sections before, and in one case I rewrote the missing portion of the novel, only to discover the original. They weren't identical, but they were close, including word choice. So maybe, then, I could have rewritten a version close to the original.

Years later the story showed up again in the dusty attic of my mind, said remember me?

I did, but was still uncertain I wanted to try and find it in my memory banks. Something didn't seem right. I had always felt a bit uncomfortable with it when writing, but loved the idea so much. I opened the metaphorical attic window and let the idea fly out.

A few years later and Lawrence Block asked me for a story for one of his anthologies, and I decided it was time to dig down and find this one again.

It had not flown out after all. I quickly shut the window that had now been open for years.

The more I thought about the original, what I could recall of it, the less I liked it. I decided the idea was right, but my previous approach was not. I came at it from another angle. A less aggressive one, and a better one. Maybe my subconscious knew the original was wrong many years back and had caused me to delete it.

I doubt that, but it's a thought.

I started writing and the story jumped out as soon as I found the voice of the narrator. I found the place and time then.

I like this story a lot, and consider it one of my best.

DEAD MAN'S CURVE

JONATHAN MABERRY STRIKES again. He was editing an anthology with George Romero, and he asked me to contribute a new story about zombies. I had already written a few and thought I might not have another on board to deliver. But as is often the case when challenged, and the impetus is there, I did come up with one.

I liked the idea of it being more about the lead character and her brother than the zombies, but I didn't want to get too far from George's original premise. This story jumped out and roared around the curb.

I'm glad I did it. I wanted to work for Jonathan and George, and in no time at all after my writing this, George was gone. This was actually the second time I had written something directly associated with him. The other was *The Book of the Dead* in the eighties, edited by John Skipp and Craig Spector. A book inspired by Romero's films about the living dead. For that one I wrote one of my better-known tales. "On the Far Side of the Cadillac Desert with Dead Folks."

This is the other one.

FILLING STATION

GHOST STORIES ARE fun. I'm not a believer in the supernatural, but I love a good story of any kind, and I'm especially fond of ghost stories.

I grew up reading them.

I grew up hearing ghost stories.

Several times, traveling, stopping for a bathroom break, I've entered into some toilets that appeared to have last been cleaned when the tile was laid and the commode was dropped into place.

Stinky, dark, foreboding.

I thought, this is the perfect place for something terrible to exist. Like a malicious ghost. The odor alone was enough to form a being so frightening it might make you hang yourself.

The idea of a haunted filling station stuck with me.

Also, my daughter, when she was a child, wrote a haunted toilet story.

I think it was an influence.

When Jeani Rector of *The Horror Zine* asked me for a story for an anthology she was editing, this one arrived in my skullcap, and letting it flow down and through my fingers, this came out.

THE HOODOO MAN AND THE MIDNIGHT TRAIN

I CHANGED TITLES on this one a few times, and never can remember which one I finally ended up with. But I remember the story.

When I wrote it for an anthology of Weird Western tales, I was sure, and told the editor, it was probably my last story of that nature. I was kissing Weird Westerns goodbye. Thing is, when I wrote it, it opened a door to a potential series, and I'm pretty sure I'm going to bite and write others.

This one was so much fun, and in my view, is my best Weird Western. My first appeared in 1985 as a serial, and was revamped for a novel the very next year. Off and on, I've been writing in the genre ever since. Actually, two Weird Westerns appeared in 1986. *Dead in the West* and *The Magic Wagon*. One definitively supernatural, the other marginally so, and more up to the reader to interpret.

I wasn't the first to write a Weird Western, but in the eighties the genre was rare, and hard to place with a publisher. I lucked out that it did find a home, and led to more work in that vein.

Now I see Weird Westerns all over. I hear from writers who thank me for *Dead in the West*, and have taken their own weird trails.

As Roy Rogers and Dale Evans sang, "Happy Trails to you."